Prison Earth

Not Guilty, as Charged

by

Clifford M. Scovell

www.prison-earth.com

*

A RED MOONS PRESS PUBLICATION

Second printing

ISBN-10: 0984732462
ISBN-13: 978-0-9847324-6-3

PUBLISHED BY RED MOONS PRESS

Printed in the United States of America

Cover artwork by Kari Angle

To Leith Robertson

For love is a more incredible adventure
than my mind could ever create.

ACKNOWLEDGMENTS

I would not have reached this point without the patient, loving help of Jessica Maxwell Andersen and her Red Moon writing group. Creating stories is an art, but getting them down on paper is a skill that requires much refinement.

The wonderful cover art is the work of a talented young woman, Kari Angle.

Though I can think up hundreds of exciting scenes for my characters, not one of them involves me being photographed. For coaxing a more-than-respectable image that even my own mirror refused to reveal, I thank Andre Lindauer.

1

"Has jury reached verdict, maybe?"

The words shocked him as he struggled to breathe the hot, heavy air, made worse by the acrid odor of perspiring bodies pressing against the railing behind him. Two-hundred people squeezed into a room designed for fifty: dusty farm workers pressing rough leather against the fine white silk of the upper class. Bodies filled every door and window, blocking circulation as fans fluttered overhead in a futile effort to move the dense air.

Breathing became even more difficult as the tall, two-headed judge moved to the front of an elevated platform, turning one shockingly ugly face to glare at him. Its ten stubby feet shuffled nervously beneath the hem of a flowing crimson robe, festooned with buttons, sashes and medals. The creature's other head faced a group of ten equally-bizarre beings standing in a small cubicle to his left.

"We have, Your Honor," answered an individual with sky-blue skin and a head that seemed to be nothing but a rainbow-colored mass of hair. For some reason, he knew it was a female, and oddly enough, the sight of her didn't strike him as strange.

The judge nodded both heads. "Defendant will be rising."

When he turned to see who was on trial, shackles rattled on his wrists and ankles. He hardly had time to react before enormous hands slipped under his arms, clamped his ribcage, and yanked him to his feet. Warm sweat dribbling off his nose, he struggled in vain to twist around for a look at whoever was manhandling him.

He jerked back when the judge's head facing the jury asked, "What be you deciding?"

Her hair curling and uncurling in rhythm with her speech, the blue female answered, "We find da defendant…"

Her words were lost in the crowd's roar. Though restrained by the enormous hands, the defendant turned his head to look at the excited mass of people, but sweat stinging his eyes blurred their faces.

A horn, barely louder than the crowd, blared somewhere to his left. Ignored, the horn sounded again, bringing only a small drop in the decibel level. Grabbing an ornate staff with the rightmost of his four hands, the judge pounded the floor as his mouths opened and closed, but the effort was wasted.

A third, much longer blast finally brought quiet to the room.

The judge scowled. "'Nother outburst and we forfeit verdict."

"He's never going to get a fair trial from a Koko judge anyway," someone protested.

"Scum like him don't deserve no trial," another person countered. "Give him to us, Judge, and you won't need no verdict."

While the crowd rumbled in agreement to one opinion or the other, the staff rapped the floor again. This time the sound traveled to the far ends of the room, bringing immediate silence.

"Next person to be interrupting proceeding go with him."

The meaning was clear. No one else spoke, or even coughed.

The judge kept one face toward the defendant, as the other turned to the jury box.

"Madam Foreperson? Please be repeating…"

A blur of green on his right startled the defendant as someone jumped up and pressed against the table separating him from the judge.

"Your Honor, this trial has been, and continues to be, a mockery of the most monstrous proportions."

The protester was tall and slender, wearing a full-length, green velvet robe that sagged loosely on his bony frame and hid all but his head and the six stick-like feet extending below the hemline. As he spoke, his tear-shaped head wobbled on narrow shoulders as if it were about to fall off. A voluminous sleeve fell back as he raised a bony hand and shook a finger in His Honor's direction.

"My client's rights have been trampled at every turn. You can't possibly consider this a fair and impartial verdict."

The judge shook his heads and sighed in stereo. "Counsel for defense be having many chances to present usual pleas for mercy at later time." He scanned the crowd. "Right now, all we wanna hear is verdict of most esteemed jury."

Both of the judge's heads turned to face the jury box. "Our apologies, Madam Foreperson, please be continuing."

The female bowed slightly and said, "Your Honor, on de charges of da willful destruction of de planet Ooertfael and da deaths of de six-and-one-half billion occupants of dat planet, we find da defendant guilty as charged."

She paused, as though expecting to be shouted down again. The judge watched as well, but not a peep was uttered.

"De jury would also like to propose special circumstances relative to sentencing, Your Honor."

Tears trickled down the defendant's cheeks as all four of the judge's jet-black eyes focused on him.

"And what those circumstances be, maybe?"

She hesitated and also appeared to look in the defendant's direction, though he could see no eyes in the vibrating mass of hair. "We propose dat de defendant be imprisoned with no possible hope of parole for da duration of de existence of his Life Force."

It seemed to him that everyone in the room gasped in surprise at the severity of the verdict. Even the judge seemed taken aback.

As his lawyer slumped back into his seat looking defeated, the defendant struggled against the restraining hands, but their crushing grip made it impossible to breathe.

"Oh God," Wyatt Simmons cried as he sat up in bed, gasping for air.

His wife, Aurelia jerked awake and fumbled for the light switch. "Honey, are you OK?"

His eyes wide, and mouth opening and closing like a dying fish, Wyatt looked at her, but said nothing.

"Was it that exploding planet again?"

He shook his head, while running fingers through his reddish-brown hair. "This was different."

"What happened?"

"They said I destroyed it."

"The planet?"

He nodded. "And I think they were right."

2

"Observation Unit 335536, this is Delta one-one-eight requesting verbal response."

Static hissed from the speaker.

"As I said, Sir," the Third-Level Monitor (TLM) said anxiously as his large, almond-shaped eyes met his superior's. "We lost contact with the observation unit's craft just before I woke you."

The Second-Level Monitor (SLM) stretched his nearly three-and-a-half foot tall body while yawning. "Diagnostics?"

The TLM moved a hand across his console to display a brightly-colored screen of data. "Everything on our end checks out, but I'm getting nothing from the unit."

The SLM's mouth snapped shut as his eyes narrowed. "Transponder?"

"No signal."

"What was its last known location?"

The TLM pointed a long, slender finger at the display. "Approximately forty-four degrees, fifty-five minutes north latitude by..."

"Don't give me numbers," The SLM moaned while rubbing sleep-filled eyes. "Just point to it on the damned map."

The TLM's screen morphed into a globe and grew in size as he zoomed in on the location. "It's the North American section, in the coastal range of their northwest region."

"The nearest major city?"

"In the foothills just west of the city they call Salem, Oregon."

"You said Salem, *Oregon*?"

"Yes, Sir, Oregon."

The SLM froze momentarily as his small mouth dropped open. "But that's where…it can't be…you're sure the observation unit is down?"

"I'm afraid so, Sir."

"Any unusual activity among the internment units in that area?"

His eyes on the monitor screen, the TLM shook his head. "The prisoners? No Sir. Nothing of that nature."

Pressing the heel of his hands into his broad forehead, the SLM flexed and clenched all twelve of his fingers twice before sighing,

"Good. I don't need to tell you the panic it would create if word got out that he was trying to escape."

"But Sir, that's impossible."

Lowering his hands, the SLM shook his head slowly and stared at the monitor. "Some believe nothing is truly impossible for that N-Tschester creature. Get someone down there and make sure of it."

3

Terry Egan and Charlie Betts stood at the edge of the deepest end of a newly-carved trench in their small plot of timber. Along the trench, downed trees lay at odd angles, looking like giant matchsticks casually tossed on the ground.

Rail thin and a head taller than his partner, Charlie scratched his unruly mop of sandy hair. “What the hell caused this?”

Terry shrugged. “A meteor?”

“Are you serious?” Charlie argued. “A meteor would have…”

He stopped when a spot of ground at the lowest point of the trench rose a few inches before settling back down.

“Shit,” Terry exclaimed. “Something’s down there.”

Both men froze momentarily until Charlie laughed, “It’s just dirt settling.” He glanced back at the several-hundred feet of trench. “What could survive a crash like that?”

“Some kind of satellite?”

“No chance.”

“And you’re an expert on secret military…”

Terry went silent as a large saucer-shaped disk rose from the ground, dirt still piled on its top.

“Shit-oh-dear,” Terry cried.

Charlie took a quick step back. “Let’s go!”

Though Charlie tugged his arm, Terry held his ground. “We’ve got to tell someone.”

“Bullshit,” Charlie exclaimed as the object continued to rise. “I’m out of here!”

“Chicken-shit.”

Charlie turned toward his friend. “Better chicken than…”

A loud hissing cut off his response as the disk rose to eye-level. White vapor spewed from one side, pushing the craft to their right as it ascended.

“Oh God, we’re dead,” Charlie moaned, but Terry remained where he was, slack jawed and staring.

They both watched as the craft stopped rising, shuddered and slowly sank out of sight.

"Run," Charlie screamed, yanking his companion into the trees behind them.

Both men ran with all their might, neither looking back until they were further into the trees.

"What do you think?" Terry gasped as he and Charlie slowed, each ducking behind a tree before peeking around to see a white mist floating over the spot they had last seen the ship.

"I think we're safe here," Charlie said just before a deafening explosion sent the whole world crashing down on them.

4

The massive black battleship slipped quickly up to the orbital station, its lights off, weapons stowed, and any remaining sign of its existence masked by powerful shields. Inside, officers worked quietly in subdued light as the captain and his superior watched their objective grow larger on the main view screen.

"Any indication that we've been detected by onboard personnel, Captain?" Supreme Commander Khephra asked softly without taking his eyes off the display.

"None, Sir," came the hushed response, "But I still don't see why we need to sneak up on our own people."

"I just want to make sure no one else knows we're here."

"Do you really think the Kokos are behind this?"

"Enough of them want us dead to make that a good assumption."

"But Sir, we're allies."

Khephra shook his head. "What would you have done if they had won the war?"

The captain looked confused. "But that was decades ago."

"Some wounds heal and others fester."

"I guess I'd have been looking for a way to turn it around."

The ship shuddered slightly as docking clamps grabbed onto the station and the navigation officer gave the thumbs up.

"I think the Kokos finally found a way," Khephra said as he rose. "And our job is to make sure they never get to use it."

5

"Sir," the TLM called anxiously as his superior rushed toward him. "We have contact with the saucer unit."

"Damaged?"

"Yes, but it's hard to tell how much."

"What's happening?"

"It's airborne, but losing coolant."

"Order it back to the ground," The SLM demanded. "We'll send another unit to retrieve it."

"It's detected Humans."

"*Shendtada*!" he swore. "Get a description before they escape."

"I'm trying but the saucer unit is failing too quickly."

The SLM pointed at the screen. "Use the Anfeld-Fortier link."

"But that might overload the…"

"Just do it!"

Fingers flying, the TLM entered commands. "The data's coming in now. We should have…"

As the display froze, his superior slapped the desk. "Now what?"

Lurching from his chair, the TLM stretched to reach a control switch on the next console but it went dark just before an ear-piercing alarm filled the air.

"*Famoach*!" he cried. "We lost the master-control antenna for that region."

"The antenna?"

The TLM looked down at the dark unit. "Actually, it may be worse than that. This system is connected to the monitoring station that controls the prisoners."

The SLM's mouth dropped open, but he quickly recovered. "Kill that alarm, dispatch a repair crew and bring the backup unit on-line."

The TLM disabled the alarm, touched a golden patch on his sleeve, and after a short verbal exchange, turned to his superior.

"The repair crew's on the way, but there is no backup."

"What?"

"The last one went to the Middle-East region during the previous solar cycle because of heavier activity there."

"So get it back!"

The TLM moved to a working console, tapped the surface several times and waited for a response.

"It's already in use and they have no backups to spare."

"Hammond's royal red rump," the SLM muttered as perspiration dotted his face. "Find the nearest facility," he demanded without taking his eyes off the monitor.

"Secor-Alpha Four, but it's over fifteen-hundred light years away."

"Kee-Hathor is closer. We've swapped with them before."

"Their sun became unstable five solar cycles ago and almost everything has been shipped to Elum, on the other side of the galaxy."

The SLM groaned. "Then see if Secor-Alpha Four has any spares."

Another operator waved at the TLM.

"What is it?" he snapped as the junior officer approached.

"A request from Secor-Alpha Four, Sir." He handed a small disk to the TLM, who passed it to his superior. As the Second-Level Monitor's fingers wrapped around the disk, a 3D image of the planet appeared in front of him. Two large rectangular areas on its surface blinked red as the subordinate continued,

"They lost two monitoring stations and want to know if we have a spare."

"They what?" the SLM cried.

"They were attacked, Sir. Space pirates, they think."

The SLM looked at the screen as a simulation of ships attacking the stations played before his eyes. When it was done, he asked, "Isn't his mate confined there?"

"Tammabet Ferrisis? That is correct, Sir" the subordinate answered. "But to be precise, she is his Second Mate. There are also about five hundred of his former crew."

"Five hundred? Was this a massive conspiracy?"

The TLM shook his head. "No, Sir. They just refused to believe he had done it."

"Really? But there was a trial. He was properly convicted."

"I don't know, Sir. That is just what happened."

"So how many of his people are here?"

"Only a few dozen, along with Saki N-Tschester, himself, and his Primary Mate, Pana-tee."

The SLM scratched his chin. "Pana-tee? But isn't that…?"

"Yes," someone behind the threesome interrupted, "but my daughter no longer goes by her full name."

The SLM jerked around to face an individual a good head taller than himself.

"It's Pana-Teelr Khephra," the speaker added as the SLM's mouth flopped open.

6

Terry awoke under a pile of dirt and wood scraps. The forest of trees that once stood all around them was now a scrambled mess of shattered logs.

"Charlie?" he moaned, shaking debris from his face before pushing a limb off his chest. "Are you OK?" Groaning from a sharp pain in an ankle crushed beneath an overturned tree, he tried to look for his mate. "Charlie! Help me. I'm stuck."

Getting no response, he attempted to use his right arm to rise, but found it badly fractured, a jagged chunk of bone poking from the torn skin.

"Why doesn't it hurt?" he asked dumbly as bile rose in his throat. Feeling light headed, he looked up to see something large approaching through the smoke.

"Help," he cried. "We're trapped over here."

Terry feebly waved his good arm until he realized the shape was floating several feet above the ground. What he took for a face had two square openings where eyes should be, no nose, and a small round hole for a mouth.

"Oh my God."

7

Tom Celdridge jumped from his father's pickup and scanned the trees to their right. "What the hell was that?" he asked as his father exited the driver's side.

"Don't know," Ed answered as he tugged his left ear and looked in the same direction, "but it almost bounced us off the road."

Tom shook his head while unconsciously mimicking his father's ear tugging. "You think Terry and Charlie were fooling with dynamite?"

"There won't be much left if they were."

Tom stepped over to a barbed-wire fence at the edge of the road, slid his short, stocky body between the wires and headed for the forest beyond. "I guess we'd better find out."

After hurrying up a steep rise through a canopy of firs, the two men found themselves at the end of a long, freshly cut trench. About three-quarters of the way down, a disk-shaped object lay at the bottom, spewing white smoke that fogged the surrounding area. In a wide, circular pattern around this disk, all trees were denuded or flattened, some sheared off only inches from the ground.

Tom turned to his father, but before he could speak, an opening appeared in the disk, and something resembling a chrome-plated ape sitting on a floating platform appeared.

"What is that?" Ed cried as the two men shied back to the cover of the trees.

"No idea of any kind," Tom responded.

After momentarily hovering over the disk, the thing moved to their left, and into the densest part of the smoke.

When it vanished from sight, Ed turned around. "I'm getting the guns."

Tom's protest died on his lips as his eyes flicked between the smoking disk and the spot where the thing vanished. He was still tugging on his ear and watching when his father returned moments later.

"Any more sign of it?" Ed wheezed as he handed a rifle to Tom.

His son nodded while pointing. "I caught a glimpse of it through the smoke, but I can't see it now."

After Ed threw back the bolt on his 30-06 and jammed a shell into the chamber, Tom put a hand on his arm. "Whatever this is, we don't want to shoot until we figure out what's going on."

His father shook his head. "And how will we know that?"

"I don't know, but let's just not get trigger happy."

Ed slipped his rifle into the crook of his left arm, adjusted the billed hat on his crew-cut head and smiled at his son. "And when did you get so level-headed?"

Adjusting his own hat in the same way, Tom met his father's eyes. "Just taking after my dad," he said before ratcheting a shell into his own gun.

Suddenly a voice came from the direction of the disk, "Help. We're trapped over here."

"Christ," Ed exclaimed. "It's got someone."

Guns raised, both men took off at a run.

8

Terror rendered Terry speechless as he stared up at the thing floating in front of him.

Without a word, the creature telescoped out an arm, grabbed a large tree and hefted it into the air. As it held up several tons of timber, its other arm lifted Charlie's limp body onto its platform.

"Charlie," Terry screamed. "No!"

Ignoring Terry's protest, the creature dropped the tree with a ground-shaking thump, pulled a thick, silver rod-shaped object from an opening in its platform and moved it over the unconscious man. After numerous passes, it stowed the rod and paused for a moment before turning its attention to the trapped human.

"Oh crap," Terry groaned as he struggled to rise.

Though held down by his pinned ankle and broken arm, Terry managed to heave a rock at the creature. The effort fell short.

As the ache in his arm intensified, Terry's brain began to numb. Moving closer, the creature lifted the tree from his ankle and tossed it aside. Picking up the silver rod again, it telescoped an arm, and passed it over the prostrate human. Almost instantly Terry's entire body began vibrating as though each cell was trying to escape its confines. Groaning from fear and pain as the vibrations irritated the injuries, he tried to crawl away, but his muscles refused to respond.

Interminable moments passed before the pain began to subside. Finally, the creature switched off the device, backed away and motioned for Terry to rise. The stunned man lifted his arm to find the torn skin healed and the bone reset. Expecting pain, he grimaced while slowly standing and was surprised to find his ankle a bit stiff, but free of pain.

Terry gawked at the thing. "You're not here to hurt us, are you?"

As though in response, the robot scooped Charlie up and gently laid him on the ground. When his body touched earth, Charlie sucked in a deep breath and began to stir. The creature backed away, allowing Terry to move in.

"Are you OK?" he asked while gently shaking his friend.

Groaning, Charlie started to rise, but jerked into a defensive crouch when he saw the dark figure hovering in the smoke.

"Damn," he exclaimed.

Terry opened his mouth to speak, but was interrupted by the crack of a rifle followed by a loud ringing. Both men dove for cover as the creature turned to face away from them and a humming sound filled the air. The rifle fired again, but this time the bullet stopped just inches from the robot's skin, The now red-hot projectile hovered momentarily before dropping to the platform with a splat. Another shot sent more lead splattering.

"Someone's shooting at it," Terry exclaimed.

"Son of a bitch," Charlie said with awe. "It's got shields."

Terry jumped from his hiding place as another shot rang out.

"Stop," he screamed. "Don't shoot!"

Charlie grabbed for his friend, but only managed to slap his waist before Terry lurched out of reach, dancing around and over downed trees while waving his hands overhead.

"Wait, damn it," Charlie cried as he scrambled after him.

Hurrying around a tall rootwad, Charlie nearly ran into Terry who had his hands in the air while staring at two men with rifles.

"Tom? Ed? It's us," Charlie yelled as the men alternately moved their aim from the humans to the nonhuman and back.

After several tense moments, Tom lowered his rifle slightly. "What is that thing?"

"I don't know, but it saved our lives," Terry answered.

The two men looked at Charlie, who shrugged while shaking his head. "It doesn't matter anyway, guys. It's got some kind of shielding that stops your bullets. If it wanted to kill us, it would have done it by now."

Ed lowered his gun. "So, where did it come from?"

All four humans turned to face the creature as Terry said, "We haven't had a chance to ask."

9

"Supreme Commander," the second level monitor cried while bowing before the newcomer. "My most exact apologies, your Excellency. I had no idea you had graced us with your presence."

"Stop bowing," Khephra ordered, his eyes already scanning the room. "I'm a military officer, not some insipid Koko king."

Embarrassed, the SLM straightened while looking around self-consciously. It was at this point he noticed a cluster of military officers jammed in behind the supreme commander in the small room. They were sharply dressed in blue-gray uniforms worn only by the Manchra division: Khephra's elite corp. Each had the traditional progressive tattoo of his rank on the side of his forehead. The SLM counted one major and four captains, but the five remaining faces were too hidden to determine their ranks.

"Yes Sir," he said. "It's just that we haven't had anyone of such high office here in such a long time…"

The SLM's voice trailed off as Khephra raised a hand, palm up, his long slender fingers spread.

"Just treat me like you'd like to be treated. After all, this isn't a military facility. I have no more authority over you than any other citizen."

Not sure how to respond, the SLM remained silent as the surprise visitor looked around the room again. "What kind of staffing do you have here?"

The SLM grimaced. "There used to be sixteen of us monitoring this region, but due to budget cuts, we are reduced to only six, working overlapping shifts."

"And you monitor how many prisoners?"

"One-hundred-and-thirty million in the western Canadian, American and Mexican sectors," he answered. "Of course, much of the work is done by the computers. We mostly supervise insertions and extractions."

Khephra moved closer to the SLM's monitor. "Did I hear you say you're having a problem?"

The second-level monitor looked nervously from the screen to Khephra and back. "Umm…yes Sir. We just lost a drone, and…" He glanced at his feet, embarrassed. "…possibly a monitoring station."

"Was anyone hurt?"

"It just happened and we've only begun to assess the damage."

"Can we help?"

The SLM glanced at his own subordinate before turning back. "We heard of an attack on Secor-Alpha Four. Do you know anything more about that?"

Khephra shrugged. "News has been sketchy, but that's why we're here. This lost drone may have something to do with that attack, and we don't want anyone thinking this prison isn't secure."

"I am relieved to hear that, Supreme Commander."

Khephra pointed to one of the officers behind him. "Pass the last known location of the drone to Captain Praetor and we'll help search for it. My people are experts at finding fleas among the dog hairs."

The SLM motioned for the TLM to undertake that task.

"Is there anything I can do for you, Supreme Commander?"

Khephra turned to one of the large windows facing the planet below. Without looking back, he asked softly, "Tell me. How does time pass for them down there?"

The SLM scrambled to his side. "This planet revolves around its sun much faster than our Primary Planet, making ninety-seven-point-three trips per *druak*. In the place your daughter is now residing, they refer to each solar revolution as a year."

The supreme commander shook his head. "She's been down there a little over thirty *druak*. What would that be in her time?"

"Roughly three-thousand years."

Khephra shook his head. "That must seem like an eternity."

"Not really, Sir. She wouldn't be experiencing it as one continuous event. The life span of the indigenous population is extremely short. While we live thousands of *druaks*, they rarely last even one. In addition, memories of her previous lives are blocked, and at the start of each cycle her Life Force is implanted in an unborn fetus. As far as she knows, she's a normal Human with no idea she's in prison." The SLM moved to another station and quickly entered a code. "According to our records, your daughter is experiencing her fifty-sixth life span."

The supreme commander's face looked pained. "You mean she's been born, lived and died over fifty times in thirty *druaks*? What can this possibly accomplish?"

"As you know," the SLM continued when the supreme commander turned back to the window, "an individual's Life Force cannot be extinguished. When a body dies, the person loses their corporeal form and the physical possessions that go with it, but their good and bad characteristics -- the essence of who they are -- carry through.

"With special manipulation provided by the artificial-intelligence behavior-modification programs in our computer system, we can manipulate the prisoner's life to make them gravitate toward good behavior while avoiding the bad. Given enough time, we can change them from the troublemaker they were to the good citizen our society wants them to be."

The supreme commander shook his head. "My daughter was a good person before she met him."

The SLM nodded. "And because of her excellent reports, you may have success petitioning the Over Council for clemency."

"The Over Council?"

"Considering the seriousness of her crime, it would take our highest Council to grant such a request."

"And you think she's ready now?"

The SLM shrugged his narrow shoulders. "Your daughter has never been a problem internee. She's only here now because her sentencing directive decreed she never be paroled. Personally, I do not believe she's a risk to anyone."

"And what about him?"

"Our records show Saki N-Tschester has also been a model prisoner, but it is highly doubtful he'll ever leave this facility."

Khephra remained quiet for some time before turning to the SLM. “You are, I assume, under the belief that he isn’t responsible for the drone that just crashed.”

The SLM’s mouth dropped open as he stared up at his superior. “I…I don’t think that’s possible, Sir. The internees do not even know such things exist. Any who actually report seeing a drone are immediately subject to ridicule by the native population. We have so deeply implanted the notion that aliens sightings are the work of unbalanced and attention-seeking individuals, most who see our drones never report it to anyone.”

Khephra looked back at the planet. “Just the same. I am sure you won’t mind if I take a look for myself.”

10

Shaded by a canopy of fir trees, the alien machine floated five feet above the ground as Terry and Charlie slowly approached it.

"This is crazy," Charlie protested as he caught up with his partner.

Terry kept his eyes on the strange visitor. "It saved our lives. Why destroy us now?"

"You're assuming they think like we do. It might just be saving us for lunch."

Terry turned toward his companion. "Our only chance to make contact with aliens and you make them out to be monsters?"

"Well, it is pretty damned ugly."

"Great, Charlie. Give it a reason to hate us."

Charlie rolled his eyes. "It's not going to hate us just because..."

The robot lurched forward, rising up and over the twosome and on toward Tom and Ed.

"See what you did?" Terry moaned as it moved away.

"You said it wasn't going to hate us."

"How did I know?"

"For a machine, it's damned sensitive."

As the robot stopped in front of the father and son, Ed and Tom raised their rifles.

"I am Observation Unit 335536," it droned in a flat, monotonous voice. "I am looking for Standard Internment Unit number 73983988223, an Antrakan derivative. Please direct me."

The men looked at each other and then back at the observation unit.

After a tense moment, Tom lowered his rifle. "What?"

The creature repeated its request.

Tom shook his head. "I have no idea what you just said."

"You want to give us that in English?" Ed asked while still keeping his rifle at the ready.

"I am communicating in the North American English vernacular," the robot responded. "I assumed you would be fluent in this language."

"North Amer…" Ed started to protest before his son interrupted.

"We are, but we don't know what this Standard Attorney unit thing is."

The creature tilted slightly forward as though looking them over then straightened. "You are Standard Internment Units."

11

"How do I get down there?" the supreme commander asked, making it sound more like an order than a question.

"You don't want to do that, Sir," the SLM said nervously.

"Make ready for ten of my men and myself to transport down," the supreme commander ordered as though he hadn't heard him. "We'll put an end to this once and for all."

"You can't. At least, not as you are."

Khephra glared at the SLM. "What do you mean?"

The SLM cowered. "I thought you knew, Sir. It's an oxygen-based system. You wouldn't last ten milli-paks."

The supreme commander's face showed surprise then anger. "My daughter's down there," he bellowed.

The SLM nodded quickly. "But her life force occupies a reproduction of the native species. As such, she's perfectly adapted to the environment.

"That's what makes this such a perfect prison. The internees need more oxygen than we do, they cannot exist in a vacuum and their bodies are hypersensitive to radiation. Even if one of them stole a ship, their body would die before they escaped the solar system."

Khephra scowled at the SLM. "I'm more concerned with someone kidnapping one of them."

"But who…"

"Never mind. Just get us down there."

"That will not be easy."

"Our environmental suits will protect us from the corrosive atmosphere."

"But Humans are quite agile. Even in our best suit, they'd out maneuver you at every turn."

Khephra turned to Major Phaa, who nodded. "No disrespect, Sir, but I believe he is correct."

"We don't need agility. We'll stun them into submission and transport them back up."

The SLM shook his head slowly. “Sorry, but it is going to be much more difficult than that.”

“What do you mean?”

“The prime objective of this facility is to rehabilitate internees using experiences that change their negative traits. This involves actively manipulating their lives, and if they knew what we are doing, the methodologies we have successfully implemented for centuries would be useless.

“In the late 1970s of their time-frame, an event occurred that almost destroyed that delicate balance. Several of our rapid insertion units, disguised as military officers, were involved in an accident that seriously exposed our operations. We had to capture hundreds of Humans and wipe their memories. Unfortunately, with some of the Humans, we failed to remove their memory of the wiping process itself. They not only recalled being tied to tables and probed, but some saw the rapid insertion units in military outfits. Despite our best efforts, stories of the Earthling military’s involvement in these abductions still circulate to this day.”

The SLM turned to Khephra. “Humans are very curious creatures and often blend fact with fiction to arrive at a conclusion that satisfies them. We keep them skeptical by inserting operatives in various official and unofficial positions that ridicule the eye witnesses, and present them as unbalanced individuals spouting unsupported conspiracy theories.”

He chuckled. “We destroy or hide any concrete evidence, either through government confiscation, blurring photographic images, or replacing items found or seen with similar, easily explained objects. We’ve been so effective that even those with strong circumstantial evidence are thought to be unbalanced or liars. Many who actually see our ships are reluctant to report the sighting for fear of being ridiculed.”

He turned to the supreme commander. “Of course, ridicule only goes so far. Our studies show that Humans want to believe in what they refer to as ‘extraterrestrial life’. If there are too many sightings, no amount of ridicule will stop them from believing. To reduce the number of exposures, the Councils passed laws restricting access to the planet surface and set strict protocols on the abduction of internment units or Humans. No matter what the cost, it is imperative that you leave no clue that the termination of these units is anything other than something they would expect to see."

"And how do we do that?"

The SLM shrugged. "I'll get you a list of acceptable methods."

"One of our fighters could destroy their dwelling while they sleep. We could make it look like a natural explosion."

The SLM shook his head. "The use of any weapon not made by the indigenous population is strictly forbidden by law. We can't even include them on emergency vehicles."

"Huh," Khephra grunted angrily. "It sounds like the system is working in his favor, not ours."

A captain raised a hand. "If we can't take weapons to the surface, a canon shot from space could be effective, though there would be considerable collateral damage."

The SLM shuddered. "The oxygen level in the lower atmosphere is too high. Even a micro canon would set off a catastrophic chain reaction."

"The oxygen level is low enough," the captain protested.

"You're not factoring in water vapor. Our weapon's hyper-energetic phasons break water apart, producing even more oxygen and flammable hydrogen. The intense vibrations feed on themselves, radiating away from the point of impact, and spreading at an ever-increasing rate."

"I doubt it's as bad as all that."

The SLM shook his head. "About one-hundred of their years ago, we did a test in the remote Tunguska region of the Russian territory. A single laser blast destroyed nearly everything in a two-thousand square kilometer area around the impact point. Of course, we convinced the local authorities to call it a meteor impact, but even so…"

"So what do you suggest we do?" Khephra interrupted irritably.

"You must meet the internment units face-to-face, and terminate them with their own weapons."

"But if wearing environmental suits is impractical, how do we accomplish this?"

The SLM looked at him warily. "There is only one way and you're not going to like it."

Khephra straightened to his full height. "We're soldiers. We often do things we don't like."

"This might be an exception," the SLM mumbled as he tapped an icon on his console.

12

"What the hell is it talking about?" Ed demanded as his eyes darted from the observation unit to his son.

"I don't know, Dad. Maybe you should ask him."

"It," his father corrected.

Tom shook his head. "Yeah. Whatever."

Ed looked up at the robot and swallowed hard. "What is this Standard Interpreting thing?"

It rotated to face the elder man. "The correct term is Standard Internment Unit."

Tom held up a hand. "Internment? Like we're prisoners?" He looked around. "Where's the walls?"

"None are needed," the creature droned in response. "You are confined by the physical limitations of your bodies."

For a moment the four humans stared in silence at the visitor until Charlie picked up a chunk of wood and threw it. The projectile bounced harmlessly off the observation unit's skin.

"What the hell are you doing?" Ed cried.

Ignoring him, Charlie grabbed a rock. "Come out of there, whoever you are. This has gone on long enough."

"Are you nuts?" Terry screamed while wrapping his arms around his mate. "He'll kill your stupid ass!"

"Someone's jerking our chains," Charlie yelled.

Despite Charlie's feeble attack, the creature kept his attention on Ed and Tom. As Terry and Charlie's struggle fizzled, Tom looked from the robot to his neighbors.

"You don't like gay Standard Interruption Eunuchs?"

"They are not Standard Internment Units. They are Human."

Ed shook his head. "Son of a bitch," he said slowly. "I feel like I'm watching some kind of Hungarian movie without subtitles." He turned to his son. "You making any sense of this?"

Tom looked at his neighbors again before turning to his father. "Crazy as this might sound, Dad. I think I do."

13

"We have to what?" Khephra demanded.

The SLM's eyes were wide as he answered, "Your Life Force must be transferred to one of these Rapid Insertion Units."

They were both looking through the transparent wall of a tank holding a gestating humanoid body. Seventeen identical tanks lined up behind this one, along with their monitoring equipment, took up most of the room. Eighteen stasis chambers filled the far wall.

Khephra pointed to the humanoid floating in front of him. "Into that?"

"It's the only way you'll be able to complete your mission."

"You're right," Khephra said while shaking his head. "I'm not liking this one bit." He looked back at his men milling outside the room's entrance. "How long will it take?"

"If we use the local terminology for time, usually two to three days," the SLM answered.

"Just to do the transfer?"

The SLM shook his head. "No Sir. It takes four hours to transfer the Life Force, and another six to complete the diagnostics and sympathetic systems coordination." He walked past the tank to a stasis chamber. "The subject is then transferred here to be slowly awakened while their consciousness adjusts to its new environment." He touched a console surface and a bank of displays lit up. "Rushing the process almost always results in a brain rupture and symbiont death."

"Death?"

The SLM shook his head. "Don't worry, Sir. We have procedures for retrieving the Life Force, but the process must then be restarted."

"Is the subject aware of this part?"

"No, but sometimes a very strong consciousness can cause problems."

"You mean someone like the N-Tschester internee?"

Blushing, the SLM shook his head. "Actually, I was referring to your daughter."

The supreme commander stiffened, but his look of surprise had a hint of a smile in it.

"How do you deal with this...strong personality?"

The SLM pointed at the colorful bank of displays. "In the case of your daughter, we needed a level-six stasis." He turned back to his superior. "I've been processing Internment Units for nearly twenty *druak*. Most go through fine at level two. Roughly ten percent require level four. Only a fraction of a percent need six."

"Hmmm," the supreme commander murmured while turning toward the nearest window to cover his now-obvious smile. "Then I guess you'd better use that level with me."

The SLM nodded. "That will add at least one of their days to the process."

Turning back, Khephra lifted a questioning eyebrow.

"The further into stasis sleep the internee must go, the longer it takes to bring them out. In addition, that extends the post-awakening recovery period."

"Why?"

"You might think of this as being reborn. You must learn to eat, speak, and walk all over again. Even going to the bathroom will be a challenge at first. The Human anatomy is so much different than ours. For starters, the males have a..."

"I'm a fast learner," the supreme commander growled.

"I'm sure you are, but even with the inserted algorithms to help with the transition, much of it must be learned by doing. A resistant mind slows the process."

"Surely the internees don't go through this."

"We get around that by inserting them into a fetus. With their past suppressed, there is nothing for them to unlearn. Their new skills develop along with their growing bodies.

"However, very strong personalities can overwhelm the immature controlling device we insert in the fetus brain. An internee judged to be too strong for a fetus is first put into a full-grown Rapid Insertion Unit to "acclimate" within a computer-simulated lifetime."

He pointed to a twitching humanoid in the third gestation tank. “This one is experiencing the forty-fifth year of his simulated life.”

The SLM frowned. “Actually, in the case of your daughter and the N-Tschester creature, the judge decreed they go through the acclimation process for their first life cycle. He even sent three KokoroTetian technicians to supervise the process.”

“Are Kokos often involved like this?”

The SLM barked a high-pitched, nervous laugh. “To my knowledge, it had never been done before or since. Just the same, since N-Tschester and your daughter are Antrakan and the destroyed planet was in KokoroTetian territorial space…well, for us to countermand the Koko judge’s order might bring on…uh, it just wasn’t an option.”

Khephra waved an impatient hand. “Yes, I know all about that, but tell me, how do you control them once they’re down there?”

“The cerebral implants act as a shunt between their present consciousness and their past.” He chuckled while tapping his forehead. “We can keep a thousand generations of existence from them, or release it as suits our needs. We can also insert thoughts, or actions to make them do things they might not otherwise do: a faithful husband suddenly cheating on his wife; a banker embezzling funds to support a newly acquired gambling addiction; a happy woman unexpectedly committing suicide.

“We don’t do these things to be cruel. It is part of the reprogramming process to give them empathy for their former victims and make them better people because of it.”

Khephra shook his head. “But the controlling station is off-line. Won’t all that control just vanish?”

“In time, yes, but the implants are designed to maintain themselves for two to three of their months without outside contact.”

“And they won’t notice a thing?”

The SLM shrugged. “There may be a short period in which memories from previous lives will peek through. In most cases, the internees will be so confused by the sudden change, they’ll hardly realize what is happening before it has past.”

“They won’t recognize their past lives?”

"You have to remember, Sir. They think they are Human and Humans don't generally believe in past lives. They will pass it off as a flash of insanity, and will likely keep to themselves."

The supreme commander turned to look at the planet. "Like a bad dream, eh?"

"Pretty much."

"And who would ever wish that for their baby girl," Khephra mumbled.

"I beg your pardon, Sir?"

Still looking at Earth's night side, he shrugged. "Oh, I was just thinking it must be a horrible existence."

The SLM shook his head. "Well, after all, this is a prison."

Yes it is, Khephra thought as his chest ached. *For them and all who love them.*

14

From the highest point on his property, Wyatt Simmons stretched his long arms skyward before running fingers through his hair. In the wide Willamette Valley below him, the grass seed harvest was in full swing. The mid-day sun illuminated great clouds of dust fogging the valley floor as mechanical harvesters wrenched tiny seeds from the dry grass.

"Wyatt?" Megan Simplott called as she approached. "We've got to get back and…" Her voice trailed off as she took in the view. "My God, that's beautiful."

When Wyatt didn't respond, she turned to him. "Hey buddy? What'cha thinking."

"Do you believe in God?" he asked while continuing to stare at the distant valley.

"What?"

"I think they've got it wrong. It's not a single God – a benevolent father who loves us – but a group of…lesser beings, watching over us, manipulating our lives like puppets in a play."

"What on Earth are you talking about?"

"It just makes no sense, is all," he continued. "Good people living lives of pain and misery while evil ones have plenty. A person's morals have nothing to do with how good their life is. Your whole world can get screwed up by someone you never see and the perpetrator walks away scott-free. Where's the love and justice in that?"

"This is about your parent's murder, isn't it?"

Wyatt shook his head. "It's not about what happened, but why."

"We'll never know why."

"Then what's the point? How do you learn? How can you be a better person if you don't know what you're being punished for?"

A good head shorter than her friend, Megan pushed a strawberry-blond lock from her slightly plump face, and looked up at him, saying nothing.

"I think the Buddhist's philosophy is closer to the truth. We live many lives to experience the true effects of greed, hatred and corruption so we can eventually return to…" He waved a hand at the sky. "…whatever existence we had before we were sent here."

Megan slapped him on the arm. "What are you smoking?"

Wyatt smiled, but didn't respond.

She was preparing to say more when a loud boom made both of them look to the west as the ground shuddered.

"What the hell?" Megan asked as she turned to find Wyatt staring into the distance, his eyes glassy and unfocussed. "Wyatt?"

His gaze remained fixed for a moment more before he turned to her, looking confused. "I'm sorry?"

"What was that explosion?"

"What explosion?"

"You didn't hear it?"

When his head shook, she moved in close, pressing a hand to his forehead. "Are you feeling OK?"

He responded by closing his eyes and putting his own hand over hers. "Your hand is cool."

He grabbed her other hand and pulled it briefly to his cheek before releasing them both and pulling her into a hug. Though surprised by the move, she soon reciprocated. Their relationship had always been close, and platonic. She had no reason to assume anything had changed.

After a moment, he pulled away. "Whoa! Danger!"

Alarmed, she looked around. "What do you mean?"

"Just now, I got this really intense feeling…I don't know, like someone is coming to hurt us."

She laughed nervously. "Who the hell would want to hurt a harmless fool like you?"

A tear dribbled down his cheek as he looked at her and shook his head. "No," he said softly, but with a certainty that shocked her. "They're coming for you."

15

"So once we get to the surface, how do we get back," Khephra asked as he stared down at the planet.

The SLM smiled. "That's the beauty of the system," he stated with a sense of pride. "Your essence is maintained within the Rapid Insertion Unit by the specially modified ethereal force emanating from the implant in the unit's brain. Our orbital system tracks each Life Force and recovers it when the unit terminates."

The supreme commander's eyes widened as he turned to face the SLM. "The only way to get back is to kill myself?"

The SLM held up a hand, palm out. "Just your body. Under normal circumstances, your Life Force would come back here for reinsertion into your original body, which is kept in stasis. Of course, someone with a longer sentence will be returned to the surface in a new…"

"What do you mean, 'under normal circumstances'?"

The SLM moved to a monitor. With a few taps on the console, the screen doubled in size, showing a 3-D copy of the planet below. Touching the screen, he rotated the planet until the area he wanted to display was facing the supreme commander. Satisfied, he pointed to two dark-red squares covering part of the North American region.

"The areas marked in red are covered by orbital control station 6236. The crash of our drone damaged this station. Drones crash once in a while, but we have enough influence with the governing bodies down there to hush things up before anyone notices." He turned to Khephra. "There was this incident in Boswell, New Mexico that just about exposed the whole…"

Khephra cut him off with an impatient wave. "Get back to the problem."

"Uh, yes Sir. Anyway, this drone initially reported contact with indigenous Humans. With Standard Internment Units, we can modify their memories from here. However, indigenous natives require physical contact for this procedure to work. Unfortunately, we were downloading information about the Humans, when the drone overloaded and blew out the station."

"How long before a replacement is in place?"

"Well…that's hard to say."

The supreme commander slammed a hand on the counter, sending cups, pens and data chips dancing across its surface. "Get to the damned point!"

"A solar month at the earliest," the now-cringing SLM answered.

Scowling at the SLM, Khephra touched an emblem on his sleeve. "Supreme Commander Khephra to lead ship."

"Yes, Sir. Lead ship here."

"Give me the technical bay."

There was a slight pause, then, "Technical bay. Sergeant Specialist Akki speaking."

"Akki, good. This is the supreme commander. Do you have any experience with the orbital control stations in use here?"

"Yes Sir," he responded energetically. "For my first doctoral thesis I recreated one and doubled its capacity. I also added an Alpha wave inhibitor that…"

"We've got a disabled station here. How long to repair it?"

"What's the extent of the damage?"

The supreme commander turned to the SLM and raised an eyebrow. It took the subordinate a moment to realize he was expected to answer.

"After our observation unit crashed, we discovered it was unstable, and initiated an Anfeld-Forter link to get the data faster."

"That's what I would have done," Akki said.

"Yes, but something went wrong and a level-seven feedback pulse blew out the semi-control antenna."

Akki whistled. "Level seven? I'm guessing it didn't stop there."

"You are correct, Sergeant Specialist. Even with the antenna acting as a buffer, it wiped out over seventy percent of the orbital unit. Our engineers say it is unrepairable."

"Ha," Akki barked. "You don't have my resources."

"You're saying it can be repaired?" Khephra asked.

"Yes, Sir, but it will take a bit of time."

"How long?"

"With respects, Sir," Akki responded. "I can't say until I've seen the extent of the damage, but I'd say no more than eight or ten paks."

"Why so long?"

"It's mostly a matter of scale, Sir. That thing is the size of a battleship, but even that isn't the real problem. My robotic maintenance units can have it cleaned out and re-circuited in short order, but there are six sections in each station, and they hold three-hundred-thousand status control regulators each. There's a lot of calibration involved."

"Would it help if the station's engineers assisted?"

"Without a doubt, Sir."

The supreme commander locked eyes with the SLM. "You're in charge, Akki. I'll make arrangements with the station director to get you all the staff that can be spared. This takes top priority."

"I won't let you down, Sir," Akki squeaked proudly.

"I have no doubt of that, Sergeant Specialist," Khephra said softly as he turned again to face the planet. "I'm putting my life in your hands."

16

"What are you thinking about now?" Megan asked.

Wyatt looked up to find her ahead of him on the trail. His walks with her were always a high point for him, but today disturbing feelings clouded his thoughts.

"I keep getting these weird memories that can't be real, but sure seem to be," he explained after catching up with her.

"Like what?"

"Like I lived another life, or maybe many lives before now."

"You're kidding."

He stopped abruptly, forcing her to turn around and walk back to him.

Seeing the confusion on his face, she put a hand on his forehead again; a move that only moments earlier brought complete relaxation, but now generated an entirely different feeling. To his surprise, he found himself pulling away.

"What's the matter?" she asked.

His mind reeled as her lilac-scented perfume aroused him.

"We've got to get back to the house," he announced suddenly and took off down the trail.

"Wyatt?" she called after him, but he only quickened his pace.

"I need to…" he started to say, but finished with the thought, get away from you!

Breaking into a jog, he was alarmed to hear her coming up behind him.

As she reached his side, he turned slightly at the waist and said, "Listen, I think you should go…" The sight of her bouncing breasts stopped his thoughts just as his toe caught and he felt himself falling.

The ground came up so quickly, he barely had time to throw out his hands. He felt his forehead strike the ground as he tried to tuck into a roll. The failed attempt threw the full force of the impact onto his shoulder before he flipped over onto his back. He was still trying to recover his senses when she dropped to one knee and bent over him.

"Your forehead is bleeding," she cried as her handkerchief pressed against his forehead. "You numskull," she laughed. "What's wrong with you?"

His eyes were chest level as a button on her blouse opened to expose part of her left breast. As the swelling in his pants became more distinct, perspiration beaded on his forehead.

"No," he muttered while trying to brush her hand away.

"Oh, stop being such a baby. The blood will clot in a minute and you can get up."

She slapped his hand down and it landed on her breast. He felt electrified as it rested there for a moment before she pushed it off and looked into his eyes.

"You're sweating."

Before she could say more, her own eyes rolled up into her head and she started to fall forward. Grabbing her under the arms, he held her up as she regained consciousness, shook her head and looked around.

"What?" she asked softly before looking at him again. "Son of a bitch," she cried as their lips met.

17

"Gentlemen," the supreme commander spoke calmly to the ten officers at attention before him. "They tell me I won't be out of the processing machine for at least a solar day after you depart. In addition, the orbital control units needed to facilitate our return won't be operational until just after that."

He turned and began pacing slowly in front of them. "Normally, we like to have all the safety measures in place before launching such an important mission. However, both the Over Council and Level Council believe we must move quickly to contain this threat or…" He paused and scanned the faces of his men. "This person has been convicted of destroying an inhabited planet, and murdering over six billion men, women and children."

Disciplined though they were, he could see emotions playing on their faces. "And now someone wants to break him out. I'll kill the bastard before I let him start another civil war."

When Khephra stopped walking, the team leader stepped forward and saluted. "Sir! We will not let you down. Sir!"

As the officer lowered his hand, Khephra returned the salute, holding it as he said, "I know you won't Major Phaa. That is why you're here."

"It's time, Supreme Commander," the SLM said as he entered the room.

Khephra turned to him and nodded. "When they're ready, send them down. I will follow as soon as you can get me out of that damned box."

The SLM nodded in acknowledgment.

"And one more thing," Khephra said as he motioned for the door and then followed the SLM outside. "At present only one of my men knows my daughter is part of this." Looking back toward the open door, he pulled the SLM closer. "I'd like it to stay that way for now."

"Sir?"

"These men are very loyal to me. If they knew one of their targets was my own daughter, they might hesitate to do their job." Khephra glanced at the door again. "It wouldn't stop them, but in battle, a slight hesitation can make the difference between the flag of victory and a field of headstones."

"Are you referring to…," the SLM's voice faded.

Khephra sighed. "Keddit's Field, yes." He shook his head slowly. "Over a thousand men died because I hesitated long enough to let two civilian groups escape the battlefield." With a look of determination, he put a heavy hand on the SLM's shoulder. "In addition, the Councils want assurances I can't provide, so they're pushing this to a new level."

He pointed toward the ceiling. "As we speak, three more battleships are settling into geosynchronous orbit around this planet. If we fail and it looks like N-Tschester will make it off the surface, those ships have orders to destroy everything in, on and orbiting this planet."

The SLM's eyes bulged. "But…but, surely you can't mean…"

Khephra nodded, his expression grim. "And this time there won't be any place left for headstones."

18

"Gaaa," Wyatt cried as he pushed Megan away. "What are we doing?"

Megan tried to rise to her feet, but lost her balance and landed on her back, her hands covering her face. After a moment, she peeked through her fingers, as Wyatt rose quickly to his feet and stared at her, his mind awash with confusion.

"I'm sorry," she cried while covering her face again. "I don't know what came over me."

"Don't apologize. I wasn't exactly pushing you away."

She sat up abruptly. "It doesn't matter. This shouldn't be happening."

"And you think I don't know that?"

He stared at her staring at him for a long moment before his shoulders slumped. When he offered her a hand, she took it and stood, but immediately stepped away from him.

"This can't happen again."

He shook his head. "This wasn't us."

She looked at him incredulously. "What?"

"What did you see, just before you kissed me?"

She shook her head. "I don't know."

"Yes you do."

"It isn't what I saw, but what I felt."

"Like you were my mate?"

"But you're not. You can't be."

He nodded. "I know."

"So what's going on?"

"I don't know," he sighed, "but that's why I'm saying it wasn't us."

"You can't just blow this off like it never happened."

He threw his hands out in surrender. "I love you like…like… no one else I know, but I love Aurelia too. I'm not looking for anyone to replace her."

Her face relaxed as she moved in and raised a hand to touch his face, but pulled back at the last second.

He grabbed for her, and when she slipped out of reach, stood with his hand out, as a forbidden longing made his heart ache.

Get to the house! a voice in his head demanded.

He looked at Megan to see if she was the one who spoke, but she was turning away from him.

Danger! Hurry! the voice cried.

It felt like a slap in the face that made his head jerk back. Megan was just turning back toward him when he did a quick spin in the direction of his house.

"We've got to get back," he cried as he started running. "Something's happening."

19

As Ed scratched his head, Tom looked around. “You’re saying all of this is a prison and we, meaning my dad and I, but not Terry and Charlie, are prisoners?”

“Your assessment of the situation is basically correct,” the observation unit responded.

“But what did we do? How did we get here?” Tom looked at his father. “Why don’t we know we’re prisoners?”

The creature paused before answering. “My database has been partially damaged in the crash of my vehicle and the following explosion. I do not have that information at present and cannot make contact with the station computers for input.”

“So,” Ed said slowly, “If we aren’t supposed to know we’re prisoners then it makes sense we shouldn’t know about you either.”

“That is logical.”

Ed gave his son a nervous look. “And since we have seen you, what now?”

“I cannot answer that question.”

Ed leaned toward his son and whispered, “What if he has to kill us because we know too much?”

Tom looked nervously from his father to the machine then both men raised their rifles.

The creature did not react to their action, except to say, “I am not programmed to destroy. My primary duty is as an observer. I must locate the Standard Internment Unit I seek. It resides in this area.”

Tom glanced at the others. “What is its human name?”

“His internment name is…” The machine paused. “I do not have access to that information, but I have a visual representation.”

“What does that mean?” Ed asked.

“Just like with you, an internment number is printed on its forehead.”

Tom and Ed looked at each other.

“I don’t see any numbers,” Ed protested.

"The imprint uses patterns in your skin that are far too subtle for a Human to detect."

Tom ran fingers across his forehead. "What do you plan to do with this…person."

"I am to retrieve it and its mate for termination."

"I thought you weren't programmed to kill," Charlie argued as he and Terry moved up beside their neighbors.

"I am going to terminate the Standard Internment Unit, not kill the subject."

"But you have no weapons," Terry observed.

Moving so fast neither man could react, the robot snatched Tom and Ed's guns.

"I do now," it said.

20

As Wyatt and Megan came within sight of his cabin, four people were coming around the barn, followed by the observation unit. Aurelia stood in the doorway, but they were too far away to see her expression or hear what she was saying. It didn't matter, as both were staring at the object floating behind the other four.

"Son of a bitch," Megan swore as Wyatt pulled her behind a bush. "What the hell is that?"

Wyatt shook his head. "This isn't supposed to be happening."

"What isn't supposed to be happening?"

He lifted his head to peek over the bush. "We're not supposed to be able to see that thing."

"How would you know that?" Megan asked impatiently while peering through the bush.

Shaking his head, Wyatt dropped down to sit beside her. "Remember earlier, I told you someone was coming to kill you? Maybe that's it."

"You think there's a person inside that thing?"

He shrugged. "No way to tell from here. I've got to get closer."

Megan grabbed Wyatt's arm as he started to rise. "And then what?"

He pulled free and peered over the bush. "I don't know. I guess I'll improvise."

"You'll improvise? What about me?"

He squatted again. "Get over to Ed's house and call the Sheriff."

"I'm coming with you!"

Wyatt shook his head. "If it's here to kill you, you need to be as far away from it as possible."

"You're just trying to get this silly girl out of harm's way."

Frowning, he shook his head again. “You’re one of the most capable people I know, male or female, but we’ve got no weapons, nor do we know what it can do. Trust me on this.”

She held his stare for a moment before starting to rise, but he stopped her.

“Stay down until I get out of sight. If this is a false alarm, I’ll call Mary and let her know.”

Releasing her, he patted her lightly on the cheek before moving into a brush patch to their right.

As she rose, Megan muttered, “And if you get your silly ass killed, Wyatt Simmons, I’ll kick your butt all the way to Hell and back.”

21

Supreme Commander Khephra quietly closed the door to the small room and stumbled back into the hospital bed he'd spent the last day in. Pulling a small box from his pocket, he placed it on the bedside table and pressed an icon on its surface. A red light flicked on, blinked half-a-dozen times before turning green.

Pressing a button on another device wrapped around his wrist, he said, "Dampening fields are in place. We can…talk freely now."

An electronically altered voice warbled as the other party spoke, "And this channel?"

"Encrypted with my own…personal code. Even I can't break it without the unique…p…program encoded into this…transmitter."

"You are very thorough, Supreme Commander."

"Why are you…contacting me?"

"You're on a mission to kill Saki N-Tschester."

"How did you know about..."

"That's not important. What is important is that you do the exact opposite."

"What?"

"All is not as it seems, Supreme Commander. Saki isn't the enemy here."

"He put my daughter in this hell-hole."

"No," the caller insisted. "It was her idea."

"Don't try to dump this on Pana!"

"The destruction of Ooertfael? No, neither of them is responsible."

"I'm not following."

"There's no time to explain, but it was your daughter who proposed they be imprisoned."

"Why?"

"Because not providing a scapegoat would have meant civil war, or even worse if the Maatiirani had invaded. It might have ended the Alliance and everything it stood for."

"Cut the histrionics. Not even the Maatiirani are that powerful."

"They aren't, but this is."

"What is?"

There was a pause before the caller answered. "You're going to have to trust me, Supreme Commander. I'm not comfortable talking about this, even over a secure link. We will meet after you've succeeded in rescuing Saki and your daughter. But you must hurry. There are others at work trying to beat you to the prize."

"It's not my in…tention to rescue…N-Tschester."

"That's no longer your choice. If you lose one, you lose both."

"What do you mean by that?"

"That they are inextricably linked. Each has a piece of the puzzle and we need both to figure it out."

Khephra shook his head. "You're going to have to do…better than that."

"For that I need Saki and your daughter. Believe me, Supreme Commander. You will not be disappointed."

"Trusting…Ghost Men isn't in my nature."

"Then this will be an unnatural experience."

Khephra grunted angrily. "Then I'd rather…"

"Is everything on schedule?" the caller interrupted.

The supreme commander paused for a moment before answering. "My men just went down. I'll be following in another solar day and w…we'll finish this."

"Why not sooner?"

"The environment is too hostile for us to…transport down in anything other than…b…bulky environmental suits. That would increase the risk of exposing our operation and I don't think you… would like that, would you?"

There was a pause before the caller answered, "No, my friend, it is quite imperative that no one ever knows what we are about to do, even long after it has been done."

"Then it has to be done a…particular way and that…takes… t…time."

"Your speech sounds rather halting. Are you well?"

Khephra frowned. "Yes, but the transfer to this humanoid b… body has not been an easy…process."

"Can you carry out the mission?"

"A day ago I c…couldn't even sp…eak. B…by tomorrow I'll be as fluent as a…native."

"I hope so, because if you don't get there in time, it is possible that their Life Forces could be lost permanently."

Khephra glared at the box from which the voice emanated. "How c…could that happen? The Life Force is indestructible."

"Not exactly. This area of space has a higher-than-normal concentration of an ethereal life form we call the Samhain. Nasty creatures, these: mindless, heartless, and relentless. They swarm their victims, sucking out the essence of who they are. When their prey is too depleted to resist, the Samhain absorb them into their collective. They'll be as good as dead because they'll never be able to take solid form again."

Khephra shook his head. "Why are there so many around here?"

"Humans kill thousands of their own every day. The higher concentration of unattached Life Forces naturally attracts predators. If your daughter's or Saki's body is terminated, we'll have only a very short time to recover them before the Samhain drag them beyond our reach."

"We've got the p…planet covered," Khephra argued. "Until we're done here, no one comes or goes."

"We believe the enemy operatives are already down there. Time is not on our side."

"My men are watching him right now."

"But I hear they're having trouble getting close, so the enemy could strike and they'd be left with nothing to do but watch it happen."

"How c…can you know this, Amph…" Khephra stopped abruptly, but the meaning was clear.

"Watch yourself, Supreme Commander," the voice warned angrily. "You've got as much to lose as I."

Khephra snorted. “I’m f…fully aware of the importance of the…situation.”

“Then let’s get it done.”

Khephra reached up to scratch his ear, but jammed a finger into his forehead instead. Frustrated, he slammed the errant hand against the bed, and hesitated momentarily before echoing the caller,

“Let’s get it d…done.”

The voice asked, “When will you be contacting me?”

“Not until this…b…business is…finished,” Khephra said angrily before breaking the link and turning toward a window filled with stars, knowing three of them were battleships. “And believe me, AmPheet. If this is one of your tricks, it won’t end in the w…way you expect.”

22

"This is embarrassing," Terry whined as Wyatt's cabin came into view. "We make first-contact with an alien and it takes us hostage."

"It's not like we didn't try," Tom argued. "What were we supposed to do against that thing?"

"How do we know you're not in cahoots with it?" Charlie snapped. "After all, it said you are aliens too."

Ed shook his head sharply. "I'm no damned alien. I was born two miles from here and my son is as human as I am."

"You are making a common mistake," the creature said flatly. "The assumption that all Humans are created equal is actually…"

It stopped as a woman appeared at the cabin door.

"Hello there," Aurelia Simmons greeted.

Because the creature was hovering low and behind the group, she didn't notice it until after she spoke.

Before she could react, the robot moved up beside its captives and said, "Greetings. I am Observation Unit 335536, and am looking for…a person."

Unsure of what her neighbors were up to, Aurelia smiled gamely. "What is this person's name, Mr. Observation Unit…uh?"

"335536." it added. "The unit resides here, but I do not have a name. I do, however, have a recent image used for observational identification."

"Oooh Kay," she said cautiously while eying her neighbors. "I'll bite. Let's see the photo."

Everyone turned to face the observation unit as its chest began to glow and slowly revealed a face they all recognized.

"Oh my God," Terry exclaimed. "It's here to kill Wyatt."

23

By the time Wyatt reached the back of the house, sweat was trickling down his cheek. He was also breathing harder than expected for such a short sprint. Though glad to finally put some distance between himself and Megan, this didn't seem to be much of an improvement.

Leaning against the house, he heard Terry saying, "It's here to kill Wyatt."

"So much for my premonitions," he muttered while looking around for a weapon.

"Terry? What are you talking about?" Aurelia asked with alarm. "Who wants to murder my husband?"

Wyatt felt his muscles freeze momentarily as he struggled to decide what to do. Seeing a large rock on the ground, he picked it up and felt its weight before tossing it away.

The observation unit can't kill you, a voice hissed in his head. It's after Megan.

"That thing does," he heard Terry say.

"How do you know this?" Wyatt asked as he stepped back from the house and looked around. "Where are you?"

You can save your friend.

"Megan?"

"But why?" Aurelia was asking.

Otherwise, it will kill her and everyone else who knows it is here.

"How do you know this?" Wyatt cried.

Don't waste time. Go now!

Shocked into action by the revelation, Wyatt hurried around the house.

"I believe you are looking for me, Observation Unit," he said upon entering the front yard. "What can I do for you?"

As the robot turned toward him, Aurelia ran to her husband, throwing her arms around him and pressing her face into his chest.

"Standard Internment Unit 73983988223," the creature droned as it aimed a rifle at the couple. "Per Over Council decree JMM44231, I am ordered to terminate you for the purpose of…"

Aurelia squeezed tightly as Wyatt tensed for what was to come. The others froze, staring silently at the Observation Unit floating in front of them.

"…for the purpose of…"

The machine stopped, its weapon still pointed at the couple. No one moved as it paused for a moment more before lowering the rifle.

"I am experiencing technical difficulties," it said. "Please maintain your positions."

Wyatt's hand shook as he pointed at the machine. "Are you damaged, Observation Unit?"

"That is correct. I cannot access information necessary for the execution of this decree and am still unable to contact the master control computer." It laid the rifle on its platform. "Therefore, I cannot terminate you."

"Shit," Wyatt exhaled shakily as he looked from his four neighbors to his wife still squeezing the breath out of him. "This has been one damned weird day,"

Aurelia relaxed her grip and leaned her head back as everyone started talking at once.

Aurelia: "Wyatt, what's this about?"

Tom: "I didn't give him my gun, honest!"

Ed: "This thing says we're aliens."

Charlie: "What happens now?"

"Are Charlie and I the only humans here?" The question silenced everyone as they turned toward Terry. "Well, are we?"

Aurelia looked at her husband anxiously and shrugged.

"I'm no damned Martian," Ed insisted.

"Me neither," Tom added.

Wyatt threw up his hands, palms out. "Everybody calm down. We've a more immediate problem to deal with." He turned to the Observation Unit. "What are you going to do now?"

The machine was silent for a moment before saying, "I must follow the order given me."

Wyatt shook his head. "But you don't know what that is."

"That is correct. I will wait for further instructions before terminating your internment unit."

Hide him, the voice in Wyatt's head ordered. If others see him, it will create panic.

"And these people aren't panicked?" he muttered while looking again for the source of the voice.

He turned back to the robot and asked, "Are we a threat to you?"

"I detect no technology that would endanger me."

Wyatt gave the area one more scan. "Listen. You shouldn't be seen hanging around my yard. How about parking yourself in the garage?" He pointed to his neighbor. "Ed will open the door for you."

"Your request is reasonable, but you must not leave this immediate area."

Wyatt nodded. "I'm guessing you can watch me from in there."

The machine nodded as well. "Then I will follow Standard Internment Unit…Ed."

Ed scowled at the machine while leading it to the garage.

No one else must know. Stop Megan.

Wyatt turned to his wife. "Get Mary on the phone right away. Megan went there to call the police, and I want to speak to her before she talks with anyone."

"But, but," Aurelia stammered.

"Explanations later," he interrupted while pushing her toward the house. "This is important."

She hesitated for a moment before hurrying away.

Running a hand over his face, Wyatt turned to the remaining threesome.

"This is so weird I can't begin to explain it," he said as calmly as he could while his hands shook. "But one thing I do know is that this cannot get out."

"You're joking, right?" Charlie asked. "This will be bigger than Area 51."

"Oh God," Terry cried. "We don't want that here."

Wyatt held up his hands and shook his head. "This is not an alien invasion, Charlie."

Charlie looked at him incredulously. "This thing could be the first of many. We need to tell someone."

"To do what?" Tom asked. "Our weapons are useless against it."

"Wait," Terry cautioned. "That thing said Tom and Ed were also aliens. How do we know they're not working with it?"

"This is stupid," Tom protested.

"So who are you going to trust?" Wyatt asked. "Neighbors you've known for years or some strange contraption that came from who-knows-where?"

When no one answered, Tom added, "It was damaged in the crash. Even it doesn't really know why it's here."

Wyatt shook his head. "It might be something our military cooked up."

Terry looked at him suspiciously. "Then why is it after you?"

Before Wyatt could answer, Aurelia appeared in the doorway.

"Honey. Megan's on the phone."

Hurrying to her, Wyatt leaned in to give her a kiss, but suddenly changed his mind and patted her cheek instead. While puzzling over this sudden alteration, he moved inside and grabbed the phone.

"Megan?"

"I just got here. What's up?"

"What have you told Mary?"

"Nothing yet."

"Good. Has she called the Sheriff?"

"No. There's something wrong with the phone lines. We can call locally, but the Sheriff's office just rings and rings and no one answers."

"Let's not involve the police just yet. I think things are under control."

There was a long pause on Megan's end before Wyatt added, "No one's holding a gun to my head. Everything is really under control."

"You're sure?"

"Yes, I'm sure."

"So what's going on?"

"Just get back here and keep quiet about it."

After a short pause, she said, "Mary says Tom's pickup has the keys in it. She'll drive me up."

"Better yet, I'll send Ed to get you. We don't want anyone else to see this just yet."

"Why?"

"The thing we saw is threatening to kill me."

24

For the first time since the conversion process started, Khephra was seeing Earth entirely through Human eyes. The experience was so dramatically different than anything he'd ever known, he spent the better part of an hour just looking out his window.

"Good afternoon, Supreme Commander." The SLM's voice sounded tinny as the wall on Khephra's right became transparent. "As we discussed earlier, since your Human body requires oxygen and a higher atmospheric pressure, we will be communicating through transparent media from now on."

From the supreme commander's new perspective the SLM looked, well…ugly. His short, hairless body bulged in the middle and was framed by long, skinny arms that seemed to droop to his knees. His legs were thin and half the length of Khephra's Human ones and the head, admittedly his most striking feature, was large in proportion to the body, with a bulging forehead, huge almond-shaped eyes, a small chinless mouth and almost no nose.

"How are you feeling today?" the SLM asked.

Khephra nodded and was happy he could do so smoothly. "Like I want to fly down to the planet and get to work."

"Your team will make contact in a quarter of a deca-pak…" The SLM paused and checked his clipboard. "If you don't mind, Sir, I'd like to use Earth-based time references from now on. It will help with your transition."

"Works for me."

"Good. Then you'll be talking with your team in one-half of an hour. Do you feel up to the meeting?"

"Absolutely, but there is something I want to understand. Why do you look so…different?"

The SLM laughed. "With short-term insertions, such as yours, we have to alter the individual's perception algorithms. Otherwise, you'd go mad trying to interact with such repulsive creatures."

The supreme commander looked into the mirror to find a pale-skinned face with tiny eyes, a bulging nose and protruding chin. He held up a hand with five short, stubby fingers and shook his head.

"The algorithms aren't working in my case," he grumbled as he turned to look at the SLM. "This is one ugly body."

The SLM nodded. "We do our best, but with strong personalities like yours, the effect is less successful."

Khephra looked in the mirror then back to the SLM. "So now everybody is ugly."

The SLM shrugged. "Is it a workable compromise?"

Khephra looked back at the mirror and nodded. "I won't go berserk and hide in someone's basement."

"I'm glad you're taking this so well. Your men had some problems at first, and we were concerned that you might as well."

The Supreme Commander smiled lamely. "If their faces are as ugly as mine, it's no wonder."

"It's difficult when the transition time is so short. If we had a bit more time, this would go smoother."

Khephra shook his head. "Ugly or not, I'm going down before the end of this solar day."

"But Sir," the SLM protested. "The control units won't be active for at least another day and the Samhain concentrations in this area are abnormally high."

Khephra frowned. "This is not a choice. You know what will happen if we fail."

Looking frightened, the SLM nodded.

"Then let's not waste time."

25

Megan jumped from the truck and hurried to Wyatt. "What the hell is going on?"

After a decade-long platonic relationship with this spitfire of a woman, Wyatt wanted nothing more than to take her in his arms and kiss her. It puzzled him that he'd not felt this way toward his wife earlier.

"It was a bit scary at first, but it all worked out."

She moved in close, and met his eyes, which intensified his uncomfortable longing.

"What happened?"

Stepping away from her he pointed at the house. "I reached the back yard without being seen, but didn't have a weapon. It was then I realized it probably already knew I was there, so I just walked around the house and said hello."

Megan looked at the others, before turning back to Wyatt. "Are you nuts?"

He rolled his eyes. "Apparently not. I'm still alive."

"So what did it do?"

"It pointed a damned rifle at him and said it was going to kill him," Terry explained excitedly, "but for some reason, it didn't."

Megan kept her eyes on Wyatt. "Why?"

He shook his head. "Its memory is damaged, and it can't remember why it was supposed to."

"What happened next?" she asked angrily.

Wyatt shrugged as Terry spoke, "It put the gun down, Wyatt told it to go sit in the garage and I'll be damned if it did just that."

Megan did a quick spin to face the garage. "It's there now?"

When five heads nodded as one, she charged up to Wyatt and slammed both hands on his chest. "Why did you let yourself be captured?"

He smiled weakly. "Because I think it can help us."

26

Khephra stopped at the door to the communications room and leaned heavily against the wall.

"Why is this body in such poor condition?" he asked no one in particular.

"It's not," the SLM said from behind him. "It's just not yours."

The supreme commander jerked around to find the SLM wearing an environmental suit.

"It shouldn't be that hard to walk a couple dozen – what do you call them? Meters? – without being rendered helpless."

He could see the SLM nodding knowingly inside the suit. "The dynamics of this body are quite different than your own. Trust me, Supreme Commander, if you gave us another day you'd be marching up and down these halls with little effort."

Khephra shook his head. "Unfortunately, there just isn't time."

"Then you must be careful not to overexert yourself down there."

The supreme commander nodded toward the communications room. "And my men?"

The SLM giggled in a way Khephra found annoying. "They have exceeded everyone's expectations, but there are some difficulties. Their dexterity isn't quite what I'd like to see, and some are having problems with nausea, but they should be able to complete their mission."

After briefly resting his head against the wall, Khephra took a deep breath and pushed himself upright. "Good. That means they won't need a long pep-talk to get their spirits up. I may not last more than a few minutes…if that."

The SLM pressed the door release and turned back to his superior. "I've heard you speak, Supreme Commander. You won't need more than that."

27

The shadowy figure pulled the curtains closed and lifted a transmitter to trembling lips. "Kronshak? That observation unit seems more interested in protecting them than helping me."

"Is necessary they trust it," Kronshak responded condescendingly. "Don't be so damned paranoid. When time come, it will do as told."

"But what about the female?"

"We not need her," he growled. "If she get in way, terminate."

"But there is no control station to recover her Life Force."

"Not your problem."

"Why can't I kill her now?"

"Our ship not in position yet. We not want to get anyone excited until everything ready."

"But what if something else goes wrong?"

"Deal with it, but don't let your body be terminated until we be ready."

"What do you mean?"

"You know of Samhain?"

The figure nodded. "Down here they're called the Specter of Death."

Kronshak laughed. "Very appropriate, no? Cold, thoughtless creatures that suck up Life Force. We love it!"

The figure shivered. "I don't."

"Maybe, if you fail, that be your fate."

"That's not part of our deal!"

"Is now."

Pausing, the figure pushed back a curtain, revealing glistening tears on a pale cheek."

"How do I know you'll recover me even if I do deliver?"

"You not got much choice now."

A sigh shuddered from the figures lips as the transmitter beeped, showing the connection had been broken.

28

Wyatt moved up behind his wife, massaging her shoulders while watching through their living room window as the Observation Unit helped Megan haul feed to the goats.

"It's been here a day and she's already got it helping with chores?"

Aurelia shrugged. "It was Megan's idea."

"But what ever prompted her to ask it?"

Aurelia rubbed her hands together and turned to face her husband. "More to the point, what are we doing about Augustus?"

"Augustus?"

She put her arms around his waist. "We had to call it something and Observation Unit 335536 doesn't exactly roll off the tongue."

"But Augustus?"

She smiled crookedly, an affectation he loved. "The robot sounds pompous as does the name." She looked back out the window. "A perfect fit."

Wyatt sighed while continuing to watch Megan and the machine. "Well if it wants to help, hopefully cleaning the barn isn't beneath our Caesar's dignity."

"You haven't answered my question."

Wyatt shook his head. "I have a strong feeling it's just the precursor of things to come."

"An invasion? But if these creatures are as powerful as Augustus, we're helpless against them."

Wyatt shrugged. "I've been wondering if its damaged circuits can be repaired."

Aurelia's eyes widened. "Are you kidding? It'll kill you."

Wyatt shook his head again. "But that doesn't jive with my feeling that the victim will be a woman."

Aurelia looked alarmed. "What feeling?"

He shrugged. “It’s just a voice in my head telling me that if I cooperate, it will help us.”

“So it’s not here to kill you?”

Wyatt barked a hollow laugh. “Either that or I’m being paroled from this prison it says we’re in.”

“But where does that leave us?”

Wyatt looked across the yard as Augustus herded sheep into a pen. “With the exception of its threat to kill me, the robot has been benevolent towards the rest of you. It rescued Terry and Charlie and didn’t hurt Tom and Ed, even after they shot at it. And now Megan has it helping with chores.” He turned back to Aurelia. “I think, if other aliens come, it’ll protect the lot of us.”

His wife frowned while waving a hand toward the sky. “Unless they sent it. After all, Augustus is just a machine and it’ll likely do whatever they tell it to do.”

Wyatt took a deep breath and exhaled slowly. “Then I guess we’d just better ask it.”

Before she could protest, he walked quickly out of the house, forcing her to scramble after him.

“Observation Unit? May I have a word?”

“Standard Internment Unit Wyatt,” the robot greeted. “How may I assist?”

“Except for killing me, why are you here?”

“I was not sent to kill you, Standard Internment Unit Wyatt; my mission is to terminate you.”

“What’s the difference?” Megan asked as she moved up beside Wyatt.

“Your body is a vessel that contains the Life Force. When the body dies, the Life Force is recycled.”

“Recycled?” Megan threw up her hands. “What the hell does that mean?”

“His Life Force is inserted into a different body.”

“But why? What has he done?”

“I cannot answer that question.”

After brushing both hands through her hair, Megan cupped them behind her bowed head. “Can’t or won’t?”

Augustus did not hesitate. “That information is not relevant to my mission.”

Hands dropping to her sides, Megan did a quick spin-about and started walking away. “This is getting us nowhere.”

When Wyatt put an arm in front of her, she pushed into it, but stopped.

“Augustus,” he said. “We think someone wants to harm Megan.” Megan looked up to find Wyatt staring at her. “If we are correct, would you protect her?”

Instead of pushing his arm away, she turned to face the robot again, letting the arm slide to her waist. She felt the urge to put her hand on his, but resisted.

“Where would these beings come from?” Augustus asked.

“Outer space.”

“That is forbidden. Unauthorized termination or mistreatment of internment units by anyone other than the natural or interred occupants of Prak a’Terra is not allowed. Violation of this statute is punishable by an internment of no less than fifty *druak* in the same facility.”

Megan squinted at the robot. “Fifty what?”

“A *druak* is a unit of time, equivalent to ninety-seven-point-three of your Earth years.”

“You’re kidding, right?”

“I am not.”

“But people don’t live that long.”

Though it seemed impossible for the robot to do so, it nodded.

“Humans do not, but when it comes to…”

“I think we need to get back to the original subject.” Aurelia interrupted. “How would they get down here?”

“In a transport disk similar to mine, or if more than six individuals are involved, a larger ship.”

“Would they arrive at night, to avoid being seen?” Wyatt asked.

“No. The craft would be shielded and almost entirely invisible to your technology, even during the day.”

Megan moved closer to the robot. “Could you see them?”

"Yes."

"Would you help us defend against them?"

"It would depend on whether or not they had an Irrevocable Council Authorization certificate."

"And if they didn't?"

"I would be required to detain them."

"Would you give us weapons to defend ourselves with?"

"Giving internees such advanced technology is forbidden. Your weaponry must be made from local resources using your own limited knowledge."

"Limited?" Megan snapped as she scooped up a rock. "Limit your ass with this," she snarled while hurling it at the robot.

Augustus did not seem to react as the projectile bounced off its skin, arched high into the air and landed only inches from Megan's feet.

"His point exactly," Wyatt said wryly as Megan grabbed the rock and threw it again.

Like before, it landed only inches from where she was standing.

"Shit," she cried, but left the rock alone.

"You can see," Augustus explained, "why it would be inappropriate to give such primitive peoples advanced technology. If that had been a halogen fusion grenade, it would have destroyed me and everyone within a hundred of your meters, including yourself."

Wyatt picked up the rock and nodded. "We'd be more of a danger to ourselves than the enemy if we were to use weapons technology we didn't understand."

Aurelia looked toward the sky and asked, "What will they look like?"

"Only one off-world species is allowed access to Prak a'Terra. However, their native bodies cannot exist for long in your nitrogen-oxygen atmosphere. To compensate, they use Rapid Insertion Units, which look very much like you, but are better conditioned."

"Better conditioned?"

Augustus nodded. "They would likely be experienced warriors: faster reflexes, stronger limbs and highly conditioned minds." It turned to face Wyatt. "In hand-to-hand combat, even you would be disabled in seconds."

Wyatt's muscles tensed as he glared at the robot, but said nothing.

Aurelia waved a hand. "Are they invincible then?"

Augustus shook its head. "No one in Human form is invincible, but the chances of your mounting a successful resistance are quite low."

"But you could help us," Megan stated.

"That very much depends on…"

"Yeah. Yeah," she said impatiently. "That Council authorization thing, but we've done nothing wrong. You've got to protect us."

"I cannot defy a Council order."

Megan looked at Wyatt for a moment then back to Augustus. "But you haven't received a Council order, have you?"

"The one I have is incomplete, and therefore invalid."

"And you don't have solid proof that anyone from outer space is coming here, right?"

"Human feelings cannot be considered proof of anything."

"Then will you help us defend against an unknown enemy which may be as skilled as those alien soldiers you talked about."

"I cannot give you weapons technology exceeding what you currently have."

Wyatt shook his head. "I suppose they'll probably have some kind of ray gun."

"Our energy weapons cannot be used in this environment."

"What about your shields?" Aurelia asked timidly.

"The equipment used to support shielding technology is too heavy for a Human form to carry. However, the shielding on a troop transport carrier would allow them to move about unseen."

"How big is this carrier?"

"In your measurements, the platform is one and one-half meters by three meters."

"We're sunk," Aurelia announced sadly.

"Maybe not," Megan said as she paced a circle in front of Augustus. "They have to use bodies like ours and guns like ours and the only advantage they really have, besides their hunky physiques, is this transport sled to make them invisible."

"What are you thinking?" Wyatt asked.

Megan looked at him, feeling more protective of her friend than ever. "I'm thinking all we need from Augustus is to know when they are coming and how big their ship is."

"That's all?" Aurelia asked incredulously.

Megan nodded. "That and we have to move everyone to my place."

29

"Major Phaa, report," Khephra demanded as he entered the cigar-shaped transport unit his men were using.

"Per your orders, Sir, we have been observing the subjects since our arrival."

"The plan was to mix with them and gain their trust."

"Yes, Sir, but there is a problem." He pointed at the screen. "They appear to have made contact with the downed Observation Unit we thought was destroyed. We cannot get any information from the unit, probably because its transmission equipment is damaged. We were concerned that if we approached the location, it might expose us and compromise the mission."

"Can you make physical contact with the unit?"

"Negative Sir. The Humans are keeping a close eye on it and we have not been able to isolate it long enough to safely do so. In addition, considering that the Observation Unit has defied its programming by allowing the humanoids to see it, we are concerned that damage may extend to its logic control circuits."

Khephra looked again at the screen to see the Observation Unit carrying a large bucket piled high with something brown and spongy.

"What is it carrying?"

The major shook his head. "It is offal, Sir. I believe it is from the creatures they keep in that building behind him."

The Observation Unit moved to a mound a short distance from the barn and dumped the contents of the bucket onto it.

"And they just dump this stuff in their back yard?"

Phaa nodded as his face registered disgust. "They collect the offal – they call it manure – and later spread it on the ground they use to grow crops."

The supreme commander shook his head as the major waived at the men seated behind him. "I thought it prudent to keep everyone on rations and avoid all contact with native food."

"A wise precaution, Major."

"Sir, we are prepared to terminate the subject on your order."

Khephra shook his head slowly. "As much as I dislike doing so, we're going to have to wait."

"Sir?"

"Work on the array is taking longer than expected. One of the primary power units is faulty."

"Something's happening," a voice behind them announced.

All eyes turned to face the main view screen as two vehicles pulled into the barnyard. After Ed and Tom appeared from their trucks, the Observation Unit turned toward them and raised a hand.

"I believe the Observation Unit is using a local form of greeting. It seems quite familiar with this group of people."

"Can we hear what they are saying?"

The captain shook his head. "We are approximately two of their kilometers from the location. We've tried audio surveillance, but this area is rife with small flying wildlife they call birds. There are so many of these noisy creatures between us and them, listening is nearly impossible."

"What about mounting a sensor closer in?"

Major Phaa looked at the scowling Captain Praetor.

"We tried that, Sir," Praetor answered. "Unfortunately, soon after it is in place, these birds push mud and grass into the listening cones. Apparently they create a bowl-shaped receptacle with this litter and place their young in it."

Shaking his head, Khephra turned back to the viewing screen. "Are we to assume the Observation Unit's programming will be of no help with terminating the subjects."

"Yes, Sir," Phaa agreed.

"Then we need to disable it."

Captain Theara stood. "Supreme Commander. I have a plan."

"Yes?"

"If I can make physical contact with the unit, it will be possible to use its internal communications system to regain control."

"How long will it take?"

The captain's eyes dropped to his notepad. "The unit would go into maintenance mode within *micro-paks*, er, seconds after contact is made. It would only take a moment more to transfer our control program."

"And if the input circuits are disabled?"

"The unit will still be immobilized."

The supreme commander looked at the screen again as Augustus put a large box into one of the vehicles. "Then we must make it our priority to get Captain Theara close enough to do his job."

"How do we do that, Sir?" Major Phaa asked.

Khephra shrugged. "We have one solar day to figure that out."

30

Augustus lowered a piano into the back of Tom's truck, sinking it nearly a foot.

"Geeze, Robot," Megan cried as she ran to the vehicle. "We won't need accompanying music."

Aurelia hurried from the house. "My fault. I told Augustus to load up the pie pans sitting on the piano. I guess it misunderstood."

Megan shook her head. "Well, take it back inside, or there won't be room for anything else."

Augustus looked at Aurelia who nodded. Lifting the piano as though it were a box of pie pans, the robot returned to the house.

"Why does Augustus always look at you before doing what I tell it?" Megan asked.

Both women watched the robot maneuver its load through the front door.

"You and Wyatt are its prisoners. It may think it's not supposed to be helping you."

Megan looked at Aurelia and was surprised to see her more as a competitor than a friend. She shook her head sharply to banish the unwanted feeling, but it remained.

"God, I wish I knew what the hell this was all about."

"That makes two of us," Aurelia said solemnly as she patted her friend's shoulder and headed back to the house.

And I wish I didn't want your husband so much, Megan thought while chewing her lower lip.

"Megan," Wyatt called as he exited the barn. "I'm going take a load to your place. Do you want to come along?"

Feeling her face flush, she shook her head, thankful that Wyatt simply turned and went back into the barn.

"Son of a bitch," she muttered under her breath. "If something doesn't happen soon, I'm going to come unglued."

Seeing Wyatt's truck pull out from behind the barn, she moved toward that building.

"Standard Internment Unit Megan. I wish to speak with you."

"What the hell is it now?" she protested.

"We are being observed."

Megan's mood shifted so quickly, she stumbled back a step. "What do you mean? By who?"

"Two Rapid Insertion Units have been observed placing remote listening devices within the range of my sensors."

"Remote listening…?"

"That is correct. It has happened on three occasions. In each case, I disabled the devices using local resources."

"Wha…What resources?" Megan asked while looking around the yard.

"Complying with the primary Council Directive 132.a.445, I used mud and twigs, similar to the technique used by the small winged creatures that dominate this area."

Megan shook her head. "You built a bird's nest in their listening device?"

"That is correct."

She gaped at the machine for a moment before smiling. "You're damned creative for a tin man."

"I did not think the situation threatening, but that has changed."

"How?"

"A large craft is positioned one-point-nine-seven kilometers from here." Augustus pointed at a low hill. "It landed outside the range of my scanning equipment, but I did observe it visually. It stopped for only a few of your minutes and then departed. I recognized the craft and determined from its descent and departure telemetry, that it offloaded approximately six-hundred kilos."

"Reinforcements? Additional weapons?"

"Such a move implies a change in strategy."

Shading her eyes, Megan looked at the hill. "They're coming?"

"That is one possibility."

"Come on, Robot," she called over her shoulder while moving toward the house. "Let's move."

31

Sub-commander Pheet looked up and down the gangway before slipping into the cabin.

"Matrina?" he called softly while hurrying through the dark room to the small bedroom illuminated with a dim light.

As he passed through the bedroom door, something moved to his right. He jerked around to find a Shentowin female dressed in a light silky shift. Unlike the thin fuzz that passed for hair on an Antrakan's head, this Shentowin's bountiful, wavy, blue-black mass flowed over her shoulders to cover her chest. Though the hair aroused him, he felt even more excited when she brushed it back to reveal hard nipples under the thin cloth.

"I was wondering if your silly supreme commander was going to let you come," she said huskily while moving close to him.

He embraced her, pushing his face into the perfumed hair.

"He's down on the planet right now," he murmured into her ear, "but Ceratha and all his demons couldn't keep me away."

Her closeness combined with an intoxicating perfume numbed his brain, so he resisted only slightly when she pulled back and started unbuttoning his shirt. For a thrilling moment, she looked at him with eyes that he knew varied in color with her changing mood. Matrina's normally green eyes were now bright lusty amber.

As he fondled her hair, she pulled off his shirt and tossed it aside before running her hands over his naked chest. The sensation aroused him even more. When he pulled her close, she kissed his neck and then ran her tongue around his ear opening.

"Tonight, let's try something different," she whispered.

He pulled back slightly to look into her eyes. "Oh?"

She moved to the nightstand and snatched up a small cube. It opened as she walked back to him, revealing two tiny blue tablets.

"Our sex has been great up to now," she announced huskily while picking up a pill and holding it out, "but this will simply blow your mind."

He jerked back, looking questioningly at her offering. “What is it?”

She giggled derisively. “Don’t be so silly. It’s just Pharmitan.”

When he shook his head, she moved in close and fondled him gently with her free hand. “It’s a very low dose,” she assured him, “but it heightens the sexual experience to an amazing level.”

He continued to look skeptical. “I think we’re doing just fine without help.”

She brought her face up to his, gently brushing his lips with hers before pulling back. He almost fell forward while trying to maintain the contact.

“Try it just this once and see if you feel that way afterward.”

Without waiting for a reply, she stepped further back and tossed a tablet into her mouth.

“I don’t want to go on this wonderful journey alone,” she pleaded softly while offering him the remaining one.

Looking at her now-pouting face, he hesitated only a few *micro-paks* before releasing a sharp breath and taking the pill.

“Just this once,” he conceded before popping it into his mouth.

At first he didn’t feel any different as they undressed and pressed their bodies together, but as time passed, the experience became more and more intense. His skin tingled with sharply higher sensitivity. Every touch was thrilling to the point of being overwhelming. After a little more time, it seemed like he was no longer making love to her, but that they were a single entity at the height of an almost permanent orgasm. He lost track of time and place, and finally consciousness.

He wasn’t sure why, but even in the total darkness, he knew she wasn’t there when he awoke. He also knew he could barely lift his head, let alone sit up.

“Lights,” he called when he could think of nothing else to do.

He was initially blinded by the light, but when his eyes adjusted he released an involuntary gasp, and with great effort, struggled to a sitting position.

He was fully dressed and sitting on his own bed.

32

Two full moons hung heavily in the sky as a pair of dark figures moved through tall brush, their presence having no effect on the loud mating stridulations of the katydids around them.

"What the hell you drag me out here for?" the old woman yelled angrily as her young companion motioned for quiet.

"You'll see, Auntie," he answered impatiently. "Just wait."

"And what is it I'm supposed to be seein', Nephew?" she protested over the raucous insect's noise. "Old women like me shouldn't be sneakin' around in the dark, crawling through brush to peek into someone's bedroom window."

"I'm no peeper, Auntie," he said while pointing to the road at the bottom of the hill on which they were standing. "You ain't gonna believe this unless you see it yourself."

"You brought me up here to watch cars?"

"No ma'am."

"Then what are we looking for?"

"Nothin'," he answered solemnly, "that becomes somethin'."

Shaking her head derisively, she barked a laugh. "Raytaan, please tell me you ain't gone completely…"

She stopped as the katydids went suddenly quiet. Seconds later, a large silver bus blasted into existence in the middle of the road and sped the rest of the way across their field of view before disappearing around a corner.

"Son of a..."

She stopped when another bus followed the path of the first.

"You fucking with my head, boy?" she asked angrily.

Shaking his head, Raytaan kept his eyes on the road below as a third bus appeared. "I have no idea who could do somethin' like that."

Gripping his arm, she motioned for him to follow. "Let's go."

"Why?"

"Because I do."

33

"Sir," Captain Theara announced as he looked up from the monitoring station. "Four vehicles just arrived at the house."

"We should take them now, Sir," Captain Praetor stated.

Khephra shook his head. "It's too early, and besides, where are they going to go?"

"Sir," Major Phaa said. "One of them is separated from the group right now. If it is N-Tschester, it would be far less risky to grab him now."

Khephra scowled. "No. They must be taken together."

The major passed his commander a puzzled look. "Sir, I know your daughter is one of that group. If this is personal…"

Khephra turned on him, his fist clenched. "Someone's trying to disrupt a peace we've struggled for decades to maintain. If they succeed, it will not only tear apart our alliance, but bring war with the Maatiirani as well. Billions of lives are at risk, gentlemen. How much more personal can it get than that?"

The Supreme Commander sagged against a chair, but quickly righted himself. "My daughter's involvement isn't a factor here, Major." He stiffened his back, straightened his jacket and stared directly at Phaa. "Is that understood?"

The Major snapped to attention and said, "Sir! Yes Sir!" The remaining officers jumped up and copied their team-leader.

Shoulders drooping, Khephra waved them at ease and trudged toward his sleeping quarters.

"Damn, it's a struggle to keep this body going," he muttered. "I can't wait to get back into my own skin."

Without comment, the men watched him move past them and disappear into the other room.

As the door closed, Phaa motioned for a subordinate to approach.

"Take three men and follow them, but be discreet."

"We have an idea where they're going, Sir."

Phaa nodded. "Then you'll have an easy time of it."

"But Sir. Should we pick up the one that has separated from the others?"

Phaa shook his head. "We'll follow orders."

"Sir?"

"How long have you been with the supreme commander, Captain?"

"Twelve *druak*."

"And if he asked you to follow him into Ceratha's burning bowels, would you do it?"

"Without question, Sir."

Phaa shook his head again. "That's good, because I'm thinking that's exactly where he's going to take us."

34

The aide knocked twice then quietly opened the door into the dimly lit room. From behind two monitors on a wide desk, the creature within raised first one reptilian-shaped head then the other. Even in the dark room, the sight of the occupant's rough, pale skin sent shivers of revulsion up the aide's spine. The three moist nostrils on the front of each snout swelled and shrank as the occupant took a pair of quick breaths and focused its large weepy eyes on the intruder.

"Senator Addy," the single-headed aide called as he leaned though the open doorway, but the overpoweringly rancid smell of the room kept him from entering. "The report from Secor-Alpha Four has arrived. I'm afraid it is not good news. Would you like it now?"

One of the senator's heads nodded silently as the other turned toward a monitor screen glowing dimly in the gloomy room. A glob of drool slowly dropped from the side of one mouth and onto his desk, but the creature seemed not to notice.

"Drop it on desk," the nodding head said. "We get to it in moment." The speaking head turned briefly toward the screen then back to the aide. "Has any udder peoples been briefed on this?"

Moving quickly, the aide put the file on the desk, and returned to the doorway, before speaking.

"We've been monitoring communications, and since the attack there has been only minimal activity in the region around that planet. Almost all of it has been ours."

The head facing the monitor moved up beside its companion. Its left ear, which looked much like a frayed tube of paper, twitched as it spoke in a much lower voice than its mate. "Any report from intervention team?"

The aide nodded. "Due to the distance there is a two-pak delay, but based on their last contact, the Secor-Alpha Four team will arrive at the planet tomorrow morning."

The senator's left head shook, but the aide couldn't tell if he was grimacing or smiling as both heads slowly lowered to stare at the monitor again.

"Be there any problems at other prisons?"

The aide nodded. "Oddly enough, we just received a report that Prak a'Terra has recently lost a monitoring station. Our intervention teams have learned that Supreme Commander Khephra is already on site. With help from his crew, that station should be online about…"

The aide stopped abruptly as both of the senator's heads snapped up, his eyes wide with surprise. "Khephra? At Prak a'Terra?"

The aide took a step back. "I assumed he was part of the team sent to prevent N-Tschester from escaping."

"But he not should be anyplace near Prak a'Terra. Our source say Antrakan fleet on udder side of region. You make mistake."

"N…no Sir. Our people arrived several pak ago and the supreme commander was already on site. The intervention team's commander was very clear on that point."

The senator's heads turned inward to look at each other.

"Let us hope he just check on daughter," the left head said.

"In thirty *druak* he been not there once," the right head countered. "That mean..."

Addy's heads froze as his four eyes jerked toward the Antrakan aide then back to their opposites.

When the two heads finally turned to face the aide, both issued a collective sigh. "Why we ever let it come to this?"

"Sir?"

Addy pointed a finger at the aide. "You be papa?"

"Yes, Sir. Two boys and three girls."

"All still live in home?"

The aide nodded. "The oldest are twins. They'll be twenty-*sirius* old tomorrow."

"That much too young," the senator said as both heads turned to the monitor again and repeated the collective sigh. Without looking back up, the creature said, "Do them favor, my friend. Go home and kill them."

35

Tammabet Ferrisis' gulped air in labored gasps as she leaned against an alley wall with her good hand. Only moments earlier, she had been walking in what she had always believed was a safe neighborhood when something completely inhuman appeared from a side alley.

Nearly blinded by terror, she ran blindly, sprinting straight into a fire hydrant. The painful impact sent her sprawling, slamming her left hand onto the concrete, the pain making her scream as she rolled. Gripping the painful wrist with her good hand, she scrambled up, and hobbled away, briefly losing sight of the creature until the sound of many feet stamping pavement made her look back to see it reappear.

Ignoring the pain in her leg, she ran with all she had, managing for a time to stay ahead of the creature's two snapping mouths as it hurried after her. She barely escaped its grasp by dashing between two moving cars, the trailing vehicle slamming into the creature, as she raced across the street to apparent safety.

Pushing away from the alley wall, she tenderly flexed the wrist, gasping at a pain that brought a sharp reality to an already too-damned-real nightmare.

She was about to move on when footsteps that sounded like a platoon marching in double time, echoed against the alley's walls. She jerked upright and stared down an empty passageway glowing with light from the largest of the planet's two moons.

God, please let this be a damned dream, she thought as blind panic contracted her chest.

The sight of her chubby silhouette on the alley wall caused her to jump back then bark an angry laugh.

"Shit, girl. You're even jumping at your own fat shadow."

Struggling on jelly-like legs, she stumbled across the next street, until her foot snagged a crack, almost sending her to the ground. Mustering all her remaining strength, she regained her balance and hurried on.

Entering the next alley, she rattled the knobs of locked doors until one gave at her push. It opened so quickly she went sprawling onto the floor, crying out as her left hand impacted the solid surface. Doubling up, she yanked the injured wing to the safety of her chest, rolled onto her back and kicked the door closed.

Tears dribbling down her cheeks, she sucked in air and listened for the footsteps, but noise from a nearby refrigerator threatened to mask them. Whimpering, she started to rise, but before reaching her feet, an inside door opened and a person appeared.

"Who are you?" he demanded of the woman crouching in front of him in the dark room.

She almost collapsed as the lights came on and she recognized him. "Bottar?"

"Tamm? What are you doing here?"

"There's someone after me," she cried, still clutching her hand to her chest. "I need to hide fast."

"Are you injured?"

Looking at her wrist, she was about to answer when she heard the tromp, tromp, tromp of her pursuer. Both of them froze as the perfectly-synchronized marching stopped outside the door. She tried to jump up and push him back through the door, but her legs wouldn't move.

"Oh dear God," she cried as the door exploded in a flash of light and darkness quickly enveloped her.

36

Wyatt's attention was drawn to the sky above his vehicle, and when he looked up through his front windshield, two large birds circled several-hundred feet above. Without knowing why, he continued to watch until one of them stopped abruptly and dropped some distance before regaining control and leveling out.

Pulling over, he jumped from the truck and stared into the sky. Seconds later, the other bird, which seemed to be higher than the first, vanished for several heartbeats before reappearing. He watched it continue to circle until it repeated its disappearing act at close to the same location.

"Christ," he swore as he looked around the area. "They're coming!"

Jumping back into his vehicle, he grabbed his cell phone and dialed. When nothing happened, he looked at the display to see "No Service" boldly displayed.

Dropping the phone, he stepped on the gas, cranking the steering wheel to wrench the vehicle into a tight turn. The road being too narrow for such a maneuver, he ran down a short bank, through a fence and into a field, his trailer of sheep bouncing and bleating noisily. He didn't look up again as he drove to the nearest opening to the road, crashed through a gate and returned to the road. Dust billowing behind him, he pressed the accelerator, and was caught off guard when the engine suddenly stopped, throwing him into the steering wheel.

"Crap," he yelled.

As he exited the truck, his foot landed on a loose rock, sending him crashing to the ground. He jumped up to continue on, but the damaged ankle rolled, sending him back to the ground.

Twisting around, he looked up as another bird repeated the vanishing/reappearing act.

"Shit man," he grunted while glancing at the blood on his scuffed hands. "They've got you now."

37

"What do you mean, the Standard Internment Unit has spotted you?" Major Phaa asked as he stared at the monitor. "Weren't you shielded?"

"Yes, Sir, but a male unit appears to have seen us because he stopped his vehicle and looked in our direction before doing a quick turnaround to head back in the direction from which he came. To keep him from exposing our position to the others, we were forced to stop his vehicle, but he appears to have injured himself attempting to escape on foot. We now have him segregated from the others, but another of their party is approaching."

Phaa shook his head. "Do you know which unit this is?"

"The Human name is Wyatt Simmons, but we're unsure which Life Force occupies the body. We are too far away to get the information from his implant with our hand-held readers."

"Then pull back," Phaa ordered. "Do not approach the subject and stay out of visual range of the Observation Unit accompanying the others."

"Yes Sir! Pulling back now."

"Phaa?" a familiar voice called from behind.

Oh no, he thought as he turned around and asked, "Yes Sir?"

"Which Standard Internment Unit are they talking about?"

"The male, Wyatt Simmons, Sir."

Instead of showing anger, Khephra seemed to pause for a moment as though deep in thought. Finally, he turned to one of the other officers and said, "Open a link to Sergeant Specialist Akki. I want to know what his status is."

As the officer acknowledged the order, Khephra turned to the Major. "Where was he headed?"

Phaa looked at his monitor. "Back to join the others. I believe their objective was to gather at the home of the unit known as Megan Simplot. The back part of that property has high-voltage electrical power lines crossing it."

"Power lines? They don't generate enough energy to threaten us."

"That is correct, Sir, but whenever our vehicles come close to these lines, interference from our tri-phase engines interrupts the flow of the electricity. It can jump from the power lines to the craft, creating a high-energy plasma field that disables our shielding, making the craft visible and vulnerable to attack. In addition, since these lines often feed power to their major cities, such an interruption, even for a minute, is hardly an event that would go unnoticed."

The supreme commander stared at the monitor for a moment more before turning back to Phaa. "Let them go onto the property."

"But Sir…"

Khephra silenced him with an upheld hand. "Somehow they know our mobile vehicle can't approach them while they are under that power line. That means they'll stay there until we route them out, correct?"

"That seems reasonable, Sir," Phaa said hesitantly.

"Once they are there, make sure they stay put until we are ready."

"Yes, Sir," Phaa acknowledged.

"And this is important, Major," Khephra said seriously as he locked eyes with his subordinate. "We don't move until the array is up."

"Understood, Sir."

Khephra patted Phaa on the shoulder and walked back to his office. Just as he entered, another officer announced a link with Sergeant Specialist Akki.

"Report, Akki."

"I've got good news and bad news, Sir."

"Start at the top, Sergeant Specialist."

"The array is operational and we're preparing to install the first fifty controllers now."

The supreme commander smiled at the monitor. "And the antenna?"

"It will be operational tomorrow about sunrise in your area. We can start connecting to units on the planet's surface as soon as it's aligned."

"Good job, Sergeant, that's a day ahead of schedule."

"I have to give credit to the engineers on this station, Sir. The threat of total annihilation is highly motivating."

"You said there was bad news?"

Akki looked around cautiously before continuing. "Something strange is happening here. The other ships gathering around us aren't allowing us to mingle with them."

"Is there no communication?"

"Yes, Sir. The basic stuff, but none of us has been allowed to visit or even communicate with friends on the other ships."

"I see," Khephra said almost too quietly for Akki to hear.

"Any idea what's going on, Sir?"

"Yes, I do, Son, but we can't talk about that right now. How long would it take to get the ship ready for high-speed transport?"

The Sergeant Specialist paused for a moment before answering. "We're in standby mode at present, so it would be at least one deca-pak before we could attempt acceleration."

"Would you say the other battleships are also on standby?"

"Absolutely, Sir. I checked their energy outputs and none are ready for acceleration."

"How short can you make that time and not let any of the other ships know what you're up to?"

Another pause as the Sergeant Specialist looked around. "We're due for a fusion purge in two days." He looked at his watch. "If I start it now, we won't be able to go anywhere for nearly two deca-paks, but at the end of the cycle, we'll be putting out so much energy that no one will notice our engines building for a jump. In fact, standard procedure is to follow this process with a full-ship maintenance check. They won't expect us to even move for another solar day."

The supreme commander also looked at his watch. "Don't start right away. I want you to be ready when this part of the planet is just experiencing sunrise."

"If I understand this time-keeping system, that would be five o'clock, your time."

"I'll leave that up to you," Khephra said. "And another thing. Tell the engineers working on the array that they are not to stop their work, even if we leave. That array must be completely operational in two solar days."

"What should I tell them?"

"I think they already have incentive enough."

"But won't the other ships chase after us?"

"It's doubtful. They believe something more dangerous than us is on that planet."

"Something more dangerous than a fully-armed battleship? What in Hammond's name could that be?"

Khephra shook his head as he stared at the face in his monitor. "An idea," he answered softly.

38

Megan poked her head through the front door of the house. "Aurelia? Are you there?"

Hearing no reply, she turned to find Augustus floating behind her. "Standard Internment Unit Megan, Rapid Insertion Unit Aurelia is not here."

Megan froze. "What did you say?"

"Standard Internment Unit Megan, Rapid Insertion Unit Aurelia is not here."

"I thought you said she was human."

"I did not."

"Shit! Where did she go?"

"Rapid Insertion Unit Aurelia advised me that she was following Standard Internment Unit Wyatt to your property."

Megan began running toward her pickup and Augustus followed. "You said the attackers would come as rapid insertion units." Megan stopped at the truck and turned to the robot. "That means she's here to kill him."

When the machine didn't respond, she asked, "Why would she do this?"

"She could then collect his Life Force for insertion into another body."

"But why Wyatt? What did he do?"

"That information is unavailable to me."

Megan slammed a fist on the truck's door. "We've got to stop them."

"I cannot comply."

She hit the truck again. "Why?"

When Augustus remained silent, she jumped into the pickup and turned the key.

Nothing happened.

"Damned," she cried while fruitlessly turning the key again and again. "Start you son of a bitch."

"Standard Internment Unit Megan, your vehicle will not start."

Megan turned an angry face toward Augustus. "What?"

"All of your vehicles have been disabled."

"Then take me there yourself."

"I cannot assist you in this matter."

She jumped from the truck and scanned the barnyard. Finding what she was looking for, she dashed to the barn and stopped in front of a bicycle. Yanking it around, she climbed on and started peddling.

Augustus pulled up beside her as she went. "You will not arrive in time."

Megan glared at the robot. "At least I'm going to try."

"To what end?"

"Because that's what humans do."

39

"Sir," Major Phaa called as he approached the supreme commander. "We've discovered something."

"Report," Khephra demanded while following Phaa into the main room.

"Sir," Captain Praetor announced as his superior officers raced into the room. "We just learned that the female we thought was Human is actually a Rapid Insertion Unit. Its controlling signal signature was being masked somehow."

"Any idea who sent it?"

"None, Sir, but we did learn that it is transmitting a signal in a very narrow band. We only discovered it when the unit left the farmhouse and passed under our observation platform. I've transferred the coordinates to our ship and they're looking for it now."

Khephra tapped the emblem on his sleeve. "Sergeant Specialist Akki. This is the supreme commander. What is your status?"

"We've been having problems with the power unit, but I think it's resolved now. We're going to take a break and then start aligning the control units. We'll have the antenna and more than a dozen units online by morning."

"We don't have until morning. The enemy agent is making her move now."

"We'll start right away, Sir, but it will take time to get these up and running."

"Can you fake the fusion purge while ramping up our engines? We're going to need to leave this area quickly."

"Yes, Sir, but I'm using all available crew to get the monitoring station up."

"Focus on getting the antenna and two control units up first, then do what you can about the ship," Khephra ordered. "We'll give you as much time as we can."

"But Sir, I can't protect…"

"You have your orders, Sergeant Specialist. Khephra out."

The supreme commander turned to his major. "Phaa, order the advance team to intercept and destroy that rapid insertion unit and disable the observation unit."

"Sir," Captain Praetor called. "I've detected a shielded craft moving in our direction. The energy signature is Koko."

"Where is it?"

"It is currently about one Earth hour northwest of our position."

"But it wouldn't have to get all the way here to do its job," Phaa added. "In less than half that time, it would only need a small control unit to extract a Life Force."

Khephra shook his head. "And if it got to within a few kilometers, it would be powerful enough to pull the Life Force out of a living body."

The room went silent for a moment before Khephra swore, "Hammond's balls! I'll not let those bastards get away with this."

All eyes turned to him and he tapped his sleeve. "Supreme Commander to lead ship. Give me the fighter squadron leader."

40

Peddling hard, Megan raced around a corner and found Augustus hovering in the middle of the road, with Aurelia and Wyatt's vehicles behind him.

"Where is he?" she screamed.

"Standard Internment Unit Wyatt has gone into the woods and is approximately fifty meters from this location. You are not permitted into that area."

"The hell I'm not," Megan screamed as she jumped from the moving bike, hit the ground running and headed into the woods.

As Augustus started to move between her and the forest, Megan heard a loud ringing sound and turned to see the robot drop to the ground and go inert.

"What the..." she started to cry, but was interrupted by a popping sound coming from the woods. "No," she screamed as her pace quickened.

To her surprise, Wyatt was still standing when she first sighted them.

"Aurelia, what are you doing?" he pleaded while hobbling from one tree to another.

Megan ran with all her might as Aurelia silently leveled her gun and squeezed the trigger again. Wyatt yelped as the bullet plowed into his shoulder, spinning him around and away from the protection of a tree. When two more bullets punched into his back, he pitched forward to sprawl onto the forest floor.

As Wyatt fell, the two women collided, but Aurelia was far more agile than she appeared. Scooping an arm under Megan's crotch, Aurelia used her attacker's momentum to heave her over her own body. Megan's head struck a tree trunk, but she still managed to do a quick roll and come up in a crouch. As her blurry vision began to clear, she could see Aurelia leveling her weapon.

"Two birds with one stone," she laughed as a puff of smoke erupted from her gun.

Feeling a painful tug on her neck, Megan staggered back a step before dropping to her knees. Warm liquid splashed onto her hands as she lifted them to cover the wound, but before she could even find it, the scene blurred and faded to black.

To her surprise, she found herself floating above her prostrate body. Though she could hear no sounds, she saw Aurelia's body jerk twice with blood exploding from her chest before a third shot ripped her forehead open. As several figures ran toward her, guns at the ready, Aurelia's corpse sprawled on the spongy ground, like a puppet suddenly deprived of its life-giving strings.

As armed men moved to surround the inert bodies, Megan watched a ghostly form rise from Aurelia's remains. It appeared to be momentarily disoriented, but quickly recovered and began rising.

"Don't let them get her!" Aurelia's Life Force screamed.

Megan turned to see what appeared to be clouds of mist swirling around a central figure, which she recognized as Wyatt.

As Aurelia rushed past her, she tried to suck air into lungs she no longer had.

"Samhain!"

"She's ours," Aurelia screamed before she slammed into one of the mist-like creatures.

To Megan's surprise, the impact knocked the creature away from Wyatt as Aurelia made a tight arc to crash into another. Her momentum somewhat reduced by the tight turn, the second impact wasn't as effective. Before she could smash into the third one, the other two were already moving back toward their intended victim.

Still not fully comprehending what was happening, Megan looked down at the men below waving their arms, and yelling something she couldn't hear. She turned back to see dozens of the ghostly shapes had appeared a short distance from them. Within seconds their numbers doubled then doubled again.

"Take that one," Aurelia screamed while crashing into yet another Samhain. "This one's mine!"

Megan turned to find two of the creatures approaching her. Without really knowing how, she moved toward Wyatt, working to gain enough speed to knock Samhain away from her mate.

As she moved, the essence of what made her Megan began melting away. By the time she impacted an ethereal creature, all of her physical features had vanished along with her sense of physical self, and gender. A pulse no longer thumped in her ears and the wounds on her body were a distant memory. Slamming into the Samhain, she felt the pressure of impact, but no sense of pain.

Turning to attack again, she suddenly realized the beings were now just sensations that gave off a dull-gray glow. She and Wyatt were splashes of green in a swirling sea of gray. Aurelia was an intense blue.

"They should have us by now," Aurelia cried.

Megan tried to turn her non-existent head. "Who should have us?"

"Fool," she screamed while knocking another Samhain from Wyatt. "We don't need a loser like you. Pana's the key."

Megan felt confusion swirling under her fear. "But I thought…"

"Because your body was female?" a voice laughed in her head. "You're Saki, idiot. It doesn't matter what your physical body is, your Life Force is male."

A Samhain scratched painfully at Saki's consciousness: razor-sharp cuts that drained energy and caused his color to fade slightly. As he pushed the creature away, several more swept in, digging in unseen claws. Though pushing them away used even more energy, the need to find his mate kept him going.

Within moments the number of invaders grew to allow only random flashes of his companion's color flickering through the swirling gray. Panic exploded inside him as more and more Samhain latched onto his consciousness, painfully gouging deeper and deeper, sapping strength and pulling him further and further from the others. Try as he might, the ever-increasing numbers were simply overwhelming.

The low roar of their empty thoughts clouded his own. Aurelia's cries soon faded to nothing, leaving him cut off, alone, desolate, and sensing the approach of a great abyss; a place he knew was devoid of love, caring,…hope.

He heard Pana's voice at the center of his being, "Hang on, my love. Father will save us. I promise you he…"

Though he fought to stay connected, her voice faded into the ever-increasing noise. Like a small fish resisting the great river, he struggled vainly against the mindless flow, trying to find her again. Even as he did, his color faded, his being merging with theirs as they tore away the remaining feelings, desires, and wants that defined his humanity.

But was he human? The shadows of his memory hinted at a different being he couldn't quite see. He was struggling to remember when Aurelia screamed a last, distant, "Noooo!"

As the infinite depths of nothingness absorbed him, he felt intensely cold and forgot why he should care.

41

Tammabet Ferrisis awoke to her worst nightmare.

Her injured wrist throbbed painfully as she opened her eyes the tiniest bit to see what looked like the head of a short-snouted alligator, its bulging eyes staring at her legs. Before she could process this, an equally ugly head, attached to the same body, appeared in her limited view. One face grimaced, showing sharp, irregular teeth. A blob of drool dropped from the left face and splattered on her exposed belly. She flinched, but did not otherwise move. It was at this point she felt the rough ground digging into her back and butt.

God almighty, she thought. *I'm naked*!

The creature lifted a device with one of four hands and squawked like a hoarse vulture. When a different hand reached down and touched her thigh, it was all she could do to keep from pulling away. Somehow Tamm knew she should play dead. Even so, it took a great effort to keep still as rough fingers moved up and down her thigh, leaving her unsure as to whether it was going to eat or rape her.

With another hand, the creature grabbed her injured wrist, causing her to whimper, but it hardly seemed to notice.

Shaking its cumbersome head, which scattered spittle the length of her body, the creature lifted the device and squawked again. However, this time Tamm was sure, though she didn't know how, she understood what it was saying.

"The flesh be damaged," said one head. "Swelling increases ever since we pick this one up."

"Whole arm be useless if not fixed quick," added the other. "Such injury sours flesh."

"Fix now," a voice squawked from the device. "And get back for others."

The first head nodded as a hand pulled what looked like a fat, silver rod from the apron-like skirt hanging from its waist. Pressing a glyph on the device's side, the creature passed it back and forth over Tamm's wrist. Her whole arm began vibrating and the initial pain made her wince, but after several passes, the creature grunted and released the wrist. Afraid to show she was conscious, Tamm let it drop, and was surprised to feel no pain as her wrist struck the ground.

Peeking again, she saw two faces leaning closer to her own. As rancid breath filled her nostrils she struggled to control her gag reflex. Another drop of drool plopped onto her breast just before the creature removed its hand from her thigh, grunted derisively, and moved off. She struggled to remain still while listening to its many drumming feet march through the gate. The lock clicked, and when she looked, the creature was gone.

"Gawd," she gasped while sitting up and wiping drool from her chest and belly. "That thing smells like rotting flesh."

Looking around, she found herself in a large cave, its broad opening covered with a fence. Lying next to her, Bottar Wak was unconscious and also stripped of his clothing. Nakedness notwithstanding, she wrapped her arms around herself as a chill came over her. Upon standing she found a small glowing device a short distance away, and next to it, a pile of cloth.

Scanning the cavern one more time, to make sure they were alone, she moved to the device and found it gave off heat. After warming herself for a moment, she moved to the pile and began extracting its contents: Two each, loosely fitting shirt, and pants.

She dressed quickly and took an outfit to Bottar, carefully laying the clothes on top of him. When she pressed a hand to his forehead to see if he was warm enough to be alive, he awoke.

"Watch it, buster," she warned. "They took your clothes."

Bottar looked down at the pile covering his groin then up to her. "What the hell?"

"Not a clue, but we need to get out of here fast."

He sat up and looked around the cave. "How did we get here?"

She laughed dryly. "You don't remember?"

He shook his head, his face blank. "I remember seeing you in the back room of my uncle's store. Nothing after that."

She moved back to the heater, held her hands out toward the welcome warmth and sighed. "You wouldn't believe me if I told you."

While pulling on the shirt, Bottar asked, "This some kind of kinky sex thing?"

Tamm's laugh had a hollow sound to it. "We should be so lucky. We've been kidnapped by some kind of alien." She pointed in the direction of the gate. "They just left and they're really creepy."

"Alien? Like in, not from this country?"

She shook her head slowly. "More likely from outer space."

"You're shitting me."

When she shrugged, Bottar lifted his head and sniffed.

"This place smells like crap," he complained.

Tamm moved to the gate blocking the entrance and rattled it. "I think you're smelling the creatures who put us in here."

Bottar grimaced while pulling on the pants. "Damn."

She rattled the gate again. "Our more immediate problem is how to get out."

Moving up beside her, Bottar shook the gate as well. "Maybe we could negotiate with them. Maybe it's a misunderstanding."

Tamm shook her head. "Trust me, friend. We don't want to be here when they get back."

Her companion turned to face the interior of the cave. "It's pretty dark back there. We'll need a light source."

Tamm scooped up a stick, moved back to the heater and held the tip close to it. After a moment, it burst into flame.

"How about this?" she asked just before the fire vanished.

Bottar sighed. "We'll need more than that."

Tamm lowered the stick and looked around. Finding nothing of use, she pulled off her shirt and began wrapping it around her stick. When she was done, she turned to find Bottar staring at her breasts.

"Find us some wire," she ordered with a laugh. "I'd rather run around naked than be eaten by those friggin' aliens."

"But we could have used my shirt," he protested.

Tamm shrugged. "Odds are we'll need your shirt, and probably our pants before we get out of here." She looked at the ceiling. "This lava tube could run for miles."

"And what if we don't find a way out before we run out of clothes?"

"Then we'll stumble along in the dark until they catch up with us and give them the fight of their lives."

As she shook the stick over her head, Bottar's eyes jerked from the shaft to her jiggling breasts and back. Without further comment, he scrambled away.

Shaking her head, Tamm moved in the opposite direction, scanning the ground for something useful. After a few paces she found a limb large enough to act as a second torch. Soon after, a wave from Bottar standing at the far edge of the entrance, signaled he'd found some wire.

As they came together, her mind was suddenly flooded with so many images she became disoriented, stumbled and fell into Bottar.

"Whoa," he exclaimed as his arms wrapped around her.

The sensation vanished as quickly as it had come, and she then realized Bottar's hand was on her left breast. To his credit, he quickly jerked it to her arm pit and lifted her back to her feet.

"What happened?" he asked while still holding her up.

She regained her legs and stepped back. "I'm not sure," she said while involuntarily folding her arms over her chest. "My head was suddenly full of things that made no sense."

"Some kind of mind control?"

She shook her head quickly, before moving toward the heater. "Until we know more, let's stick with our plan."

Working as she walked, Tamm wrapped the wire around the shirt and lowered it close to the glowing device. When it quickly lit, she lifted it over her head and turned back to find Bottar gaping at her.

"What?" she asked just as she remembered she was topless.

"You…you look like the goddess Liberty."

She forced a laugh, turned and headed into the cave. "Oh get a grip, man. It's not like you've never seen boobs before."

Bottar paused momentarily as he struggled with feelings of both lust and respect for the half-naked woman walking away from him. Finally coming to his senses, he snatched up the extra stick and wire and ran after her.

We're probably doomed, he thought, *but at least I'll have something to die for.*

42

Sergeant Specialist Akki jerked as his communications link beeped. A data cube and an empty cup clattered to the floor as he jumped from his chair and scrambled to his main console to hit the speaker icon.

"Sergeant Specialist…uh, good morning, Sir," Akki greeted as the ugly Human face of his superior appeared on the screen.

"Progress report."

"The antenna's power supply is still giving us trouble, but we'll have five control units ready as soon as it is up again."

The supreme commander shook his head. "We need to capture their Life Forces now."

Akki frowned. "The power supply's an old design and we don't have a replacement."

"Do you have anything on board that can substitute? We only need to extract two Life Forces quickly. There are Samhain in the area."

Akki looked shocked. "I think we can reroute the signal through our main antenna."

"Do it now, Sergeant Specialist," Khephra said grimly. "*Micro-paks* count."

"Yes Sir," he said as he broke the connection and switched to a local relay.

"Communications Maintenance here," announced a familiar face. "Hey, Akki. What's up?"

"Kimmo," Akki blurted. "I need to take over your antenna right now. Direct order from the supreme commander."

"Not a problem. We're transmitting status reports to the other ships. You can have it in about five milli-paks."

Akki typed a command at his terminal. "No time."

Cutting off the transmission, he pressed another key and took control of the antenna. A few more key-presses reoriented it to align with the newly refitted control station.

Flipping on his communications link again, he called, "Akki to control station."

The SLM's face appeared on the screen. "Control station here."

"We've had an unplanned termination. I need two controllers online as soon as you can get them powered up."

"Five are running right now, but we have no antenna," the SLM protested.

"I'm going to route the signal through our own antenna. We'll handle the transfer."

"But this is not according to protocol!"

"No time for rules," Akki cried. "We move now, or the enemy gets them. I don't need to tell you what will happen next."

Akki watched the SLM's face go pale as he barked instructions to a subordinate.

"We're transferring control to you now, Sergeant Specialist," he announced. "May Hammond guide your hands."

Without responding, Akki cut the connection and jumped to another terminal.

43

"Sir," Captain Praetor called. "We have control of the Observation unit."

Sweat beading on his humanoid forehead, Khephra hesitated for a moment before nodding. "Have it take everyone else back to their homes." He paused to refer to a device in his hand. "I'm sending memory modifications to make them forget this ever happened."

"Good enough, Sir, but what do we do with the bodies?"

"Leave them in the woods, but arrange things to look like a murder/suicide incident. The Humans won't have any reason to question something like that."

"Yes, Sir."

"Once that is taken care of, we'll pick you up. Since there aren't enough monitoring control relays, we'll be flying back to the ship."

"Will we be reporting to the station for reprocessing?"

Khephra shook his head. "There won't be time. We're moving out as soon as we've recovered the Life Forces."

"Sir? Are we taking him from the planet?"

"That is correct. And another thing. There will be no further communication with the ship until we are back on board."

"Sir?"

"Much depends on what we do here, Captain," Khephra said gravely. "For the sake of my family and yours, we must not fail."

"With all due respect, Sir," the captain said cautiously. "Is this a coup attempt?"

Khephra's face turned grim. "I'm no tyrant, but there are others who want to be, and our job is to stop them."

The Supreme Commander's communicator beeped and Akki's face appeared on the screen. "It's crude, but everything's connected, Sir. We're starting the extraction process right now."

"How's it going?"

"Their signals are very weak, and we're having trouble distinguishing them from the Samhain."

Khephra struggled to maintain his composure. "I know you'll do your best, Sergeant Specialist," he said with a calm voice that covered the screaming terror raging in his head. "That's all I can ask."

"Sir," Captain Theara called. "Our fighters will not get to the Koko ship in time."

"Can we fire on them from here?"

"No Sir. We are too low in the atmosphere."

"Move us into their path and engage full shields," Khephra ordered. "That should keep them from locking onto someone."

As their ship lifted off, Khephra looked at his men -- the best the military had to offer -- all working to outwit the enemy and save his daughter. He wanted to believe that skill alone was enough, but his cramping gut told him no one controlled the luck factor.

However, if they were to have a chance, his men needed a strong leader and that was a role he was born to play. Straightening to his full height, he moved among them, barking orders and watching their progress. He was doing what he'd always loved, but this time it felt painfully surreal. There was no exciting adrenaline rush. His legs felt rubbery; his heart thudded dully. This time the prize was too precious and the confusion of uncertainty clouded his thoughts.

"You're no quitter," he mumbled angrily to himself before calling for more speed from the engines.

The muscles in his neck were hard as rocks as the ship moved far too slowly to where it would block the Koko's extraction beam. He should have felt the thrill of the challenge, but there was none.

The cabin was awash in noise as the crew passed information back and forth, but everyone went suddenly silent when the Koko ship vanished from their screens. Khephra's mind went blank as the sudden realization of what that meant stripped the air from his lungs.

Who has Pana? was the only thought in his head.

Though no one looked his way, Khephra knew they were waiting for him to say something dramatic -- something to make their effort sound heroic -- but he could only turn to Phaa and whisper,

"Pray for them Major. It never should have gone this far."

44

He awoke in an endless blackness, devoid of any sense of space or time. He was a child unborn: a blank slate with no past or future. And then they appeared: white dots against the ebony background. As the first few reached him, they felt like snowflakes pelting a windshield, but he quickly realized they were thoughts. The few became many, the many became a flood and the flood a torrent that merged into one long-running, disorganized movie with him at the center. A billion-trillion snowflake/thoughts enveloped him, burying him until its energy became a solid mass that dissolved and reformed in repeating cycles until it took on a new form.

Fleeting moments combined into continuous hours that evolved into days then weeks, years, decades and finally lifetimes so numerous he began confusing one with the other. It was nonsensical and yet made perfect sense. He knew it all and yet was lost in its sheer volume.

Eventually, the memories merged into a hazy white glow, making time transparent, as the past became contemporary with the present. He was a soldier, a farmer, a prince, and a pauper. He had been fat and skinny, happily penniless, and miserably rich. He ran naked through an ancient forest in pursuit of a fleeing buck, fought hand-to-hand with a vicious enemy, made love to the woman of his dreams, prayed devoutly in a great cathedral wearing scratchy monk's robes, and struggled with a body distorted by cerebral palsy. He had succumbed to old age, been killed by an enraged husband, died bravely in battle, and suffered the agony of the Black Plague. It was all there and yet…how could it?

In time he couldn't measure, he absorbed, organized and cataloged the memories. Half-a-hundred or more lives all put in their places. Slowly, as he accepted them, his mind grew calmer and he once again floated in space, alone.

While drifting in the calmness of the moment, he saw a memory much different than the rest. It came, not as individual, unorganized thoughts, but as one continuous stream, seemingly prepared for him in advance. A fearful chill stabbed the depths of his soul as it played out.

An alarm sounded.

"Incoming debris," someone screamed.

The planet in the view screen was breaking apart, but most of it still rotated around an invisible center. Smaller pieces were flying everywhere, including directly at the station in which he was standing.

"Engage the deflecting shields," someone else cried.

"They're out," a third person responded, "We're defenseless!"

"This wasn't supposed to happen," he could hear himself saying in disbelief. "This isn't…"

The station shuddered as a console lurched up to knock him across the room. As he tried to pick himself up another console to his right exploded sending dust and debris flying. The floor continued to lurch as smaller impacts shook the station.

"Pana?" he called desperately while struggling to rise. "PANA?"

He grabbed for a handrail, but couldn't grip it with his blood-soaked hand. Pushing off the floor, he walked unsteadily on the trembling surface to Pana's station. She was sprawled on the floor like a dropped doll, blood oozing from her forehead. When he picked her up, a cry of anguish gurgled in his throat as her head lolled back. Struggling to maintain his footing, he pressed an ear to her chest, gratefully sensing the beat of a heart slightly out of synch with his own.

Another impact knocked him off his feet. As he struggled to right himself without letting go of her, an airlock burst open. Soldiers, their weapons drawn, surged into the station and overtook the terrified and unarmed occupants.

"All clear for the general," someone shouted, just before a tall figure hurried through the airlock, and marched right up to him. Saki was still on his knees as General Khephra's hard eyes glared down at him and his burden.

"I hope you're ready for a very long stay in Ceratha's burning bowels, N-Tschester," he said coldly while glaring down at the girl. "I just wish you hadn't taken her with you."

With a wave of the general's hand, two soldiers lifted Saki up, with Pana still in his arms. A rifle barrel jabbed his back as he stumbled forward, clutching his precious burden and feeling all hope vanish as they entered the dark airlock.

45

Akki's face appeared in the SLM's monitor. "Sir. I've just received a communication from the supreme commander. The mission was a success. Only three individuals killed. We've recovered two of them."

"We're prepared to process them," the SLM said eagerly. "When shall I expect the transfer?"

Akki shook his head. "We've been called away on an important mission, and will be taking the life forces with us. However, it is important that you continue to work on the array."

"Is N-Tschester among them?"

"No, Sir. We've returned him to his home, though he and his primary mate have been injured."

"Can I know when you'll be back?"

"I'm afraid not, but we'll handle the return of our people to their bodies."

"I've seen enough to know you can accomplish that without much difficulty," the SLM acknowledged. "Is there anything we need to know about him?"

Akki looked at his monitoring screens. "It should take them a while to recover, but they aren't so seriously damaged that the indigenous doctors can't handle it. None of them will remember our visit, so there shouldn't be any need to change protocols."

"What about the problems at Secor-Alpha Four? Have their control units been restored?"

"I don't know, Sir. I'm just a lowly sergeant. They don't tell me much more than I need to know."

The SLM nodded with a knowing smile. "On that point, I can relate entirely."

Both men laughed before Akki raised a hand. "Well, I must get back to my duties, Sir. We're departing very soon. It's been a pleasure working with you."

"The same here, Sergeant," the SLM said. "Who shall I report to now?"

Akki shrugged. "I'm told someone will be contacting you."

The SLM shook his head. "I'm glad I don't work for the military. Too much secrecy for my taste."

Akki swiped a hand at the screen and a different face appeared. "Captain, all pleasantries have been dispensed with. You're back in control now."

"Thank you, Sergeant Specialist."

Without further comment, the screen went blank and Akki smiled at the hum of engines revving for launch. However, his smile quickly vanished as he looked at the two coffin-like capsules sitting in his storage room.

"I sure hope the Supreme Commander knows what he's doing with this lot," he muttered just as his monitor beeped.

"Sorry to bother you, Sergeant Specialist," The SLM announced, "but I just thought I'd ask."

Akki's heart sank as he struggled to keep his feelings from his face. "Oh?"

"Should I have our observations units paying closer attention to N-Tschester from now on?"

Akki shook his head. "That won't be necessary. We believe all the perpetrators of the escape attempt have been rounded up."

"Escape?" the SLM squeaked. "They were actually trying to leave the planet?"

"Don't worry. The situation is under control."

"I am relieved to hear that, but how did it manage to get this far?"

Akki shrugged. "Space pirates."

The SLM looked puzzled. "Maatiirani? In this sector?"

Akki nodded. "If the prize is rich enough, even they will take the risk."

"I can only shiver at the ramifications, Sergeant Specialist. How did they bypass our security?"

Akki shook his head. "It seems they modified your computer system so it couldn't see them. I've made changes that will prevent that from happening in the future. However, it is important to keep this secret. Rumors would sprout like infectious weeds and quickly blossom into wholesale panic."

The SLM nodded energetically. "I remember what it was like just before he was captured. I shudder to think what would happen if this were to get out."

Akki nodded as well, playing on the obvious fear shadowing the SLM's face. "The pirates may still have spies hidden among the staff of our fleet. It's critical they not know what we've done here until we route them out."

"What else can I do to help?"

"Just keep your status reports normal, like he's still working and playing as before. He'll be down for about two of his weeks. Then all will be as it was and no one will be the wiser."

The SLM frowned. "I don't like subterfuge."

"Nor do I," Akki said softly, "but it's a small price to pay for preserving our way of life."

The SLM hesitated for a moment before giving a quick, but decisive nod. "You make a very persuasive case, Sergeant Specialist. I'll do the best I can."

Akki thanked the civilian and signed off. Working at his console, he uploaded several new algorithms to make the fake Wyatt and Megan routines more active over time.

"Hopefully, this boob won't try to make visual contact with either unit," he mumbled while wiping perspiration from his brow.

46

Sub-commander Pheet leaned against the bulkhead and sucked down another gulp of *thoapa* as he struggled to muster enough energy to continue on. At that moment, Matrina rounded the corner.

"Well, hello there," she purred with a lecherous smile.

Pushing away from the bulkhead, Pheet lifted his spill-proof mug and shook it. "This damned thing has enough caffeine to kill a giant rock sloth and I'm on my fourth mug this morning."

Matrina laughed. "Did our lovemaking take all the strength out of you?"

Pheet shook his head. "It was that damned pill you gave me. What was it again?"

She waved a hand dismissively. "Just a sex stimulant." She took a step back and spread her arms. "I'm not having any problems."

Pheet growled angrily while slumping against the bulkhead again. "Well, that's not how I'm feeling."

After looking around conspiratorially, Matrina pulled a small packet from her fanny pack. "Try this," she said while tearing the top off the bag.

Before the sluggish Pheet could react, she flipped the mug's lid open and poured the contents in.

As she snapped the lid closed and shook the mug, Pheet scowled angrily. "What is it this time?"

Matrina laughed. "It's just an herbal caffeine booster. Totally safe. My mother takes it when she's down."

Looking around again, she moved close to him and ran a hand down to his crotch. "Maybe we can get together when I get off shift. I had a simply wonderful time last night." Though Pheet reacted to the pleasure of her touch, his skeptical look made her scowl. "Well, if all you can do is lean against this bulkhead, and look hostile, I'm not sure I want to spend time with you." She patted the bottom of his mug. "Drink up."

Though he wanted to resist, his hand rose automatically until the hot liquid was pouring down his throat. Within *micro-paks*, he began to feel normal again.

Pushing away from the bulkhead, he barked a laugh. “Wow! This really works.”

“Well, I’ve got work to do,” Matrina announced abruptly as she moved past him. “I’ll see you tonight.”

She was gone before he remembered to ask her about how he got back to his room the last time they made love. Not wanting to make a scene by chasing her down, he just shook his head and took another sip from the mug.

“Guess I’ll talk to her about it tonight,” he murmured while continuing on his way.

47

For Saki, the gray ceiling of his hospital room was a welcome relief to the constant barrage of memories. Anxious voices echoed dully in his ears, but he could not make out words. His body remained frozen, limiting his sight to one small patch of ceiling.

More excited speech reached his dulled consciousness just as sensation came into his chest, spreading quickly to his arms and legs. He could now feel and hear his rapidly-beating heart gradually slowing.

"Can you hear me?" a distant voice asked.

He tried to nod, but his eyes blinked instead.

"Don't be afraid," the voice assured him. "This is just temporary. You'll be OK soon."

He gave a nod/blink but knew from the recent flood of memories that it was only a lie. If he really killed all those people, he'd never be OK.

Can you hear me? echoed in his head, though he intended to speak it.

"Yes," the voice answered. "I'm Doctor Paquet. How are you doing?"

I'm not sure I know how to answer that.

"Your brain will have to learn how to communicate with your body," the doctor explained. "It won't take long, now that you're conscious."

Why am I here?

"I don't know. Supreme Commander Khephra thought it was important, but I've no further explanation than that."

Do they intend to kill me?

"I doubt it," Paquet answered. "They could have done that on the planet."

Where are we going to next?

"Angrolicat."

May Hammond have mercy on me.

"I'm sorry? What is the problem?"

That's where the survivors of Ooertfael went after their planet was destroyed.

"But certainly the supreme commander didn't go to all this trouble just to sacrifice you to the survivors."

He might. After all, because of me, his daughter… Saki paused as he struggled and failed to sit up. Where's Pana?

"I am not sure where your wife is."

They didn't recover her?

"They recovered a female, but I don't know anything more."

Would you find out and let me know?

"I'll take care of it personally, but in the meantime, you need to focus on your recovery."

The doctor stood, spoke briefly with a technician and left the room. As he moved down the hall, a dark figure approached from a side room.

"How is he doing?"

Though startled by the question, the doctor recovered quickly. "I'm not sure I should be talking with you."

The figure shook his head while handing him a data chip. "The supreme commander has authorized you to keep me informed."

After reading the authorization, the doctor shrugged. "He's just become conscious, but we're still communicating with him telepathically. He'll be verbal and mobile by tomorrow. You can see him then."

"Did you tell him about his wife?" the figure asked.

The physician shook his head. "Not a good idea in his present state."

"When will you tell him?"

"I think it's best to wait until he's stronger."

The figure nodded curtly. "And how will you go about it?"

Frowning, the doctor shrugged as he handed the chip back. "Maybe I'll leave that bit to you."

48

With a labored sigh, he settled his frame onto a small stool facing the stasis chamber that held Pana's body. Around him lights blinked erratically as the machines hummed, but his attention was on the face showing through the observation bubble.

"I know you're not in there," Khephra sighed softly, "but I have to talk with someone, and in my position there just isn't anyone else."

He quickly scanned the room before putting his hands on his knees and leaning toward her.

"I can't chase after you," he whispered guiltily. "Lord knows if your mother ever finds out, she'll poke out my eyes, but there's too much at stake."

He dropped his head, shaking it slowly for a moment before looking at her again. "Maybe old Senator Patatior was right. After the last war we should have just wiped those damned Kokos from existence instead of making an alliance with them. Patatior knew the Councils couldn't keep them in line forever and he was right.

"But now I have to get to them before they can use you against us. Even though it may mean…"

His voice broke as he once again did a quick survey of the room. Finally satisfied, he turned back to her.

"As soon as I can, I'll come looking for you." He swallowed hard, steeling his resolve. "The day of regret is coming for the saterhi who kidnapped my girl." He shot quickly to his feet, shaking a fist in the air. "I speak true, Daughter."

His enthusiasm vanished as his eyes once again fell on the still face.

He watched a moment longer before sighing deeply, and quietly leaving the room. After the door hissed closed, the only remaining sounds were the life-giving hum of the stasis chamber and the slightest of beeps made by a hidden transceiver denoting the end of its transmission.

49

"Supreme Commander on deck," the captain announced as Khephra stepped onto the flight deck. "Glad to have you back, Sir."

"What's our status?"

"We caught the other ships off guard, Sir. No one has followed us, nor could they."

"Are we tracking the enemy ship?"

"Yes, Sir. Once it was outside the atmosphere, they turned off their shields."

"Estimated destination?"

"If they maintain their course, it will be the same as ours: Angrolicat. Are we planning to get there before them?"

Khephra hesitated for a moment before shaking his head. "Have we made our first course correction yet?"

Letting his concern show only briefly, the captain quickly blanked his face and nodded. "We left passive sensor range two *deca-paks* after departure. I waited another *deca-pak* before making the change." He looked at his watch. "Our next course correction will be just after shift change tomorrow morning."

Khephra smiled. "Very good, Captain, but I'll be altering that heading."

"Yes, Sir. Will we be intercepting the Koko ship before they reach their destination?"

"No. Our destination is Secor-Alpha Four, and I want all sails at full mast."

"Will we have time for refueling at our destination?"

"No, but we should make Todulous Station, don't you think?"

"Do you anticipate resistance, Sir?"

The supreme commander shook his head. "I don't expect it, but we'll plan for it anyway."

"What do you expect, Sir?"

The supreme commander's lips curled into a smile not reflected in his eyes. "To meet some very old friends."

"Shall I announce our new destination to the crew?"

Khephra shook his head. "Let's keep this party small for the time being. Make the change slowly so as not to attract attention and have your security boys listen in on the internal chatter."

"You think we might be carrying a spy?"

The supreme commander shook his head. "Of the three-hundred-and-twenty people on board, there has to be someone with loyalties contrary to our own."

The captain turned to the communications officer. "Chief, let's go silent."

As the chief worked at his station, the captain turned back to his superior. "Would you mind if I run a battle drill? If they're going to spy on us, they might as well do some real work at the same time."

The supreme commander nodded. "It's your ship, Captain and it looks like you've got it well in hand."

"And where will you be, Sir?"

Khephra smiled grimly. "Visiting a different old friend."

50

He tried to open his eyes, but the brightness of the room forced them closed again.

"Did someone call for me?" he asked while shading his eyes and peering at the two shapes by his bed. "I thought I heard someone say my name."

"Do you know what your name is?" asked a voice he immediately recognized, and for reasons he did not fully understand, feared.

"I don't know," he said cautiously. "There seem to have been so many."

"Your first one," a tall person wearing a uniform asked as he moved to the foot of the bed. "The one you had before this all happened."

"Saki…uh…something or other."

"Saki N-Tschester," the person announced with a hint of irritation.

Saki sat up for a better look at the speaker. "And what am I supposed to have done to you?"

"Don't you remember any of it?"

Saki shook his head. "Bits and pieces, but it makes little sense. I couldn't be responsible for what happened."

"You make a habit of avoiding responsibility?" the person asked sarcastically.

Saki shook his head uncertainly. "I…don't think so. But of all the things I remember, that part is so…jumbled and incomplete."

The tall person turned to his short companion, who wore a dull brown robe of a style Saki didn't recognize. "How long before he's past this phase?"

The short one shook his head. "A couple *pak*, maybe more. It's too early to tell at this stage."

The taller person turned back to Saki. "You've got three *pak* to figure this out, Son. If you don't, I'm going to have a hard time making the rest of my plan work."

"But I don't even know exactly what happened. How can I possibly help?"

The soldier turned and opened the only door in the room. "One way or the other, you've got three *paks*."

"But…" his protest was cut off when the person slipped through the door and snapped it closed.

"Don't worry," the shorter person was saying. "I'm confident you can do it."

Saki stared at him. "How can you know that?"

"You said all the other memories came in a flood. In time, these will do likewise. Your brain just needs time to absorb it all."

Saki shook his head. "This is different. The other memories came without hesitation, like old friends at a reunion. But I'm afraid of this last one. There's something there I don't want to know."

"Then I'll do what I can to help you."

"And who are you?"

The figure pushed away from the wall and extended a hand that slid from under his long sleeve. The skin was nearly transparent, clearly showing muscles, bone and green blood vessels.

"Forgive me, Saki N-Tschester. I've been working with you for so long during your transition, I forget that you don't know me. My name is Doctor Forrtess Makhaman. My friends and comrades call me Makh. I am here to help you through this."

Ignoring the hand, Saki shivered and slipped down under the covers. "What does it matter? Everyone thinks I'm the mastermind behind this thing. If I was even just part of it, I deserve to die."

Lowering his hand until it slid back under his robe's sleeve, the Makh nodded. "Yes, but if someone else planned this, they could strike again."

Saki threw off the covers and sat up. "It's been thirty *druak* since this happened. Wouldn't he have done something else by now?"

Makh shrugged. "Maybe he has. The people he destroyed were primitive and only just experimenting with space flight. If we hadn't been tipped off to what was happening, he would have wiped them all out and we'd never have known. In the meantime, this is a vast galaxy. He may have destroyed another hundred planets and we'd be none the wiser. Worse yet, he could be building a fleet, using these primitive creatures as slaves and has one large enough to take on the Hierarchy of Councils."

"But, if the Councils are so worried about this guy, why kill me?"

Makh shook his head. "Because everybody else thinks you are him."

Saki shook his head as well. "But I'm not. I can't be."

"It doesn't matter. The act of destroying an entire planet stunned the Maatiirani and stopped a galactic war just as it was starting. Your capture and imprisonment kept the war at bay because neither side wants to risk the instability that might set you free."

"Just because of me?"

He sighed. "Let's just say some very smart people made you out to be somewhat more evil and clever than you really are."

"Somewhat?"

He laughed softly. "OK, a hell of a lot more, and it was very effective."

"I don't get it."

"He who hates my enemy can't be my enemy. If you and your allies were seen as more dangerous than the other side, it made sense for both sides to parlay a peace just to keep you bottled up."

"And it worked?"

Makh's smile faded. "Until now, yes."

"Is the fear factor losing its effect?"

He frowned. "On numerous levels, I'm afraid."

"What of my comrades?"

"Your second mate, Tammabet Ferrisis and about five hundred members of your old division vanished from another prison planet called Secor-Alpha Four."

Saki's face clouded. "Is Tamm OK?"

Makh held up both hands, palms up. “All we know for certain is that they’re missing. However, the fact that the array controlling them was destroyed just before they disappeared is quite telling.”

“What do you mean?”

The doctor shrugged. “There are those who will benefit by the resumption of the war.”

“Remove the threat. Remove the peace.”

“There might be another way of looking at it.”

Saki shook his head. “If one side thinks the other has me they’ll feel compelled to attack in self-defense.”

The doctor smiled grimly. “You know, you’re every bit as smart as the Supreme Commander said you were.”

“That was him in here earlier, wasn’t it?”

Makh nodded. “When the Secor-Alpha Four array went down, he seemed to be the only one who realized what might be happening and made straight for you.”

“So I’m a bargaining chip?”

Makh moved to the side of the bed so quickly it startled Saki.

“You’re much more than that, my foolish friend,” he said seriously. “You may be the only hope we have left.”

51

"Senator Addy," the aide called softly as he shook what he hoped was the creature's shoulder. "Sir, I've got news from the intervention teams."

The bed was wide enough for four KokoroTetians and Addy was sprawled sideways on it. The aide was thankful the senator's heads were closest to the bedroom door, so he didn't have to crawl up on the bed to make contact with him. Though the first Koko to ever sit on the Over Council, Addy had been forced to accept an Antrakan aide. It was rumored that the senator had eaten the previous one when he disturbed him in bed.

Unwinding from his voluminous covers, Addy rolled over, revealing both faces at once. "Since you risk wrath by waking us, We guess it not good news."

"No, Sir," the aide answered as he took several quick steps back. "They're gone."

"Who gone?"

"All of them, Sir: N-Tschester, his two wives and all his men."

"That not possible! They light-years apart. How it happen so fast?"

"It was two different teams. Of that we're sure."

"Well, spill out!" Addy snapped angrily as he rolled out of bed. "Don't make us crankier than We already be."

"The first team, at Secor-Alpha Four blew out two control stations, disabled the Observation Units and shut down all sensor arrays in that region of the planet. No one is sure how they did it, but they lifted about five-hundred Standard Internment Units off the planet before the defense teams could arrive."

The senator's heads turned toward each other.

"Impossible task, maybe?" one said.

"Militia strike force?" asked the other.

The first head shook. "Even so, that a lotta butts to move."

The second head jerked toward the aide. "How long this take?"

"One, maybe two *paks*."

"Not possible."

The second head lunged at the aide forcing him to jump back, "What about other prison?"

"At Prak a'Terra, the station's SLM reported that Supreme Commander Khephra went down to the planet to secure the prisoners. He later told the SLM that the pirates had been defeated and all was as it had been. However, after he left it was discovered that the internment units holding N-Tschester and his mate, Pana-Teelr Khephra had been terminated. Their control units had been modified to hide that fact."

"That Khephra always be smart for Antrakan," said the right head.

The left head shook. "But attacks be so much different. Maybe not coordinated effort."

The right head shook as well. "Khephra not traitor. This gotta be pre-emptive strike."

The left head's mouth dropped open. "We be in negotiations with Council about our increased fleet size. He not dare attack us while they still talking about…"

Both heads suddenly turned to face the doorway. Raising a hand to silence the aide, the senator reached under his pillow and extracted a weapon. As he moved toward the door, a third hand carefully moved a chair out of the way. Jumping forward, he fired twice into the wall to the left of the doorway. A dull thump followed as a single-headed body fell across the doorway.

"But Sir, that's our janitor," the aide squeaked as Addy rushed to the body.

Without comment, the senator rummaged through the corpse's clothes.

"Ceratha's ass!" he exclaimed while lifting a small device to the light. "Transmitter."

"Lord Hammond," the aide cried. "That means…"

Both heads nodded slowly as they turned toward the aide. “Yes, my friend. That mean we in race against time.”

“Yes Sir, but it is our understanding that Supreme Commander Khephra has N-Tschester. Surely he won’t side with a traitor.”

The aide hoped the expression on the senator’s face was a smile, though he hadn’t been with him long enough to really know for sure.

“Only Khephra truly know his intentions, maybe?” the left head said grimly.

“He not work under Council orders now,” the right head grumbled.

“We can only hope he not in league with somebody else,” the first head added.

The aide looked nervously toward the door. “But I thought you said he wasn’t a traitor.”

The heads shook quickly. “What We want to believe and what be real may be different things,” the left head said.

The right head nodded. “Maybe he on our side, maybe not. Still got big asses to cover.”

The aide took two steps toward the door. “Then the Over Council should be notified at once.”

The senator looked shocked as both faces paled noticeably. “Now we at war,” he said, whipping his weapon around and firing.

As the Antrakan crumpled to the floor, Addy hurried to his monitor, punched several keys and stared into the screen until two faces much like his appeared.

“Get guards in here on double,” he growled. “And prepare our shuttle for departure quick.”

“Yes Sir!”

Addy punched several more buttons as two frightened Koko Marines rushed through his doorway.

“Secure apartment,” he demanded. “Nobody to go in or out, but us.” He swept a hand at the corpses. “Clear this garbage out, but leave guard to help carry our things to shuttle.”

“Yes Sir,” responded the first Marine as he grabbed the aide’s feet and started dragging him toward the door.

"Not that way, idiot. You spread blood all over carpet. Pick it up and carry out."

Just then two faces appeared in his monitor.

"Major. What activity on Maatiirani front?" Addy asked abruptly.

One of the Major's faces turned away momentarily before he answered, "No activity in demilitarization zone for weeks and even then, just cargo ship."

"Ship? What ship?"

Both heads left the screen this time, followed by hushed, but urgent whispering.

Returning, they glanced at each other before the left one spoke hesitantly, "It be …Elktaterian ship. They be authorized to trade with Maatiirani, so…apparently, uh, since this be regular visit, we not track them once they…leave zone."

The senator stared at the screen with an expression of mixed rage and terror.

With a calm that was obviously forced, he asked, "What name of ship?"

The Major nodded eagerly. "It be the…"

"Then send battle cruiser to find damned thing and interrogate crew!" he shouted angrily.

Though a well disciplined soldier, the major still paused briefly before answering, "Yes Sir. If they follow flight plan, we have them in half *deca-pak*."

As the faces moved off the screen the senator spoke again. "And Major," he said, showing obvious restraint. "They will lie to you at first. Before interrogation team leave ship, make undoubtedly certain they have truth."

The major's faces reappeared in the screen. "Undoubtedly certain, Sir?"

"Even to point of skinning alive and slow-roasting on spit," he said angrily.

The Marine guard was certain he saw both of the major's mouths curve up into a smile as he saluted. "Yes Sir!" he barked in stereo.

For a moment after the screen went blank the senator continued to stare at it. When he finally turned to the Marine, his eyes were inquisitive.

"You ever eat roasted Elktaterian, maybe?"

Looking puzzled, the guard shook his heads.

"It be over century ago now, during Boortstoor wars. We lead division against those devils. After each battle, we got in habit of cooking captives, both as psychological tactic, and because we low on food. It turn out they be really quite good, and it not be long before we put more effort into capturing than killing." Letting his gaze drift to a random point on the far side of the room, he rubbed his stomach. "After war end, we take some thirty thousand home, but before we have celebratory feast the Council make us give them back."

He sighed and looked back at the guard. "Even so, a black market thrive for many *sirius* after and We have to admit We never lose taste for them." Turning to the blank monitor screen, he smacked his lips. "You know, this might be long interrogation, and We think Major could use hand, maybe?" he said with a smile while moving to his dressing room.

52

"Oh Damn," Pana said as she awoke for the first time.

Her vision cleared quickly and she found herself staring into the face of the ugliest person she could ever remember seeing. The oversized face was distorted with a large almond-shaped eye on its right side and a shrunken and somewhat recessed eye on the left. A scar ran from his right temple, through the small eye and across his mouth. His nose had obviously been broken at some distant time and not healed well. In addition, his right ear was only a flat scar on the side of his head.

"How are you feeling?" the face asked.

"Like curdled pig shit," she snapped through the mask covering her face.

When he reached for her face, she pulled back against her pillow.

"Do not be afraid," he said in a soft, reassuring voice. "I'm only going to remove your breathing mask."

She didn't relax as he lifted the mask over her head. Without another look at her, he moved to a side table and worked a console. With his back to her, she slipped her legs from under the covers and tried to rise, but the room started to spin as she did. Falling back against the pillow, she struggled to resist the threatening urge to vomit.

His hands quickly but gently pulled her back into the bed. "Don't move so quickly, Pana," he said while pulling the blankets over her. "Most who do end up puking their guts out."

She tried to shake his hands off. "You drugged me!"

Without much effort, he continued to restrain her.

"You were not sedated. This is just part of the transitional trauma. It will pass soon, now that you're awake."

Lifting her hands, she noticed her skin was no longer pink, but a greenish-gray with six long, slender, fingers that felt stiff as she flexed them.

She looked into the speaker's face which, though still scarred, seemed more attractive. In fact, she had the impression she'd seen him somewhere before.

"What have you done to me?"

"There's much to explain," he said almost too quietly to hear. "Most of it you're going to remember soon."

"What do you mean, I'm going to remember?" she asked as a memory of a child running toward her flashed in her mind.

Before she could process it, another memory followed. She saw someone standing in a crowded control room as an overhead panel exploded into his face.

"You're Kappa," she said softly as another thought cut off anything else she planned to say.

She was a Human male standing by a bed and looking down at the naked Aurelia. She was both excited and repulsed by the sight.

"Shit," she exclaimed while shaking her head.

As Kappa moved closer, the undamaged side of his face now looked almost handsome, but another memory filled her head so powerfully she lost sight of him again. She was staring at a different person for whom she felt a powerful attraction. They were in a space station and he was looking shocked.

"This wasn't supposed to happen," he was saying in disbelief. "This isn't…"

The room lurched and her last thought was a sense of falling.

"What just happened?" she cried as Kappa's concerned face reappeared.

"Don't be alarmed," he said. "You've made it through the initial flood of memories, but there are still a number of suppressed ones to come. They may be a bit overwhelming, but will explain a lot."

He could see her face contort with the beginnings of a protest before her eyes suddenly glazed over. Kappa sighed as he glanced at the screens above her bed. Her pulse rose and fell in tune with the changing pace of her respiration. Brain waves were spiking all over the chart.

Shaking his head, he walked to a chair and picked up the tablet he had been reading.

"How she doing?" a voice squawked in his ear.

"Nothing unusual for someone trying to absorb a billion memories they didn't know they had." He sighed. "Let's keep the release of memories slow for the moment. It's not going to be an easy ride for her."

"Negative," came the insistent reply. "In two *paks* we reach destination. What she know not as important as what someone pay for her."

"It's not a good idea to rush this part of the process. She has over fifty lives to absorb and process. No one can do that in two *paks*."

"So what? It doubtful she survive anyway."

"What do you mean?"

"You not know?"

Kappa shook his head. "What?"

"She mate of N-Tschester," came the reply. "Ooertfael are mad to get hands on either of them. By the Ooertfael old solar cycle, they observing one-hundredth anniversary of destruction of home planet." The voice laughed maliciously. "Ironic, no? We get money to snatch her from Samhain and then sell to Ooertfael so they can send her back to them. Primitive races be so bloody profitable!"

"But she can't be as culpable as he is?"

"Who care? We only paid to get her there on time."

Kappa shook his head slowly as he looked at the sleeping female. "You think I could take a bathroom break?"

"She be secure?"

He nodded. "She won't regain consciousness for some time."

"Take all time you need. None of us be going anywhere until after rendezvous."

Kappa rose and waited for the guard to release the door. Walking briskly toward the restroom, he glanced around before lifting a device from his pocket. Cupping it inside his hand, he pushed through the door, relaxing only when he saw the room was empty.

"It's me," he said into the device. "We've got a problem."

"What?" asked a gravelly voice.

"We've got less than two *paks* to make our move."

"Are they on to us?"

"No, but they're going to rendezvous with the Ooertfael. Once she's in their possession we won't get another chance."

"Understood."

Footsteps in the hallway.

"Regular meeting place in a few *milli-paks*," he said quickly.

Not waiting for the response, he shoved the device back into his pocket and moved to a large oval opening in the floor the Kokos used as a urinal. Just as he started to relieve himself, two Kokos entered.

"We tell you, Monik. The sooner we rid of that vermin, the better," said the taller of the two.

Monik stepped over the urinal next to Kappa, and squatted down before turning one head toward him. "You Antrakan, right?"

Kappa zipped up, stepped away from the urinal and nodded.

Orkid looked past his comrade. "Shit. They only got one head…"

Monik stopped him with a sharp slap on the arm.

"But We never see one before," Orkid protested.

Both of Monik's faces glared at him. "Geeze," he cried while slapping Orkid again. "You gotta forgive stupid friend, maybe?" he said while turning both faces toward Kappa. "My comrade not often mix with other peoples. Of course, that probably why peace last so long."

"We say We sorry," Orkid whined. "But We still wants to know why we risk Antrakan wrath by doing this?"

Monik nodded toward Kappa. "You restoring N-Tschester mate?"

Kappa nodded. "She just woke up this morning."

"How you feel about selling your kind to Ooertfael?"

Kappa shook his head. "I'm just here to do a job. It's nothing to me."

Monik finished his task and rose. "But why not do this thirty *druak* ago, maybe? How many millions be spent incarcerating these peoples?"

Kappa shrugged. "No idea, but I'm guessing it has something to do with politics."

Orkid nodded. "That probably right. We be told his capture stop war with damned Maatiirani and keep it stopped. Antrakan commander find way to make that permanent, maybe?"

Monik slapped his comrade on the shoulder. "Maybe he likewise find way to make everybody rich. That make Us happy."

As the two Kokos laughed, Kappa followed them out of the restroom. When the pair turned left, chatting as they went, he hurried in the opposite direction. Within *micro-paks* he was around a corner and letting out a huge sigh as his pace slowed.

He fondled the communication device in his pocket while thinking, *We need to get out of here and soon.*

53

Stopping at the doorway to Matrina's apartment, Pheet leaned heavily against the door frame before pressing the call button.

Matrina looked surprised to see him. "I thought we were meeting at the usual place."

Without answering, Pheet pushed past her. "I need some more of that herbal stuff you gave me earlier."

"Still feeling a bit down?" she asked as the door closed.

"Very," he gasped while crashing into the nearest chair. "That stuff you gave me only lasted a *deca-pak*. Nothing else seems to help."

"Poor baby," she said mockingly while moving into an adjoining room. "Better let Matrina fix up something to get your lazy butt off the floor."

"No more of the sex stimulant stuff," he said loudly. "I've had enough of that."

"No," she agreed while reappearing with a frothy looking drink. "This has nothing to do with stimulating your sex drive."

He grabbed the drink from her hands and gulped down half of it before even taking a breath. Lowering the glass, he smiled at her briefly before his eye lids started drooping. As his hands and the glass settle into his lap, Pheet's eyes closed and his head slumped against the chair back.

Smiling, Matrina lifted the glass from his hands. "And now, my love, our relationship is going to change for the better." She chuckled while sniffing the fragrant drink. "At least for me that is."

54

"Something's wrong here," Saki announced as he sat up in bed.

"What?" Makh asked from his chair in the far corner of the room.

"You're not a doctor, are you?"

Makh's face betrayed no emotion, but he didn't speak for several moments. "What makes you think that?"

"Because you don't dress or act like one."

Makh lifted both arms away from his body. "Ah, the robe."

Saki shrugged. "That and the questions you ask seem more geared toward helping the general than me."

"Well, we are on a tight deadline."

"But a medical doctor would put his patient's needs first."

Makh shook his head slowly. "You always were quick to figure things out."

"Why would you know that?"

He waved a hand dismissively. "It doesn't matter. What we need to…"

"The hell it doesn't," Saki shouted. "My head is so full of senseless blarth, I can barely remember my name. Everything matters to me."

Makh was quietly shaking his head when the room's only door opened. The tall person Saki had seen earlier entered.

"Do you know who I am?" he asked, his eyes locked on Saki.

Saki's anger was instantly replaced with regret.

He nodded. "You're General Khephra."

"It's Supreme Commander now. Anything else?"

Shaking his head, Saki looked at Makh. "What is your real name, anyway?"

Looking indecisive, Makh hesitated until the supreme commander answered, "We call him AmPheet."

Behind Khephra, AmPheet's mouth curled into a sneer, but he said nothing.

Saki turned to the Supreme Commander. "I have the impression that stands for donkey urine."

Khephra nodded. "I see you're good with useless information. How about something that can save your entire species?"

Saki's eyes dropped to his hands. "If I could tell you, I would." He looked up at Khephra. "I honestly don't have any reason to keep secrets from you."

The tall soldier turned abruptly and marched to the door. Holding it opened, he turned back, staring directly at Saki.

"I don't care about reasons, Son," he said softly. "I need answers."

The two remaining stared at the door as it clicked closed and held that pose for several moments.

"So, what name would you like to be known by?" Saki finally asked.

"AmPheet will do for now."

"No it won't," Saki insisted. "I can't work with anyone I don't trust and that certainly applies to someone who won't tell me his real name."

AmPheet sighed. "That's difficult, because I don't really know myself."

"How can that be? I've been through dozens of lives and I still know who I am."

"You have an advantage," AmPheet said sadly. "You actually knew your original name. I was but a pup when my parents were killed in the Dekstert Rebellion. There were millions of us orphans roaming the streets of PanPher looking for anything to stay alive. Trouble was never something I went looking for, but it found me often enough. Whenever things got too hot, I'd change my name and move to another part of town. Let's just say, I made a lot of moves."

"So what do they call you now?"

AmPheet's eyes drifted to the floor. "Now might not be a good time for this."

"It doesn't look like I've much time left, so out with it."

His mouth opened and closed several times before he finally said, “AnKat Ta-Tschester.”

A memory flashed in Saki’s mind, knocking any response out of reach. He was a child hopelessly entangled in his crashed bicycle, his left elbow scraped and bleeding. Someone appeared above him as Saki struggled to rise, but his legs were painfully entangled in the bicycle’s frame. Finally, big hands reached down and pulled him free. As he was lifted up, the person’s face came into view.

“Damn,” Saki exclaimed. “You’re my father.”

55

While scanning the hallway, Kappa knocked on the door with three light taps. *Micro-paks* later the door opened quietly, but the entryway was empty. Without hesitation, he hurried inside and stood in the entryway as the door quickly closed behind him.

"This is foolhardy," a dark figure complained from the shadows as he slid something shiny into his belt.

Looking up at a person nearly a third-of-a-meter taller than himself, Kappa shrugged. "I know, Baroque, but we're two *paks* from Angrolicat space. By this time tomorrow, she'll be in lock down, so we do it now or she's lost to us."

His wide mouth curving down, Baroque glared down at his comrade. "If those Koko bastards even think we're about to betray them, they'll literally eat us alive."

Kappa nodded slowly. "It's risky, but there's no other choice." He walked across the room to his comrade. "If you want out, now's the best time."

"And who will fly the shuttle?"

Kappa shrugged. "Guess I will."

The taller male laughed dryly, his eyes mirthless. "Sorry, friend, but you couldn't fly a mosquito through an open window."

Kappa looked hurt. "I'm not that bad."

"You're probably worse, and that won't save us."

Kappa's shrugged. "If you leave, it won't be your problem."

As Baroque's head shook, his silver-gold hair glistened in the low light. "I promised your mother I'd look out for you." The hint of a smile appeared on his face. "At the very least, I've got to get you out of that shuttle bay."

"After this, we'll go to Gibbron and rest for a while. We can reconnect with our families and settle down. I promise. No more adventures."

Baroque mouthed a silent laugh. "We both know that if these guys are dealing with the Maatiirani, this could start a war."

Kappa frowned. “They’re going to sell her to the Ooertfael.”

“You’re kidding. But they’ll…”

“Pay much more than the Maatiirani,” Kappa interrupted. “Is everything ready?”

“As much as it can be, considering the security protocols in place around her.”

“That will have to do.”

“I’ve checked the shuttle bay and they don’t have anything here that can outrun this ship.”

Kappa shrugged. “I think we may be able to come up with something that will keep them occupied long enough to get safely inside Angrolicat air space.”

Baroque rolled his eyes. “What scheme has the Lord Hammond put in your head?”

Kappa motioned for Baroque to go into the living room.

“I’m not dressing up as a damned Koko,” Baroque stated as they walked.

“I have, or rather had an uncle who was a conman. He said that even the lousiest plan will work if the distraction is good enough.”

“What happened to your uncle?”

“What usually happens to his kind? He conned a guy with the resources to get back at him.”

“And you think these Koko pirates don’t?”

Kappa shrugged. “If we can get to Gibbron, they won’t follow us.”

“We’ll be lucky to make it to the priest’s protection on Angrolicat, so why take her to Gibbron?”

Kappa was silent for a moment as he stared at nothing in particular. “Because it’s close and the Kokos fear Gibbi’s worse than death.”

Shaking his head, Baroque opened his mouth to speak, but a triple tap on the door made both men freeze.

After another more insistent knock, Baroque slipped a knife from his belt and moved to the door. Both men released a sigh of relief as the thin Wat Wat hurried in carrying two large bundles.

"I got the stuff you wanted," he announced as the door zipped closed.

Sheathing his knife, Baroque moved up beside the new arrival. "I'm risking my life with a pile of electronics? We need weapons."

Shaking his head, Kappa looked into the bags. "Is everything working as expected?"

Wat Wat nodded. "I've got a link into their main computer system, but what does that get us?"

Kappa smiled. "With the right programming, we're going to send their heads spinning."

56

"Your light is going out," Bottar observed as he caught up with Tamm for the umpteenth time. "And could you slow the pace a bit? An antelope couldn't keep up with you on this rough ground."

Tamm lowered her torch and looked at it. "Prepare your stick," she ordered. "You can light it from mine."

Yanking off his shirt Bottar started tying it to the stick. "This damned thing is pretty wet," he complained. "I've been working up a good sweat climbing over these rocks."

Tamm was turned slightly away from him, obscuring her breasts, but he could see beads of sweat reflecting the light she held.

"It will have to do," she said, "or we go ahead in the dark."

"That's going to be a challenge," he observed while wrapping the wire around his shirt. "I can barely get around with the light we have."

Tamm shook her head. "I've been in caves like this without light. You move slower, but you can get along pretty well after a while. We can use the sticks to tell what's in front of us."

"But those aliens are going to have lanterns and weapons. What chance do we have against that?"

Tamm turned to face him, and the light illuminated her bare chest in a soft warm glow. The sight caused him to miss a wrap and slug himself in the gut. As Tamm laughed, her breasts jiggled even more, turning the poor man's mind to mush. His second attempt at wrapping the wire missed its mark.

"Shit, Bottar," she chastised. "Hold this thing and let me do it."

She held out the torch, which he took begrudgingly, embarrassed by his failure to control himself. Shaking her head, Tamm finished the task and touched the new torch to its predecessor. When she turned her attention to Bottar, he was looking further into the cave.

"I don't see any end to it."

Tamm shook her head, and looked up at the ceiling now only a meter above their heads. “It’s going to end soon, one way or the other. Let’s just hope we find daylight and not solid stone.”

Bottar nodded as she handed him the lit torch but said nothing as they continued on. However, around the next corner they found a solid wall of rock. At the sight of it, Bottar stopped in his tracks, but Tamm marched straight up and hit it with her stick.

“Damn it,” she screamed as the stick broke in half. “Damn, damn, damn.”

In desperate frustration, she threw the remainder of the wooden shaft at the center of the wall. Both of them stared in wonder as it disappeared from sight, and clattered against rocks somewhere beyond the wall.

“What the hell?” Bottar swore. “Do that again.”

Tamm snorted while marching forward. “I think once is enough.”

Without even hesitating, she walked through wall.

“Get your butt in here, lummox,” she yelled. “I need that damned light.”

Startled into action, Bottar lurched forward, but slowed as he approached the wall. It looked as solid as the stone around it, but when he pressed his hand against the wall, it went right through. Before he could react further, Tamm grabbed the hand and yanked the rest of him in.

“What are you? Some kind of caveman?” she chastised while taking the torch from him. “It’s just a projection system.” She spat on the ground. “Shit, these guys aren’t as clever as I thought. Even I could put something like this together.”

Recovering quickly, Bottar stared at the path ahead.

“Look,” he cried. “This shaft intersects another one.”

Tamm laughed. “If they haven’t beat us to it, we’re out’a here.”

The ceiling of the intersecting cave rose to their right, so they turned that way and walked until they came to a stream crossing their path. Beyond it, the way narrowed as it climbed steadily and curved to their left.

"I see light," Bottar cried as he waded through the cold water.

"Then let's get up there and find out what it is," Tamm insisted as she splashed past him and raced up the path.

Once again on dry ground, Bottar hesitated. "But what if the aliens are there?"

Tamm stopped and turned back. "If they are up there, we're screwed," she said, matter-of-factly. "On the other hand, if we cower down here long enough, they will find us and you can bet we'll be screwed then."

When Bottar looked indecisive, she added, "Up there, maybe screwed. Down here, certainly screwed. Move it!"

Not waiting for a response, she charged up the path with Bottar close behind. They continued on until the passageway opened into a larger space. Hesitating at the edge of the opening, they peeked in to find the cave beyond empty and the entrance only partially covered with fencing.

"We got here just in time," Bottar said as he moved cautiously into the opening.

Tossing her torch aside, Tamm rushed past him toward the entrance. "Well, let's not wait for them to finish it."

57

"I was told you were dead," Saki said, not sure if he should be angry or happy.

AnKat shrugged. "Your mother wasn't pleased that I left." He rolled his eyes. "But then she wasn't happy when I was there either."

"But you never came back."

His father's head shook slowly. "Some time ago, I made a mistake that lead to my exposure. If a ghost isn't invisible, he and his family will soon be dead."

"You were a Ghostman…a spy?"

AnKat wagged his eyebrows and looked down at his hands. "Though there were many spies before me, I am the original Ghostman. My upbringing made me the perfect candidate. No one was better at getting into and out of trouble."

"There seems to be quite a bit of animosity between you and the Supreme Commander."

"He doesn't care for our lot, but he needs the information we provide."

"Does he know you're my father?"

AnKat nodded.

"Do you know what happened to put me here?" Saki asked.

His father's head jerked a quick no. "I was in the Sokar sector when it happened."

"But surely there were news reports."

His father sighed. "There are always news reports, but in my line of work you quickly learn they're less about accuracy and more about capturing eyeballs with money to spend."

"Do you believe I did this…thing?"

AnKat shrugged. "I nosed around a bit, but found a great void where there should have been someone with an ax to grind or a self-defined moral reason to tell what they know. It's impossible to keep something this big bottled up unless the number of people involved is very small."

His mouth opened then closed quickly as he pressed a hand over his left ear.

"I'm afraid this conversation will have to wait for another time," he said after a short pause. "Work beckons."

"What kind of work?"

AnKat's only response was a knowing smile as he moved quickly through the door.

58

Senator Addy rushed through the entry of his transport shuttle. "Let us be going," he demanded, "and give us secure line to Fleet Commander Brak."

The craft was a modified commercial shuttle, redesigned for the larger KokoroTetian bodies. On the left side of the cabin, every other row of seats had been replaced with tables. KokoroTetians do not nibble at food, but gulp large quantities at a time. The regular, pathetic seat-back tray simply would never do.

On the other side of the cabin, was a sleeping bench wide enough for two. Kokos do not mate for life. In fact, once they finish mating, they go their separate ways. The women carry the fertilized eggs to term and then deposit them in a safe place to hatch on their own. Those children who live long enough to make their way back to civilization are raised by the community until they are old enough to strike out on their own. Those that do not are usually eaten by the survivors.

Moving to his usual seat, Addy looked out the transport's window to see his former aide's corpse through his office window.

"Damn," he muttered as the vehicle started to rise. "We hate to kill stupid bastard. He not much smarter than dog, but at least he not pee on furniture."

"Antrakans not taste good as dog though," someone behind him said, "but as general rule, we better off when they dead."

Addy jerked around to find the two heads of Senator Dec peeking from the aft restroom doorway.

Oh no, he thought angrily. *Biggest jabbermouth in galaxy!*

"Dec?" he asked. "What you do on our shuttle?"

Dec waved a hand dismissively. "Ours be on blink and yours be convenient. We got couple of girls up there that need…uh, tending to and since it not far from your ship, We availed ourselves of hospitality."

Turning one head, Addy shot a withering glare at the attendant who quickly slipped into the galley.

"But…"

Large, even for a KokoroTetian, Dec waddled toward his host. "While We got your attention, there be some serious thing We wanna discuss."

Addy looked out the window at the quickly vanishing heliport. "What that be?" he asked, pretending a disinterest he certainly didn't feel.

"Well, We hear you be very naughty boy, maybe?" Dec answered haughtily.

"In…what way?"

"It be said you smuggle hundred cases of illegal Andreatite sour grape on last visit to their system." Dec smiled broadly. "Your secret safe with us, but We pay handsomely for case of that wine."

"Yes, well, like you say, Antrakans not be good tasting, but the wine help when stuck at private dinner with nothing else to eat."

"You should try Human, maybe?" Dec laughed. "Saltier than local fare, but juicier and lot more flesh. Of course, they be expensive 'cause you gotta import them. We sure you know they not grow without oxygen, which make challenge to cooking. Our chef soak in bittew juice for whole week to get caustic crap out of meat."

"With such trouble, be they worth it, maybe?"

Grinning, Dec nodded eagerly. "After one been stewing in own juices for day, kitchen smell like heaven." He gurgled something like a laugh. "God, We get all slobbery just to think about it."

"We try one sometime," Addy said as he settled back into his seat to the sound of Dec's muttering and lip smacking.

"Just let us know," Dec gurgled. "We got rock-solid source for them."

Picking up his communicator, Addy pressed it to one ear and spoke, "Is Fleet Commander on line yet?"

"Yes Sir," came the reply, "but he be, uh, sleeping. He be there quick."

The senator pressed the video icon and a virtual screen materialized in front of him. After a moment watching the dark screen, he yelled, "Get up, Brak! You try our patience."

Within *micro-paks* two heads appeared: one with a sleeping cap heavily skewed to the left, and the other topped with women's underwear.

The Fleet Commander snatched away the underwear as he spoke, "Sorry Senator. We be…otherwise occupied."

Addy nodded. "That obvious, Brak, but time be of essence. Get entire fleet on full alert quickly."

"What happening?"

The senator looked around. "We fill you in after We get to our ship. Just get things in motion."

"Is there nothing you can tell us, maybe?"

Addy sighed. "Oh well, it get out soon enough." One of his heads looked back at Dec who had settled in behind him and was still slobbering over his thoughts of a Human dinner. "He has escaped."

"You don't mean…?"

"Precisely. We also hear Khephra got him and that mean you be really busy very soon."

The fleet commander blanched. "But Khephra be one to bring him in. Why this mean trouble for us?"

"Because he gonna find out who behind kidnapping. Was it you, maybe?"

Though he didn't know how Brak's face could turn any whiter, it did.

"Hammond save us," he moaned. "He know?"

Addy sighed. "What precisely do he know?"

Jaws open, Brak's faces stared blankly on the screen.

"Brak?"

The fleet commander remained blank for a moment more before snapping out of his trance. "We gotta go."

Before Addy could react, his screen went blank.

"Hammond's red rump," his left head cried. "That idiot be death of us all, maybe?"

"Having some trouble with fleet commander?" Dec asked eagerly. "We not help overhearing. Who escaped?"

Without responding, Addy pocketed his transmitter and pulled out a silenced pistol. Turning in his seat, he fired two rounds into the still-drooling Dec, shaking his own heads as his victim slumped forward.

After watching for a moment more, to make sure Dec was truly dead, he settled back into his own seat and signaled for the attendant.

"Clean up mess behind us," he commanded. "Dump everything in recycling processor and set for maximum demolecularization. When done, bring us sour-grape wine. Make it tall and dry. This not one of our better days."

As one of the attendant's heads looked at the slumped Dec, the other responded as though he'd been asked to bring a bag of peanuts. "Yes, Senator. We get right on it, Sir."

"One more thing," he said as the attendant started to leave. "Another surprise visitor on shuttle, and you be joining him."

59

“Alpha One base, this be KokoroTetian Transport nine-one-six-six available for guided approach to planet.”

“We see you, Transport nine-one-six-six,” Alpha base responded. “Set your autopilot for frequency two-two-one. Your present course and speed will bring you in range of our controls in thirty-three *milli-paks*. We’ll contact you again just before takeover commences. Welcome to Angrolicat.”

“Thank you, Alpha One. We looking forward to arrival,” the pilot said while shaking his heads as he switched off his microphone. “And being rid of little bombshell in sickbay.”

Pressing a glyph on his console, he said, “Timer. Count down twenty-five *milli-paks*.”

Shaking his heads again, the pilot pulled out a digital clipboard and started clicking off items on his checklist. He was only two items down when his communications/scan officer yelled,

“Captain. Maatiirani ships approach at high speed.”

Almost dropping his clipboard, the captain looked at his scanner where six Marauder light cruisers almost filled his aft view.

Though both of his hearts were thumping wildly, he managed to keep his voice calm. “They just fly by, maybe? We check it out.”

“Yes Sir.”

The captain glanced at his timer while grabbing his radio. “Angrolicat, this be Transport nine-one-six-six. Maatiirani raiders approach our position. Be they on scheduled flyby, maybe?”

“That’s a negative, Transport nine-one-six-six. We’ve had no contact with them.”

“We not have business with them either and we just transport shuttle. Could you send help, maybe?”

“Increase your speed to 116 and lower your angle of approach by ten degrees. Hopefully, that will put you inside our protection zone by the time they make contact. We’ll send ships to support you, but you’ll have to hold them off for a few *milli-paks* until they can get...”

"Koko ship, stand down your engines or be fired upon," came the unmistakably Maatiirani demand. "We will not repeat this order."

The Koko captain released a quick whimper before squeezing his microphone. "This be KokoroTetian Transport nine-one-six-six to Maatiirani ship. What are intentions, maybe?"

"To blast your fat, two-headed ass into space if you do not shut down your engines now."

"But we under Angrolicat planetary security protection. You no have rights to interfere with us passing."

A fist of light streaked from the Maatiirani ship, striking the Koko's light shielding on the starboard engine. The impact rattled every one of the captain's teeth.

"You want we should use our heavy canon next?"

"But we have nothing you want," the captain pleaded.

"In ten *micro-paks*, no one else will want it either."

The captain scanned his console screen. "Where is help when We need it?" he cried.

"Sir," his co-pilot announced. "Angrolicat fighters just leaving atmosphere, but even if arrive in time, they not risk war by attacking Maatiirani outside Angrolicat security border."

With a shuddering sigh, the captain grabbed the throttle control and slid it down to minimum. "And we not have firepower to take on six Maatiirani light cruisers."

Pressing his communicator icon, he announced with as calm a voice as could be managed, "We be peaceful people. With you we no have quarrel."

"Then you will have no problem with us paying you a visit," the Maatiirani captain snarled.

His KokoroTetian counterpart swallowed hard. "We meet in starboard shuttle bay."

"My boarding party is on their way," came the brusque reply. "You should hurry because they do not like to be kept waiting."

* * * * *

As the captain scurried toward the starboard shuttle bay, Wat Wat was squeezing his own communications device in a sweaty hand.

"We've got serious trouble," he said without preamble.

"What the hell hit us?" Kappa asked.

"Maatiirani boarding party is on its way to the starboard shuttle bay."

"Get Baroque and meet me in the port bay."

"Right," Wat Wat acknowledged as he dropped his communicator.

"Aren't you going to need that?" Baroque asked while pointing to the dropped device.

His thin companion shook his head, grabbed a black bag and lurched toward the door. "If we don't make it to that bay, it'll be because we're dead."

With a quick nod, Baroque ran after him.

They entered a corridor filled with terrified crew members rushing to escape pods.

"Word travels fast," Baroque observed as they dashed down the hallway, crashing alternately into running Kokos and corridor walls. They finally came to an intersection jammed with bodies trying to go in all four directions. The terrified crew members were pressed so tightly together, no one could move.

"Hammond's Royal Red Rump," Wat Wat exclaimed as Baroque rattled the handle of a door next to them.

Pointing across the corridor at an open passageway, he yelled, "Get in there."

When his comrade hesitated, he gave him a shove before screaming, "Maatiirani in the starboard and port shuttle bays. They're heading this way."

As Baroque threw himself through the open door, a mass of screaming, squawking KokoroTetians pushed past. Both men watched until the flow decreased enough to allow them back into the corridor. However, as Baroque reentered the hallway, a large Koko knocked him to the deck, and he had to scramble to avoid being stomped by its many stubby feet.

Wat Wat jumped through the door, just avoiding another terrified Koko as he helped Baroque to his feet. Running to the intersection, they turned right as Kappa appeared from the medical bay with a blanket-wrapped bundle in his arms.

They rushed to catch up with him, but Wat Wat's black bag snagged a tool in a Koko's belt pack and was yanked from his hands.

When he turned to retrieve it, Baroque cried, "Leave it."

Ignoring him, Wat Wat scrambled between two panicked Kokos, taking several hits from flailing arms as he tried to pick up his bag. Baroque raced back, grabbing his companion's arm and pulling him up just as another Koko kicked the bag further down the hall. Wat Wat ripped his arm free and chased after the bag again.

This time he managed to get it, but as he turned back, two large Kokos, running side-by-side down the hall, blocked his way. When he tried to push between them, they shoved back, unwilling to slow even for a *micro-pak* to let the hapless Antrakan past. Two legs were no match against twenty and Wat Wat was carried to the intersection where they dumped him as they turned right. By the time Baroque saw him again, Wat Wat was running in his direction.

Baroque did an about face and saw Kappa, his precious bundle over his shoulder, entering the port bay. While glancing back occasionally, to make sure Wat Wat was still coming, he also made for the bay.

As the two men burst into the almost empty space, Kappa was nowhere to be seen.

"What was so important about that bag?" Baroque demanded as they gasped for air and looked for their friend.

"It's our only chance of getting out alive," his companion answered. "That is, if we can find a shuttle."

"They've taken them all," Baroque said in disbelief.

"Not all of them," Kappa countered from somewhere to their left.

"Where are you?" Wat Wat asked as he and Baroque moved in the direction of his voice.

As both men peeked into a small bay, Wat Wat cried, "Shit, Kappa, that's a maintenance rig. It's only designed to carry two people."

Kappa stuck his head from the rig's small door and smiled. "Two Kokos take up as much room as four of us. I've tied Pana into the cargo space behind the seats."

Baroque peered into the tiny craft. "You ever fly one of these?"

Kappa shook his head. "That's what you're here for."

"Strap in beside Pana," Baroque advised. "She might wake up before we land."

"You have your gear, Wat Wat?" Kappa asked while climbing in.

Nodding, the thin male entered via the passenger side and kneeled into a space designed for ten Koko feet.

"We're going to die, aren't we?" he asked while unpacking his gear.

Baroque shrugged. "Probably."

Shaking his head, Wat Wat grunted. "You skipped leadership class in school, didn't you?"

Baroque started the rig's engine. "I used the time to practice my piloting skills."

Wat Wat yanked a controller unit from his bag. "If we're still on plan, then I need to get the ship's main laser canon on-line."

"We're still on plan, buddy," Kappa announced as he buckled in beside Pana, "but now we're going to be shooting at Maatiirani instead of satellites."

"Prepare for launch," Baroque called as he continued to tap the surface of the console. Just as the small engine engaged, the ship shuddered. "What was that?"

Wat Wat jutted his chin toward the front of the ship. "The main laser canon moving into position."

"Shit," Baroque laughed nervously. "You are fast."

"I did the programming earlier today," his companion announced while watching the small screen on his controller unit. "Let's hope you're as fast with this rig." Quickly thumbing a joy stick, Wat Wat pressed an icon and the whole ship vibrated. "Direct hit on the lead Maatiirani ship, but their shields deflected it. You've got less than twenty *micro-paks* to get us out of here."

The rig burped, jumped forward, jerked to a stop then jumped again. While being alternately slammed against the console and the seat back, Baroque struggled to activate the rig's booster drive.

"Ceratha's Holy Hell," Wat Wat cried as he held the laser canon's controller to his chest.

Smoke billowed into the bay as the rig shot straight for the opposite wall. Pressed back into the poorly-fitting seat, Baroque struggled with the controls, barely managing a left turn that slid them past a support beam. As the hanger door loomed ahead, the ship shuddered again.

"That would be the Maatiirani returning fire," Wat Wat cried as the bay doors opened. "Ten *micro-paks*."

The tiny craft shuddered violently as it burst from the ship's hold. Baroque worked quickly to dodge the debris filling their view as the Maatiirani's heavier-duty canon fire tore into the KokoroTetian ship.

"Hold her steady," Wat Wat screamed as the rig barely missed a large piece of shielding.

"What in Ceratha's Name do you think I'm doing?" Baroque screamed back.

"I'm trying to get another shot off," Wat Wat protested as the Maatiirani lead ship began moving into a better firing position.

When the enemy ship tilted slightly for a turn, Wat Wat thumbed a control, sending a blazing pulse of energy at an unshielded cover plate on its starboard engine. Smoke spewed out as the other Maatiirani joined in with combined firepower of their five remaining ships, sending more debris into the space around them.

"I can get off one more shot," Wat Wat announced, "if you can hold this thing steady for half a *micro-pak*."

Baroque banked the rig up as a large chunk of the Koko's port engine flew past them. "Do it now! Their deflectors are down."

All three men watched as the shot collapsed the lead Maatiirani ship's cover plate. It veered sharply to the right as engine parts flew into space.

“Head for the planet, boys,” Wat Wat commanded as the Koko ship disintegrated behind them. “And hope they don’t notice that this little bit of debris has engines.”

60

Fleet Commander Brak looked up from his work to watch three bodies being carried from his bedroom. “Feed them to poor,” he sighed to the men carrying the women. “It what they would want.”

The lead carrier nodded to the fleet commander who watched until they disappeared into the front room.

“Damned waste,” Brak muttered as he turned back to his console’s screen.

He hadn’t been working long before the high-priority communicator light blinked on his monitor. Pressing an icon, he turned one head away to spit on the floor as the senator’s faces appeared on the screen.

“What is status of fleet, maybe?” Addy asked as Brak’s second head moved back into view.

“All fired up and ready to move out,” Brak answered solemnly, “but We had to kill our three favorite women.”

“They overheard?”

Both of the fleet commander’s heads nodded.

Addy sighed. “You get over women, Fleet Commander. You know they spill plans with only tiny threat of torture.”

Brak sniffled. “But one was with eggs. We not fertilize female’s eggs since before this whole damned mess start. All this stress is bad for our virility.”

“Shereeta, Brak,” Addy swore. “We not have time for soap opera. If you not get Khephra before he built up fleet, he chop off more than egg fertilizing parts.”

Brak’s two heads looked at each other, his fear more apparent in profile.

“We hear Khephra got six ships only,” Addy continued, “and he be in southern district.”

“How you know this?”

Addy waggled his heads. “We have source on his ship, but now he go dark, so we not know more than that.”

Brak brightened. “We got thirty light cruisers less than *pak* from there.”

“Then get them hunting. If they not defeat his heavy battleships, at least they keep him bottled up until rest of fleet can overtake.”

“Well… it not wise to send whole fleet, maybe?” Brak argued nervously. “That leave our rear unprotected.”

“He only got six battleships,” Addy screamed. “You got fifty, along with over three-hundred light cruisers. How he ever get to your fat butt?”

“Remember,” Brak argued. “Those who underestimate Khephra, he defeat. That not happen to us.”

The senator shook his heads. “Well then, save couple of ships to protect precious butt, but get others moving toward southern district quick. Your advantage in numbers not last long.”

“We take care of it,” Brak announced as he broke the connection and paged his assistant.

“Yes Sir,” Styxx announced as he entered.

“Supreme Commander Khephra be in southern sector. We have thirty light cruisers there, maybe?”

“Correct, Sir.”

“Break into three groups of ten and search for Supreme Commander. Tell them to report to us when he be found.”

“Should they engage enemy, maybe?”

Brak shook his head. “No. Just report back, but keep safe distance.”

“Yes Sir,” Styxx acknowledged.

“In addition, send another thirty light cruisers and twelve battleships to reinforce.”

“How many are ships of enemy, Sir?”

Brak drummed his fingers on one of his chins. “We hear maybe six battleships, but should expect more.”

“We take care of it right quick, Fleet Commander,” Styxx said. “Anything else?”

“Just one thing,” Brak said as he approached the aide. “Have rest of fleet form defensive sphere around this planet.”

"Entire fleet, Sir?"

Brak nodded. "Every ship that fly must be ready to defend."

"Sir?" Styxx asked, looking puzzled.

"There be something here Khephra want, and We not intend to let him have it."

"What that be, maybe?"

Brak nodded both heads as he stared intently at his subordinate.

"Your Fleet Commander."

61

"So what do we do now?" Bottar asked as they hid behind bushes and scanned the area in front of the cave.

"Where the hell are we?"

Bottar looked back at the cave entrance. "As far as I know, the only lava tubes close to our home are in the Pittston Basin."

"Shit," Tamm exclaimed. "They moved us over three-hundred miles? What for?"

"No idea. I'm just hoping they're somewhere else right now."

Tamm shook her head. "I don't see anything moving. Let's go."

"Where?"

"We've got to contact the authorities," Tamm insisted. "We need a phone."

Bottar shook his head. "Who will take us seriously? It's a good bet that, 'Excuse me folks. My half-naked comrade and I were kidnapped by aliens. Can we borrow your phone?' might not be received well. Especially in the Pittston Basin where you're more likely to get a Bible bounced off your head than a helping hand."

Tamm glared at her companion. "You got any brilliant ideas?"

Bottar looked around while rubbing his chin. "You know? I just might." He moved past the bush while motioning for Tamm to follow. "Let's find an empty house."

Stumbling through dry grass, sharp rocks and sticks with feet too soft for the task, they moved to the top of a ridge where a cluster of trees provided both protection from the glaring sun and softer ground to walk on. Starting down the other side, they came upon a small tent. From the sounds reaching their ears, the couple inside were doing anything but sleeping.

After Tamm scanned the campsite, she turned to catch Bottar staring at her chest.

"Would you stop doing that?"

He pointed past her breasts toward a clump of bushes below the campsite. "There's a vehicle down there."

"Oh," Tamm said, feeling her face blush.

"Let's cut around and see if they have any spare clothes in there."

"Could you hotwire their rig?"

Bottar shook his head. "Tamm, I don't think..."

"Listen, stupid," she interrupted. "We don't know how many those aliens have taken. The faster we get the word out, the sooner the authorities can start doing something about it."

"Who is going to believe us?"

The groans from the couple in the tent began climbing to a higher pitch.

Tamm stood. "They're almost done. Let's go."

Moving as quickly as their bleeding feet would allow, the twosome reached the vehicle just as climatic screams came from the tent.

"There are clothes in the back," Bottar announced. "Get in. We can dress later."

Climbing in, they closed the doors quietly as Bottar reached around to hotwire the car.

"Son of a bitch," he exclaimed. "They left the keys in the ignition."

"Then get this thing rolling," Tamm demanded as she twisted around to search the bags in the seat behind them.

Bottar twisted the ignition key, slipped the car into gear and pressed hard on the accelerator, raising a dust cloud as the vehicle lurched forward.

Sitting back into her seat, Tamm pulled a T-shirt from the duffel bag in her lap.

"I like you better topless," Bottar joked as she pulled the shirt on.

"Yeah," Tamm responded with a laugh. "The free peepshow is over. The next peek is going to cost you a knee in the nuts."

Despite the stress of their situation, Bottar couldn't help thinking how nice it would be to have Tamm naked next to him in a small tent. To his embarrassment, his body responded to the thought as well. To make matters worse, Tamm stripped off her cotton pants before scrounging in the bag and lifting out a pair of jeans.

"This girl is a bit bigger than I am, but it will do." Digging some more, she found a pair of panties. Tossing the bag into the back, she began pulling them on, which caused Bottar to almost miss a turn in the road.

"Watch where you're going, damn it," she protested as she fell against him.

"Sorry," was all he could think to say as he guided the car back onto the narrow track.

Embarrassed, Bottar kept his eyes forward while Tamm finished dressing. She then twisted around and grabbed the bag again, extracting a man's shirt, shorts and pants.

"Pull over and let's get you dressed," she announced while pointing to a wide spot in the dirt road.

Stopping the car, Bottar locked the brake, took the offered clothing and jumped out. As he pulled them on, Tamm exited the other side to tuck in her shirt and roll up its sleeves.

"Just so you know," she said while finishing. "I'm married."

"When did this happen?" he asked while buttoning his pants."

"I don't know."

"You don't know?" he asked incredulously. "How could you not know something as important as…"

A tear trickling down her cheek stopped him. For a moment they stood frozen, staring across the car at each other until Bottar looked down.

"Well then, I guess we'd better get home so you can find him."

"That's another thing," Tamm said as they settled into the car. "I don't think we belong on this planet either."

"You mean we look like those aliens?" Bottar asked as he shifted the car into gear and stepped on the accelerator.

She shrugged. "It's all rather muddled, but I don't think so."

"There's more than one kind of alien?"

"Why wouldn't there be?" Tam answered. "There are billions of suns out there and we're already finding planets around many of them."

"Then why haven't we made contact with them before now?"

Tamm shrugged. "Apparently we have. It's just that most people refused to believe the people who report it."

Bottar shook his head. "And I used to be one of those disbelievers."

Tamm looked around. "We've got to ditch this car quickly."

"Why? We're just getting going."

"Don't you think that couple heard us drive off?" she argued. "If they have a cell phone it's a good bet they've already called the cops. Who's going to believe us if we get picked up driving a stolen vehicle?"

Bottar shook his head as Tamm opened the glove box.

"What are we going to do?" he asked. "Steal another car?"

"Maybe we don't have to," Tamm responded while pulling out a wallet fat with bills. "There's got to be a couple thousand bucks in here."

"We still can't buy or rent a car without ID."

"Look at this," Tamm said as they passed a sign announcing that they were entering a town. She held up the wallet. "This guy's license says he lives here."

"Yeah, so?"

"It also says he's married. Would a married couple drive five miles into the woods just to have sex?"

"I would."

Tamm laughed. "Yeah, but I'm not talking about deviants like you."

"You're the one taking her clothes off."

"And you couldn't give a lady a little privacy?"

Bottar shook his head. "So where does this get us?"

"If there's a missus and little kiddies at home, maybe lover boy will be willing to let us borrow his car."

Tamm dug into the glove box as Bottar tried to locate the address on the driver's license. Finding nothing more of use, she unbuckled her seatbelt and climbed into the back seat.

"Well, looky here," she announced triumphantly while holding up a cell phone. "This big thing's gotta belong to a guy."

"How does that help us?"

Tamm grinned. "I don't see another phone back here, or the woman's purse, so it's a good bet she has it in the tent."

She fiddled with the phone's controls as Bottar announced, "I found his house."

As he parked the car and pointed at a house three doors down, an attractive woman lifted a baby from the back seat of a SUV.

"If that isn't the wife, I'll sleep with you myself," Tamm stated.

Bottar started to get out of the vehicle but Tamm grabbed his arm.

"I thought I'd ask her."

Tamm shook her head. "Don't you think the woman's going to notice you're wearing her husband's clothes?"

"I wouldn't."

"Yeah, but you're a hormonal accident waiting to happen. All you see is a pretty face, boobs and an ass. Women pay more attention to clothes. Especially that shirt with…" She checked the driver's license again. "…his initials embroidered into it."

He looked down at the letters. "So this was a gift?"

Tamm nodded. "And maybe from her."

"Bad idea?"

"Yup!"

Bottar sank back into his seat as the woman unlocked her front door and went inside. "So what do we do?"

Tamm began fiddling with the phone again. "It's a good bet this guy's last call was to his girlfriend. If she still has her phone, maybe we can reach him through her."

She pressed a key and held the phone to her ear. Bottar heard three rings before a woman answered. Though he couldn't make out words, the tone of her greeting implied she was not a happy girl.

"I'd like to speak to Eldron, please?" Tamm asked. There was a pause before a man spoke. "Eldron, you don't know me," Tamm continued, "but I have your car." She jerked the phone from her ear until the screaming stopped. "Eldron, I'm sitting three-doors down from your house and just saw a beautiful woman and her baby go inside. Who were you just screwing?" She waited for a moment before continuing. "Are you still there, Eldron?"

After the man grunted a yes, Tamm continued, "Have you called the cops yet?"

Bottar heard a loud, "No."

"That's good, because we need to borrow your car and we don't need any complications. I'm pretty sure you know what that would mean, don't you, Eldron?"

Tamm held the phone away from her ear as Eldron babbled on about what an inconvenience it would be and that they surely misunderstood what was going on and that he was sure an understanding could be reached, if only…

"Eldron!" Tamm yelled. "Does your girlfriend have a car we can bring you?"

While listening, she signaled for something to write with. After digging around in the glove box, Bottar pulled out a pen and paper.

Tamm scribbled something and smiled.

"Eldron, you've got yourself a deal."

She closed the cell phone. "We're going to get his girlfriend's car and drop it off where the gravel road meets the highway. We'll give him back his wallet and half the money."

Bottar shook his head. "Should we be helping a guy who cheats on his wife?"

Tamm shrugged. "I'd like to whack off his manly privileges, but this gets us wheels and money. Besides, it will only take a few minutes, since she lives close by."

Bottar sighed. "So should we find the nearest police station and report what happened?"

Tamm looked out the window for a moment before turning back to her companion. "Let's get back home and find out who else is missing?"

They dropped the girl's car at the agreed upon spot, and as the sun dipped behind the western hills, started driving home. Tamm turned on the car radio, but could not find a station. After trying for a few minutes, she dialed information with the cell phone, but was told all the circuits to their home town were busy.

With nothing else to do and no way to get information about what was going on, Tamm eventually fell asleep. Less than an hour later Bottar felt his eyelids grow heavy as well, but when he looked at Tamm, she was leaning awkwardly against her door, still asleep.

"Tamm," he called while nudging her. "I need some coffee."

When she didn't respond, he scanned the empty highway ahead for some sign of civilization. By the time the lights of a rundown motel appeared along the road, he knew his battle against sleep was lost.

He pulled into the lot, parked and shook Tamm again. When she still didn't respond, he exited the car and looked at the single-story building. A lit sign over the manager's office indicated they had a vacancy, but he could see no sign of a coffee shop.

Leaving her to sleep, he stepped out of the car and stretched, but all his tired body wanted now was a warm bed.

"Guess this is as far as we go for now, hon," he said to the still sleeping woman.

62

"This is Pecta at-Hammond," Baroque explained. "Hammond's oldest temple is here."

To Wat Wat, the city sprawling across the broad plain below looked anything but holy. Smoke rising from the myriad of simple huts created a hazy view of horse-drawn wagons sharing congested, narrow roads with motorized vehicles and pedestrians wearing colorful, broad-brimmed hats. The roads formed a concentric set of rings radiating out from a central hill on which the religious complex sat. South of the hill, an even larger collection of buildings provided a sharp contrast to the diminutive dwellings peppering the hillside and plain below.

"You mean that big red one against the eastern wall?" Wat Wat asked while wiping his breath off the rig's small window.

Baroque shook his head. "The small one in the middle. It's over ten-thousand *druak* old. Legend has it that He built it with His own hands, just prior to ascending to Heaven." He laughed. "No one would dare try to improve on God's handiwork."

"Whoa," Wat Wat whispered. "Are we going to land inside the complex?"

Baroque smiled sympathetically at his companion. "Civilians only rarely land there."

"Not even the Maatiirani?"

"Especially not them."

"Surely they don't fear Hammond's wrath."

Baroque tilted the rig to give Wat Wat a better view of the pentagonally shaped complex. "You may notice that there are four other temples to match the one you first pointed out."

When his companion nodded, Baroque added, "Since the pentagon, and therefore the number five, is sacred to Hammond, the temples have five sides and are situated at the center of each of the main complex's five walls."

"Each temple has five towers armed with a heavy laser canon. That's twenty-five canons with ground-based shield generators to protect them. In addition, there are ten other complexes much like this positioned around the planet to make sure that any craft entering Angrolicat space without permission will be vaporized before reaching the planet's surface. Even a division of Maatiirani fighters wouldn't stand up to that."

"Is that clustering of large buildings to the south part of the complex?"

Baroque chuckled. "That's a shopping mall."

Wat Wat shook his head. "Greed follows need."

"With over a ten-million pilgrims coming to this site every year, it's only surprising that there aren't more of them."

"How do you know so much about this place?"

"It was my home for nearly twenty *druak*."

"You were a priest?"

As Baroque nodded, Wat Wat looked back at the temples.

"Uh, Baroque? Why are those tower roofs opening?"

Kappa's head appeared between their seats. "Are you sure we've got the clearance we need?"

"Of course I'm sure," Baroque argued. "We're not even… wait." He tapped a spot on his console.

"…I repeat. Maatiirani vessels. You are not authorized to enter our air space. Return to neutral territory."

"Those cerapas attacked us, and stole our cargo," came a gruff response. "We have the right to pursue."

"On our planet, you will obey the laws of our Lord Hammond."

"Your pathetic god be damned," the Maatiirani captain growled. "We take what is ours."

Before the Angrolicat authorities could respond, all six of the attacking Maatiirani ships fired on the temple towers. After several *micro-paks* of intense, yet impotent bombardment, the Angrolicatian heavy canons returned fire, quickly overwhelming the enemy's shields.

"Maatiirani vessels. You are ordered to stand down your weapons or be destroyed."

"If we can't have her, then you can't either," came the angry reply.

"*Shendtada*," Baroque exclaimed as he jerked the rig to the left.

The craft lit up like a flashbulb as a burst of energy pulsed to their right. The intensity of the attack so polarized the hull that dozens of tiny arcs jumped from the cabin walls to the occupants exposed skin.

"Get us out of here," Kappa screamed as their tiny vessel bounced and shuddered in the resulting turbulence.

"And go where?" Baroque cried, banking the craft sharply to the left as a second shot jostled them even more violently.

So terrified that they no longer noticed the arcing energy burning their skin, Wat Wat and Kappa turned to gawk through the craft's tiny rear window at the Maatiirani's lead ship bearing down on them. As Baroque started to make another evasive maneuver, five balls of light streaked up from the ground, each hitting a different part of the Maatiirani vessel. The craft vaporized into trillions of tiny shards that hung momentarily in the air like an ominous black rain cloud before falling as one toward the earth below.

"My God," Wat Wat cried.

As the threesome watched, invisible forces pushed the descending shards of metal and glass into a stream that flowed down and over the populated areas before crashing into an open field.

"The others are moving away," Baroque announced.

His companions looked up to see the remaining five ships turning toward space. Even though each ship was completing its own evasive maneuvers, another series of shots rose from the planet's surface, striking and buckling the shield plate on each ship's left engine compartment.

"If that don't make you believe in the power of the Great God, I don't know what will," Wat Wat whispered as smoke billowed from the retreating ships.

"Little Piquit," a voice called over the radio's speaker. "Are you alright?"

Baroque looked pleasantly surprised. "Ansen?"

"Yes, old friend," the speaker replied. "It looks like you still have an attraction to the troubled life."

"No matter what road I travel, it is my constant companion."

"As it always was, so shall it continue to be. The brotherhood welcomes you home, An' Detertch."

Baroque gave a strained smile. "Thank you, old friend. If possible, I'd like to see you as soon as we land."

"I look forward to it, but the Shendeah insists on seeing you first."

Baroque bowed toward the console. "Then I will comply. May Hammond's praise be yours."

"And yours, my brother."

Breaking the connection, Baroque turned to find Wat Wat and Kappa staring at him.

"Once a priest of Hammond, always a priest of Hammond," he said.

"But, but," Kappa sputtered. "We've fought countless battles together. How can this be?"

"Hammond is the warrior God. It is only natural that his oldest sect of priests be warriors as well."

"KokoroTetian maintenance shuttle C-three-oh-four, this is Pecta at-Hammond traffic control. You are being redirected to the Temple landing field. Prepare for accelerated descent."

"KokoroTetian maintenance shuttle C-three-oh-four acknowledges the change in destination," Baroque responded as the little rig banked right.

63

"How are you feeling, my Love?" Matrina cooed as Sub-commander Pheet's eyes slowly blinked open.

"You know you're going to be the death of me," he mumbled as she kissed his forehead.

"I brought some of my special tea," she whispered. "I don't want you dying just yet."

His head moved sluggishly from side to side. "No more of that stuff. I can get along without it."

He pushed himself up on his elbows, but the feeble attempt to sit up collapsed on him as he fell back into the pillow.

Matrina moved in close, holding the cup next to his face. "I put your favorite spices in it."

He looked at her with weepy eyes, the hint of a protest on his lips before he took a deep breath and let it out loudly.

His eyes fell to the cup. "It does smell rather good."

Matrina lifted his head and pressed the cup to quivering lips. Pheet took two sips before lying back down. He could feel the warm liquid flowing down to his stomach. Within *micro-paks*, the sluggishness seemed to fade from his limbs.

When Matrina offered him the cup again, he pushed it away. "I don't need any more."

She lifted the cup and held it in front of him. "Oh yes you do," she insisted. "You won't make it through your shift if you don't drink the whole thing."

Pushing it aside again, he rose from the bed and headed for the bathroom. He hadn't gone five steps before his energy started to fade. Slumping against the bathroom's doorframe, he sighed and turned back.

She rushed to his side and held up the cup. "See, I told you."

Taking a sip, he looked at her. "I'm going to the med station and see what's happening to me. This just isn't normal."

"Oh, I wouldn't do that," she warned as her head shook slowly.

Her demeanor alarmed him. "What is that supposed to mean?"

"You don't want to go anywhere near a med station," she answered. "Not if you want to keep your job."

He had started to take another sip, but the cup stopped at this lips. "What?"

When she didn't answer, he lowered the cup, and almost immediately his eyes started to roll up into his head. Anticipating the action, Matrina moved in and grabbed the falling cup. Ignoring the spilling liquid, she quickly set the cup on a nearby table and grabbed Pheet as he started to slump over.

As she hurriedly rushed him toward the bed, another figure entered from a side room. Without speaking, Matrina dropped the sub-commander onto the bed and the other person held up an injection device. He moved swiftly to Pheet and pressed the thing against his neck.

"How much time do we have?" the gruff voice asked.

"His shift starts in about thirty *milli-paks*."

The other person smiled wickedly while lifting another device from his pocket. "Plenty of time to get what I need."

64

The lights in his cabin dimmed to a crimson red. “All hands to battle stations,” reverberated in the room as Saki pulled on a fresh uniform. “We are now flying dark. I repeat. All hands to battle stations. We are now flying dark.”

Saki buttoned his top collar as Khephra entered the room wearing full battle dress.

“How are you feeling?” he asked while waving the attendant out of the room.

Confused by the plethora of mixed emotions swirling in his head, Saki hesitated a moment before nodding. “I’m doing fine, Sir.”

“Humph,” Khephra responded. “You don’t look so fine to me, Son.”

Saki shrugged. “At present, I have very little to compare it with, Sir. This *milli-pak* is better than the last one, but whether or not that makes my condition good or bad, I can’t say.”

For a brief moment the supreme commander’s face contorted in a way Saki couldn’t read, but quickly returned to his usual stoic expression.

“For thirty-three *druak*, the entire federation thought you and my daughter destroyed Ooertfael. Recent events made it clear that was a lie.”

The two men’s eyes met, but Saki remained silent.

Khephra smiled grimly. “Our knowledge of how the mind stores memories has improved quite a bit in the last thirty *druak*. We can now identify implanted memories because they degrade far faster than real ones. We can also recover erased memories, but part of that process involves the victim putting the fragmented pieces together themselves.”

“What have you learned from me?”

“The Kokos found an ancient vessel, which they called the Aken. According to them, it contained an energy source beyond anyone’s imagination. When they tried to test this device on a remote moon four light-years from Ooertfael, it destroyed that planet, two of its four moons, twelve Maatiirani cruisers and all the scientists involved with the test.

"My predecessor, Supreme Commander Pitheta somehow learned of the test and was close enough to get to the moon ahead of the Koko rescue team. All they found on its scorched surface was that vessel and a dozen or so disembodied Life Forces."

"Where is it now?"

"The Kokos have it."

Saki's jaw dropped. "Why would the Councils give them such a device?"

Khephra shook his head. "The Councils know nothing about it. Pitheta hid the vessel on an out-of-the-way planet called Xamti. Addy stumbled across a document that should have been destroyed, and learned about the vessel and where it was located."

"But why didn't the supreme commander take both and deliver them to the Over Council so they could…" Saki stopped as the realization came to him. "…kill each other fighting over it."

Khephra nodded slowly, as Saki remembered Aurelia's words during their struggle with the Samhain.

And he implanted the key in Pana.

The supreme commander nodded again. "Apparently, it was Pana's idea."

"But where is she?"

"Supreme Commander to the bridge," a voice called over the intercom. "The enemy has been sighted."

"We'll have to finish this later. For now, I want you on the bridge."

"Sir? You can't just…"

Khephra's face grew stern. "As long as I'm in command, I'll determine the order in which we do things, Mister."

Saki looked into his superior's eyes. "And what of the rest of the crew, Sir?"

"They have been briefed as to your situation, but they know nothing of my daughter's involvement."

Saki nodded curtly. "Then I'll do as ordered, Sir."

His eyes betraying sadness, Khephra reached for the door control, but stopped and turned back to Saki.

"There's something else you should know. We've got a spy network on board that has been feeding information to the Kokos, and I may need your help in rooting them out."

"Me, Sir?"

"Someone on my senior staff is part of it. You're the only one among them I can be certain isn't involved."

"How can I possibly help?"

Khephra shook his head. "Right now, just your presence is enough to shake them up. In addition, we've gone dark, so they can't get any messages out without our spotting them. I'm hoping that will be enough to force them to make a mistake and expose themselves."

"I'll hold myself alert for them, Sir."

Khephra nodded. "Then let's get to work," he said while motioning for Saki to take the lead.

"I'm not sure I know where the bridge is."

The supreme commander smiled. "And I'm betting you still do. Basic ship design hasn't changed that much in the last thirty *druak*."

Confused, but compliant, Saki moved through the door, and without knowing why, took an immediate left. To his surprise, the deck plates vibrating under his feet felt familiar, as did the red emergency light reflecting off the corridor's gray walls. He fell in step with the slow, melodic sound of the churning engines, and quickly realized the supreme commander did the same. The two officers marched down the corridor, and Saki was pleased to realize he knew the cross corridors they came to did not lead to their destination, though he wasn't always sure where they did go. Other officers and enlisted men stopped and saluted as he led his commander straight to the bridge.

When they entered, a Marine sergeant shouted, "Supreme Commander on deck," and the entire staff snapped to attention.

"As you were men," Khephra ordered while approaching his station. "Captain, I'd like permission to stow this officer at the Marine's station for the duration of the battle."

The captain's eyes jumped briefly to Saki. "Yes, Sir. Sergeant of the Guard, please escort this…person to the Marine's station." He turned back to the supreme commander. "Will he require restraint, Sir?"

Khephra shook his head slowly before turning to Saki. "Will you need to be restrained, Sub-Commander N-Tschester?"

Saki suddenly realized the significance of the uniform he had been given. Without even willing it to happen, his back stiffened, shoulders squared, heels clicked together, and hands jerked flush with his side.

"No, Sir," he snapped back. "The captain has my assurance that I will not interfere in the command of his ship during this or any engagement."

As Saki remained at attention, the Supreme Commander turned to the captain. "That's good enough for me, Captain. Let's focus on the task at hand."

Giving Saki one more glance, the two superior officers moved to the command console. As the other officers returned to their duties, Saki relaxed but soon heard muttering. He turned to find half-a-dozen nervous Marines watching him.

"Am I in anybody's way, gentlemen?" he asked the six young faces.

A sergeant stepped forward. "No Sir, but I am bound to inform you, Sir, that if you attempt to interfere with the operation of this ship in any way." The Marine looked hesitantly at his men. "Well, Sir, we're ordered to vaporize you."

Saki felt the urge to smile, but forced it down. "Then gentlemen, that is exactly what you should do."

Turning to face forward again, Saki heard faint whispers and the nervous sounds of soldiers checking their equipment. The memory of himself, Bottar, and Kappa on their first battle assignment flashed in his head. It had been a terrifying, yet exhilarating time for them, as it would be for these young men. And they had the same advantage he had in serving under a leader whose legendary command prowess would get them through this to fight another day.

He turned back to the men. “Do you know who we’re fighting and how many of their ships we’re facing?”

The sergeant looked nervously from his men to Saki. “It’s the KoKos, Sir, and I’m told they have thirty light cruisers against our six battleships.”

“Thirty? Have they spotted us yet?”

The sergeant shook his head. “It seems they’ve split up into three groups.”

“You’re kidding.” Saki laughed. “They had us outnumbered five to one and now they’ve reduced that advantage by a third? With tactics like that, the Supreme Commander could take them with a single battleship.”

“Really, Sir?”

“The Heal of Hammond will be on our side today, gentlemen. We might even pick up a few ships in the bargain.”

“With six against thirty?” one of the other Marines asked incredulously.

Saki smiled. “It’s not numbers that win the battle, but how you use them. Do we have any idea where they are yet?”

The sergeant pointed to the main view screen. “Two of their groups are on our left beyond that protostar, and the other just went behind the magnetic storm we’re approaching. If we can see them, why can’t they see us?”

Saki chuckled as the huge black storm loomed larger in the view screen. “The storm and the protostar mask our electronic signals. Running dark hides our heat signature, while Kokos always fly with all lights on.”

“But Sir,” the sergeant asked. “We’re in open space. Even running dark, they’ll see us long before we get in firing range.”

A thunderous rumble rattled its way through the ship.

Saki turned to look at the view screen. “We’re entering the magnetic storm.”

Overhead, an alert sounded, “All hands to battle stations. Secure for rough passage. I repeat, all hands to battle stations. Secure for rough passage.”

The ship jerked again as Saki motioned to the Marines. "Buckle in guys. This may be more dangerous than the battle."

The sub-commander remained standing, his feet apart, hands clasped behind his back. After weathering a few more impacts, he noticed the sergeant standing steadily beside him.

"You should buckle in, Sergeant," he said to the white-faced young soldier.

"I was ordered to guard you, Sir," he responded, sounding much calmer than his blanched face implied. "Where you go, I go."

"But it's going to get rough."

"Before I went into space, I served on the sailing ship Praticia. We mostly sailed in the Straights of Gentanticor."

Saki smiled as color seemed to return to the sergeant's face. "I did my sea duty on that same patch of water. As I remember it, a calm day was thirty-foot swells. Has it changed much?"

"No Sir," the sergeant said with a knowing smile. "If anything it's worse." The sergeant eyed him cautiously. "You served on the Praticia?"

"No, the Hem-dat, but I remember your ship. Rumor has it that she was haunted."

The sergeant shook his head. "It's no rumor, Sir. Captain Mat-Thor kept a Samhain spirit below in a shield-bubble, and threatened to let it loose if any of us died. It sure kept us motivated to stay alive."

A sudden impact sent both men skidding, but they caught themselves quickly and remained standing.

"Attention. Storm's edge in one *milli-pak*," the intercom announced. "Prepare to engage the enemy."

"Hammond protect us. Here it comes," the sergeant muttered as stars reappeared on the view screen.

"Thirty degrees to port, fifteen degrees up and full throttle," Khephra announced when the Koko fleet appeared on his screen. "Prepare all forward heavy canon for firing. Fire to wound, not destroy."

"Location of our ships?" the captain shouted.

"Captain Pike's on our starboard, Sir," announced the scan officer. "He came out a few *micro-paks* behind us and is moving down and to their right. The others haven't appeared yet."

Khephra jumped from his seat. "Navigation: adjust our speed so we'll both come into weapon's range at the same time. Fire control: coordinate weapon's fire with the other ship. Scan: let me know when our remaining battleships appear."

Though no one looked up, three officers cried, "Yes Sir" as the Koko ships grew larger in the view screen.

"Why aren't we flying directly at them, Sir?" the sergeant whispered nervously.

"The Kokos always fly in a flat oval formation. Attacking edge-on only gives us a shot at those on our side. Flying over or under them, exposes all of their ships."

"Weapons range in ten *micro-paks*, Sir," The scan officer announced. "Two more of our ships have appeared from the storm and the Kokos are starting to scramble."

"Have those ships fly directly at the enemy to keep them confused," Khephra ordered. "Prepare to engage."

A display clock on the screen counted off the last few *micro-paks* as two Koko ships collided while hurrying to move clear of their battle group.

"Fire," Khephra yelled when the screen counter struck zero.

The ship shuddered slightly as energy from six heavy canon streaked toward the enemy, Feeling the excitement of the attack, Saki took a quick step forward.

"Sir," the sergeant called as his hand went to his laser pistol.

Keeping his own hands behind his back, Saki stopped and quickly stepped back.

"Sorry, Sergeant. An old reflex."

"To interfere, Sir?"

Saki shook his head and turned toward the non-com. "No. To participate."

Before the sergeant could say more, two more Koko ships collided.

"The enemy is turning to return fire, Sir," the scan officer announced, "and our last two ships are out of the storm."

"Have one of the ships follow our path and the other go under the enemy," Khephra commanded. "Weapons Station, disable any ships that try to leave."

"Incoming!"

"Hard to port," Khephra cried as an instrument panel near a weapons station exploded, knocking the officer over.

The captain started moving toward the station, but Khephra stopped him with a raised hand. "N-Tschester! Replace the downed officer. Marine Sergeant, help the injured soldier to the med station."

Though the sergeant hesitated momentarily, Saki rushed to the console, lifted the unconscious officer up and passed him to the non-com. As several of the sergeant's men helped haul the soldier away, Saki threw debris off the console and began scanning the controls.

"Aim control is on your left, firing lock on right," Khephra shouted as Saki pulled his chair into position. "Red circles show which ships the other operators have a lock on. Green circle is yours. Any problems, Sub-commander?"

"None, Sir," he answered sharply while watching the red circles dance across his screen.

Picking a ship moving away from the group, Saki locked his target and fired into its left engine. His shot no sooner hit home than all but one of the Koko ships started going dark.

"Cease fire," Khephra commanded as four red circles overlapped the fleeing ship. "Engineering? Has the payload been released?"

"Yes Sir," came a voice over the intercom. "Contact in ten *micro-paks*."

"Good job," Khephra announced before turning to the communications console. "Directive to Captain Pike: Give pursuit to the escaping ship, but let it get away."

He turned back to his intercom. "Engineering, we've got damage up here, what's your assessment?"

"The hull breach has been secured and replacement circuits are on their way up now. While we're safe to fly, I'd like about thirty *milli-paks* to clean things up, Sir."

"You'll have to do it while we're moving. We're not done yet."

"Understood Sir."

"Sir," the communications officer called. "Crews have been dispatched from the other ships to put disabling devices on the Koko's main computers."

Khephra frowned. "Scan officer, this was too easy. Make sure we aren't in a trap of some kind. Communications, find out what that escaped Koko ship is telling his friends."

Scan officer: "Nothing in sight, Sir."

Communications officer: "Just the standard cry for help, Sir."

Khephra scanned the screen in front of him. "Communications. When Captain Pike returns, he is to provide support for the boarding crews and watch the Kokos. The rest of the ships are to follow me back into the storm as planned."

At just that moment, the Marine sergeant reentered the bridge with an officer.

Khephra motioned the officer to Saki's station. "Sub-commander Saki, you are relieved. Return to your original station."

Saki, who had been studying the controls of his console, gave the supreme commander a surprised look, but said nothing as he rose and approached the sergeant.

"What just happened, Sir?" the sergeant asked when they were back at station. "I thought you were a prisoner."

Saki shook his head. "It's complicated, but you could say that was a test."

"Of your loyalty?"

"No. Of my ability to deal with new situations in a crisis."

"Sir?"

"Weapon's consoles have changed quite a bit in the last thirty *druak*. He wanted to see how I dealt with it."

"To what end?"

Saki looked at Khephra. "I think the supreme commander has an assignment for me."

"Attention all hands," the intercom announced. "Prepare for rough passage."

"Where are we going now, Sir?" the sergeant asked as they bounced through the storm.

"As I'm sure the supreme commander expected, the escaping Koko ship took the long way around the storm, so we're taking a short cut. About the time it comes into communication range of its comrades, we'll be in position to attack."

"But if we went the other way, we could easily get away."

Saki shook his head. "The supreme commander has no intention of running. They are divided and we still have the element of surprise. I believe he is also setting up…"

"All hands to battle stations," the intercom blared. "Exiting storm in twenty *micro-paks*."

"All quiet on the bridge," Khephra announced while glaring at Saki. After holding his stare for a moment, the supreme commander turned toward the scan officer. "Passive scans only."

As they exited the storm, the dust surrounding the protostar filled their entire view.

"Are all ships out of the storm?" Khephra asked.

"Yes Sir," the scan officer responded.

"Send the Kantita, and Floursha around the port side of the star. The other two will go starboard with us. Stay in the dust to avoid detection. I want them in position in no more than sixty *milli-paks*."

After a short pause, the communications officer twisted around. "Orders confirmed and accepted, Sir."

"Then let's get moving."

As their ship plowed through the dust and debris surrounding the developing proto-system, the Marine sergeant moved closer to Saki.

"Sir?" he whispered. "We're going to surprise them by popping out of this dust, right?"

Saki nodded. "Cutting through the storm gets us into position before the escaping Koko ship clears the storm and warns his comrades."

"But Sir, they'll surely make it before we get to them."

Saki smiled. "I'd say the supreme commander is counting on that."

"Sir?"

"Watch and learn."

"Sir," the communications officer called. "The escaped Koko ship is just clearing the magnetic storm. He's reporting that they were attacked by twenty battleships and that we came out of nowhere."

"Ten *micro-paks* to open space," the scan officer announced.

"Hard to port," Khephra ordered, "and bring us out towards the middle of the system. Have the other ships maintain their present course."

"Sir," the scan officer called. "Ten Koko light cruisers dead ahead."

"Maintain this course and prepare to engage the enemy."

"Five *micro-paks* to open space. The enemy will be slightly below us and within firing range when we clear the dust."

"Weapons officers. Pick targets, but don't fire until you get the command from me."

As their ship burst from the dust cloud, chatter from the enemy ships stopped abruptly. Before the Kokos could react, the other two pairs of Antrakan battleships appeared and made straight for their flanks. Suddenly the airwaves were filled with urgent cries, the Koko word for retreat being the most dominant. Without a single shot being fired, the entire group turned and fled in disarray.

"Sir," the scan officer announced. "They are turning toward the remaining battle group."

Khephra grabbed his communicator. "Engineering, disable the decoy."

Within *micro-paks* the "escaping" light cruiser went silent and less than a *milli-pak* later, the fleeing ships changed direction and both groups headed for their home planet.

"What the hell just happened?" the sergeant asked Saki.

"Think about it," Saki said. "Twice, we've appeared out of nowhere and caught them completely off guard."

"Yeah, but why did they change course instead of regrouping with the other ships?"

Saki nodded eagerly. "What would you think if one of your ships appeared to have been destroyed, but the enemy was nowhere in sight."

The sergeant whistled. "I'd think we were fighting ghosts."

Saki smiled. "And that's how the best military mind in the galaxy works."

"This is how you guard someone?" Khephra growled from behind them.

Both men snapped to attention.

"Sir, at no time did the subject attempt to interfere with the operation of this ship. Sir!"

"That's not what I asked, Sergeant."

Saki snapped his heels together. "With all due respect, Sir."

"Respect is all well and good, Sub-commander," the Supreme Commander interrupted, "but right now I need discipline. Without which we'll all be dead."

Saki opened his mouth to speak, but Khephra's angry stare stopped him.

"Understood, Sir!" the sergeant shouted. "It won't happen again, Sir!"

The Supreme Commander paused, but Saki now knew it was more for effect than anger.

"Sergeant, take Sub-commander N-Tschester to his new quarters and make sure he stays there."

"Yes Sir," the non-com snapped before quickly stepping to the side and motioning Saki toward a corridor.

Unable to think of anything further to say, Saki complied quietly.

The officer's cabin Saki had been assigned was little more than an oversized closet, but at least he had a room alone. For the sergeant guarding his door, it would be worse. The corridor was barely wide enough for two people to pass, so there was nowhere for him to sit.

After half-a-*deca-pak*, the door suddenly burst open and Khephra stepped in.

Holding up a hand to stop Saki from standing at attention, he turned back to the sergeant. “Return to your unit, Sergeant.”

After the sergeant saluted and left, Khephra closed the door and leaned against it. “In response to your earlier question, Pana is missing.”

Saki jumped up, banging his head on the storage locker over his bunk.

Holding a hand over the injured spot, he looked at his father-by-law. “I thought she was aboard ship.”

Khephra sighed, “We thought we had her as well, but it turned out to be the Koko assassin. When we made our next attempt, she was gone.”

Saki’s eyes widened. “Did the Kokos get her?”

The Supreme Commander looked grim. “At this point, we can only hope they did.”

Khephra pulled an electronic pad from under his arm and handed it over. Saki examined it as his superior spoke, “They hid a ship in the planet’s magnetic north pole, where we couldn’t see it.”

“What if the Samhain got her?”

Khephra shook his head. “Our technicians said parts of her aura should still have been visible, but they found no sign of it.”

Saki looked up from the tablet. “They kidnapped Kappa as well?”

“Kappa has gained quite a reputation for his skills in reprocessing internees. However, they probably didn’t know he’d do everything in his power to save her.”

The Supreme Commander held his hand out and Saki returned the tablet.

“This ups the ante considerably. The only reason they’d go to so much trouble to kidnap Pana, is if they knew about this vessel and its key.”

Saki shook his head. “They have both pieces of the puzzle.”

Khephra's shoulders sagged slightly. "But not yet in the same place."

Saki paused to stare at his father-by-law. "Since we don't know where Pana is, we have to get the vessel before they can put them together."

Nodding sadly, Khephra pressed several keys on his pad and passed it back to Saki. "There's something I need you to do."

Saki looked at the pad. "Secor-Alpha Four?"

"Back when you were being processed for internment, the division under your command staged a protest."

"A protest? Over what?"

"Not one of them believed you did it."

Saki's eyes shifted from the electronic pad to his superior. "Not one?"

Khephra nodded. "Emotions were high and it didn't take much for a small group of senators to convince the Over Council to send the lot to Secor-Alpha Four." Shoving his hands into his pockets, he leaned back against the bulkhead. "Some of them, like Kappa, managed parole after a few *druaks*, but about half were still there, until just recently."

"They were released?"

"Nope. Someone disabled the monitoring system and by the time it was reinitialized, they were gone."

"How many transport ships did they use?"

"As far as we know, only one ship went down and one ship came back out."

"That's not possible."

Pushing away from the bulkhead, Khephra lifted his hands with the palms up. "Then they're probably still down there somewhere."

Saki gave the Supreme Commander a questioning look.

"Sir, are you ordering me to find my people?"

Khephra shook his head. "You're an escapee from a maximum security prison. I'm not even talking to you now."

Saki paused for a moment before asking, "The Kokos built those monitoring stations, didn't they?"

Smiling, Khephra nodded.

"How many light cruisers did you capture?"

"Some may have been destroyed during the battle. We haven't taken an official count yet."

"How long before you do."

"Just as soon as you get out of my hair."

"I'll need a crew."

Khephra shook his head. "I can't order anyone to help you. However, I won't penalize volunteers."

"How do I find volunteers?"

The supreme commander smiled. "Go to launch-bay six and try to narrow it down."

"Narrow it down?"

After opening the cabin door, Khephra turned toward Saki. "It seems that just before I undertook this mission, a number of your paroled crew members were transferred to my ship. They seem eager to serve under you again, but please try to leave some men for me to work with."

65

They walked through a towering stone door, its polished surface and lintels completely covered in ornate, gold-inlaid carvings and glyphs. Beyond the door, an enclosed courtyard was filled with a forest of brightly painted stone columns, ten elaborate side altars, five splashing fountains and even more ornate carvings and glyphs on the walls. Small furry creatures scurried across the open floor as fragile-looking butterflies fluttered around them.

Wat Wat tried several times to catch a butterfly, but each time it quickly flew just beyond his reach.

After his last failed attempt, the thin technician turned to find his companions had vanished into the stone columns.

"Eeeeaakk," he squawked before sprinting around an enormous vase. "Wait up, friends. We're only through the first doorway and I'm already lost."

Catching sight of his errant comrade through a gap in the columns, Kappa gently shifted the sleeping female in his arms as he leaned toward Baroque. "Can we go straight to your infirmary?"

Baroque waved at a person in a sleeveless sackcloth shift. All of his hair was shaved except a jet-black ponytail attached just above his left ear. A scarlet circle of makeup ringed his left eye, and seemed to hang from an ornate design painted on his forehead. As the person approached, Baroque put both hands over his own face, before moving one hand to each shoulder and bowing. The approaching person did likewise.

Wat Wat was just catching up with them as Baroque said something unintelligible, and the other person bowed again, but did not speak.

"This novice will take you to the infirmary," he said to Kappa. "Ask for Ansen Paraka. He's the best healer I know."

"What is our guide's name?"

Baroque smiled. "Just call him Novice. They are nameless until they pass the first level. They don't speak either."

Kappa nodded at the novice. “Lead the way, kind Novice, but please hurry.”

As they moved off, Wat Wat looked nervously from the departing Kappa to Baroque.

“What about me?”

His companion smiled. “You can come with me. This is something very few people outside the priesthood ever see.”

Wat Wat pointed at the novice. “What do they have to do to pass the first level?”

“They must draw blood in battle.”

“Really?”

“An initiate goes through six phases, of which the Novice level is first. He must study, pray and train for five *sirius* before taking the initiation test.”

“What if there aren’t any wars to fight?”

Baroque laughed. “They don’t fight in other people’s wars. The initiates are separated into four divisions of one hundred each. For their battle, each novice is given a loin cloth, staff and jug of water. They are marched to the Crimson Field, about twenty kilometers from here, where they engage each other in a mock battle.”

“They march all that way wearing nothing but a loin cloth and then attack each other with sticks?”

Baroque nodded slowly. “There’s nothing more terrifying than the sight of one hundred screaming, naked warriors charging at full speed.”

“But how bad can it be? They only have sticks.”

Baroque stopped and turned toward his companion. “Each and every one of them has been trained to kill with his bare hands,” he said softly. “Think how much more dangerous he would be with a weapon and then multiply that by one hundred.”

“Do a lot of them die?”

Baroque’s hand flicked up and enveloped one of the butterfly creatures.

He turned to Wat Wat. “No one dies. To a Warrior of Hammond, fighting is an art…” When he opened his hand, the butterfly spread its wings and flew off. “…and precision is the key.”

Wat Wat's mouth dropped open, but before he could speak they were approached by four older men wearing ornate robes, towering headdresses and each carrying a scarred and stained walking stick. They bowed as one to the approaching men and Baroque bowed back. Wat Wat, not sure of what he should do, half bowed, half shrugged while keeping an eye on his companion.

"An' Detertch. We welcome your return to the House of The Shendeah," said one of the men. "The Glory of God be with you."

"Your greeting warms my heart, my brothers," Baroque responded. "The Glory of God be with you as well." He waved a hand toward his companion. "I present my friend, Wat Wat Tsee, an outsider, but a deserving one."

"Friend, Wat Wat Tsee, you are also welcome in the House of The Shendeah. The Glory of God be with you."

Wat Wat gave Baroque a nervous glance. "Cool. Yeah. That's, uh, thanks guys."

Neither Baroque nor the other four reacted to Wat Wat's nervous response. Without speaking further, the foursome split into two pairs, stepping to either side of the visitors to let them pass.

As Baroque and his companion moved through another golden door, Wat Wat started to speak, but Baroque lifted a finger to his lips and shook his head. They continued in silence down a long hallway that ended with two ten-meter-tall doors made of polished stone.

Like the other doors, their entire surface was polished and elegantly carved, but with no gold or silver overlays, except for that covering one tall figure on each door. On the left door, the figure held up his left hand, palm up as though holding the clouds above him in abeyance, while the right hand gripped a golden chalice overflowing with fruit and grains. The right figure held a shield across his chest and a massive spear in his right hand.

Even though they were still some distance from the doors, Wat Wat had to lean his head back to read the glyphs next to each figure. He found himself whispering the magical words:

"Master of heaven.
Controller of sky and firmament.
Deliverer of sustenance to the needy.

Leader in the battle against evil.
Lord Almighty over all.
Who lives forever and ever.
Our Holy and Loving Father, Hammond."

As they drew near to the right door, it began to slowly, noisily grind open.

Baroque leaned close to his companion and whispered, "Don't say anything while inside this room unless you are addressed directly. I will speak for both of us."

After opening enough for the two men to pass, the door stopped moving and the room went silent. Wat Wat felt his stomach rumble as they entered a room that at first seemed to be completely devoid of furnishings or decoration. It was only after his eyes adjusted to the dim light that he realized each stone wall was divided into four panels. Inscribed at the top of each panel was one of the sixteen known virtues. His eyes scanned the titles topping each panel: strength, charity, knowledge, compassion,...

His review was interrupted when men dressed in elaborate, colorful full-length robes appeared from the shadows of each corner of the room. Their heads were covered in tall ornate headdresses, their waists wrapped with a golden belt bearing a sword in a bejeweled scabbard and each held a walking stick in his right hand.

Another person, as elaborately dressed as the others, but without headdress or walking stick, sat at an ornate desk. The chubby male looked up from the many tablets and ledgers in front of him, but said nothing. To Wat Wat's surprise, Baroque ignored all of these people, choosing instead to approach a small slender figure sitting on a low bench in the middle of the room. Unlike the others, this person wore only a simple linen smock, died bright red, but devoid of any decoration.

As he looked up, Wat Wat was struck by the intense blue of his large eyes.

"An' Detertch," the person said with a voice so soft, Wat Wat wasn't sure he'd really spoken. "It is so good to feel your presence again in our humble halls."

"It is good to be here, my Father," Baroque answered while bowing low. "There is much to tell you."

The Shendeah raised a rail-thin arm, spreading six nearly-skeletal fingers wide. "That can wait, Little Piquit. Have someone attend to your injury first. Then we can talk."

Wat Wat gasped when he realized the blue eyes were unfocused and unseeing. Then, as the words of the Shendeah sunk in, he turned to see a spot of blood staining Baroque's pants leg.

"Considering the urgency of my message, my injuries can wait."

The elder shook his head. "I am blind, little brother, but even from here I can smell your blood, and hear the shortness of your breath."

"Please, Shendeah, let me tell you what I must. Then I will seek out Ansen to tend my wounds."

The Shendeah paused for a moment before lowering his hand. "You are concerned about the aggressiveness of the Maatiirani? They have been testing our defenses for some time now."

"It is not the pirates that should concern you, my Father. There is another force that may be as powerful as the Good God Himself."

Hearing Baroque's words, the priest at the desk jumped up, knocking over his chair with a clatter. All four guards took a step forward and hammered their staffs onto the stone floor.

"Careful, Little Piquit," the Shendeah warned as he raised a hand again to stop his subordinates from further action. "To imply anything made by a mortal hand is as powerful as our Lord is heretical."

"And I would not speak thus if it weren't for the danger threatening all that I hold holy. I may need your help in defeating those who strive to control this force, and through it, the entire universe."

"You have seen this evil in action?"

"No, Father, but I have proof enough it is real. Those who possess it lack only the key that opens it. At this very moment, she is in your infirmary."

"Your key is a female?"

"It is mingled with her Life Force. I do not know how."

"And she wishes to rule the universe?"

Baroque shook his head. "No, Father, but others, by possessing her, would do so."

The Shendeah rose, signaling as he did for his robe. A colorfully dressed female hurried from a side room and settled the intricately patterned garment over his shoulders.

"Well, Little Piquit," the Shendeah said calmly as the female buckled a golden belt around his waist. "I'd like to meet the key to the destruction of our universe."

66

When Matrina opened her door, Pheet shook his head and stumbled into her apartment.

"What have you done to me?" he asked weakly before crashing onto her couch. When she didn't answer, he looked up to see she was smiling. "What?"

"I need your help with something and I know you won't say no," she answered confidently.

He gave his head a sharp shake, as though to knock something loose. "What do you want?"

"Oh, it's nothing really, just a little message to my friends."

He pulled himself into a sitting position, but despite his best effort, his head lolled to one side. His vision was so blurry he could barely make out her features.

"What friends? Where?"

"Your supreme commander is blocking all outgoing transmissions. I'd just like to get a message out to tell them I'm OK."

"Who do you need to contact? Where are they?"

Shaking her head, she squatted down in front of him. "Don't trouble yourself with all that right now. I have everything ready, but I need someone on the bridge to send it out with the other communications going between the ships."

His eyes widened. "A piggyback signal? Not a chance!"

Standing, she shrugged. "You should know that we have your daughter and ex-wife. I supposed you should also know that you are now addicted to Pharmitan."

She threw up her hands in mock frustration. "My friends are tired of waiting. If you don't cooperate, your ex-wife, your daughter and your career will all be dead."

He tried to rise, but a cramp in his gut made him double over instead.

"You can't fight this," she warned. "Your choices are very limited."

"I won't betray my…" Another cramp stopped him.

"What?" she asked incredulously. "You won't betray the very person who is right now defying the will of his people? He's prepared to start a war nobody wants."

"He's my…" he jerked forward slightly, his hands pressing against his stomach. "supreme commander."

She shook her head sadly. "I was afraid you'd be uncooperative."

As she rose, another pair of hands pulled Pheet back. He was so disoriented by the sudden movement, he didn't have time to react before he felt a disk pressing the side of his neck. He reached up to tear it off, but his hand stopped just short of his objective. In fact, his whole body went rigid at that very moment.

"Sorry to have to do this," Matrina cooed mockingly while nodding to the shadowy figure behind the couch. "I like a male who knows what he wants, and now you want to do anything I ask of you."

Pheet's eyes moved slowly up to hers. "I am a male who knows what he wants," he said flatly. "And I'm going to do what you ask of me."

"That's my little soldier," she said sarcastically. "And now let me tell you what it is you want to do."

67

The figure moved through the dark room quietly, ignoring the many plaques, gold-plated weapons and oversized self-portraits covering the walls. Such was his familiarity with the space, he had no trouble expertly side-stepping a small desk topped with a disorganized collection of trophies and the bleached skulls of more than a dozen different species.

Moving quickly to the huge bed taking up a third of the large room, he searched its voluminous folds for the snoring life form within.

"Sir," the orderly called as he located and nudged Brak's shoulder. "News from front, Sir."

"She had eggs," Brak muttered sleepily. "Fertile eggs!"

"Wake up, Sir."

Brak's eyes snapped opened as he reached toward the orderly. "And you be such a pretty…what?"

"News from front, Sir," the orderly repeated. "Battleships soon to be returning."

The Fleet Commander looked at his clock with both heads. "So soon? We not hardly think they be back by now. Khephra defeated already?"

"No, Sir. He surprise light cruisers before fleet arrive."

"Surprise…? What?" Brak sat up in bed and rubbed both pairs of eyes before looking at the orderly again. "Ceratha's piss! Get watch commander!"

The orderly shook his heads. "He wait in first conference room with captains of remaining battleships. Some say it pretty bad, Sir."

"Remaining battleships? Bad? What you mean? We send damned armada against six lousy ships."

The orderly shrugged. "Sir, you gotta get dressed. They wait."

Brak quickly rolled out of bed, knocking the orderly to the floor. "Get up, moron, and put all ships on full alert."

The orderly sat up. "But Sir, they already on full alert."

Ignoring him, the Fleet Commander yanked off his night shirt and tossed it aside as he ran naked into his dressing room. “Our dress uniform! Our dress uniform!”

A bleary-eyed aide opened a door on the other side of the dressing room. “You gots problem, Sir?”

“Problem?” Brak screamed. “Do We make habit of screaming for dress uniform at this craziness of hour?”

The aide nodded both heads. “Quite often, actually.”

“Don’t give crap, idiot! Get us dressed.”

Easing into the room, the aide waved at the orderly and said, “Go tell others, maybe? He be right out.”

Gratefully, the orderly nodded and left the room.

Forty *milli-paks* later, Brak arrived in the conference room in full-dress uniform with a myriad of medals, ribbons and buttons, most of which the audience knew he’d purchased, stolen or bestowed upon himself.

“Gentlemen,” he announced as he swept in, smelling heavily of alcohol and perfume. “Give full report.”

A small officer at the far end of the conference table stood. “Armada in full retreat, Sir. Supreme Commander Khephra surprise them with whole fleet of ships. Considering we outnumbered two to one, it show superior tactics that we lose only ten light cruisers.”

“Did our battleships engage him?”

“They not get chance, Sir,” answered another officer. “His ships be invisible. Captain Arak say they destroy one light cruiser right before his eyes, but he never see enemy ship. Ships of Khephra also appear from nowhere and almost surround his battle group. They only barely escape with lives.”

“How many ships do we destroy?”

Everyone in the room looked at everyone else.

“Well?” Brak asked insistently.

A brief silence followed until one officer spoke, “It difficult to say, Sir.”

Someone else added, “Invisible ships hard to fight, you know.”

Brak shook his heads. "But when ship destroyed, it break into little-tiny pieces. Surely stealth technology not built into damned atoms!"

"Oh definitely," the first officer cried.

"We only guess," added another, "but ten battleships, maybe"

"Another twenty light cruisers disabled or destroyed," announced a third officer.

"They not soon forget encounter with us," the first exclaimed.

"Fantastic," Brak cheered just before his smile vanished, "but why we retreat?"

After another prolonged silence someone said, "We don't be retreating, Sir. We just…regrouping, maybe?"

"We take time to understand stealth technology so we can get 'round it," said a second officer.

"Next encounter gonna be great victory," spouted a third.

Brak clapped his hands and laughed. "Put commander of armada on comm channel, maybe? We congratulate in person."

The room erupted as everyone spoke at once. Finally, the officer at the far end of the table rose again. "Sir, we not in communication with armada. They, uh, traveling though magnetic storm."

Brak's eyebrows squatted low over his eyes. "Why they in magnetic storm? Don't that be dangerous?"

The standing officer gaped at his superior until the one next to him answered, "Stealth technology of Supreme Commander not work there, Sir. They want make sure he not be followed, maybe?"

"Excellent," Brak cried while clapping his hands again. "We know stupid orderly just pulling our legs." He did a little KokoroTetian dance before returning to the head of the conference table. "Tell armada commander to keep after enemy until they be thoroughly routed. We want him to bring Khephra and his officers to us personally, so we all can eat them in communal feast."

The whole room erupted in applause as the Fleet Commander happily marched back to his quarters, completely ignoring the communications room where they were receiving repeated distress calls from the fleeing armada captains.

68

Soft hands pulled her into a heat she longed for.

"I love you," she sighed when lips kissed her neck.

The room swirled as her passion rose until she could hardly stand it.

"I've waited so long..." she groaned.

"Me too," he sighed. "If only this were real."

"What?"

Tamm awoke with a start to find herself naked and hugging a warm body, the room smelling like warm musk and sweat.

"Damn you," she cried upon seeing she was intertwined with Bottar's body. Pushing him away with one hand, she slapped his head and shoulders with the other. "Damn you. Damn you," she repeated with each blow.

It took three slaps before Bottar was fully awake. In self-defense, he grabbed Tamm's arms, realizing for the first time why she was so angry.

"What the hell is going on?" he cried as the angry woman struggled against his grip.

"You fucking well know, bastard!"

Though a naked woman writhing against him should have been arousing, the realization of what had happened kept his libido in check.

"Tamm," he cried as he pushed her back down to pin her arms against the mattress. "Calm down. This can't be what it seems."

"Why did you stop the car? We could be home by now."

"I was falling asleep and couldn't wake you."

"And you thought a sleeping woman would be easy prey?"

"No," he protested. "It's not like that at all."

Struggling to make sense of the moment, he noticed a large hickey on her left breast. Looking down at his chest, he saw three on him as well.

"I think we made love."

She growled, “That’s not what I’d call it.”

“Then who put these hickeys on me?” he said while jutting his chin toward his chest. As her eyes fell on the indicated spots, her struggles stopped.

“But why?” she cried. “I don’t…”

He released her arms. “I think it’s the memories.”

Crossing arms over her breasts, she twisted away from him. He rolled back to let her go and then sat up, unconcerned by his nakedness.

“Listen, Tamm,” he said softly as she sat on the edge of the bed, facing away from him. “These memories flooding my head are exhausting. I don’t know what’s real and what isn’t. You can’t tell me you’re not plagued with them too.”

“That doesn’t make this right,” she cried. “I’m not like that cheating bastard back there. I don’t do this kind of crap!”

He put a hand gently on her shoulder, but she jerked away.

“Listen, maybe if you took a shower, it might make you feel...”

“You take the damned shower,” she interrupted, “and then get out of my room.”

Bottar looked around. “Uh, Tamm,” he said softly.

“Just do it and go!”

“This is my room. It looks like you came to me.”

She twisted around to face him, scanning the room as she did. “Oh shit,” she whispered.

Before he could respond she jumped from the bed and began pulling on her pants and shirt.

“Tamm, it’s OK for you to take…””

“No,” she interrupted. “This is your place and I shouldn’t be here.”

Bottar shook his head. “It’s no big deal, really.”

She grabbed her coat and slammed it on the bed. “The hell it’s not! I just screwed my partner and I don’t even know why.”

With tears running down her cheeks, she ran to the door, yanked it open and charged outside.

Bottar took a deep breath and exhaled slowly. Before he could do more, there was a knock on his door. Without even bothering to cover himself, he hurried to the door, standing behind it as he opened it.

Tamm looked sheepish. “What room am I staying in?” she asked while moving inside.

Closing the door, he walked toward the bed and looked around. Finding nothing, he pulled the bed covers taught, the keycard flicked onto the floor.

After picking it up, he turned to hand her the card. “It’s the room next door.”

“Shit, Bottar,” she protested. “At least you could cover yourself.”

He laughed. “We just made love, Tamm. What else could I have to hide from you?”

His comment seemed to confuse her, and instead of responding with a wise crack, she snatched the keycard and fiddled with it as he walked her to the door.

Opening it, he turned back to her. “We’d better get going.”

Nodding self-consciously, she stopped in the doorway and looked into his eyes.

“Thanks for not giving me crap about this.”

“I should thank you, actually.”

Her face turned cautious. “Why?”

“Because you said the next time I saw you naked you’d knee me in the nuts.” He smiled. “Thanks for not doing it.”

She pressed her forehead into the door for a moment before looking at him with an impish smile. “OK, you got a pass, but if it happens again, I’ll castrate you.”

Without comment, he closed the door behind her.

Half-an-hour later they were in the car.

“Listen,” he said before starting the engine. “About what just happened...”

Without looking at him, she held up a hand. “I don’t want to talk about it right now.”

“But Tamm…”

"What's the point?" she interrupted while jerking to face him. "My whole world is upside down. My head's full of crap I don't understand and I'm sleeping..." She hit his shoulder with the back of her hand. "...with a guy I shouldn't be sleeping with." Pushing back into the seat, she stared at the ceiling. "Worse yet, I'm married to a guy whose face I can't remember." She slapped her thighs. "How the fucking hell can I talk about this when it's all just a muddle?"

Bottar shook his head slowly. "Tamm, I'm sorry. You have to believe I didn't plan for this."

She slammed her head against the headrest. "Yeah, well that's how it's been going, isn't it?"

"I don't follow..."

She turned to face him, her hands fluttering beside her face. "We don't know if these memories are real or imagined. We don't know why some creepy two-headed monsters scooped us up and stuck us in a cave. We don't even know if we escaped or they intended for us to get away." She collapsed back into the seat, looking exhausted. "Do we actually make our own choices or are we just puppets in an already written play?"

He stared at her for a moment, wanting to take her in his arms, kiss her forehead and promise it would be OK. He almost laughed when it occurred to him what her reaction would be.

Firing up the car's engine, he slipped it into gear. "Then I guess," he said while pressing the accelerator pedal, "we'd better get out there and find some answers."

Tamm remained silent as they turned onto the highway and sped for home. To Bottar's surprise, the next time he looked, she was slumped against the door, sound asleep.

He turned to look at the road ahead, the memory of what Tamm had said nagging at him. He struggled to stay focused on driving, but random memories kept popping into his head. Some were just snaps of people or places he couldn't place, yet seemed familiar to him. Sometimes they were continuous scenes of something from his unknown past, such as walking through a park, playing and bantering with people he didn't know, and yet, felt he should.

Twice he had to pull off the road when the memories came so quickly he couldn't pay attention to the traffic in front of them. Tamm snored softly as he struggled to regain control of his thoughts. He longed to curl up with her and sleep as well. Unfortunately, that hadn't worked well the last time he tried it, so he shook his head to chase the thoughts away and drove on.

After the longest four hours of his life, he finally saw the sign for their home town.

Shaking Tamm's shoulder, he called softly, "We'll be home in ten minutes."

Tamm's eyes popped open and she quickly jerked upright and looked around.

"It feels good to see familiar scenery, but it also feels…" Her voice faded as she continued to stare out the window.

"Like it's not home anymore," Bottar sighed.

She sighed. "Yeah. Something like that."

"So what do we do now?"

She shrugged. "Let's go to my house and see if…" Tamm slapped her forehead. "Damn! Marrett must be going out of his mind."

Bottar stepped on the gas, accelerating down the highway and cutting a sharp right onto their street. He immediately slammed on the breaks to avoid hitting a police officer flagging traffic.

"Do you folks live in this area?" the officer asked as Bottar stopped the car and rolled down his window.

"Yes, Sir," he answered while pointing to Tamm. "She lives at 2285 Watershed and I live next door."

The officer checked his clipboard. "Mister Bottar Watt at 2295?"

"Yes, Sir."

He peered into the car. "How long have you folks been gone?"

Bottar looked at Tamm as she shook her head.

"Actually, we don't really know. Maybe a couple of days."

The officer shook his head. "According to this, there hasn't been anyone at either of those houses for over a month."

"You're kidding," both of them said simultaneously.

"May I see your ID?"

Bottar held up both hand, palms out. "We don't have any. You see, we just woke up a couple of days ago in a cave about three-hundred miles south-east of here and there were these…"

Tamm put a hand on his arm. "We really have no idea how we got there, Officer."

"Ma'am, is your name Tammilyn Perpatton?"

Tamm's mind froze at the mention of a name that was familiar, yet alien. She finally nodded. "Yes, Sir. I live with my son…" Her face registered shock. "Oh my God," she exclaimed. "I've been gone over a month? Where's my son?"

The officer checked his clipboard again. "Ma'am. Marrett Perpatton is with his father."

Tamm held up both hands. "I swear, Officer, I didn't leave my son alone on purpose."

The officer shook his head. "Under any other circumstances, I might not believe you ma'am, but right now, I wouldn't be surprised if you said you'd been abducted by aliens."

"Really?" Bottar asked. "How's that?"

The officer swept a hand out behind himself. "Over three-quarters of the people in this ten-block area have gone missing, and it all happened in one night. The same thing's happened in Hetson and Delvintown. We think somewhere around five-hundred people went missing."

"Have any been found?" Tamm asked.

The Sheriff nodded. "About thirty, so far. Most were in the old Dattson gold mine down by Wipsomville, but they don't know how or why they got there."

Bottar looked at Tamm before turning back to the officer. "You might want to look in the Pittston Basin on the other side of the mountains. That's where we escaped from."

The officer nodded again. "I'll pass that on, but you need to get over to that Federal van just down the block." He pointed to a black van with Federal Department of Security, on the side. "They'll want to chat with you before you go home."

Bottar looked at Tamm again before nodding. "We'll do that, Sir," he said while slipping the car into gear as another officer moved the barrier back.

"Let's go home first," Bottar said as they approached the van. "They're going to keep us for hours and I could use a change of clothes and a shower."

"No," Tamm insisted. "They might make a fuss about my leaving Marrett. His father would love to deny me custody, if only just to pull my chain."

As they approached the van, Tamm scrunched up her nose. "What's that smell?"

Bottar's eyebrows shot up as they both stopped. "The cave?"

She nodded. "When the aliens were there."

The van's side door slid open and a frazzled-looking man stuck his head out and waved them in.

"Get in the car," Bottar ordered as he started backpedaling.

Already retreating, Tamm looked back to see a gloved hand grab the man's jacket and yank him back into the van. Stumbling, she fell against the car, but turned back when she heard a sharp crack. A loud squawk -- which she somehow knew was a swear word -- preceded the man flying from the van to land in a crumpled pile on the pavement.

Bottar let out a startled cry as Tamm jumped into the car, and slammed her door. At that same instant a tall, horridly ugly, two-headed creature rush from the van and stopped on top of the dead man's body.

"Drive!" she screamed as Bottar slammed his own door and shoved the keys into the ignition.

The engine roared to life just as the two-headed creature stuck one of its four hands into the pocket of his oversized coat. The alien fumbled briefly with an odd-shaped device as Bottar slammed his foot on the accelerator. The car lurched forward, knocking the creature onto its back. Bottar kept his foot pressed down as the vehicle rammed into the bulky alien and shoved it ahead of them.

"Christ," Tamm exclaimed as they heard a long, loud squawk, cut off sharply by dual thumps when the creature's heads slammed into the van's rear tire.

As they sped on, Bottar looked in his rearview mirror. "There's another one coming out. Get down!"

Seeing the creature level its weapon at them, Bottar swerved left just as a ball of fire shot past them. Tamm pressed into him as the paint on the passenger side burst into flame.

He tried to maintain control of the car, but both right tires exploded, pulling it into a parked car at the corner.

Shoving his own door open, Bottar rolled onto the pavement, grunting as Tamm landed on top of him. Without hesitating, she rolled and pulled him between two cars as another ball of hot flame shot overhead.

Jumping up together, they scrambled behind another vehicle as their own car exploded in a ball of fire.

"To the houses," Tamm screamed as another car burst into flames.

In the next house, a woman stepped onto her front porch. "What the fu…" she started to scream as a third volley turned her and half the porch into fine ash.

Adrenaline pumping, hearts throbbing, the twosome cut a sharp left and sprinted between two houses.

"Find a car to boost," Bottar yelled.

"No time," Tamm panted. "He's too close."

Keeping low, they rushed across the next street, quickly crossed in front of a house, and were cutting a sharp left between it and the next one when another car exploded behind them.

As they sprinted down a narrow alley, Tamm spied a shovel leaning against a detached garage. Snatching it, she ran around behind the garage while motioning for Bottar to continue on.

Despite its many short legs, the alien motored along at a good pace. As it appeared from between the houses, one head looked in the back yard, while the other watched Bottar run behind a row of cars. It quickly turned both faces toward him and aimed its weapon.

Sucking in a deep breath, Tamm heaved the shovel around with all her might. The creature started to turn in her direction as the shovel impacted the bridge of both snouts at once.

Its weapon discharged as the creature instinctively jerked its hands across its body. Several balls of energy cut an exploding arc into the ground before the last one burned a notch in Tamm's left thigh. Dirt and burning debris rained down, as both she and the alien fell screaming to the concrete.

Bottar raced to them as the alien sat up, holding both snouts as lavender goop gushed from them. Seeming to ignore them, it started scrambling on hands and stubby legs with both heads dipped low to the ground, as though searching for something.

Bottar located the weapon first and snatched it up, but the alien didn't seem to care. After only a few moments of searching, the creature turned and lurched towards them.

"Eeaapisk! Eeaapisk," it cried while pointing to its snouts.

Unable to use the weapon, Bottar tossed it at Tamm. He snatched up her shovel, but before the creature reached them, its eyes rolled up and it fell onto its huge rump. Its arms waved wildly as it desperately gasped and slowly fell onto its back. While the Humans stared dumbfounded, the creature kicked its legs spasmodically in every direction, took several more desperate breaths, and went still.

"Gahhh," Tamm groaned.

When Bottar turned to find her sagging against the garage, he dropped the shovel and hurried to her.

"Are you all right?"

Gritting her teeth, she shook her head. "It burns like the devil."

Dropping to one knee, he pulled her hand back to see blood pouring from a blackened spot on her thigh. He yanked a cloth from his pocket and pressed it against the wound.

"Yaahh!" she screamed while grabbing his hand.

"Sorry, kid, but we've got to stop the bleeding."

Biting her lip against the pain, Tamm struggled to look past the garage. "Are there any more of them?"

Still holding the cloth to her leg, Bottar looked as well. "I don't see anyone."

"Then get its weapon."

He looked puzzled. "But I don't know how to use it."

"If there are more of them, we don't want them to have it."

Nervously, he moved to the device and picked it up.

"I hope this damned thing doesn't go off in my hand."

Still leaning against the garage, Tamm held out a hand. "Give it to me and see if that thing has any more of them."

Bottar looked at the creature then handed her the weapon.

"You sure it's not just playing dead?"

Instead of answering, she turned her attention to the device. "I think I've used one of these before."

Bottar shook his head. "How could that be possible?"

Still staring at the weapon, Tamm shook her head, but before she could answer, she gasped again and slumped to the ground.

"We've got to find a doctor," Bottar cried as he grabbed a piece of cloth from around the alien's waist and rushed back to her. "You're losing too much blood."

He wrapped the cloth several times around her thigh before tying it off. As he was just finishing, someone called from beside the house.

"What's happening down there?" the officer asked as he slowly approached their position.

"Over here, Officer," Bottar called while waving a hand. "We've disabled the alien, but my..."

He stopped when the officer lifted his gun and aimed it at him. "Step out where I can see you and throw down your weapon."

"But Officer," Bottar protested while pointing toward the alien. "That thing attacked us. We were only defending ourselves."

"Do as you're told, Sir or I'll be forced to shoot," the officer warned.

"What do you mean, shoot me?"

The officer looked at the body and shook his head. "Sorry, Sir, but I see an FBS officer with his face bashed in, and you're the only one here."

Bottar straightened and stepped into the alley. “You can’t see that creature has two heads?”

The officer raised his gun to shoulder level. “Get down on the ground. Now!”

Bottar took another step back. “Yes Sir, but I want to get away from this thing first.”

“Move slowly, Sir,” he said while following Bottar step-for-step.

As the two men moved in unison, Tamm felt the alien’s weapon in her hand. Without knowing why, she adjusted it so her thumb matched a worn spot on one side. As the officer’s gun appeared in her line of sight, she aimed the device and pressed her index finger into a slight depression.

Light shot from the weapon, the front of the gun vanished and the officer fell back.

“Christ!” all three people cried simultaneously as the remains of the weapon clattered on the concrete.

Groaning, Tamm limped into the alley as Bottar stared at the policeman lying on his back, holding up burned hands.

“Are you OK?” she asked the officer as she leaned heavily against the garage.

His eyes wide, the officer looked from his singed fingers to her. “What the hell was that?”

Tamm held up the device and pointed at the alien. “This belonged to that thing you call an FBS agent.” Glancing back at Bottar, she motioned him over. “I won’t hurt you any more if you’ll give my friend your radio.”

Without uttering another word, the policeman fumbled clumsily with the device and eventually passed it to Bottar. Something squawked on the device as he took it.

“Are they calling for you?” Bottar asked.

Still wide eyed, the officer shook his head. Bottar released the battery cover lock, slipped it off and extracted the battery. Dropping the radio onto the ground, he looked down at the officer.

“We’re going to leave now. If you’ll stay here for a bit, we won’t hurt you. OK?”

After looking at the remains of his gun, the officer nodded.

"Shouldn't we cuff him or something?" Bottar asked.

Tamm shook her head. "Let's just get out of here and leave him be."

As Tamm limped back toward the street, Bottar leaned over the officer. "Are you with the Sheriff's Posse?" The man nodded. "You really should do as she says. She might be a great looking gal, but trust me. She's a total bitch when crossed."

The officer looked at his hands and quickly nodded again.

"Where are we going now?" he asked after catching up with the staggering woman.

"To the FBS van," she grunted as they reached the street.

"They won't need it."

Movement down the street caught his attention, and he briefly watched the people gathered around the burning cars. When Tamm released a high-pitched whimper, he quickly turned back, and grabbed her arm to keep her from slumping to the ground.

"It's bad?"

She jerked a nod. "Like a raging bitch!"

"You're looking quite pale. We need to get you to a doctor."

She half laughed, half cried. "That's the first place they'll look for us."

When she stumbled again, he scooped her up at the knees, flinching when he heard her groan.

"We'll make better time," he explained while breaking into a trot.

Gritting her teeth, she tried her best not to cry out with each footfall, but one or two whimpers made it out as they progressed.

They skirted the crowds and made their way to the van where Bottar deposited his moaning companion in the front seat. After digging the keys from the dead agent's pocket and finding another weapon next to the alien they'd run over, he ran to the driver's door and jumped in.

"No time to get anything from the house," he said while starting the van. "The cops are probably on the way."

Turning the van around, he raced past the police car and onto the main highway.

"Gotta ditch this thing," Tamm groaned as they raced along. "They'll call us cop killers."

Bottar nodded as they took an exit to the downtown district.

Racing through the city streets, Bottar looked sharply left and right until he sighed with relief and pulled the van over.

"Raytaan," he called while jumping out.

A short, dark-skinned man separated from a group of young men, looking puzzled as he waved. When Bottar motioned him over, Raytaan said a few words to his companions, who all looked briefly at the van before turning back to whatever they were doing.

Bottar fidgeted nervously as Raytaan sauntered to them.

"What you doing here, man?" the dark man asked while looking past Bottar. "And where did you get that?"

"I need a favor," Bottar answered. "It'll be worth a hundred."

Raytaan waved a hand dismissively. "Your money's worth nothing to me, man. What will it be?"

"Someone to drive this van to the docks and a quick replacement. Nothing flashy, just reliable."

Raytaan smiled, turned half-way back to the group, and whistled. "Jockan! I gotta job for you."

A tall, wiry boy separated from the group and raced over.

As he approached, Raytaan turned to Bottar. "Got a fiver?"

Pulling a small wad of bills from his pocket, Bottar separated one from it, and handed it to his friend who held it out to Jockan.

"Take this van to the docks. Drive nicely and park it safe." He held the fiver up. "This will cover your fare back and a bit more."

Without a word, the boy snatched the bill and jumped into the driver's seat. Tamm opened her door, but groaned as she tried to swing her legs out. Bottar rushed around to lift her out, and shut the door. As he stepped back, the van lurched forward so fast, their clothes were still rustling when it took the first turn.

"Thought I was a fast driver," Bottar said dryly as the vehicle disappeared.

Raytaan nodded lazily. “He’s one of my favorites, but I’m not about to tell him. The kid’s ego is bigger than the Silver moon.”

Tamm moaned while pushing her face into Bottar’s neck.

“Do you know of any discreet doctors around here?” he asked while looking at her pale face.

Raytaan shrugged and motioned to where the van had disappeared. “What’s the deal?”

Tamm shook her head as Bottar said, “She’s got a chunk out of her leg. I’d take her to the hospital, but…it’s complicated.”

“This got anything to do with all those people going missing?”

Bottar felt Tamm’s arms tighten around his neck, but he nodded anyway.

Raytaan shook his head. “And the Feds are in on it?”

Tamm lifted her head and glared at Bottar’s friend. “Look. If you don’t want to help us we’ll just fine someone…”

“Tamm,” Bottar interrupted. She jerked her face toward his.

“Raytaan and I got history. If we can trust anyone, it’s him.”

Raytaan looked down. “Your friend’s bleeding pretty bad, Bot. She’s going to need something done quick.”

“Can you help?”

Raytaan grinned. “Well, I can’t get you a doctor, but maybe the next best thing. Maybe even better.”

“It will have to do,” Bottar answered without hesitation.

Raytaan nodded and turned toward his group. Giving out a sharp whistle, he made some hand signals and another boy jumped up and ran down the block. A minute later, he was back with a small car.

When the car stopped, Raytaan opened the back door. “I hope this will do.”

Tamm whimpered as Bottar lowered her onto the seat. As she gritted her teeth against the pain, he tried to fasten her seat belt.

“Don’t bother with that, man,” Raytaan called from the driver’s seat. “We ain’t going that far.”

Bottar hesitated until Tamm nodded curtly. “I don’t know why this hurts so much,” she panted. “It isn’t that deep a wound.”

He looked at her pale face as an unbidden panic surged inside him. “Tamm, there could be something in the…”

She jerked a hand up and slapped his arm. "So let's find a doctor with a boatload of pain medicine." She shoved at him and he backed out of the car.

As he buckled into the front seat, the car surged forward.

"I told one of my boys to call ahead," Raytaan said as they took a sharp left turn that made Tamm grunt. "Things should be ready when we arrive."

"How far is it?"

Raytaan laughed. "Just a right at this next street and it's an easy half-mile to her door."

Raytaan's smile vanished when he stopped at the corner. Traffic was backed up to almost where they were and it was obvious from the people standing beside their cars, that things were moving very slowly.

Instead of turning, he drove through the intersection, and as both men looked down the street, blue, red and yellow lights flickered off buildings several blocks down. Whistling, Raytaan pulled over in front of a small cluster of men.

"Hey, Mattee," he called.

A small man, whose skin was even darker than Raytaan's moved to Bottar's open window.

"Yo, Rayman," Mattee greeted before nodding silently to Bottar. "What's doin'?"

"What's those barrelheads up to?"

Mattee shook his head. "Don't know, man. They just showed up a minute ago. Started going through people's cars, even grabbin' cousins off the street. Maybe someone robbed a bank or something."

"Or something," Raytaan muttered then said in a louder voice, "Thanks, Mattee. See you around."

He pulled back onto the street and turned left at the next intersection.

"Aren't we supposed to be going that way?" Bottar asked while throwing a thumb over his shoulder.

"Those cops looking for you?"

Bottar did a shrug/nod. "Probably."

The car slowed and pulled to the curb where the streetlight was out.

Raytaan turned to face Bottar. “How deep does this go?”

When Bottar hesitated, Tamm cried, “Tell him. We need someone on our side.”

Bottar looked at his comrade and hesitated for a moment before responding. “The report will be that three Federal agents were killed just a short while ago. In reality, two of those so-called agents are some kind of alien, and they’re part of the same group responsible for the disappearance of people all over town.” He looked at Tamm again. “We know about them because we were among the people kidnapped, but we escaped and made our way back here.”

Though he paused to gauge Raytaan’s reaction, the man showed none, so Bottar continued. “When we got here, a cop sent us to the FBS van to be debriefed, but I smelled something that reminded me of that cave we were in.

“When we started to run, the aliens killed the real agent and shot at us with some kind of ray gun thing that spit a ball of fire. We only killed them in self defense.”

Tamm groaned and both men turned to see her slump over.

“She get shot with this ray gun thing?” Raytaan asked.

Bottar nodded. “It’s just a nick, but it’s getting worse by the minute.”

Raytaan looked back at Tamm again. “Well, she’s bleeding on my seat, so like it or not, I’m in for the ride.” He smiled. “You’re going to owe me a couple of cases of Crock juice.”

Bottar tried to smile, but could only manage a grimace. “Save Tamm and I’ll give you a damned warehouse full of that shit.”

Raytaan stepped on the gas. “This means plan number three.”

“Number three?” Bottar asked uncertainly as they made a sharp right.

“It’s a good thing your friend is unconscious.”

69

The scan officer snapped a salute. "I am detecting no active scans of the area, Sir."

Khephra nodded in acknowledgment but continued to stare at the nebula filling their view screen.

"Communications," he barked. "Are we still running dark?"

"Yes, Sir," came the quick response. "No communications have left this ship since a *pak* after leaving Prak a'Terra."

"What is that wily fox up to?" he asked no one in particular. "Considering my previous tactical moves, surely he expects me to come at him through that nebula."

"If I may, Sir," the scan officer answered. "He's probably half-way across the galaxy by now."

Khephra shook his head. "Son. A venomous snake may have only a limited intelligence, and be totally incapable of conceptual thinking. Yet, when cornered, only a fool would underestimate the deadliness of its bite."

"But we don't have him cornered, Sir."

"Yes," he sighed. "We do."

"Sir?"

The supreme commander shook his head. "Did the two captured ships we commandeered manage to catch up with the retreating armada?"

The first mate nodded. "Considering the enemy was flying in the wrong direction for almost a *pak*, it wasn't hard."

"Any reports so far?"

"The only message they've received from the Fleet Commander is to turn back and finish us off."

The supreme commander raised an eyebrow, but betrayed no other reaction. "And their response?"

"They continue to plead for reinforcements, but no one seems to be listening."

“They’re listening all right,” Khephra muttered. “But I wonder if any of them have the guts to tell Brak how badly I routed them.”

“I’d offer a negative on that, Sir.”

“How long before the armada arrives at the KoKo home world?”

“They should have arrived just before we did.”

“How many other ships were we able to properly crew?”

“We have one with enough people to run at full strength and two more minimally manned.”

The supreme commander turned to face the first mate. “Send all three around the other side of the nebula from the retreating armada and have the two poorly manned ships fake damage from our fight.”

“Yes Sir.”

“Captain Pike will follow them, but he is to remain dark, so they aren’t likely to notice him.”

“We can have the ‘damaged’ cruisers release radiation from their N-Drives,” the first mate offered. “It’ll interfere with the Koko’s scans, so they won’t see the battleship until she gets into visual range.”

Khephra nodded. “Make it happen, Son.”

“And what are we going to do,” Sub-commander Pheet asked as the first mate moved away.

“I’m going to show Brak why he needs to pay attention to his captains.”

“But Sir, they have a vast superiority over us.”

“No they don’t,” the supreme commander responded seriously. “They just have a lot more ships.”

70

Raytaan led Bottar down a dingy, dark hallway and knocked on a door covered with more scratches than paint. Further down the hall, a door opened slightly and then quickly closed. The unpleasant smell of urine assaulted Bottar's nose as he shifted his precious burden and looked cautiously around. Somewhere in the rooms around them, a baby cried, a dog barked, and a TV blared.

"Not exactly the Ritz, but Auntie Bezzle's been mending people here since the big war." Raytaan knocked again. "She says the government gives her medicine and supplies to help people with, but I'm not sure it all comes from them. Leastways, I know she doesn't sell the stuff to users."

"I hope she's up to dealing with this mess," Bottar sighed as he shifted Tamm again.

"Actually, there's something else you should know about Auntie Bezzle," Raytaan said as he rubbed his nose. "That alien you described on the way over here?"

Bottar nodded. "Yeah?"

"She told me about something like that once. She said they are wicked bastards that'd as soon eat you as look at you, and they wouldn't bother to kill you first." He shook his head. "Damned woman's stories gave me nightmares for months."

"And now you know they're real," Bottar added.

Raytaan wiped his face. "I can kiss off another month of sleep."

He turned to knock again but hesitated when someone spoke from behind the door, "Who is you?"

"Auntie, it's me, Ray."

"I know lots 'a Rays, honey. Which one be you?"

"Meta's boy. I got an injured woman out here. She's bleeding bad."

The door swept open, revealing the rail-thin silhouette with long frizzy hair and loose-fitting clothes. Fuzzy yellow slippers covered her feet and she held a broom out front as though she planned to shove it into their faces.

"Ray-boy, was that you who called earlier?"

"Yes, 'em." Raytaan swept a hand towards Bottar. "This woman's been shot with some kind of ray gun."

"You shitting me, Boy?" she asked angrily.

Bottar moved quickly forward, causing the woman to step back and brandish her broom.

"Ma'am, my name is Bottar Wak." He nodded down to Tamm. "My friend here has been shot with some kind of weapon I've never seen before. It didn't look like that much of a deal, but the damned wound has gotten inflamed and…"

The woman leaned forward and turned her head left to look down the hall before doing a quick 180 degree turn and staring in the other direction. Seemingly satisfied, she looked at Raytaan. "Get them into the front room, and I'll be with you directly."

With that, she vanished into the gloomy interior of her apartment. Shaking his head, Raytaan led them down a short hallway to a surprisingly clean room.

"Put her there and let's get her pants off," Raytaan instructed as he pointed to a stainless steel table in the center of the room.

Bottar did as told and started to unbuckled Tamm's belt when his friend moved in with scissors and began cutting away at the pants.

"No time for niceties," he said. "Auntie'll be back in a moment and she's not to be kept waiting."

"You've helped her before?"

Raytaan nodded. "When I'm not with the kids, I help her out."

Setting the scissors aside, he pulled the cut-up pants out from under Tamm and tossed them into a bin behind the table.

"It's mostly delivering babies, but we do get the occasional bullet wound or broken bone."

"You should go to school and take up medicine."

Raytaan shook his head while working Bottar's bandage off the wound. "Can't afford it and don't need it. I'll learn more from Auntie Bezzle than I'd ever get out of a school book."

As the cloth came off the injured spot, Bottar flinched, feeling bile rise up in his throat. The center of the original injury was now a black bubbling goo. All around it, the skin was dark blue with streaks of red.

Raytaan shook his head. "I've seen lots of wounds, but nothing like this."

Bottar turned away, taking a deep breath and letting it out slowly. "It's hard to believe that happened only an hour ago."

Raytaan started to say something, but was cut short when Auntie Bezzle burst into the room, her arms filled with a jumble of equipment.

"You did say it was some kind of ray gun, didn't you?" she asked while dumping her load onto a counter next to the table.

Bottar pulled one of the weapons from his pocket. "Yes, ma'am. This is it, in fact."

Pulling on rubber gloves, she whirled around to look at the device. "KoKo hand weapon," she announced. "Those two-headed shits are the stupidest creatures ever to breed." She pointed at Tamm's wound. "Their weapons mess with the atoms in the skin and bring on this kind of ugliness."

Moving back to the counter, she pulled a stubby, silver rod from the pile of equipment. She then extracted a putty-colored box, and plugged a cable from it into the tube. Moving back to Tamm's side, she pressed a bump on the tube, causing it to hum.

"Straighten out her leg," she said to Raytaan, who did as told.

"Can I do anything to help?" Bottar asked.

Aunt Bezzle shook her head. "I just cleaned this floor. You feel the urge to puke, use the sink."

As the tube moved over the wound, Tamm's body stiffened noticably, though Bottar couldn't see any reaction in her face. Aunt Bezzle waved it back and forth slowly, at first running it up and down the full length of Tamm's leg, but gradually focusing it directly over the wound. As she worked, normal color gradually returned to the area around the injury, but the center stayed black.

"Get me some towels and that goop in the orange container," she commanded.

When Raytaan returned with the requested items, she took the towel and passed the tube to him. "Keep moving this over the wound slowly. I've got to get that black shit out of there."

Frustrated, Bottar danced nervously around them, struggling against an overpowering urge to dive in and help.

"How is it you know about all this stuff?" he asked as she wiped the wound.

She shrugged. "Just do, is all."

"Do you know what's happening?"

She shook her head as she refolded the towel to find a clean spot. "All the people being picked up seem to be from the same group." She pointed to her forehead. "You can tell by the number printed here." She saw Bottar's confused look. "You can't see it?"

He shook his head. "Are Tamm and I part of that group?" When she nodded, he looked surprised. "Are you?"

Continuing to work, she nodded again. "But whatever made the others go to sleep doesn't work on me."

"Why?"

"Don't rightly know, but then I've always been able to see the aliens when other folks couldn't. Some kinda bug in the system, I guess."

"But you've seen them before. Why was this different?"

She shrugged. "Oh, I see 'em from time to time, but when Ray-boy done showed me those buses appearing out of nowhere, I knowed somethin' was up."

"Buses? Appearing out of nowhere?"

She shook her head. "I suppose it does sound kinda strange, but I figure they's a lot more advanced than us, so it stands to reason they can do things we don't understand. Anyway, later on, those buses come up our street and they started takin' people out of their homes. I seen Molly Tesser, across the way, just get up out of bed and go off with them. They took a couple of bus loads from our block alone. I hear they took people from other parts of town too."

At her signal, Raytaan passed her the orange container. With gloved fingers she scooped out a measured amount of gel-like substance and worked it into the wound.

"But you escaped?" Bottar asked.

She shrugged. "I told you those KoKo's was stupid, but they's also a nasty sort of predator. I tell you sure, I ain't goin' to be part of their dinner plans." She barked a humorless laugh. "Shit, I'm only ten years off my release date. I ain't about to let them do me in now."

"Release date? What do you mean?"

She gave Bottar a questioning look. "You can see 'em, right?" He nodded. "Then you must know what's happening here."

"I…uh, no. Not really."

She shook her head slowly. "The aliens call this planet Secor-Alpha Four." She pointed to the ceiling. "They're up there watching over us, messin' with our lives, playing games that only they understand. I guess it makes more sense if you know one thing." Pressing a clean gauze bandage into the wound, she held it in place with strips of tape Raytaan was handing her. "You and your woman is prisoners in the most elaborate jail ever imagined."

71

Ansen Paraka's eyes were closed as he listened to the rhythm of Pana's breathing, but they popped open at the soft sound of bare feet on the stone floor.

"Welcome, Father," he said while slowly turning and bowing to his visitors. "Are you here to see my patient?"

The Shendeah returned the bow. "Is she in danger, Healer?"

Ansen shook his head. "She is strong, quite stable and may well awaken at any moment."

"Then our brother needs your attention."

Baroque held up a hand to stop the healer's approach. "With all respect, Father. Every moment we delay endangers you."

"You can speak while he is attending you," the Shendeah said.

Baroque nodded. "The KokoroTetians will pay any price to possess the key that releases the force I told you about."

"Then we will have to make the price very high," the Shendeah said calmly. "But you will be of no use to anyone if this wound isn't properly dealt with."

Ansen moved in and put a hand on Baroque's shoulder. "Let me help, Brother. You will be healed and back to your adventure before Piquit sets." He looked out the room's only window at the smallest of Angrolicat's six moons. "Your namesake watches over you."

Grinning, Baroque shook his head. "That doesn't give you much time, my friend."

Ansen smiled knowingly. "I'm very good at what I do."

Wat Wat sucked in a breath as Baroque dropped his pants. The handle of a screw driver protruded from the back of his left leg. The tip tented skin in the front.

"Lord that has to hurt," he exclaimed.

Ansen shook his head while pointing to a plaque on the wall titled The Sixteen Holy Virtues. "The eighth Holy Virtue is

Endurance. A warrior must endure pain, and Little Piquit here has always been an exceptional soldier."

"Little Piquit?"

As he examined the wound, Ansen answered, "He may not look it today, but Hammond's Warrior was the smallest of his initiate group."

"So he got picked on a lot?"

Extracting a device from one of the many cabinets surrounding them, Ansen shook his head. "Smaller does not mean weaker. During his initiate training, An' Detertch, which was his given name, was always at the top of his classes, especially in hand-to-hand combat."

Baroque grimaced. "We don't need to dredge up the past."

Ansen laughed. "Humble Brother, I think your friend has the right to know he's keeping company with the only trainee who not only drew blood at his first trial, but managed to do so with all one-hundred of his opponents."

"And more than a few got hits on me as well."

Ansen leaned down to examine the view screen on the device in his hand. "As did this screwdriver, my brother. You're lucky it didn't punch through something vital."

Baroque grimaced. "I didn't see the damned thing on the Koko seat." He waved a hand at the injury. "This happened while we were being attacked by the Maatiirani."

"How're you going to get that out?" Wat Wat asked.

Ansen turned to the questioner. "Like magicians, we healers like to keep some of our techniques secret. It looks like you're going to have to leave."

"But I'll get lost out there."

"I'll have a novice guide you."

"That won't be necessary," a female voice announced from the doorway. "I'd love to show him around."

Wat Wat did a quick spin to see the most beautiful female he had ever set eyes on. In fact, it was her penetrating blue eyes that struck him first.

“Hammond be praised,” he muttered while gawking at the new arrival.

Smiling, Ansen rolled his eyes. “Greetings, Sister Ba’ Tereso. Word travels fast in this temple.”

Wat Wat gave Baroque a questioning look, but his friend’s attention was on the female.

“Hello Husband,” she said with a tone that implied he’d just come back from the grocery store.

“This is your wife?”

Baroque nodded. “The one and only.”

72

"How are we going to approach the planet, Sir," Captain Fakat asked as Saki studied a map of the solar system containing Secor Alpha-Four.

"Has anyone challenged us?"

"No Sir," the captain answered. "With Fleet Commander Brak engaged in a battle with Supreme Commander Khephra, there's enough tension between our species to make everyone cautious of unnecessary snubs. I must say, Sergeant Specialist Akki has done an admirable job of reprogramming our transmitters to make us look like those macabre devils. And no one seems to be questioning that we're here to help fix the damaged arrays."

"Has there been any attempt to send someone out to look us over?"

"None, Sir."

Saki smiled grimly. "Leak some chatter about Pourandian leg lice. The KoKo's are quite susceptible to that kind of infestation, and no one else wants to deal with them either. If anyone asks about the conflict with Khephra, say we've just come from that sector and he's taking quite a beating. Add the usual KoKo blustering and bullshit. Everyone will know you're lying, but that's what they'll be expecting."

The captain's smile slowly transformed to a look of caution. "Just to let you know, Sir. Sub-commander Petish is in charge here. He's no Khephra, but he's a stickler for details and I've never met a more paranoid mind. We won't be able to stay here long before he'll be sending someone down to check us out."

Saki pointed to the fifth planet. "Call central control and tell them we're passing behind this gas giant. Explain the need for our science team to study the unique nature of something or other in its atmosphere. Sergeant Specialist Akki can tell you what chemicals or processes would excite the scientific mind." He looked up at the captain. "After we pass that, keep your approach high," he pointed to a 3-D representation of the solar system, "so this asteroid field will be between us and them for a while. The less time they have to scan our ship for anomalies the longer we'll be able to keep up this charade. Hopefully, by the time they find anything worth questioning, we'll be on our way."

Fakat looked nervous. "I hope you are correct, Sir."

Saki smiled broadly at an soldier he knew had spent most of his career doing administrative work. "A life without risk is hardly one worth living."

The officer nervously adjusted his collar. "This is a little more living than I'm used to, Sir."

"Don't worry, Fakat. I didn't come here to die. If we stick to plan, we'll be in and out before they even know what happened."

The captain looked at the gas giant nearly filling the view screen. "How do we get those people off the planet, Sir?"

"Once we achieve orbit, we'll request permission to send shuttles to the surface to 'reprogram' the Standard Internment Units. We'll use those trips to bring up as many people as we can."

"It'll take days to shuttle them all up."

Saki shook his head. "We'll only need enough crew to fly our ships. The others will stay here until we can sort this out."

"But, Sir? They said the missing internees aren't on the surface."

"That's because they aren't looking for the right thing," Akki announced as he approached the officers. "I did as you instructed, Sub-commander, and they started popping up on the scans."

His face reflecting astonishment, the captain looked from his superior to the sergeant specialist. "I'm sorry. What was that?"

Saki gave the sergeant specialist a steady stare until the non-comm snapped to attention and saluted. Returning the salute, he turned to Fakat.

"The controlling devices built into the Standard Internment Units give off a form of radiation not present in real Humans. Since Sub-commander Petish is working on the assumption that the detainees have been removed from the planet, he hasn't bothered to look for this little clue.

"I had Akki tap into the monitoring station's computer and do a scan of his own."

Fakat turned to Akki. "And?"

"Four-hundred-and-seventy-six life forms that show on normal scans as Human are actually leaking this radiation. We have exact locations and identities of every one of them, Sir."

Saki nodded solemnly. "Which is very handy, since our mobility is going to be very limited."

The captain smiled. "Good job, Sergeant Specialist."

Akki nodded acknowledgment, but didn't return the smile.

"There is something else, Sir."

His smile vanishing, Fakat muttered, "I knew this was going too well."

"Report, Sergeant Specialist," Saki ordered.

"There are also KokoroTetians on the planet and they're not working with Sub-commander Petish's recovery teams. In fact, two of them were recently killed in a firefight with your second wife and Captain Bottar."

Saki's eyes narrowed. "Tamm and Bottar? Are they all right?"

Akki shrugged. "They are together, and our last report has your wife unconscious, but stable. I do not believe they are currently in any danger."

"And what else did you find?"

"The Koko insertion team's mother ship is here as well."

"You found it?" Fakat asked.

Akki shrugged. "It wasn't hard. There's only one place it could be: the magnetic north pole. As low as they are in the atmosphere, regular scans would never see them and the ship is small enough to be missed by visual unless you know what to look for."

"What type of ship is it?"

"I can't identify it, Sir, but it seems to have lots of power and enough cargo space for their purposes."

Looking impatient, Captain Fakat snapped, "Which is?"

Akki's eyes flicked to the view screen, a look of disgust on his face. "According to what we can glean from their transmissions, there are three shuttles on the planet. Their people have been kidnapping both internees and Humans for transport to their own planets where they sell them to the highest bidder."

"There must be some mistake," Fakat protested. "Humans can't live in that environment for more than a few *milli-paks*."

"Captain," Saki said solemnly, as he put a hand on the officer's shoulder. "They aren't slaves. They're food."

73

As Tamm's eyes opened, the sight of Bottar's face aroused the same warm feeling she'd felt when she first awoke after they'd made love. However, like before, her mood changed suddenly as she remembered what had happened.

"What's going on?" she cried while struggling to sit up.

Bottar's hands went quickly to her shoulders and he pushed her back down.

"You're safe for now," he whispered. "But keep it down." He nodded toward a crib on the other side of the room. "They just got the baby to sleep."

Tamm yanked the covers up to see that the only thing she was wearing was the large bandage covering her wound.

At least I've still got a leg to bandage, she thought.

Feeling both relief and embarrassment, she pulled the covers up against her chest and asked, "What is this place?"

Bottar shook his head. "No time to explain right now." He held up a shirt and a large pair of pants. "These are a bit big for you, but you don't want anything rubbing on that wound for a while."

Looking puzzled, she took the clothes and slipped them on under the covers. Finishing, she tossed the blankets aside, and sat up. Bottar took off his own belt, leaned in close and weaved it through the belt loops. As he worked, Tamm felt an embarrassing warmth as thoughts of making love to him made her blush.

She wasn't sure if she was thankful or disappointed when he straightened and simply extended a hand to help her up.

"This is incredible," she laughed while gingerly testing the leg. "The last thing I remember, I wanted someone to cut this damned thing off."

Bottar motioned toward a door. "Come meet your savior."

They walked down a short hallway to another room where Raytaan lounged on a couch, reading a magazine. When they entered, he jumped up and grabbed a pair of shoes from a heater vent.

"Here," he said as he held them out to her. "I cleaned 'em best I could, but they's still a bit stained."

Tamm took the damp shoes. "Thanks. I don't know what to say."

"Say you'll help whack some of those two-headed shits," said someone behind her.

All three turned to face Auntie Bezzle, dressed from head to foot in black. "I'm told they have a dozen testicles. Think they might taste like Rocky Mountain oysters? I'm much partial to Rocky Mountain oysters."

Tamm's jaw dropped. "Who are you?"

"This is the woman who saved your life," Bottar explained. "And she's got some very interesting theories about…well, just about everything to do with this planet."

Tamm raised an eyebrow.

"You'll have to wait 'till later to catch up, honey," Auntie Bezzle stated. "These Kokos got huge butts and all I want to do tonight is kick them clear to hell and back." She smiled crookedly while cocking her head slightly to the left. "OK, maybe we can forget the 'back' part."

When Tamm didn't react, Bottar put a hand on her shoulder. "I know this is coming rather fast, but the gist of it is that if we had gotten into that van, those creatures would have eaten us."

Auntie Bezzle laughed. "But now we got weapons and surprise goin' for us. If we're quick about it, we might even get more weapons before they call up the reserves."

"Yeah, but we ain't got much time," Raytaan added. "They's already huntin' for the two of you."

The older woman moved close to Tamm, gripping her arm with a frail-looking hand that was anything but. "Ray-boy's been askin' around. It seems your son went missin' two days before you come back. Same with your ex."

Tamm's eyes widened. "Fuck!"

Auntie Bezzle let out a whoop. "That's the attitude I'm looking for, honey. Give it to those alien freaks with a laser pistol!"

"I'm in," Tamm exclaimed.

Auntie Bezzle turned to the men. “Get our gear in the van. Missy and I’ll collect the medical supplies.”

As the two women headed down the hall, Auntie Bezzle asked, “That man of yours is quite a hunk. You had him yet?”

Tamm hesitated for a moment, wanting to say no, but realizing her head was nodding. “It’s complicated.”

Her companion laughed. “Oh honey. I’ll take that kind of complicated any day of the week.”

Shaking her head, Tamm stopped and turned to her. “What about my son? Why would they take him?”

Auntie Bezzle shook her head. “How much do you remember about the KokoroTetians?”

Tamm shrugged. “Nothing except they’re disgusting and I never want to let one touch me.”

“That’s instinct talking and it’s a good thing, ‘cause those filthy creatures are as cruel as they come.”

“And my son?” Tamm cried.

The older woman shook her head. “We’ve got an advantage over them there. Oxygen is poison to them, so they can’t kill him here.”

“But we killed two and they didn’t seem to be affected by it.”

“Their skin doesn’t have a problem with it, but it’s murder on their lungs. They wear some kind a’ nose plugs to filter it out. If you ever get in a scrap with one of ‘em, punch their snout hard.”

Tamm nodded. “I think I’ve already done that.”

Nodding, Auntie Bezzle led the way into her surgery. Grabbing a box, she handed it to Tamm.

“Why are we bringing all of this stuff?”

“We’re at war and someone has to fix up the wounded.”

Grabbing another box, the old woman rushed into the hallway to find Raytaan coming their way.

“You found any others?” Auntie Bezzle asked.

The young man nodded. “Sixteen so far. Most can see the aliens for what they are, but it’s kind of freaky. They’re talkin’ ‘bout memories of lots of past lives.”

Tamm nodded. “Bottar and I are experiencing that too.”

Auntie Bezzle looked at Tamm. "That wasn't one of your dreams you was talking about earlier, was it."

Tamm blushed and looked down at her feet. "No, it was real."

Grinning broadly, the old woman winked. "Let's go see if any of these new people will be of any use to us."

74

"How long have you been with my husband?" Ba' Tereso asked with a voice that was as perfectly lyrical as any Wat Wat had ever heard.

They were just outside the temple walls, strolling around a large pond bordered with blooming flowers, birds and insects the likes of which he had never seen. Despite the wonders around him, he couldn't take his eyes off of the tall Shentowin beauty walking beside him.

"Not quite a *druak*, but we've been through some exciting times."

Ba' Tereso looked quickly away, and when she turned back, small tears beaded the corners of her eyes.

"From the beginning, I knew my husband wasn't made for domestic life. Many join our priesthood for the prestige or to improve their self-discipline. Even in this age of religious skeptics, a good many are here to deepen their understanding of our Lord's teachings. My Ba' Roque came because he was only a common soldier and wanted to be a True Warrior of Hammond."

Wat Wat blushed. "I don't wish to be disrespectful, but I've never seen him in that light. I mean, he's smart and all, but he isn't the kind to go looking for a fight."

As Ba' Tereso smiled, her beautiful eyes sparkled and the effect spread across her face like a wave of ecstasy. Wat Wat thought his poor heart would melt into a puddle at his feet.

"There's an ancient saying: 'He who fights for atheism, fights for nothing. And he who fights for God, fights only for himself. Peace comes with the realization that your beliefs are truly your own.'

"Our Lord Hammond doesn't train His warriors to be mindless killers. He values peace and love above all else, but He also believes that fighting for the freedom to believe is the most important fight."

"But if Baroque's always out there doing his warrior thing, do you have another husband here to, uh…you know, cover all the bases?"

Ba' Tereso giggled musically while shaking her head. "Most outsiders aren't aware that the correct pronunciation of my husband's name is Ba' Roque. In the ancient language, 'Ba' refers to a special kind of closeness only experienced by two people with a shared soul. We chose it as our common name because Ba' Roque has always been my only true love and I his."

"Wow," Wat Wat almost whispered. "Is that common around here?"

She shook her head. "Not as much as Father would like."

Wat Wat's eyes went wide. "Father? As in the Shendeah?"

She nodded.

"And what does he think of his wandering son-in-law?"

Ba' Tereso giggled. "He couldn't be more proud."

75

"Excuse Sir," Brak's aide said while peeking both heads around his office door. "Senator Addy here to see you."

Brak tore a chunk of flesh from a Human leg and scowled at the aide. "Can't you see We in middle of lunch? This stuff never as good reheated."

"Sorry, Brak," Addy said sarcastically while pushing Styxx aside with his belly. "You preparing to lose battle and it time for change of strategy."

"Lose battle?" he asked angrily. "That devil, Khephra is running and We be toasting over his carcass very soon now."

Addy sighed. "Do you ever go to communications room and listen to what actually be happening, maybe?"

Simultaneously biting off two more hunks of flesh, Brak shook his heads. "Pshaw," he growled through his food. "Flunkies do that for us."

Addy shook his heads. "You mean those who know you'll cut off useless heads if they bring bad news, maybe?"

Brak grunted loudly. "It makes our captains less inclined to lose battles."

Addy frowned. "Or more apt to lie when fleeing for lives."

"What you mean, maybe?"

"We just spoke with captains of silly armada you send to surrender to Khephra."

"We do nothing of kind!"

"And doing nothing lost you ten light cruisers, while other captains shit collective drawers and run screaming all way back."

"That be Antrakan crap," Brak protested. "Our fleet kick sorry excuse for supreme commander all over near-space and back."

"And when do glorious victory happen?"

"First encounter be two *pak* ago." Brak held up a batch of papers. "Our morning report show he got only four battleships and be running for life."

"Who from, maybe?"

"What say?"

Addy sniffed lightly, like a predator about to finish his prey and flashed two mouthfuls of razor sharp teeth. "If We just visit with all surviving captains of armada, who be chasing Khephra all over near-space and back?"

Brak froze at his desk, both mouths hanging open in shock.

"What you mean, you visit with armada captains?"

Smiling wickedly, Addy moved in and leaned over the monitor to Brak's left.

"We show you," he said while pressing several keys on the console. A 3-D image of a battleship appeared on the screen. "Recognize ship?" He paused while Brak glared at the screen. "Maybe we point out that station behind him be…"

"We see ID marking," Brak yelled. "What he do there?"

Addy shook his heads. "Let us see if We can explain."

Reaching over, he pressed several more keys. "This recorded at communications office, day before yesterday."

"This be Captain Kornan. We be in full retreat. Khephra got stealth technology and we not be seeing his ships. Send reinforcements! Send whole fleet! He gotta be right on our asses but can't see him. Please help! Please…"

Addy cut off the message. "Sorry Fleet Commander, but We not feeling same level of arousal over such resounding…" He leaned both heads close to Brak's. "…defeat!"

"But…but…but," Brak repeated as he struggled to grasp the situation. "There be no hint of this tragedy. No one peep word to us."

"As We hear, your orderly tell you when he wake you."

Brak shook his head. "But that fool is idiot. We rarely listen to what he say."

Addy sighed. "And watch commander say you not listen to him either."

"He liar and thief," Brak protested. "We not ever trust that person."

"And yet, you make him watch commander. Why so?"

"Well…uh, he got family connections."

"Nice try, Brak, but watch commander be Sunder class. What kinds of family connections do such impoverished peoples have?"

Brak's heads were swiveling in opposite directions looking for a quick way out, but before he could react, Addy sighed, "We be tired of this, maybe?"

Pulling out his pistol, he put a single bullet in each of the Fleet Commander's foreheads and watched smugly as the dead KokoroTetian's snouts hit the desk with a double thump.

Moving around the desk, he pushed one of Brak's inert hands aside, and pressed an icon. While waiting for Styxx to peek through the door, he took a nibble on the leg Brak had dropped.

"Hmmm," he murmured. "Human not so bad, maybe?"

"Sir?" Styxx asked as he appeared

Addy pointed to Brak's slumped form. "We be Fleet Commander now. Get this body in cooler. We deal with it later."

Moving to the desk, Styxx stared down at the body. "Was lead bullets you use, Sir?"

Addy shrugged. "Some of brain can be salvaged, maybe."

Drool dripped from the corner of Styxx's mouth. "Not need refrigeration. If We call chef now, he be ready for dinner, Sir."

Addy shook his head. "Supreme Commander Khephra almost here. We gotta move fast, if we to have chance." He pointed to Brak's body. "Unlike this useless lump, We intend to use our ten-to-one advantage to add even more variety to next meal."

"You want all captains come in for conference, maybe?"

Addy shook his head. "No time. We be calling each personally."

"Will that be all, Sir?"

Addy raised a finger. "Another thing. Brak have ornamental vessel, shaped like pyramid, with lots'a jewels and glyph carvings on surface. Do you know where that be, maybe?"

Styxx nodded eagerly.

"Bring to us right away quickly."

"Yes, Sir," Styxx responded as he started to leave.

"Oh, and Styxx. This be very important, maybe?"

"Yes, Sir?"

"Whatever you do, don't let vessel slip through fingers."

76

"Sir," the communications officer called as Khephra entered the bridge. "I'm getting a voice-only communication coming from the ship we planted with the retreating Kokos."

"Where is he located?" the supreme commander asked as he looked up at the image of the dense nebula filling the main view screen.

"They're on our port side, just outside of visual range," the scan officer answered. "Currently, all of the Koko ships are on the planet side of the nebula, so we can't see his exact position."

"And none of the ships with him can see us," Khephra said solemnly. "Put him through to my station."

There was a slight pause before the communications officer said, "He's all yours, Sir."

"Khephra here," the supreme commander hailed as he sat at his console.

"Sir, I can't talk long, so I'll be brief," the other side responded. "Something has changed here. Brak is repositioning his ships."

"Any hint as to why?" Khephra asked as he watched the upcoming nebula.

"Not at present, Sir, but he's setting up sentries and guard posts beyond his original perimeter. He's also bolstering the region facing the nebula. If you come through that way, you'll be flying into the densest part of their formation."

"That doesn't sound like Brak. His butt has always been his most precious asset."

"Our group is being repositioned as lookouts at the eastern edge of the nebula. We've been told to challenge anyone who approaches, even if they are KokoroTetian. In addition, we're using a more aggressive formation that is somewhat similar to yours."

The supreme commander shook his head slowly. "Has anyone new arrived in the last *pak* or so?"

"Senator Addy arrived early yesterday. He brought a couple of shuttles of people with him and a *deca-pak* later, two cargo vessels arrived from beyond the nebula. I'm told they contained food and prisoners."

"Prisoners? From where? That bastard hasn't won any battles yet. How could he…" The Supreme Commander stopped and scanned the faces watching him. "Navigation, what occupied planets are directly beyond the nebula from the planet?"

The officer checked his screens before turning back to his commander. "That area of space is pretty barren, Sir. The only occupied planet is…"

"Secor-Alpha Four." Khephra finished for him. "Damn it. It was Brak who raided that planet. He's been bringing them here as food."

A number of mouths dropped open as the Supreme Commander hesitated for a moment before adding, "Captain, I'm going to assume Senator Addy has taken command of the KokoroTetian fleet. Hold your position while I rethink my strategy. If I decide to withdraw, I'll not do so before we can extract you from that position."

"Yes, Sir," came the enthusiastic response. "We'll await further orders, Sir."

Khephra cut off the transmission and turned to Sub-commander Pheet. "I may have sent Saki into a trap."

"With all due respect, Sir," the sub-commander said. "He is an able leader. He'll do as well as anyone could."

Khephra nodded silently before turning back to the main view screen.

All hands waited for several tense moments before the supreme commander turned to his communications officer. "How long before Captain Pike reaches their defenses?"

"His last communication put it at one *deca-pak,* Sir, but the nebula's radiation is interfering with our transmissions. He fell out of contact twenty-five *milli-paks* after that update."

Khephra turned to his sub-commander. "Take us under the nebula at full throttle. We've got some catching up to do."

"But Sir, there's nothing down there to hide us," Pheet protested. "We'll be horribly exposed."

Khephra shook his head. "You know, there's one thing I've learned about people who've lived all their lives on planets, as Senator Addy has. They tend to be afflicted with two-dimensional thinking."

"But after we come out from under the nebula, we'll have quite a ways to go before engaging their fleet. Surely their proximity alarms will pick us up before we can engage them."

Khephra smiled. "If I'm right, they won't be paying close attention to those alarms."

"What is your plan, Sir?"

"We're going to provide a little distraction to occupy their attention."

"Distraction? We're out manned."

The Supreme Commander lifted the sleeve on his left arm, displaying four bite marks just above the wrist. "Remember the viper, my friend. It is not adverse to risk."

As Pheet's eyes widened with amazement, Khephra turned to his communications officer. "As soon as you can re-establish contact with Captain Pike, let me know. In the mean time, get me the captain of the light cruiser. I've got some interesting work for him to do."

77

"How are we going to stop those Koko pirates, Sir?" Captain Fakat asked as they settled into orbit over the damaged monitoring stations.

Shaking his head, Saki stared at the screen Akki had configured to show the heat signature of the pirate ship. "I doubt Sub-commander Petish would let us just pop up there and shoot them down, but maybe we can come up from below."

"But all of our shuttles are going to be busy uploading refugees. Why not tell Petish and let his people deal with them."

Saki pointed to the faintly glowing blob that was the pirate's ship. "I have another idea that might allow us to use their own craft against them."

"Sir," someone called from the observation console. "Two cruisers are moving toward our position."

"On screen," Captain Fakat ordered.

Sergeant Specialist Akki rose from his console. "They're going to run a scan on us."

Saki looked up as the main view screen switched from a view of the planet to the two ships moving toward their position.

"That'll make things difficult."

"They've started scanning!" an officer yelled from the observation console.

Saki turned to his captain. "Full shields for all ships and then put us between the lead ship and the rest of ours." He turned to the weapons officer. "Ramp up weapons and open a channel to Petish's ship."

A rising whine emanated from the walls as the communications officer signaled to Saki, who turned to his console just as a face appeared on it.

"What meaning of outrage?" he demanded loudly. "You wanna provoke battle?"

Saki signaled for the other ships to arm their weapons as he turned again to face the surprised person he was addressing.

"No Sir, we were just…"

Saki slammed his hand on the console. "We give help and you threaten us with warships? Get bastards off our back or We blow hole size of Hammond's eye in hulls."

Saki turned to see his other three ships coming about to face the pair.

"Hold your fire," Petish commanded as his face replaced the junior officer's. "This is Sub-commander Petish speaking. Stand down your weapons. No offense was intended."

"We not like being treated as traitor by people We try to help."

Petish glanced quickly to the side before responding, "I'm sorry Captain Broz. There's been a misunderstanding here. I'm sure we can straighten this out without violence."

"Not when two warships scan our vessels."

Petish's face went off screen again and just as it reappeared the two ships began turning away.

"As you can see, our ships are returning to their original positions," he said. "We thought we saw an energy leak from one of your engines and wanted to check it out before reporting it to you."

"And you not think we do our own scans? Officer like you might know better, maybe?"

Petish nodded. "You can rest assured, Captain Broz, that I will look into this offense personally and punish the officer responsible."

Saki signaled for his ships to power down and return to their stations. "In interest of cooperation between our peoples, We accept apology, but your ships keep their distance or We not responsible for what happen."

"I understand, Captain and it won't happen again."

As Petish reached to cut the transmission, Saki raised a finger. "Oh Sub-commander?"

Petish sucked in a deep breath and pulled his hand back. "Yes, Captain?"

"When punishing officers, you be eating them, maybe?"

Petish's eyes widened. "Uh, no Captain. We don't eat our people."

Saki shook his head. "Pity. It have dramatic effect on junior officers when superiors meet such fate. Of course, it also help with food supply on long voyages, you know."

Saki was sure he could see Petish's face turn a darker shade of green as he terminated the connection.

"Good touch," Captain Fatak said as the communications screen went blank.

The sub-commander nodded. "That pretty well assured that neither he nor his officers will want to come here for a meal."

78

Naked as on the day of her birth, Pana fell for what seemed like an eternity, rolling, spinning, tumbling into the endless black void. A chilling air rushed past her body, and even without seeing them, she felt goose-bumps as her toes and fingers grew numb. Her first fear was of hitting the ground, but when quite a bit of time passed and nothing came up to hit her, the fear passed and she found the experience rather tame, dull, unexciting. Damned cold, but boring just the same.

Just as she started to fall asleep, a spot of light appeared in her vision. It was tiny, but intense, and growing larger at an ever increasing pace until it completely filled her vision. When she rolled over, the blackness from which she'd come was still there, infinite and cold.

As she descended toward the brightly-lit surface, it seemed as smooth as a billiard ball with only occasional puffs of yellow light from other objects that passed her and burned up in the atmosphere.

Suddenly, panic rose in her throat as she realized she too would be just burned ashes filtering down to the surface.

"God help me," she cried as miniature patterns began to develop on the surface. In an instant they grew from mere specks to monstrous size.

She waved her arms in a circle to foolishly put her feet below her, as if they would soften the blow. However, since she was falling at close to light speed, there was nothing that could save her. Nothing that is, except…

She struck the ground as though she'd only jumped from a low stool, landing in a knee-high white mist that seemed to roll across the surface like low waves over a calm ocean. Other than that, the surface of the star was smooth to the distant horizon.

"What brings you here?" a ghostly voice asked from close behind her.

Cupping hands over exposed breasts, she jerked around to face the speaker, but only found a pair of black spots drifting in the flowing mist.

"What? Who are you?" she asked hesitantly.

Silence greeted her question as the mist rose up her naked thighs. She tried to step clear, but it matched her movement, acting more like a liquid and continuing to rise to her waist, then her chest and up to her neck. It now felt more solid, pushing her one way then the other as though she were standing in surging water.

With only her head exposed, the black spots reappeared. "How did you get here?"

Panic filled her as pressure from the fluid pushed her back and forth. She flailed her arms in an attempt to keep her head above the fluid, but its movements were too unpredictable. A sudden current stripped her feet from beneath her and she went down, holding her breath and struggling to make it back to the surface.

As she slowly floated down, murmurings filled her head. She could not make out any words, but the emotion of the sounds felt like an argument was taking place. She could see no one in the milky liquid, but she felt as though many hands were pushing to keep her off balance.

Just when she was afraid she would drown, she found herself lying on the surface with a wall of liquid around her.

And then the black spots reappeared…and blinked. "I know who you are, but why did you come here," it demanded.

She shook her head and started to rise, now more concerned for her life than her nakedness. "I don't know why I'm here. Where is this?"

The eyes vanished as the liquid pulled further back, forming a tube around her. As she straightened, the black spots appeared on the other side of her.

"You might say this is the edge of the universe," it said sadly. "A place from which we can never return."

"And where is that, exactly?"

The eyes blinked again as most of the liquid pulled back further, leaving a humanoid-shaped blob in which they floated.

"You are on the surface of magnatar, a super-dense neutron star from which nothing but light can escape." The bubble-shaped head shook slowly. "Not even a Life Force can leave here."

Its humanoid shape made her once again conscious of her nakedness. She looked briefly down at her unclothed body, but no longer felt the need to cover herself. At the same moment, her fear vanished.

"And why are you here?"

A sigh -- so sad it made her heart ache -- filled the air as the liquid head shook. "I tried to claim a prize that wasn't mine."

"And what was the prize?" she asked as the liquid around her receded rapidly until it vanished into the horizon.

The bubble creature slowly melted into the star's surface until only the two eyes were left.

"You."

Pana-Tee jerked up in bed, her eyes wide, teeth grinding. Two men sitting in chairs at the foot of her bed, turned to look at her.

"Is she awake this time or is this another phase?" Ba' Roque asked.

Kappa moved closer. "Pana? Are you with us?"

She blinked twice and looked around the room. "Where's my husband."

79

"Sir," Styxx called while leaning through the partially opened door. "Your appointment be here."

Addy nodded as Lopto, a former KokoroTetian warrior, walked in, his off-balanced gait revealing the absence of several legs. A roughly-truncated stump stood where his left head had been, and the right one tilted noticeably toward the void. After giving the senator a quick bow, he stood and scratched his scarred, rough cheek with the two remaining fingers on his upper-right hand.

"Begging pardon, Sir, but We has something special for you," Lopto announced with a gravelly voice. "We be thinkin', at time like this, Senator could use pet that more than just ornament."

Saying nothing, Addy darkened his console screen, nodded toward the remains of a soldier and gave his full attention.

"As you gotta already know, Sir," Lopto continued with a bow, "We fight in Great War. We give all for cause, Sir, as do all of our comrades, but it just not enough, maybe?"

"We all appreciate sacrifices you make, Lopto," Addy said. "We only wish Antrakans be more generous with medical services and help recover lost body parts."

Lopto shook his remaining head. "Wouldn't take 'em if they did, Sir," he said defiantly. "Them devils be near as likely to suck out Life Force and feed it to Samhain. Ain't no way We let them put hand on us, and We not mind telling, Sir, there be plenty others that feel as We do."

Both of Addy's heads nodded. "And what can We do for you, maybe?"

"Well, Sir, since War, We be training animals, mostly for games, when Antrakans allow 'em. Sometimes, We find beast that warrant, err…special attention." As though on queue, a dog-like creature with iridescent scales and glowing red eyes appeared next to him and sat obediently.

"He look like dog, but really be a *Werunke*. We call him KonPita-Peck, after illustrious Koko general. You may know, Sir, We had great privilege of serving as his aide right up until…" Scowling, he gently touched his truncated stump, and looked down at the creature. "KonPita here have his unpredictable nature, but he be fiercely loyal to his master."

"And you wanna make us his master?"

When Lopto whistled twice, the creature's head snapped up and watched his hands flutter. After several quick movements Addy found incomprehensible, Lopto pointed at the senator and nodded. Long sharp claws on three pairs of feet clicked against the floor's tiles as the *Werunke* padded noisily to his new master, sat quietly in front of him and looked up expectantly.

Though he tried not to, Addy gulped reflexively as the creature's mouth opened, showing sharp, glistening teeth that curved back towards his throat. Its muscular forelegs jerked nervously as a club of a tail scratched an arc into the floor's finish. Of the four scale-plated ears on his head, two faced forward and the remainder to the rear, making it clear that, even though its eyes were on him, it was listening to everything around it.

"Whistle twice to get attention." Lopto held up one crooked finger. "One finger for greeting stranger friendly-like; two mean confront and hold at bay. For him to kill, shake fist and point." He chuckled wryly. "He do it quick-like."

"Do other fingers mean anything, maybe?" Addy asked while eyeing the dog nervously.

Lopto nodded. "Yes, Sir. Hold up two finger and point to ground to make sit. Same movement with all six finger make him lie down. That be enough for now, maybe?"

Addy jerked his eyes from the creature to the old warrior. "For now?"

Lopto looked down at the *Werunke*. "We hear Khephra be coming." He slowly lifted his eyes to meet Addy's. "He crafty devil, that one, with more lives than Hammond himself. If his people get past your clever defenses, Kon make short work of them."

"Does he eat his prey, maybe?" Addy asked because he could not think of anything else.

Lopto shook his head. "Only what you say is his, Sir. We not have dog that interfere with post-battle feast."

Addy looked back down at the beast. "One more thing, Lopto? If We sic on someone, and then change mind, how We make him stop?"

Lopto shook his head again. "That not be good idea, Sir, 'cause he faster than light when put on someone." He looked at the dog as well. "To stop anything he do, just whistle twice and yell 'box'."

Addy's faces showed confusion as he looked at the old warrior. "Box?"

Lopto smiled while nodding. "Well, Sir. We not make it 'stop' 'cause that probably what victim screaming just before he rip throat out. Just yell 'box', Sir and he run right back to you."

"Err, uh, thank you, Lopto," Addy said uncertainly. "We sure he come to good use, if need arise."

"You can count on him, Sir," Lopto said proudly. "He best We ever work with."

"Where you find such beast, maybe?" Addy asked as Lopto turned to leave.

"Oh, We get him off first trainer's estate, Sir."

"First trainer?"

Lopto nodded eagerly. "Yes, Sir. It common with *Werunke*."

"What, uh, be common, maybe?"

"They only found in wild. Can't be bred in captivity," Lopto explained, "so they most always kill first trainer. We suppose that why they be so rare, Sir. Who the hell want to be first? Right?"

"Yes," Addy responded nervously as he took a quick step away from the panting beast. "Perfectly."

Lopto laughed. "Worry not 'bout a thing, Sir. You safe with him as can be. Just keep him fed proper, which We guess not be problem, at least for near future."

"It not?"

"A battle be coming, Sir. We remember Khephra's lot ain't all that tasty, but this little feller eat pretty much anything. Just toss him a body and he be happy puppy for whole day."

Addy faked a laugh he certainly didn't feel, "Oh really?" he said while moving to the old warrior.

Lopto opened the door and paused. "You have question, Sir, just holler. We be down in refuse bins, sortin' things out." He shook his head. "It sometimes surprise us what people throw out these days. Maybe two-hundred people can eat on stuff we pull from them bins. It might be a bit rotten, but poor don't much care. It better than nothing, that be sure."

Addy muttered what he thought was appropriate as he gently shoved Lopto out the door. Pushing it closed, he leaned his heads against the polished wood and took a deep breath to collect himself. As he exhaled, the sound of retching made him do a quick spin to see the dog puking up a bone.

Addy gasped as he realized it was a leg bone.

A KokoroTetian leg bone.

80

"Your friend is awake and waiting for you," the Shendeah said without looking up from a desk as simple and unadorned as its user.

Ba' Roque moved quietly through the dimly lit room, feeling the familiar coldness of the stone walls and floor.

His fingers still running over Braille tablets before him, the Shendeah lifted his head. "You are leaving again so soon?"

The warrior bowed low. "My primary duty is to protect Hammond and all he holds precious."

Lifting his hands, Ba' Roque's superior smiled sadly. "No one can harm our Lord. He is power itself."

The warrior straightened. "As long as we remain here, there are many who will attempt to steal what we possess. You know that not everyone is as limited as the Maatiirani."

The Shendeah sighed. "Then we will help you in any way we can."

"I need the Ship of Horritiff."

For a long moment, the Shendeah said nothing, but when he finally spoke, his tone was cautious. "What do you know that your comrades don't?"

It was Ba' Roque's turn to pause. "I won't waste time with details. I recently learned that KokoroTetian pirates planned to kidnap Saki N-Tschester and his mate. The Kokos are not skilled at restoring Life Forces to bodies, so it wasn't hard to get my team hired to do it. Though they only retrieved the one called Pana-tee, it was during her transfer that I discovered another Life Force intertwined with hers."

"Another Antrakan?"

The warrior shook his head. "None that I've ever seen, but the Kokos weren't surprised."

"You told them?"

"No, but I overheard their doctors talking about it."

"And why did this make you suspicious that a great power was involved?"

"Before their imprisonment, Saki and I served together with the then General Khephra. Saki was a brilliant commander, tough, but scrupulously honest. I, along with the entire division serving under him, refused to believe he had done this thing."

"The destruction of the planet Ooertfael?"

"Yes, My Father," Ba' Roque stated emphatically. "And now, with people fighting over them, I have to believe their trial was a sham to cover up something far more dangerous."

"And as the cover-up is being exposed, our Ba' Roque is in the middle of it."

The warrior dipped his head and bowed. "A small player in a larger scheme, Shendeah."

"Two small players," said someone behind them.

Ba' Roque whirled around to find his wife's beautiful blue eyes fixed on him. However, it wasn't just her eyes that caught his attention. She was wearing the uniform of a Warrior of Hammond.

81

"Sir," the navigator called. "We are approaching the edge of the nebula. In twenty-five *milli-paks* we'll be in sensor range of the enemy.

Khephra looked as his screen a moment longer before speaking, "Fire control: launch the missiles. Detonation in exactly twenty-four *milli-paks*."

Captain Praetor shook his head. "Do you really think this will work?"

The supreme commander shrugged. "I'm counting on the Koko's overwhelming sense of self-preservation. With our embedded light cruiser leaking rumors of our coming straight through the nebula, it's my guess that's where most of them will be looking."

"But they'll surely have automated systems scanning in every direction," Praetor warned.

"And I'm going to give them something that they'll think is more important than those beeping alarms."

"Exploding missiles?"

"Even better than that, Captain."

"Sir?"

"Absolutely nothing."

82

"Sir?"

"What it this time?" the irritated KokoroTetian captain snapped at his communications officer.

"Another report say enemy attacking very soon."

The captain wiped sweat off his brows and grunted. "Same story for last two *paks* and yet nothing. Where be this great supreme commander?"

When the question was met with total silence, he grunted and looked down at his screen.

"With planet so close to nebula, don't it make sense to invent way to see into damned thing, maybe?"

Before anyone could answer, a bright light flashed in the middle of the nebula. Instantly, all twenty-two members of the bridge crew froze as their forty-four heads jerked around to face the screen. When a small opening the size of a battleship appeared in the dust, forty-four mouths gasped and eighty-eight eyes bulged.

"He comes!" someone's whisper shouted in the intense silence on the bridge.

Suddenly an additional flash appeared on each side of the first with the dust parting just as before, but again, nothing appeared in the openings.

"They invisible," another person cried just before the bridge erupted in a cacophony of orders, wails, counter orders and rattling chairs. In fact, it was so noisy and confusing that no one even noticed the proximity alarms beeping on their consoles.

To Khephra's credit, this same scenario played out on each and every ship in the KokoroTetian fleet.

83

Supreme Commander Khephra's battle group came out from under the nebula's cover at close to light speed and found the enemy fleet spread out in a broad, off-balanced disk shape that filled their view screen. Though the bulk of the battleships were close to the nebula itself, they seemed to be moving away from it.

Khephra turned to the communications officer. "What's going on up there?"

"I'm hearing a lot of chatter," the officer said with a smile. "As best I can make out, our little trick worked."

Khephra smiled. "Send a tightly focused beam to Captain Pike. He is to engage the enemy now."

Sub-commander Pheet looked at the view screen. "I can't believe that no one in that entire fleet will be looking our way."

Khephra shook his head. "If I've learned anything about Kokos, it's that they've turned blind panic into an art form."

"What about the light cruiser we have on the other side?" Pheet asked. "Aren't we going to send him a signal as well?"

"Too risky. He's so close to the other ships, we wouldn't be able to stop you from piggybacking a signal on our transmission."

Pheet's face went pale. "What?"

Khephra looked at the surveillance officer, who nodded sadly. Sighing, he turned to the Marine station and signaled the sergeant over.

Before Pheet could react, Khephra's right hand shot out, grabbed his jacket and yanked it open. Pheet pulled back, reflexively grabbing the now-exposed transmitter attached to his blouse. With a growl, Khephra covered the junior officer's hand with his own, crushing the edges of the device into his fingers. As Pheet cried out, the supreme commander yanked the bleeding hand toward him while slamming a fist into Pheet's stomach, doubling him over.

The Marine sergeant held Pheet as Khephra stripped away the transmitter.

"I think you and Addy have talked enough."

Gasping, Pheet jerked his head from side to side. "This is treason. The Councils are near a negotiated settlement with the Kokos. What you're doing will destroy that."

Khephra growled angrily. "Well, your little group of conspirators has already been rounded up. You can discuss this to your heart's content in the brig."

The supreme commander jerked his head toward the door, but as the sergeant yanked Pheet off the bridge, he cried, "You are betraying your people."

After the door closed, Khephra commanded, "Marine guard, at the ready!"

As the remaining eleven Marines hurried into position behind their leader, the Supreme Commander tossed the disabled transmitter onto his console and turned back to the remaining crew.

"Everyone on the bridge, except navigation, report to this station on the double!"

Without hesitation, the crew rushed to where Khephra pointed as the Marines activated their weapons.

As the last of the crew members lined up and snapped to attention, the Supreme Commander spoke,

"We will soon be engaged with a deadly enemy and I want all of you to be absolutely certain you can trust your fellow officers." He walked in front of the group. "No one, including myself, will be excused from this search for contraband equipment."

Khephra stepped over to the first Marine and gave him the signal to proceed. The soldier hesitated only a moment before running a scanning bar up and down both sides of the Supreme Commander's body. Once done, he turned toward another Marine monitoring the process on his screen.

"Supreme Commander Khephra is clean, Sir."

Khephra nodded and motioned for the next officer to step forward. The soldier marched quickly to where his commander had been standing, saluted him and then stood at attention while being scanned. When he was cleared, Khephra returned the salute and ordered him back to his station. Every other bridge officer repeated the first officer's steps exactly.

When they were all cleared, Khephra returned to his station. "Please have Major Phaa report to me immediately."

"Yes Sir."

"Time to initial contact?"

"Two-hundred-thirty-five *micro-paks*, Sir."

"Navigator, keep us on track for that planet. Communications! Keep our companions in close formation and let them know of the time left."

The main bridge door opened behind Khephra. "Major Phaa reporting, Sir."

Khephra kept his eyes on his own console's screens while Phaa's attention went straight to the planet growing ever larger on the main screen. "Is your team ready for deployment, Major?"

"As ordered, Sir."

Khephra turned to Phaa. "I thought you should know, we think Senator Addy has taken over command of the enemy fleet. It may be a rougher ride than we anticipated to your demarcation point."

Phaa smiled. "Just get me close, Sir. I'll take care of the rest."

Khephra nodded. "Kick butt, soldier."

"With pleasure, Sir," Phaa responded while saluting.

"Dismissed, Major."

"Yes Sir."

His face showing mixed emotions, Khephra watched the Major leave the bridge. When the door hissed close, he turned back to his console and shouted more instructions to his crew.

84

"Sir, the holding bays have been properly oxygenated for the internees," Captain Fatak announced as Saki worked at his command desk. "Additional shield generators have been added to help with radiation and a dozen space suits have been configured for Human use."

The sub-commander nodded. "Make sure the first people brought up are engineers. We have to appear to be making some kind of progress on these arrays or this is all going to fall apart."

"Understood, Sir, but with all our pilots running shuttles, who is going to go after the Koko pirates?"

"I'm pretty sure that would be me," a female voice announced from behind them.

Both men turned to find Pana wearing a pilot's uniform.

"Good Lord, Pana," Saki exclaimed as he rushed to embrace her.

After quickly hugging her husband, Pana turned to Kappa, Ba' Roque, Ba' Tereso and Wat Wat standing just inside the doorway. "You have my friends to thank for my freedom."

Saki followed her gaze. "But how did you get here without being seen?"

Pana shrugged. "The priests of Hammond have a little wonder-ship that's hard to describe."

Saki barked a laugh. "We sure could use a ship like that."

Ba' Roque stepped forward. "I'm afraid it had to return to Angrolicat. My people have a pressing need for it."

Unable to hide his obvious excitement, Saki pulled Pana aside, speaking in hushed tones as her four companions moved next to Fatak.

"Is there any way we can contact Supreme Commander Khephra?" Kappa asked in a loud whisper.

The captain shook his head. "I'm afraid any communications is out of the question right now."

"But this is of vital importance. He doesn't know we have his daughter, and...well...it's really important."

The captain shrugged as he waved a hand toward the main screen. "We're in a hostile situation. Sending such a message would seriously compromise us."

"Shit," Wat Wat laughed. "I could get a dozen messages past the likes of them with one mini-microprocessor tied behind my back."

Fakat shook his head. "That will be for Sub-commander Saki to decide."

All heads turned toward the couple as Pana jerked back from her husband. "I'd rather drink Ceratha's fiery spit!"

Saki shook his head. "But we don't yet know if you're fully..."

"It doesn't matter," his wife argued. "You don't have anyone else for the job."

Saki waved a hand at her companions. "Any one of your team is quite capable of it."

Pana shook her head. "You're only saying no because I'm your wife."

Saki tried to shake his head, but it wouldn't move. His mind struggled for a good argument, but he knew she'd find a way to counter it.

"Sir," the communications officer called. "Our shuttle teams have made contact with people on the planet. They've been mounting a resistance against the pirates."

Everyone jerked around to face the officer.

"Are they our people?" Fakat asked.

"Most are, and their memories are returning."

"Do they know where the pirate's transport ships are?" Saki asked.

The communications officer turned to his console and asked several questions before turning back. "Yes Sir, and it appears there are three of them."

"We'll need all three," Pana announced as she grabbed Saki's arm.

When he started to shake his head, she pleaded, "You've got to let me do this. That pirate ship will get me to my father faster than anything you have."

Saki looked shocked. "What?"

"There's no time to explain, but I've got to get to him before it's too late."

"Too late for what?" Saki demanded.

Pana gripped tighter. "Do you know what caused the Big Bang?"

His head shook slowly as he scowled. "Pana. This is no time for..."

"Because I do," she interrupted.

"You what? How?"

"It is one of my most ancient memories."

Saki looked at the blank faces around him before turning back to his wife. "And what caused the Big Bang?"

"Me!"

85

Addy just finished dictating a memo when the room reverberated with a deep grumbling roar.

"What in Ceratha's Name?" he cried while pointing at the young assistant he'd been dictating to. "Stitto. Get Styxx."

As the female rushed into the outer office, her boss reached for his communications console.

"What that?" he asked when an officer's confused faces appeared on the screen.

"We not know, Sir," the left face responded as the right one turned to speak to someone next to him.

Before Addy's eyes, the ceiling of the communications station exploded downward and the screen went blank.

Stitto returned just as he was screaming, "Styxx!"

"He be coming, Sir," she announced as the aide entered the room.

Seeing someone new enter, KonPita rose to his feet, a growl rumbling deep in his throat.

When his aide stopped at the doorway, Addy resisted the urge to jump away from the creature, whistled twice and cried, "Box! Stupid beast."

Despite the creature's quick drop back to the floor, Styxx remained at the office doorway. "Sir?"

Addy waved all four arms in the air. "We just see communications room destroyed. What happening?"

As Styxx opened his mouth to speak, the doorway exploded into the room. Addy was knocked backwards and instinctively rolled under his desk as debris rained down. When the noise dissipated, he heard panting behind him and turned one head to find KonPita's toothy muzzle only centimeters from his own.

"Hammond's sweet ass," he screamed while scrambling away from the beast.

Choking on the smoke and dust filling his office, he slowly stood to find everything that had been on his desk was now pushed into a pile against his sofa. Sifting through the mess, he extracted his communicator.

"Commander Gox," he yelled into the device. "What be going on?"

A gray face appeared on the mini-screen of his communicator. "We not know how he get through, Sir. Everybody watch for him, just as you command. His ships just appear from nowhere. It gotta be new stealth technology we see earlier."

"He not have…" Addy stopped as another explosion shook the room. "What you doing about him now?"

"We pull back when he come through nebula. That pack us pretty tight near planet. We try moving battleships into position, but other ships and heavy debris be in way, which make much trouble maneuvering."

"Debris? What you talk about?"

"He already destroy six of innermost light cruisers. There be debris everywhere and it hard to see what's what."

"Blast away at him. You gotta hit something."

"We have, Sir, but…well, only thing we hit is…your compound…maybe?"

"You blow up our office?"

Both faces on the screen released anguished cries. "That be true, Sir."

"So what Khephra doing?"

"Since creating debris field, he damage or destroy five more light cruisers and disable a battleship. Our right flank collapses as his ships surprise them. All other divisions pulling back to a better defensive position."

"You mean running like cowed dogs, maybe?" Addy growled.

"They be invisible! We not see them even after ships starting to explode."

"He have only six ships," Addy screamed. "How he attack on three fronts at same time?"

The commander shook his heads. "Our information gotta be wrong, maybe? We gotta retreat until we can better assess situation."

Addy shook his heads as his eyes fell on Styxx's crumpled body lying in a pile of shattered pieces of door and furniture. "And how we get off damned planet if enemy control skies?"

The silence of Gox's response was more unnerving than the explosions that earlier destroyed his office.

Footsteps yanked Addy's attention from the communicator. His eyes first went to Stitto as she rose unsteadily from the debris. Then a noise in the outer office pulled both his heads in that direction.

"Sons of bitch," he exclaimed under his breath while searching the room for a weapon.

As the footsteps drew nearer, Addy nearly fell over the panting KonPita.

Giving two sharp whistles, the senator shook his fist, and pointed a finger at the shadows moving across the far wall outside his office. KonPita sucked in his wagging tongue and jumped a pile of debris. He had no sooner vanished into the outer office than Addy heard screams and laser fire.

"Commander," he whispered into the communicator while waving Stitto toward the back of the office. "We run now, but if you not get us out soon, Khephra eat us all for dinner."

Without waiting for a response, the already running Addy shut off the device and pushed Stitto through the back door of his office. Once outside, he looked at the bright exit sign pointing left and tugged his companion in the other direction.

86

Fondling his long thick braid of jet-black hair, festooned with dozens of the teeth of his unfortunate victims, Maatiirani Commander Ehar stared at the long-range display and muttered to his companion, "What in Ya Ya's names are those stupid creatures up to?"

His brother, Uhua's head snapped around, the thick, rope-like muscles in his neck flexing nervously under skin the color and texture of scraped tendon. After making several quick motions with his hands -- somewhat equivalent to the Human's Christian sign of the cross -- he complained,

"Blasphemy will bring damnation on us." He stabbed at the dual suns shining through the window. "They hear all."

Ehar's reddish-amber eyes narrowed as he made the required motions of apology toward the suns. "Surely the twin Gods will forgive my frustration when those Antrakan dogs deny us war and yet can't stop fighting among themselves. The least they could do is invite us in."

Uhua shook his head and looked down at his shorter brother.

"They might just be holding war games."

Laughing derisively, Ehar pointed a claw-tipped finger at the screen. "These scans show explosions consistent with a real battle."

Uhua shrugged. "You know scans can be misleading. Remember the one that showed a power source larger than a trillion suns at the edge of Koko space?"

Crisscrossed scars, so plentiful on Ehar's white cheeks they looked like reddish pickup sticks, flexed as he gritted his teeth and glared angrily at the screen.

"One does not easily forget the day of our father's death," he growled. "Lust for that particular revenge has burned in my gut ever since."

"Your desires are mine as well, but it is not to be. Lord Tha-Ya-Ank believes this power source is real and would never allow mobilization of the full fleet."

Ehar shook his head. “There are too many pacifists whispering in Tha-Ya-Ank’s ear. It is time for a purge.”

“Civil war? You can’t be serious!”

His brother laughed heartily while pointing at the screen. “Well, I’d rather fight those pathetic people than our own, but we need bloodshed to keep us strong.”

Uhua sighed. “But a civil war would take too long to sort out.”

Ehar tapped a long, curved claw on the screen. “We could take on these worthless Kokos with our division alone.”

Uhua’s braid of teeth rattled as his head shook. “That’s unwise. The Antrakans will side with them.”

Ehar slapped Uhua hard on the shoulder. “Not if we pick our battles wisely. Our sons need teeth before they can breed. If we don’t do something soon, they’ll be too old to take mates and we’ll have to kill them.”

Uhua laughed dryly, revealing a double row of crystal-clear teeth behind white lips. “Their mothers would bite off our balls.”

Releasing an ear-piercing war cry, Ehar shook a fist at the screen. “Then let’s chew someone else’s balls.”

87

Pheet's eyes wouldn't open, his mouth was as dry as a sand pit and he could hardly lift his head.

"Who's there?" he called as a stomach cramp doubled him over.

When no one answered, he managed to crack open one eye to see a row of round, horizontal bars, each spaced fifteen centimeters apart. As he stared blankly at the bars, a being, so out of focus its features were unrecognizable, walked on the left wall toward him.

As the figure approached, Pheet suddenly realized he was lying down and the whole scene was ninety-degrees out of kilter.

"Ah," the being he now recognized as a corporal, said. "The supreme commander will be pleased to know you're awake."

"Where am I?" Pheet asked without lifting his head.

"Where else, but the brig."

"The brig? Why?"

He tried to rise, but the nauseating throbbing in his head forced him back down.

"You don't remember?" the guard asked incredulously. "I heard it was a pretty dramatic scene."

The ship shook just before Pheet felt himself being pushed to the left, and then down into his cot.

"The ship is maneuvering. Are we in a battle?"

The corporal shook his head. "Oh no," he said adamantly. "I'm not telling you anything, just in case you've figured out a way to get a signal out of this jail cell."

Pheet tried to push himself up, but only managed to reach the sitting position before the ache in his head made him vomit.

The corporal groaned. "You're the spore of Ceratha. You are," he complained. "You'd have to make a mess just before I get off shift."

Pheet slumped back onto his cot, hardly feeling the wetness that seeped through his shirt.

"Don't lay in it, pig," the corporal protested as he yanked the cell door open. "Now you've made your little mess even worse."

He slipped into the cell and tried to sit Pheet up, but the prisoner only threw up again, spraying vomit all over the corporal's pants and boots, and then collapsing onto the spew-covered floor.

He slipped into unconsciousness as the corporal spouted a tightly packed stream of obscenities.

88

"I don't trust these people," Bottar muttered as the spinning disk settled into the open field in front of them.

"Honey," Auntie Bezzle said while leading them toward the vehicle. "They've been a damned site better to us than those two-headed creeps and we need all the help we can get at this point."

As Tamm moved along with the small group toward the shuttle, its disk stopped spinning and a door opened from its bottom. A being, wearing a skin-tight suit with a transparent bubble for the helmet, descended the stairs and approached them.

"Shit," Raytaan cried. "That thing looks like those drawings on the UFO shows."

As they moved to within hearing range, their new ally raised a hand. "Greetings. My name is Pana," its translator squawked flatly. "Auntie Bezzle?"

The elder woman stepped forward. "That'd be me."

"Thank you for helping us. I understand you are aware this planet is a prison." Auntie Bezzle nodded. "For your assistance, we are offering early parole."

Auntie Bezzle pointed to her nephew. "What about him?"

Pana shook her head. "He's not an internee."

"So, if we go, we'll have to leave our families behind?"

Pana tried to shrug inside the heavy suit. "In most cases, yes, but you will be leaving eventually anyway."

The old woman shook her head. "I can't speak for the others, but I'd rather it wasn't my choice."

"As you wish."

Bottar stepped forward. "What do you need us to do?"

"And your name is?"

"Bottar Wak."

"Bottar?" she asked excitedly, but the translator made it a simple statement.

"Yes."

"Is Tammabet Ferrisis with you?"

Hearing a name that sounded very familiar, Tamm stepped forward, looking hesitant. "I think that's me."

"By the Spirit of Hammond, Sister. I'm your sister-by-law, Pana."

"Huh?"

As Pana turned around, another opening appeared in the disk's underside.

"Please, come inside. The shuttle's translator is much more sophisticated than the one in this suit."

"What's a sister-by-law?" Tamm asked.

Tamm saw the edges of Pana thin mouth curve up slightly and wondered if she were smiling

"We are both married to the same person."

She felt her mouth drop open, and quickly snapped it shut. "Are you talking about Saki? Doesn't he know I'm still alive?"

Pana motioned toward the shuttle bay. "Please, Sister. Come inside so we can talk properly."

Tamm looked at Bottar, who himself seemed stunned at the announcement, but before he could say anything, Auntie Bezzle pushed them both toward the shuttle bay.

"You don't remember much about your lives before you was sent here, do you?" Auntie Bezzle asked as they moved inside.

Tamm shook her head as Pana climbed into the shuttle's cockpit. After pulling off her helmet, Pana moved to the window separating the two rooms.

"Tamm, Saki is going to be so excited to see you. He's been worried sick."

Tamm shook her head. "I don't understand. If he knew I was alive, why did he marry you?"

This time Pana's grin was more obvious. "He and I were married for three *druak* before he met you."

As Tamm stared at her sister-by-law in disbelief, Bottar stepped forward. "Uh, what's a *druak*?"

"It's the equivalent of about one-hundred of your years."

"I married your husband?" Tamm asked. "Weren't you upset?"

Pana shook her head. "I was first assistant at your wedding. You are one of the best friends I've ever had."

Tamm's mouth dropped open again as she looked at Bottar, but he was staring at Pana.

"You're over three-hundred years old?"

Pana shook her head. "In terms of your time frame, I am much older than that. The lifespan of Humans is incredibly short."

"Damn," Auntie Bezzle exclaimed. "I want whatever drugs you're taking."

Pana turned away from the window and spoke to someone in the cabin. After a moment, she turned back.

"Tamm, I'm sorry, but this reunion will have to wait." She looked at Auntie Bezzle. "I need to find those alien shuttles. Any ideas?"

The old woman nodded. "They keep them in a warehouse in an abandoned coal-mining town about twenty miles from here. One of the people they kidnapped escaped from there."

"Can you show me on a map?"

Without answering, the old woman stepped out of the shuttle and waved at a small group standing a short distance away. When they moved to her, she ushered six of them into the shuttle and ordered the others back.

After everyone was in, she turned to Pana. "We're going to do more than that," she said while waving a hand at the people behind her. "This is my assault team. Since we don't need those clumsy suits you wear, we can move faster and quieter."

She reached into her pocket and pulled out a KokoroTetian weapon. "Got any more of these? They're quieter and make a bigger splash than bullets."

Pana hesitated. "We'll need them all back when this is over."

Auntie Bezzle laughed. "You think I want these loose in my neighborhood? Those stupid gang bangers and junkies don't need something that can level a city block. They do enough damage with what they have."

Turning briefly to pat the shuttle pilot on the shoulder, Pana nodded as the craft shuddered and began rising. Soon after the shuttle-bay doors closed, the craft moved forward and banked into a turn.

Auntie Bezzle moved up to the window and pointed. “Fly past that water tower, but stay low going over the hill. If we keep down, they might not see us.”

“What would be the best approach angle?” the pilot asked.

“There’s a low ridge to their east. If you can get close to the top of it, we shouldn’t have to cover much ground on foot.” Auntie Bezzle nodded toward the floor. “That’s a good thing too, ‘cause these feet of mine don’t take as much punishment as they used to.”

On the far side of the bay, Tamm turned a confused face to Bottar.

“I’m married to a bigamist and his other wife is my best friend.” She shook her head. “Dear God, this is weird.”

Bottar shrugged. “At least they haven’t tried to eat us.”

Tamm barked a mirthless laugh. “You’re a lot of help.”

“Are you sure you’re up for this?” he asked. “People might be shooting at us in a few minutes, and we need to focus on getting the job done.”

“Don’t worry about that. My son’s in there somewhere. I’ll kill anyone who gets in my way.”

“That’s my girl,” he said while kissing her forehead.

“Attention,” a voice boomed in the bay. “We’ll be setting down in…two of your minutes.”

Pana appeared in the window. “I’m going to slide a box of weapons through the door. There are simple instructions on how to use them under the lid. Please note the instructions for arming and disarming of the weapon. Don’t arm until after you disembark, as I don’t want any discharging prematurely.”

She leaned down for a moment before returning to the window. “Oh, and I also included four hand-held communicators.

There are no buttons to press, just squeeze the box and the display will show you are transmitting. When you are done speaking, just relax your hand and it will stop.”

Pana vanished from the window, the door slid part-way open and the promised box appeared. Auntie Bezzle and Raytaan moved in and pulled the box into the center of the bay. The older woman started reading instructions as her nephew tried to open the box.

She slapped his wrist. “Don’t go touching anything until we learn how to use ‘em.”

Raytaan rocked back on his heals and scowled at her. “Well then, tell us what we need to know.”

After reading for a moment, she laughed. “This is really easy.”

Pulling off the lid, she grabbed a weapon and did a quick demonstration while giving Pana occasional glances for confirmation. Once done, she and Raytaan distributed them to the others. By the time she handed the last two to Bottar and Tamm, the craft was landing.

Pana appeared in the window again. “We don’t think they are aware of our presence, but activate your weapons once you’re outside the bay and be prepared to defend yourself at any time. These Kokos are stupid beasts, but as my father used to say, ‘A venomous snake may lack our intelligence, but it can still kill.’”

“I’ve dealt with enough snakes in my day,” Auntie Bezzle declared. “Tell your pappy we get the message.”

Tamm watched as Pana nodded and waved them out of the bay. She wasn’t sure if she should love her or hate her. However, when her feet hit the ground, her thoughts went to her son, and she felt a sudden surge of energy. Hurrying to the top of the ridge, she was soon one of ten heads peering over the ridge top at the dark warehouse below.

“What do ya think?” Auntie Bezzle asked as she scanned the area.

“I think we should split into two teams,” Tamm answered. “Five of us will enter via the back. Since only a few lights are on, it’s quite possible the place is empty or they’re asleep. If there’s someone in there, we might be able to surprise them.” She squeezed the communicator in her hand. “Pana? How do we lower the volume on these things?”

"There is no volume, Sister," Pana answered. "Just speak softly."

"What about the light from the screen?"

"It is narrowly focused, and only transmits to the person holding the unit. Unless you point the screen in someone's direction, they won't see it."

Tamm held the communicator at an angle and squeezed the device. No light gave away its position. Rotating it back, the light suddenly reappeared.

Bottar leaned over her shoulder. "You know, I think I knew that."

Tamm nodded distractedly. "Yeah. Me too."

"I'll take the rest of us around to the front," Auntie Bezzle announced. "I'm thinkin' we should wait until you are half-way down and then move in so we can catch anyone trying to escape."

It was her turn to squeeze the communicator. "Hon? Can you tell us if they have any kind of defenses or alarms we should watch out for?"

"Oddly enough, we don't see anything," Pana answered. "However, a passive system would be virtually undetectable. If you get into trouble, we'll fly in and cover your retreat. Just remember, we need at least one vehicle to capture their spaceship. If they get away, there's not much chance we'll be able to help those on board."

Tamm jerked around to look at Bottar while holding up her communicator. "What do you mean, you can't help them? My son is on that damned ship."

Pana sighed. "I'm sorry, Sister, but it's a hostile situation up there. We have four virtually unmanned light cruisers against a battleship and twelve cruisers. If they discover our real mission, it's quite likely we'll all be killed."

Tamm slapped a hand over her mouth, and struggled to keep a primal scream from escaping. After regaining her composure, she asked, "So our only hope is to get you one of these ships?"

"Preferably all of them, but at the very least, one."

The enormity of what she was undertaking suddenly shut Tamm's brain down and she felt herself slumping into a sitting-fetal position, her arms around her legs and face on her knees, as the others stared at her.

When she felt Bottar's hand on her shoulder, the world came back into sharp focus. She jerked upright and squeezed the communicator.

"We'll get you that damned ship, if I have to kill every fucking alien on this planet."

Without waiting for a response, she jumped up and charged over the top of the ridge. She could hear Bottar urging the others to follow as she sprinted down the slope. Seconds later, he grabbed her arm, forcing her to stop.

"Tamm, you can't do this alone."

"They've got my son, damn it!"

He pulled her behind a nearby bush. "And our best chance is to do this together."

"Yeah, well this is all just one big screwed-up mess," she declared, tears running down her cheeks. "All I've got left is my son and those damn monsters have him."

She jerked her arm free. "I can't trust anyone else to do this. It's my job to take care of him."

Instead of running on, she continued to stare at him, frozen in the tension of the moment.

Finally, Bottar shook his head. "It's our job to rescue him."

His statement stopped her, but for only a moment. "But I'm married."

Bottar shrugged. "Let's worry about that later. Right now, it's you and me on a mission." He gripped her arm again, but this time she didn't try to shake him off. "Are you with me?"

She nodded as the rest their team approached.

"What the hell's going on?" Raytaan asked angrily.

Bottar shook his head. "Just getting our emotions under control."

The young man shook his head as well. "This ain't no time to be throwing a hissy fit, lady."

Tamm dipped her chin to her chest. "Sorry. It won't happen again."

Raytaan eyed her for a moment before pointing at the building. "I think each of us ought to sneak up and peek in a different window. If you find someone in there, nod and hold up fingers to tell us how many there are. If you don't see nobody, shake your head, but no speakin' while we're down there."

"Sounds like you've done this before," Bottar said while watching the building.

Raytaan shrugged, but said nothing.

"One more thing," Tamm added. "The friendly aliens need those shuttles to get our people back. If one of them makes a dash for a shuttle, bring him down."

"But don't destroy the shuttle," Bottar added.

"The more we talk about this, the more complicated it gets," Raytaan complained. "I just want to lop off some alien heads."

The other four nodded, and the group fanned out, working their way down the slope. They were nearly to the building when Tamm turned to see Auntie Bezzle's team moving toward the front of the building.

She was about to tap Bottar's shoulder when a bright red streak of light shot from a window and hit their far-left team member dead center. Unattached arms and legs thumped onto the ground as both Bottar and Tamm fired at the window, cutting a large hole in the wall.

Seconds later, another shot from a different window struck the ground, pelting them with steaming dirt. Bottar responded faster this time and they heard a scream as the blast burned through the wall.

"Fire at will," Bottar cried as Tamm started running.

She sprinted toward the first opening their volley had created while Bottar shot at a shadow in the next window and heard someone yelp in surprise.

As his footsteps thudded behind her, she heard him cry, "Watch out on your left!"

Seeing nothing, Tamm fired wildly into the left edge of the opening before bending low and rushing through billowing smoke and dust. Two shots behind her briefly illuminated an alien taking aim at her. She lurched to the left as the room flashed red and something hot passed only centimeters from her head. Striking the floor, she rolled and released a wild shot that just grazed the creature's left shoulder. The impact caused it to hesitate long enough for her to get off a second shot that vaporized its chest.

As the corpse crashed to the floor with a hollow thud, Bottar hurried through the opening. With a wave of her hand, Tamm crouched low and led him into the main area. The outside windows glowed with flashes of light as Tamm motioned for Bottar to move along the left wall while she went right.

Peering into the first room she came to, Tamm found an alien sprawled on the floor, one head badly burned while the other was only a sizzling stump. Reacting to the overpowering stench, she hurried on as bile rose in her throat.

She moved quickly to a portable equipment shed. After finding it empty, she started to move past it when a noise close to a shuttle caused her to crouch down and scramble behind the shed.

Looking back, she saw that Bottar had already vanished into the darkness. Fear sent perspiration dribbling down her face as she gulped air, and pressed her head against the shed's wall.

This is for Marrett! screamed in her head as she willed herself back into the open.

Moving quickly, she slipped from hiding place to hiding place until she saw the broad backside of an alien leaning over a large box. Looking around, but finding no others in the area, she moved up behind the creature.

"Hands up," she demanded, because she could think of nothing else to say.

Straightening quickly, the alien bumped one head on the lid of the box, but the other turned to stare at Tamm's weapon.

"Eeeaaap," the creature screamed with a vulture-like voice as the other head came around and it lifted all four hands into the air. "Eeeaaapp! Eassp sssaaatik."

Surprised by the loud noise, Tamm took several quick steps back and tripped over a landing strut. Her weapon discharged as she fell backwards, sending a pulse through a ceiling skylight. Molten chunks of glass and metal rained down as the alien disappeared under the shuttle. Scrambling to her feet, Tamm ran in pursuit, but lost sight of it in the darkened interior.

"Tamm! Where are you?" Bottar's voice echoed in the huge room.

"Look out," she responded. "One of them may be coming your way."

Tamm moved out from under the craft and crouched down as she saw the silhouettes of Auntie Bezzle and two others move toward her from the front of the building. Somewhere in the dark, a door sighed open.

"Shit," she yelled while pointing her weapon into the darkness. "It's getting into a shuttle!"

"The hell he is," Auntie Bezzle cried as a beam of light cut through the darkness, illuminating the gray-skinned creature hanging from the side of the next craft.

Tamm leaped up and wrapped an arm around each of the creature's necks. As the alien let out another ear-shattering squawk, she heaved back on the necks, pulling the creature free, and sending them crashing to the ground.

"Get him!" Auntie Bezzle screamed as Tamm glance up to see four people rushed toward her.

The creature proved to be much more agile than Tamm anticipated, grabbing her arms with its two upper hands, it yanked free of her grip and rolled quickly away. Tamm fell to the floor, but quickly jumped up and chased it. When the creature rolled into one of the craft's struts, she stuck her weapon into one of its faces, screaming,

"Freeze!"

Though it undoubtedly had no idea what she said, the alien froze anyway, holding all four arms away from its body.

"Son of a bitch, these buggers stink," Raytaan announced as he hurried around the shuttle. "We got two more outside and I'd just as soon wallow in sewage as stand close to them. Let's just shoot 'em and be done with it."

Tamm shook her head. "They might be useful."

"For attracting flies, maybe."

"We could swap them for my son."

When no one else responded, Tamm shook her head. "Let's look in the shuttles and see what's there."

Without waiting for her comrades, she scrambled up the side of the ship and climbed through the door the alien had opened. She felt herself go through some kind of barrier and was quickly caught off guard as the air in her lungs forced its way out her mouth. She turned quickly and shoved her head out the opening, gasping as she looked down at her companions.

"There's no air in there."

Stunned faces stared up at her until she realized what that meant.

"No," she cried before taking a gulp of air and ducking back inside.

Her eyes began to water almost instantly as her ears popped. Before she could take two steps in the lower atmospheric pressure, the air in her lungs burped out her closed mouth again.

She could hear someone climbing the outside of the craft as she stumbled forward on jelly-like legs, almost blinded by tears flooding her eyes. She searched desperately for an opening to where the captives were kept, but nothing stood out as a possibility. Stupefied, her mind was just shutting down as a strong pair of arms wrapped around her waist. She wanted to struggle against them, but her arms and legs no longer worked, leaving her feeling much like a rag doll as she was dragged from the cabin.

Seconds later, the negative pressure was off her lungs and she sucked in great gulps of air. As she vaguely felt herself descending, Raytaan's face came into view, followed by Auntie Bezzle's.

As Auntie Bezzle slowly lowered her to the ground, Tamm looked back to see Bottar making a slow unsteady descent, and nearly falling when he finally reached the ground.

"Did you see anything?" Raytaan asked as he helped Bottar over to sit beside her.

Tamm turned to see Bottar shake his head as his arms wrapped around her.

"Before I took two steps, something just sucked the air out of me. It was all I could do to find her."

"My son," she moaned dreamily.

"We ain't so sure he's in there, honey," Auntie Bezzle said as Tamm felt the woman's cool hand pressing against her forehead.

"Anyone found a basement or locked room anywhere?" Raytaan asked.

Tamm looked up as the others shook their collective heads.

"Then let's look around and see what we can find," she heard Bottar say.

He rose unsteadily to his feet, but almost immediately started to fall backwards.

Raytaan was a blur as he rushed in and steadied him. "Watch it, man. You ain't ready to be doin' anything right about now."

As Bottar slumped back down beside her, Auntie Bezzle lifted her communicator. "Bezzle here. We've got those shuttles you wanted and three of the creatures. What do we do now?"

Pana's voice was faint and tinny. "We're moving in now. How did you fare?"

When the old woman passed a questioning glance at the others, Tamm looked up to see several holding up fingers while shaking their heads.

"I think we lost three," she finally answered while looking at Tamm and Bottar. "And I think," she whispered, "your sister's boy is dead as well."

Despite Auntie Bezzle's effort, Tamm heard every heartbreaking word. She felt so numb, she wasn't sure if she even reacted as her heart dropped into her stomach.

89

The empty hallway echoed the drumming of Addy and Stitto's many feet as he softly read out the names on the doors.

"What we look for, maybe?" the young female asked.

"Astrometrics," he answered without missing a step. "Did nobody wonder why that idiot Fleet Commander put astrometrics department in damned basement?"

Padding along with one head reading each side of the hallway, Addy worked his way to the end before spinning around with his hands in the air.

"It not here," his mouths cried in stereo. Slapping both pairs of hands together, he reared his heads back and yelled, "Where in Ceratha's Name is…"

Addy froze as Stitto pointed to a door attached to the ceiling above him.

"Praising to Hammond," he said sarcastically while staring up at the words, "Astrometrics Lab," painted on the door.

"How we get up there, Sir?" Stitto asked nervously.

Addy lowered one head to look at her. "You not ever been down here?"

Wide eyed, Stitto jerked a quick no.

Scratching his right head, Addy searched the area with his left.

"If bastard Styxx not already dead, maybe We be killing him right now," he announced before turning and smashing through the door of a nearby supply closet.

Finding nothing useful, Addy threw his bulk against the next available door. Four smashed doors later, he marched back to the end of the hall and looked around.

"It gotta be something around here," he muttered while checking behind pictures, upsetting statues and yanking on anything that looked like it might be a hidden control device.

Stitto stood in the middle of the hallway with both mouths open as Addy danced around her.

"Why do we want to get up there?" she asked.

"Our protection be there," he answered without stopping. He made two more trips around her before turning to the girl-statue.

"Well don't just stand there to look stupidly beautiful. We give boost up to you. Maybe you get open."

Stitto hesitated momentarily before rushing up to put two feet in each pair of hands he presented. As she grabbed a lip at the top of the wainscoting and started to rise, it twisted in her hand and the ceiling door started down.

"Son of bitches," Addy swore as the poor female fell backwards onto the floor.

Before the elevator stopped its descent, Addy jumped in and waved urgently as the young female scrambled to her feet. She squeezed in just as Addy punched the control panel's only button and nervously watched the hallway as they rose.

When the elevator's floor sealed out the hallways' light, they found themselves in the dark. Scrambling out, Addy fumbled around for a light switch. As her eyes adjusted to the darkness, Stitto began to notice the walls and ceiling were covered with glowing planets, stars, and galaxies, all moving slowly in procession, just like their real counterparts.

While the effect seemed to awe Stitto, Addy grumbled angrily.

"We need light," he screamed in frustration.

To his surprise, the room lit up.

"As Hammond say," Stitto muttered as Addy's heads swiveled in opposite directions, scanning the room. "Ask for illumination and it be given."

While the representations of heavenly bodies vanished in the brightly lit room, the pair found themselves surrounded by a jumbled collection of equipment ranging from ancient optical telescopes to more modern long-range computer-controlled scanners.

"Where be Light of Ages?" he shouted.

As the room went suddenly dark, Stitto muffled a scream while Addy snorted derisively and yelled, "Lights!"

The room was again brightly lit.

"We gotta stop watching stupid wizard movies, maybe" he muttered while padding across the room. "We expecting things magically to appear whenever We ask."

A far-off explosion shook the room. Dust drifted from the high ceiling as a large cabinet shifted from the wall. Though it had moved only centimeters, Addy now realized it was on wheels. Rushing to it, he pressed his shoulder against the wall and pushed with all four hands. Realizing what he was doing, Stitto grabbed an edge and pulled. Ever so slowly, a gap opened to reveal a small door in the wall behind the cabinet.

When they'd managed to create nearly two meters of clearance, the senator hurried in, yanked the door open and squealed with delight. "Hooo Haahhh."

"They chase us for pretty box?" Stitto groaned as Addy shook his head.

"It more than pretty, honey. It save our lives, maybe?"

"How?" Stitto asked as the senator reached for his prize.

"It might," he said as the sounds of people moving below pricked his ears, drawing his eyes to the floor, "if maybe We get it opened before bad guys kill us."

Quickly sliding the heavy object out, he lugged it to the middle of the room and sat it on the floor.

"You not run far lugging this, Addy boy," he muttered. "They catch you before you get fifty meters.

"Why they kill us?" Stitto asked while following him. "What in there?"

Ignoring her, Addy grabbed an ancient optical telescope and passed its tripod's legs through the elevator's cage. Running back for another, he repeated the process.

"Start finding way out," he ordered while picking another tripod. "Coward like Brak not go anywhere there not be back door."

As Stitto disappeared into the mass of equipment at the back of the room, Addy shoved the last tripod into the elevator cage.

"Make that to work," he sneered at the noises below before scooping up the vessel, and rushing back to find Stitto running in circles.

"We find three doors, but all be dead ends," she whined while flailing all her arms at once.

Should We kill her now, maybe? Addy wondered as he eyed her shapely figure.

After a short pause, he gave his heads a single, sharp shake. "Hold this," he said, handing her the vessel. "But not be dropping it."

Passing off the burden, he began pulling on the nearest tall bookcase. When it proved unmovable, he moved to the next and tugged at it.

"What in this?" she asked again.

Addy shook his head. "Entire universe, maybe?"

Stitto giggled nervously. "That gotta be really, really heavy?"

"Yes…and no," he said testily as the last bookcase refused to budge.

Wiping sweat from his furrowed brows, Addy let out a long breath. "Brak not smart enough to make this complicated." Turning back to Stitto, he asked, "You sure there be nothing in those rooms, maybe?"

She shrugged. "We saw nothing."

Addy's eyes narrowed. "How hard you look?" he asked before rushing to the bathroom and smashing open the door.

As he scanned the room, the elevator in the outer room clunked as it jerked downward, and its metal cage groaned when it stopped against the telescope tripods. Stitto squealed as panic cramped Addy's stomach. Desperate, he swung both heads around in search of an exit.

"If We be that idiot, what we do, maybe?" he muttered. "He not creative, so…Yessss," he hissed as his eyes fell on a portrait of Brak in full dress uniform and so heavily covered in medals and ribbons he looked like he'd been dressed by a cadre of psychotic junk store owners.

Charging forward, he turned one pair of eyes toward the ceiling while the other watched the picture.

"Be switch," he prayed as he dashed across the room. "Be switch."

Grabbing the frame, he rotated it ninety degrees. To his delight, something above him clunked and a large light fixture in the middle of the highest part of the ceiling started to descend.

"Praising Hammond for simple-minded, yet depraved fools," he cried as the cage appeared.

Suddenly remembering the vessel, Addy ran back to Stitto. Just as he reached for it, an explosion shook the room. They both turned to see the entire mass of elevator cage, telescopes and tripods drop through the floor

Snatching the vessel, he turned to find their escape elevator had stopped half-way down.

"Son of a..." Noises in the room behind him stopped his remark as Stitto moved closer, looking as terrified as Addy felt.

"They coming," she whispered loudly.

Addy rushed to the picture and twisted the frame, sending the elevator back up. Before it reached the top, he reversed its direction, one head nervously watching Stitto while the other followed the elevator's progress.

As it descended, the cage jerked momentarily at the same point, but to his relief, continued its descent. This time it stopped only centimeters from the floor.

Without a word to Stitto, Addy jumped on board and smashed the control icon.

Nothing happened!

Terrified, Stitto squealed as Addy repeatedly pressed the button. He was so focused on it, he hardly noticed when she jumped on board. The elevator sank the remaining inches under their combined weight, and a loud clunk emanated from the ceiling. Within *micro-paks* the lift jerked noisily and started rising. Footsteps echoed in the outer corridor as their view of the room vanished into yet another dark room.

"Lights," Addy barked as he stepped from the cage.

Sudden illumination revealed a long hallway bordered on each side by half-a-dozen doors. Addy rushed to the first door and opened it. Rather than stop, he rushed to the next.

"Open all doors, but not go inside," he ordered as Stitto exited the cage.

"What for?"

"Just do!" he snapped. "And quick."

When they reached the last door, Addy forced it open to find a hallway he was familiar with.

"This lead to main lobby," he announced as his companion poked her head out the door. "They gotta have that covered, but We know better way out."

"But Sir?" Stitto asked while pointing.

"Shut up and follow," Addy snapped as he rushed to a door marked "Stairs".

"Wait, Sir." she protested. "There be something on…"

An alarm sounded, causing Addy to do a quick spin to find a small black box attached to the door frame.

"Ceratha's burning buns," he swore while pulling Stitto down a side hallway. "Quick-like! We gotta get through door at end."

Unwilling to be slowed by a bumbling female, he released her, leaned both heads toward his destination and ran as fast as his many legs would go. The distant sound of bipedal footsteps added adrenaline to his effort.

Throwing his body against the door, he was surprised to feel Stitto pushing from behind. When the flimsy door collapsed, she almost ran over him as they rushed inside.

Shouting somewhere behind them spurred them on as they turned sharply left and sprinted down another corridor to a landing bay, where a small, jet-black shuttle sat.

"This be kind of escape option Brak build for himself, maybe," Addy muttered as he cautiously approached the sleek black vehicle. "It most likely Khephra's men assume We not know how to get it going." He slowed as a realization came to him. "And maybe we not."

To Addy's surprise, Stitto rushed to the shuttle door, slamming a hand onto the release icon. Hefting his box to a more secure position on the top of his protruding belly, the senator rushed to follow her in, and was even more surprised when she climbed into the pilot's seat.

"You fly shuttle, maybe?" he asked while dropping into the co-pilot's seat.

She nodded. "We got over five *sirius* flying time, and mostly in this ship."

"But why you be secretary?"

She shrugged. "Brak see us on rare review of our division. He come back later and make clear that We either be lover or lunch." She flipped several switches while simultaneously fastening her seat belt. "Obviously, We play along."

"But We thought all mistresses be dead."

Stitto patted her belly. "After killing pregnant Ustilla, he come to do us in too. We tell him We also got eggs, and he not can do it."

"You with eggs, maybe?"

She nodded with a smile. "One-hundred-and-twenty-four and all be fertile."

"And they be his?"

The shuttle's engines came to life as Stitto barked a laugh. "You think We make eggs with that freak, maybe?"

"But you sleep with him…"

She shook her head slowly. "A girl got lotta ways to control who fertilize eggs." She turned a dial as the shuttle lifted into the air. "Fasten up, Senator. Back there, it necessary to play dumb female, but now We be girl on mission." She patted her stomach. "In very-short time, We be laying these puddle-jumpers and want to be somewhere safe when it happens. We be thinking you have such place in mind, maybe?"

Grabbing his seat belt harness, Addy grinned. "As matter of fact, We do."

"Then hang on, Sir," she laughed. "'Cause we be showing Antrakan bastards how real pilot thread needle."

90

Tamm knocked on the windows separating the bay from the shuttle cockpit. When Pana's face appeared, she spoke, "Is there any chance…"

As her voice broke, she looked at the floor.

"Don't give up hope, Sister. They store their victims in a form of suspended animation for transport to their planet. If it hasn't been too long, we might be able to revive him."

Tamm looked up. "Can I go with you?"

Pana shook her head. "There's nothing you can do here. This shuttle will take you back to our ship where we can restore you to a more compatible body. But that takes time and this mission can't wait."

"If I go back, will I forget him?"

Her sister-by-law shook her head. "You'll not forget any of this. That's why you're so confused right now. The restoration process usually takes weeks and is never supposed to happen while you're in Human form. They're too emotional and have too limited a scope of memory retention."

"Is that why I can't remember much about my life before…"

Pana nodded. "I'm really sorry this happened, and that's why we need to get you up to the ship as quickly as possible."

Tears rolled down Tamm's cheeks as her head shook. "But what about my son? Who's going to take care of him after I'm gone? His father's a total flake, my parents are dead and…"

"Tamm," Bottar said softly as he put his hands on her shoulders. "They say we have to go now."

Her head started shaking faster. "But I can't go. I've got to stay here and wait for Marrett. He's not one of them, so he can't go with us."

Bottar looked at Pana who nodded. As Tamm babbled on, he pressed a small disk against the back of her neck. Her speech slurred then turned to a murmur before she slumped against him.

Lifting her in his arms, he turned toward Pana. "I want you to know, I respect her marriage to this Saki guy, but I really do love her."

Nodding, Pana moved away from the window and leaned close to the pilot. "Take care of them, Jokko. I want them back in one piece."

Jokko nodded as she put her helmet on. "Why didn't you tell him he was also her husband?"

Pana shook her head. "Humans have a fairly simplistic view of relationships. I'll wait until they are back in their own bodies before breaking the happy news to them."

"What about her boy?"

Pana sighed as she pulled her helmet's sealing latches into place. "Some news is going to be bad no matter what kind of body you occupy. I've just got too much on my plate to deal with that right now."

Jokko sighed and nodded. "Well, we'll get them to the ship safely. Good luck."

Nodding, she disembarked and moved to the remaining un-piloted shuttle. Climbing into the cockpit, she turned to look into the back. With most of the cargo area converted into a special hold for its gruesome cargo, there was little room left for passengers. A bench seat ran down one side of the narrow space, with enough room for three bipeds, or two Koko's. On a short bench along the back, an ugly, two-headed creature sat with both pairs of hands manacled and a rope strapped around his many feet. In front of him sat two Antrakan guards. A technician from Pana's own crew was kneeling over a disassembled control panel just behind her seat.

"Are we ready yet?" she asked while removing her helmet.

The technician lifted his head and nodded. "Just about. Thankfully, these Koko transmitters haven't been updated much since the last war. They'll think you're one of their own once I get this last fix in place."

"What about him?" she asked.

The technician frowned. “No good,” he sighed. “Apparently, his boss has threatened far worse than we’ll ever do. He’ll never cooperate with us.”

Pana shook her head. “Lovely people, these.”

The technician nodded. “Yeah, well, I’ll put him in stasis when I’m done here. Personally, I’d rather shove him out without his nose plugs. That’s more than he did for the people in the…”

The expression on Pana’s face stopped him.

“Any chance?” she asked softly.

He shook his head. “Sorry, ma’am. We’ll eventually be able to recover the Life Forces of our people, but the real Humans…” He sighed. “…sorry.”

Pana leaned against the shuttle’s bulkhead for a moment before slipping into her seat. Her thoughts went to Tamm and the grief she would feel at the loss of a Human child.

“Why don’t these Humans have a Life Force like we do?” she asked no one in particular. “What makes them so different?”

“Ma’am?” the technician called as he replaced the last cover on the control panel. “You can fire up the engines now. I’ll put the Koko down and get out of your way.”

She twisted around and looked at him absentmindedly for a moment before nodding. “Thank you,” she sighed. “Are the other shuttles ready?”

“Yes, Ma’am. You’re the last.”

Seeing the technician approach, the KokoroTetian squawked loudly, and struggled against his bonds. As the other two held him steady, the technician pressed a small disk against his chest and both heads slumped forward.

After saying something to the two guards, the technician moved to the exit and stopped.

“Good luck, Ma’am,” he said before dropping out of sight.

His departing greeting brought Pana back from her musings and she revved up the engines in preparation for departure.

“All secure, gentlemen?” she asked.

“Yes, Ma’am,” they answered in unison as she pulled back on the control stick and moved the shuttle toward the hanger door.

She lifted her arm and pressed an emblem on her sleeve. “Let’s get these guys.”

The three shuttles slipped out of the hanger, climbing steadily while angling toward the magnetic north pole.

“Ma’am,” Mako, one of the guards asked as they reached altitude. “Why can’t our ships spot these guys in the air?”

“There’s some kind of special plating on these hulls that dissipates our scans, making them virtually invisible. Their small size makes them hard to spot visually as well.”

“If the Koko have this technology, what chance does the Supreme Commander have against their fleet?”

Pana shook her head. “Koko smugglers aren’t big on sharing.”

“But how did they come up with this?”

“Most likely they bought or stole it.”

Mako whistled. “The Supreme Commander would give his right…uh, eye for something like this.”

Pana laughed. “When this is over, I intend to see he gets their whole damned ship, and it won’t cost him any body parts.”

Frattee, the remaining guard, moved up behind his comrade. “What do we plan to do with the, uh, cargo?”

She shook her head sadly. “We’ll transfer them back to the surface where they can be buried properly by their friends and family.”

“But what’s the point,” Mako asked. “They’re dead.”

Pana checked her instruments before turning back to the pair. “The objective of our prisons is not to be cruel, but to change their Life Forces so they’ll be better people upon their release.

“One event that affects people more than almost anything is death. Because we live so long, and can be rejuvenated by putting our almost-indestructible Life Forces into new bodies, we tend to forget what it’s like to lose someone you love…permanently. It almost never happens to us, but Humans experience it often and within a very-short time frame. Most of them live less than one *druak* and then they’re gone, forever.”

Mako’s mouth dropped open. “Less than one *druak*?”

"Damn," Frattee added. "I was barely out of school by the end of my first *druak*."

"So, when we get these Koko's, are they going to be sent here?"

Pana chuckled. "Are you kidding? Over three-fourths of the internees on Secor-Alpha Four are Kokos."

A disembodied voice announced, "Automatic guidance locked. Approach vector set. Docking will commence in sixty *micro-paks*. Please, stow your gear, fasten your seat belts and make sure your food trays are properly stowed and locked. Thank you."

As the pair moved to their seats, Pana peered through the front windows, and after a few *micro-paks*, spotted the growing black dot that was their destination.

As her craft passed under the ship and turned to approach it from the rear, she looked back to see the other two craft following.

"Gentlemen," she announced as the mothership's rear doors began opening. "The third shuttle is going to disable their automatic controls at the last *micro-pak* and veer past the mothership. While they're distracted, you'll jump out and overtake anyone remaining in the bay. You take the left side. The second shuttle's team will go right."

She twisted around to face them. "If things go badly, get back inside as quickly as you can because I'm determined not to let them leave here with this cargo."

Mako looked at his comrade then back to Pana. "I guess that's our incentive to make sure this works."

Pana nodded as the two faces were suddenly replaced with a mist rushing wildly around in waves, like a frothing ocean during a hurricane.

"What's the matter?" she yelled though she could not hear herself speak.

A huge wave rose up in front of her, the eyes directly in the middle. "Time's running out. You must hurry."

"What do you mean?"

The wave crashed on top of her, knocking her down with its tremendous weight.

"What are you telling me?" she screamed while still floundering in the dense liquid.

"We got problem here, maybe?" an entirely different voice announced as Mako and Frattee's worried faces appeared in front of her again. "We be disengaging automatic control and veering off."

Her shuttle was just entering the bay when Pana turned to see three of the five Kokos there hurrying toward the exit. Sucking in a deep breath as the craft settled onto the deck, she exhaled slowly and pressed the side-door's release icon.

"Good luck boys," she called while turning to watch them jump out.

The almost simultaneous sounds of laser fire preceded the two Koko crewmen dropping to the floor. Pana fiddle nervously with the shuttle's transmitter controls as her men disappeared through a door leading into the ship. The voice of the mother ship's captain squawked from the speakers as he continued to demand response from the third shuttle. *Micro-paks* later she heard a loud crashing noise, followed by overlapping screams, and squawks. After a tense moment, a single burp of laser fire brought silence.

"The bridge is secured," came the announcement that finally allowed her to breathe.

As Pana relaxed, she unfastened her seat harness, closed her eyes, and felt the waves crashing inside her head.

"I'm coming, Father," she muttered as her eyes reopened. "I won't let you down this time."

91

"Excuse for asking, Sir," Stitto asked as their home world grew rapidly smaller behind them, "but what big deal with vessel?"

"You not here during the last war, maybe?"

"Uh, no Sir. We only twenty-three *druak* old."

"A century ago, KokoroTetians lead coalition of races against devious Antrakans." He turned to Stitto. "We assume you read this in history classes?"

She nodded.

"The war start well, but that not last long. We might think it not possible, but predecessor of Brak be even bigger moron than recently-deceased Fleet Commander. Even so, if it not been for unending Antrakan luck, we maybe trounce them."

"They do have lotta luck for bi-pods, maybe?"

Addy rolled his eyes. "Well, it someday come back to bite them on collective asses. It sure not last forever."

"But Sir, what that gotta do with N-Tschester destroying Ooertfael home planet?"

Sighing, Addy rested one elbow on the arm of his chair and cupped his right chin in it, his eyes staring blankly out the window. The other head turned toward the pilot.

"That really happen at much later time. You see, after war, Antrakans create three governing bodies: the Over, Level and Under Councils. For many *druak*, only Antrakans and allies can be members of Over Council. You too young, maybe, to remember this, but We be first KokoroTetian to be senator on Over Council.

"Anyway, being senator give access to inside information most peoples not ever be seeing. We love secret stuffs and spend all free time in archives. One day We find top-secret report that maybe nobody ever supposed to see." His right head drifted toward the window as well, but a moment later, he turned back. "We show it to some friends and it be decided to raid…er, visit old shaman's village where this odd little curio be kept." He tapped the vessel.

"Shaman tell me it something we could use to win war, maybe?"

"He just tell you?"

Addy's second head came around and both rocked from side-to-side as he fluttered his hands. "Well…yes, with little friendly persuasion, maybe?"

Stitto looked puzzled. "But what it be, Sir?"

Addy shook his heads. "That be getting ahead of story."

"Sorry, Sir."

"We bring it home, and our scientists eventually open box just only tiniest of bits. Whoa! Big surprise. It unleash burst of energy that exceed anything we ever see before."

"Like supernova, maybe?"

Addy shook his head. "Like billion supernovas."

"By the Gods!"

Addy shrugged while looking down at the box. "Well, maybe We fail to mention that energy from this thing not easily focused."

"What happen?"

The senator shuddered. "It vaporize division of Maatiirani battle cruisers, two moons and entire Ooertfael planet, along with scientists we send to test it."

Stitto's jaws dropped as all four of her eyes nearly popped out of her head. "Hammond's Holy Bare Butt." Her eyes fell to the box. "Why not we…you know…dead, maybe?"

"We not really know. Somehow, covering contains it." He sighed. "We be studying it for last forty *druak* and not yet figure that part out."

For a long moment, both of them stared silently at the box.

Finally, one of Stitto's heads looked up. "So why not use to break free of Federation Councils?"

Addy sighed. "That be catch, maybe. Ultimate power be useless if you not be able to get at it. After fiasco with 'experiment', Antrakans get hands on it. To make sure no one can use it, they separate vessel from only key."

"Key, Sir?"

"Yessss," he hissed as his eyes lost focus. "Though we try everything, we not able to find any other way in, but that be changing very soon."

"You find key, Sir?"

Snapping out of his trance, he turned to the aide. "We always know where it be," he said offhandedly. "But only ourself and one other do."

"So we go to get it, maybe?"

Addy chuckled. "If all go as planned, key come to us."

92

The small room was cramped as the five Maatiirani warriors finished dressing for battle. Ehar laughed loudly at something his brother had said when Uhua's eldest son, Ahau announced,

"We're ready."

"Then tell me, boys," Uhua said as he turned to his three sons, "What's the first thing you must do upon boarding the enemy's ship?"

"Dad," Ahau protested loudly. "We've been through this like, a hundred times."

Ehar burst from his seat, swatting the dissenting youngster hard enough to knock him down. "And we'll go through it another hundred until it's a part of your being."

Ahau quickly bounced up, throwing a playful fist at his uncle. "No fair!"

Ehar blocked the blow and held a handful of claws close to his nephew's face. "There's no fair in war, little one. It's all about killing or being killed. Being a 'fair' fighter won't bring you back from the dead."

Ahau's face showed fear, but only until he jammed a fist into his uncles stomach and lurched back.

Unfazed by the attack, Ehar slapped his hardened stomach and laughed. "Good try, but that wouldn't have saved you. Go for the testicles and jam them hard."

"What about the Kokos?" Ahau's brother Hantu asked. "Where are their testicles?"

Ehar laughed again. "Don't worry about the Koko's nuts. They've got too many of them. Just cut off their worthless heads. Going through a division of those losers is like running a knife through warm cheese."

Oola, the youngest, shook his head. "But I thought we weren't supposed to underestimate our enemy."

Uhua stood. "Correct, Son. On the other hand, no matter how strong they might seem, you must always believe you can defeat them. Attack with determination and vigor. They'll break and run every time."

"And what if they don't?" Ahau asked.

Ehar shook his head and smiled. "Then greet them with open arms, Nephew, because you're fighting your own people."

As everyone laughed, a junior officer snapped to attention in the doorway and saluted. "Commander, Sir. There is a private KokoroTetian shuttle approaching our position."

Ehar waved a hand dismissively. "Leave them be. They can do us no harm."

"They are on an intercept course, Sir."

Ehar shook his head slowly. "What would a Koko private shuttle be doing way out here?"

"They could be spies, Sir."

Uhua nodded. "Could be."

Ehar shrugged. "Any signals coming from their ship?"

"None, Sir, except their ID tag, which is definitely Koko. In addition, they are running dark and at an abnormally high rate of speed."

Uhua looked at his brother. "Trying to get away?"

The officer shook his head. "They appear to be coming right at us, Sir."

As Ahau displayed his teeth, the officer could see his tongue brushing against the inside row. "Let me blast them to dust," he shouted enthusiastically. "I'm an ace with the laser canon."

Uhua held a hand up to silence his son. "That would attract attention to our position and spoil the element of surprise." He turned back to the officer. "How long before they are in contact range?"

"If nothing changes, about fifteen *milli-paks*, Sir."

In one swift movement, Ehar pulled his braid around, rattling the teeth as he did so. The action brought the remaining occupants of the room to silence as his eyes wandered over the victory mementos embedded in the glossy weave.

After a moment, he threw the hair over his shoulder, and as it rattled into place, turned to the officer. "Go to defensive position three and remain dark. We'll be up in a moment."

The officer snapped a quick salute and left as Uhua and his sons watched their relative.

"What are your thoughts, Brother?" Uhua asked.

Ehar shook his head slowly. "I don't know for sure, but it's just a hunch."

"What?"

Uhua's brother looked at him with unfocussed eyes. "That maybe your sons are going to win their teeth a bit sooner than planned."

93

"Status report, Captain," Khephra demanded as he entered the bridge.

Captain Praetor handed him an electronic notepad. "We lost the two minimally manned light cruisers and four men. The Koko fleet managed to inflict some damage on our ship, and two others, but it's nothing that can't be repaired quickly. Major Phaa lost three men to that beast Senator Addy unleashed on them, but still managed to accomplish all his assigned tasks before leaving the planet."

The supreme commander looked at the notepad for a moment before nodding. "Any sign of pursuit by the KokoroTetian fleet?"

"None, Sir. They lost twenty-two light cruisers, most destroyed by friendly fire. One battleship destroyed and another badly damaged. In addition, while shooting at us through our smoke screen, they destroyed dozens of buildings on their planet, including an entire communications complex and part of the defense department."

"Any word on the other mission?"

After Praetor shook his head, Khephra paused for a moment before looking at the tablet again.

"How are we doing on fuel?"

"We've used quite a bit during our recent activities. We'll surely want to re-supply before getting into another skirmish."

The supreme commander shook his head. "It's a cinch we can't use our own refueling stations. We'll need a neutral planet."

Praetor smiled. "There's always Everona. It's not in anyone's territory."

Khephra smiled. "Let's give them a try."

94

Saki watched the KokoroTetian ship rise from the north polar region of the planet and head into space.

"Good luck, my love," he muttered as the tiny thermal blip grew ever smaller until it vanished.

"We have all the people we can carry, Sir."

Saki turned to Captain Fatak. "How many did we lose to the Kokos?"

"About thirty. We've recovered sixteen Life Forces, and created a force field that should keep the Samhain at bay until we can return."

"What about original bodies?"

Fatak nodded. "They've been replicated and are also on the ships, along with twenty-two others."

Saki raised an eyebrow. "Twenty-two?"

"The one who calls herself, Auntie Bezzle had quite a team. They were a big help recovering the missing people and getting them on board."

"I'd like to meet this person. We can always use a good leader."

The captain shook his head. "She decided not to come up, Sir.

Unlike her teammates, she doesn't want to leave her Human companions."

Saki looked out the window at the planet and nodded. "I think I understand that."

Fatak shook his head. "It makes no sense to me. They live less than a *druak*."

Saki shrugged. "Yes, but when life is short, you don't take it as much for granted. I really liked the Human passion for living. That's just something we don't feel any more."

The captain shook his head. "I'm passionate about stopping these Kokos."

Saki shook his head. “When this crisis is over, and we no longer have a defined enemy to fight, what then?”

When Fatak didn’t immediately answer, Saki jumped from his seat, pacing the room as he spoke, “You see, we’re not really fighting for our lives, because our Life Forces are not dependent on these bodies. We’re just trying to achieve some kind of stability.

“When you look at our history, it seems that every thirty or forty *druak*, someone gets so damned bored they lash out and turn everything upside down.”

Fatak nodded. “That would be Senator Addy, in this case.”

Saki nodded. “And it was the Maatiirani before that and the Great War. It doesn’t matter who causes it, because we all just keep going on and on and on.” He plopped back into his chair and sighed. “But Humans get only one shot at it. They live for the moment because they might not get the next one.”

“Terrifying,” Fatak whispered.

Saki shrugged. “It’s all they know.” He barked a scornful laugh and jumped up again. “And we mix our hardened criminals with their confused population, creating even more havoc in their short, fragile lives. How moral does that make us?”

The captain’s jaw dropped as he raised a hand, palm out. “Sir?”

Saki stopped in mid-stride, his eyes on Fatak’s face. Without further comment, he gave his head a quick shake and leaned against a nearby station.

After a moment, he looked at his captain. “Sorry,” he sighed.

“It looks like I’ve got some more work to do before my Human side is under control.”

The captain opened his mouth, hesitated and then shrugged. “Maybe you should spend some time in a processing chamber. A few *deca-paks* would do you a world of good, Sir.”

Saki shook his head. “There’s no time. Pana’s on her way to find her father and we’ve got to get out of here as well.”

“Where to now, Sir?”

Saki rubbed his chin in silence for a moment before speaking, "We've got to locate an old shaman and find out what he knows about the big bang."

95

Ehar's boots clapped loudly against metal plating, the noise echoing in the short corridor leading to the bridge. Thoughts of past battles raged in his head as he prepared mentally for the coming engagement.

An alarm blared. "High alert! High alert! All hands to battle stations. All hands to battle stations."

Ehar tapped his wrist-comm. "Sub-commander! What's' going on?"

His subordinate's face appeared on the small screen. "The Koko ship has vanished, Sir."

"Explain," he demanded as he broke into a trot.

"It just blipped out, Sir."

"Full spectral scan?"

"Done, Sir. Nothing."

"Ships don't just…" He stopped speaking while making a sharp turn. "I'm on my way. Keep looking!"

"Yes Sir!"

His bridge was a busy place when Ehar arrived, but there was no hint of panic. His men were all hand-picked and had faced almost-certain death at some time in their lives. For them, each day was stolen from the devil god, Epthra, and since they'd already met the devil, they had no fear of his return. He liked that his men thought less about dying and more about cutting out their enemy's hearts.

"Sub-commander Hellic, Report!" Ehar barked while moving to his station.

None of the men looked up as he entered. Ehar considered such formalities as saluting or announcing the arrival of every officer to be wasteful bullshit. His men respected him or at least feared him enough not to challenge his authority. And if anyone did, he killed them quickly. There was no place for rebels under his command.

"Still no sign of them, Sir," Hellic answered as his fingers moved back and forth over his console.

"Based on their last known speed and trajectory, where should they be?"

Hellic pointed to a blinking red point on the screen. "That's the location, Sir."

Ehar watched the dot for only a moment. "They should be in visual range of our left flank very soon."

"I've got the captain of that ship watching," Hellic announced. "Should he destroy them?"

Ehar pulled his braid around and played with it as he continued to watch the blinking dot. "Not unless it fires first."

"Sir?"

Standing, he released the braid and let it rattle back into place. "A shuttle against our division? Unless he's completely suicidal, I don't think he's here to attack us, Sub-commander. It's more likely he wants to do a trade."

"Trade what, Sir? They shouldn't even know we're here."

"Think about it," he said slowly, eyes still on the dot. "He's got cloaking technology we've never seen before. What else is inside that ship: an infinitely powerful scanner, superior weapon's technology, or impenetrable armor? If we fire on him first, he might destroy us all."

"I'll not run from a fight, Sir," Hellic stated adamantly.

Ehar shook his head slowly without taking his eyes off the screen. "Nor will I, Sub-commander, but sometimes the winning strategy calls for diplomacy and assessment."

"I see your point, Sir, but I…"

"Senator Addy to commander of Maatiirani fleet," a voice interrupted. "We come in peace to discuss alliance with you."

Ehar raised a hand to silence everyone on the bridge. His black eyes flicked from one face to another as they all turned to him. His smile grew as he pointed to the communications officer and nodded.

"This is Commander Ehar, Senator," he said with a calm voice that did not reflect the excitement in his eyes. "I trust you remember me?"

When no response immediately followed, Ehar grinned until all of his crystalline teeth glistened.

"Ah, Commander Ehar," Addy finally answered. "Even if we not have met, your reputation as fierce warrior be known throughout our region."

"You are well known to us as well, Senator. You can rest assured, I've been looking forward to this meeting for a long, long time."

When another pause halted the conversation, the still grinning Ehar raised both fists into the air and shook them so violently the teeth on his braid hissed.

"We be, uh, aware our past be…somewhat contentious," Addy finally continued, "but We have proposition that make up for that, maybe?"

The commander's eyebrows shot up as his smile vanished. Lowering his fists to chest level, he held them there. "What could you have that would interest me, Senator?"

"We think you know, Commander," Addy said seriously. "And We be also thinking you know what happen if it fall into hands of Supreme Commander Khephra, maybe."

Ehar scowled as his fists clenched and unclenched. "That thing vaporized my father and his entire division."

"Along with two moons and entire planet with over six-billion people," the senator added. "In our way of seeing, there be but one way to assure it never be used against your people again."

"And what is in it for you?"

"Just one thing, maybe?" Addy answered. "Help us rid galaxy of Antrakan peoples and their Supreme Commander once and forever."

Ehar's head tilted to the left as his face contorted with confusion. "But what about their Life Forces? I'm told they will just come back in another form."

Addy laughed. "With this thing, their Life Forces maybe be blown so far away they never find way back. That is, of course, if they not completely and utterly vaporized."

"And is that all you want, Senator?"

Another pause. "Well, maybe we discuss finer points over dinner."

Ehar motioned to his communications officer to mute the transmission then turned to Hellic. "When this is over, I'm going to gut that bastard, throw his nuts to my dogs and broil his carcass over an open spit until it's nothing but charcoal."

The sub-commander laughed as his superior motioned to the communications officer again.

"I think we might have a deal, Senator," he said pleasantly. "Why don't you stow your ship in my hold so we can meet in person."

"Actually," Addy countered. "We be thinking to meet someplace more neutral, like Everona, maybe?"

Ehar shrugged. "Suits me fine. Just lead the way, won't you?"

Addy laughed. "Since you not seeing our craft, We think it best you lead."

Ehar smiled. "As you wish, Senator, but if you have trouble keeping up, let us know and we'll slow down."

"Thank you, Commander Ehar." Addy's said, sounding irritated. "That not be problem."

As the communications officer cut the transmission, Ehar turned to his scan specialist. "I don't care if you have to blow white powder out your ass. Find that ship!"

96

When Pheet awoke, his whole body, from the top of his head to his nail-less toes, ached with such ferocity he was afraid to move. His mouth tasted like vomit, as did everything he smelled.

He had planned to ignore the shadowy form blocking his light until the all-too-familiar voice said,

"I'd like to know why."

Pheet sucked in a sharp breath and held it for a moment before pushing himself into a sitting position.

"I don't even know what I did."

"What do you mean?"

"Matrina drugged me. She was in control the whole time."

"Matrina?"

"The female who seduced me."

"We apprehended no females."

Pheet's head jerked up. "Then she's still on board?"

Khephra shook his head. "We've searched everywhere. No women are unaccounted for, except…"

"What?"

"Phaa lost three people on the planet, but only managed to bring the bodies of two back. The other was a female and she just disappeared."

His mouth open in shock, Pheet stared up a Khephra. "She got away?"

"And left you behind."

His whole body sagged as Pheet lowered his face into his hands. "It was never her plan to take me along." He looked back up at his superior. "When I wouldn't cooperate with her, she threatened the death of my daughter and ex-wife. When I still wouldn't do what she asked, she drugged me. I think someone helped her with that. It is quite obvious she had no intention of letting me live."

"And yet you're alive."

Pheet shook his head slowly. "This was treason, and I'm told it happened during a battle." He stomach cramped, doubling him over. "I'll be lucky..." he panted, "...if my Life Force isn't...interred so long my body will die in stasis. That's as good as being dead."

"You haven't answered my question," Khephra said without emotion. "Why did you go along with her?"

Tears streamed down his cheeks as he strained to sit upright against the painful cramping. "Why don't you ask the doctors?"

97

Kappa jerked his head around to see Pana's eyes roll up just before her lids covered them.

"Pana?" he asked cautiously.

"It's OK," she said softly. "I'm just tired. I haven't had much sleep lately."

"But what do I do if…"

She rolled her head on the seat back to face him. "There's nothing you can do. Just keep me from hurting myself and wait for it to pass."

"But…"

She laughed softly. "Don't worry. It's just a mental connection. I can hear his thoughts, but he can't actually touch me."

"There's more to it than that," Kappa argued. "Earlier, you experienced some kind of fluid pushing you around."

She nodded as her eyelids drooped. "Yes, but it's just a sensation. I'm not actually under the…water, or whatever it is." She touched his cheek lightly. "Trust me, friend. I'll be fine."

She pulled her hand back and settled into her seat. Within *milli-paks*, he could hear her regular breathing and knew she was fast asleep.

Turning to Baroque and Wat Wat, he used hand signals to indicate that they should be quiet.

He was just settling back into his own seat when her hand gripped his arm with a strength he'd never experienced from her before.

Her eyes popped open but remained unfocussed. "Turn around!" she demanded in a voice he didn't recognize. "You've got to get her out of here."

"Pana?" he asked as his two comrades rushed forward.

"She can't do this," the voice insisted. "It's too dangerous."

Kappa's wide eyes danced from his comrades to Pana and back again. "Are you her father?"

"You must go back," the voice insisted more loudly. "I can't protect her if she gets too close."

Kappa finally yanked his arm free, but still had to contend with her flailing arms.

"She said you wouldn't hurt her," he yelled while grabbing her arms and struggling to hold them.

"It isn't me you need to worry about."

Kappa fought to control his own hysterical fear. "Who then?"

Struggling against his grip, Pana almost lifted him out of his seat, but he refused to let go. When no answer came, he asked again, "Who is threatening your daughter, Sir?"

The struggling stopped so suddenly Kappa almost fell onto Pana. As he righted himself, she was facing him, her eyes still unfocused.

"You are," the voice answered sadly.

Kappa pushed back against the bulkhead but his eyes stayed on Pana as she slumped forward then jerked back up.

"Father?" she moaned while moving her hands to her face and crying.

98

"Sir," Sub-commander Hellic announced. "We'll begin our deceleration for Everona in five *milli-paks*."

Ehar shook his head. "That Koko senator is a wily fox. Let's assume he's leading us into a trap." His eyes scanned the upcoming solar system. "Send probes to each planet to make sure no one's hiding behind them or their moons." He slowly tapped a claw on the console surface. "Let's use system defense plan five."

Hellic's eyebrows rose. "That will spread us quite thin, Sir."

Ehar smiled. "Yes, but I've got eleven of the best captains in the fleet. If it's Khephra we're fighting, our lighter fighters will fly rings around his battleships until the rest can collapse on them."

Slipping from his seat, Ehar moved to the scan station. "Any luck finding that ship?"

The officer's eyes narrowed as he smiled wickedly and pointed to his screen. "I think so, Sir."

A small red blip pulsed just above the officer's claw.

"What can you tell me about it?"

"The design is totally unfamiliar, but it's definitely not Koko military. It's been flying just above and behind our left wing since I first detected it. The engine is way more efficient than anything they have. At the speed we've been traveling, a craft that small would have run out of fuel long before now. In addition, I'm pretty sure it can match our speed and maneuverability."

Ehar shook his head. "And since this technology isn't available to their military, we have to assume he's working with Koko smugglers."

"Everona is a well known smuggler's safe house."

Ehar patted the officer's shoulder. "You know, I'm glad I didn't kill your father in the last civil war. I'm not sure what I'd do without your quick wit."

The officer smiled. "Thank you, Sir."

Ehar stood. “Scan for any other cloaked ships. If he is double-crossing us, maybe we can turn his little trick to our advantage.”

“Yes Sir.”

He turned back to his commander. “Implement our defensive plan and get Senator Addy on the comm.”

“Sir?”

“It’s time to discuss a change in our arrangement.”

99

"Where Fleet Commander Brak find craft, Sir?" Stitto asked while looking around.

Addy shook his head. "No idea. We only learn of it when threaten serving Styxx at next officer's banquet. Once he talking, that boy hold nothing back."

"He tell you about vessel, maybe?"

Addy shrugged. "We know it be at war office. When Brak hear Khephra go rogue, he hide it, quick like."

"Where that be, Sir?"

The senator smiled while shaking his heads. "Moron hide it in bottom drawer of dresser, under pile of oversized shorts."

Stitto barked a laugh.

Shaking his heads again, Addy continued, "We get Styxx to move box to safer place in Astrometrics lab, but before he say where it be, damned Khephra blow him up."

"Lucky you smarter than Styxx."

Addy opened his mouth to respond but stopped when the communicator light blinked.

Stitto pressed the call icon. "Senator Addy vessel. Commodore Stitto here."

Addy touched the mute icon. "Commodore?"

She smiled. "Well, We in charge of vessel and," she patted her belly, "We got battle group worth of future captains under our command, maybe?"

Addy smiled. "We really be liking you…" His left head looked down at her belly as the right one smiled at her, "… Commodore Stitto."

She pressed the mute icon. "How we can help you, maybe?"

"Senator," Ehar responded. "We've noticed you are flying just above and behind my left wing." Stitto took in a sharp breath. "It is customary for my allies to fly on my right side. Would you be so kind?"

Four heads jerked to the right as Addy and Stitto watched the three ships lining up off Ehar's right side.

It was Stitto's turn to hit the mute. "One big advantage in toilet, maybe?"

Addy shook his heads and released the mute. "Slight not intended, Commander. We be glad to accommodate change in position."

"Thank you, Senator," Ehar responded. "And Commodore, my captains and I would very much like the opportunity to chat with you about your ship. We find it fascinating."

Stitto shot a panicked look at Addy, who shook his head.

"We appreciate interest, Commander," she finally said, "but such information be classified."

"Hmm," Ehar said as all of his ships suddenly slowed, sending the small craft ahead of them.

Stitto's eyes bulged as she pointed to a screen showing eight powerful laser canons armed and locked on them.

"I think that's something we should discuss before we enter the system," the commander said in a tone dripping with malice. "Don't you?"

Stitto hit the mute icon again. "They not match our maneuverability," she said while gripping the control stick. "Give us two *nano-paks* and they be shooting at vacuum!"

Shaking his heads, Addy grabbed her arm. "We keep this particular secret between us for now," he said with a calm voice that surprised his new commodore. "We hear what commander has to say, maybe?"

Still holding her arm, the senator touched the mute icon. "Commander," he said, as though speaking to a long-lost friend. "The cafés on Everona be much more comfortable, but if you wanna talk here, We be willing to discuss arrangement."

"Come aboard then and we can talk face-to-face."

Addy rolled his eyes. "Ah, Commander Ehar, that not be working for us. You see, We not think you trust us and We understand your feelings, definitely."

"What makes you think I don't trust you, Senator?"

Addy laughed. “Eight armed and locked laser canon be first clue, maybe?”

Stitto’s bulging eyes darted around her instrument board as nothing but static came from the speakers. She was just about to hit the mute icon again when Addy’s upheld hand stopped her.

“And what assurances do we have that you won’t attack us?” Ehar asked.

“If that be our intention, We do it when we first meet.”

The senator smiled at Stitto, and indicated that she should remain quiet while he allowed the static to continue.

“Be assured, Commander,” he finally said. “We need you as much as you need us. If we can put mistrust aside for only short while, we both be immensely rewarded, maybe?”

“What would our reward actually be?”

“We think you not muchly impressed by money,” Addy answered. “But how about one-on-one combat with Supreme Commander Khephra, maybe? His teeth not as big as ours, but We hear they have more of them. Would make excellent addition to collection, maybe?”

“You’d help me find Khephra?” Ehar asked eagerly.

“No, Commander Ehar,” Addy responded. “If plan go as we think, he find you.”

100

A small, fuzzy blur of blue shot past Saki, grabbing at his hat as it went. A quick move on his part deflected the beast, producing a loud shriek as it hit the ground, rolled and went airborne again. Keeping a careful eye out for any more flying fur balls, he and Akki moved slowly into an ancient forest. Intermingled with the trees was a primitive village with no occupants.

"Hello," he called as he approached the first hut. "Anybody here?"

The hut's walls were bundled reeds, its roof grass and the door a gaping hole in its front. Inside, Saki found a single sparse room with a lone sleeping mat on the earthen floor. Unrecognizable roots and skins were partially woven into the far wall and to his left, a small reed alter was adorned with crudely carved figurines in a circle of unlit candles.

"These are really primitive conditions," Sergeant Specialist Akki said as he looked over his commander's shoulder. "We didn't even have it this bad in boot camp."

Saki shrugged. "This isn't bad." He pulled back from the hut and looked around the village again. "There are times when I'd give my right arm for this kind of simplicity."

Akki smiled. "Like right about now?"

Saki chuckled. "Right about now could be one of them, yes."

A sudden movement to their right made both men jump. Saki's hand went up to stop the sergeant specialist from drawing his weapon. Moments later, three short, squat, dark-skinned men, naked but for their loin cloths, burst from a clump of tall grass and walked to within three meters of them.

They stopped and looked over the newcomers, making faces and gesturing to each other. After a moment, the center person lifted a stubby hand, and pointed at Akki.

"We got nut'in'. You not take it."

Akki threw a questioning look at his superior.

Saki shook his head. “I'm sorry for the intrusion, Sir. We're not here to…”

All three small heads turned toward the sub-commander, as the central one stabbed a short, thick finger at him. “You not take nut'in' eedder.”

Saki pulled a shell necklace from his pocket and held it out to them. “Actually, we want to give.”

The leader turned to each of his comrades in turn and they shrugged. Pausing, as if to consult himself, he finally shrugged as well, and moved closer to examine, but not touch the necklace. He ran his eyes the whole length of the offered gift, counting the shells, eying their quality and sniffing them.

He finally nodded and stepped back. “What you want.”

Saki smiled. “Knowledge.”

The threesome looked at each other in turn, but said nothing.

“I want to speak with your shaman…your priest, if I may.”

The leader grunted then turned and gave one low then two higher-pitched whistles. A broad, but equally-short female appeared wearing a similar loin cloth and several dozen shell necklaces. Moments later, two younger female came out from behind trees wearing maybe a quarter the number of necklaces as the first.

“We got 'nuff necklaces,” he grunted. “You wanna to talk wit' shaman, give us Antrakan beer and those cheesy-squiggly bread things.”

Akki shook his head as the sub-commander muttered, “These guys aren't as out of touch as we thought.”

“We got deal?” the leader asked.

When Saki nodded, the three men clapped as one and the large female began yipping and dancing in a circle. Her two younger companions, one of them obviously pregnant, showed less enthusiasm.

Akki moved closer to his commander. “Why aren't those thinner female celebrating like the others?”

Saki eyed them. “Most likely the men get first dibs on anything we give them. What's left will likely go to the larger female, who is probably the chief's first wife. I'm guessing the last two only get enough to sustain them for bearing children."

"That's not fair."

Saki shrugged. "Primitive cultures rarely are."

Akki looked indignant. "Shouldn't we do something?"

The sub-commander shook his head. "The last alien race to visit here probably killed and ate half the occupants before their shaman gave them the box to make them go away. Now you want to shake up their lives again by making them comply with your cultural morals? What makes us more right than them?"

Akki's protest died on his lips.

Saki smiled. "We have more important issues to deal with right now. Let's leave them to live as they see fit."

After a moment's pause, Akki nodded.

"Have the rest of our team come here with their beer and cheese pretzels," Saki ordered. "Then we'll talk with that shaman."

After suitable gifts had been exchanged, the three men lead Saki and his team out of the forest and up a hillside littered with more primitive huts. As they proceeded, people began appearing along the path, until a sizable crowd lined the way. Naked babies clung to their mothers; dog-like creatures barked; men gathered in groups, pointing and muttering among themselves; children laughed and ran ahead of them; and those soft, fuzzy creatures flew through the air, occasionally grabbing at clothes or equipment as they zipped by before landing in a tree or on someone's shoulder.

Saki's men were no less awed by the sights they beheld.

"Sir," Akki whispered to his commander. "With such a concentration of primitives, wouldn't sanitation and disease be a problem. Where do they, uh, you know, go, Sir?"

Suddenly, the three men leading their party stopped and turned to face a patch of brush to their left. A person, with one side of his face badly scarred and a missing arm, stepped onto the path and looked up at Akki. He was easily twice the height of the others, with a larger head, big, amber eyes, a narrow nose, and generous mouth. To Saki he appeared to be very old, yet his hair was jet black. Around his neck, a sea-shell necklace held a large gem that was so bright red it seemed to glow.

He motioned over his shoulder and smiled. “There’s a pit in the center of our village. We built a sturdy hut over it and that’s where we pee, poop and dump our garbage. If you drop a stone from the middle, you’ll never hear it hit the bottom.”

Akki blushed. “Oh…wow.”

The person shrugged. “If you need to use it, I’ll have someone show you the way.”

The sergeant specialist shook his head.

Saki stepped forward. “I am Saki N-Tschester, from the Alliance of Councils. We are sorry to bother you, but we seek information.”

The person’s face was bland as he nodded. “I am Tot. What do you wish to know?”

“Many years ago, a group of two-headed creatures raided your village. I’m not sure who your shaman was at that time, but they tortured him and took something of great value from your people.”

“I remember them,” he said while rubbing the scarred side of his face. “They called themselves the Kokoro, or something like that.”

Saki looked surprised. “You remember them? But that had to be close to two thousand of your solar cycles. How long do your people live?”

Tot shrugged and nodded toward the crowd to his right. “We call the solar cycles am-mara. The people here live about two hundred am-mara, but I’m not originally from here. According to their records, I’ve been here just over four thousand.”

“Who were your people originally?”

While pointing past Akki, Tot shook his head. “About an hour’s walk east of here is a large crater. The people tell of a great fireball that fell from the sky. When they went to investigate, they found me a short distance from it. Unfortunately, I have no memory of the time before then. These people taught me to speak and I eventually became their shaman.”

Akki raised a hand. “Maybe I can discover something of who your people were. Could someone take me to the crater?”

Tot nodded without emotion and called over the three men they'd met earlier. After a rapid exchange that Saki's translator could not understand, he motioned to Akki. "They will lead you. It is not a difficult path, as the people make a pilgrimage to it every am-mara to celebrate my arrival." He chuckled. "They don't have much to entertain themselves here, so any excuse for a holiday celebration is welcome."

Saki nodded at Akki's questioning look and the sergeant specialist hurried off after the three men.

After his subordinate vanished around a corner, Saki turned to Tot. "Then I must assume it was you the Kokos tortured until you gave them the vessel shaped like a pyramid."

The shaman shook his head. "They already had the vessel and were still killing people left and right. I organized an attack on them, but it was doomed to fail. They had powerful weapons and trained soldiers. We were but a rabble with sticks and stones."

He rubbed the scarred side of his face again. "They killed almost everyone. The light beam from one of their weapons took part of my arm, and burned my face for days afterward. Since I was different than the rest, they assumed I knew how to open the vessel, but I told them I'd never tried." He shook his head. "The vessel was already on this planet, and my people had been worshiping it for ages before I arrived." He held up the jewel. "This necklace was the only thing found with me by the crater. When brought close to the vessel, it began to glow, as though it had some kind of affinity with it. However, for some reason, I knew they should never come together."

"So the gem is the key?"

Gripping the necklace, he shook his head sadly.

"It was some sort of energy stored in the gem that became excited when it was close to the vessel. To my utter surprise, when they brought the gem close to the vessel, its energy jumped to one of the two-headed aliens."

Two of the women brought a stool and Tot almost collapsed onto it.

"Their anger at my keeping secret something that was unknown to me, cost me the rest of the arm. They were brutal, Saki

N-Tschester. Even after discovering the key, they kill." He shuddered. "Those monsters tore flesh from their living victims and gulped it down."

He paused as tiny hands rose up to pat him gently on the back, chest and arm while those around him muttered soothing sounds. He smiled down at the concerned faces for a moment before continuing. "Once they had the vessel and its key, they torched what remained of our village and left me lying in the middle of a burning hut. The survivors came back from the woods and rescued me once again."

Speechless, Saki looked at his men, who appeared to be equally stunned.

Turning back to Tot, he asked, "Why didn't they take your necklace?"

He shrugged. "The real key was no longer in it."

Saki shook his head. "I'm very sorry for what happened to you and your people, but I'm afraid this vessel is at the center of a larger problem. We were hoping you could help us stop the Kokos from using it for their own ends."

The small hands vanished as a collective gasp came from the people crowded around their shaman.

Tot stiffened. "We want no more dealings with those terrible creatures."

"But that's what you're going to get, unless we can work together to figure out exactly what this vessel is and how to control it."

Tot pulled back, along with the others. Shock and alarm registered on the faces of his companions, but Tot's reflected mistrust.

"But I already told you I don't know anything about it."

Saki held up both hands, palms out. "We're not here to harm you or your people. We want to help, but our people are on the verge of a civil war, so time and resources are limited."

Looking confused, Tot's eyes fell to the milling, nervous crowd.

After a moment, he turned back to Saki, looking more determined. "Then maybe you should leave and let us defend ourselves as best we can."

Saki shook his head. "You may be our only hope for stopping the Kokos and protecting your people."

"But I already told…"

Saki stopped him. "Come with me to our ship. We have medical equipment that can restore your arm and repair the damage to your face. We might also be able to learn more about your original people. Maybe they know what is in the vessel."

Tot's mouth dropped open. "You can find my…"

A nervous murmur from the crowd stopped him in mid sentence as his eyes fell to them again.

When he again looked at Saki, his smile was crooked. "They're afraid I'll leave them."

"They should be more afraid the KokoroTetians are coming back, because this time, they'll surely try to kill you."

To Saki's surprise, Tot looked puzzled. "Can they do that? Can they actually kill me?"

"I…" Saki paused, unsure of how to answer.

"I ask only because I don't think I had any idea of what death was before coming here. It may seem odd, but the thought that I might die some day has never occurred to me before now."

101

“Sir?” the sergeant specialist called. “You should see this.”

Khephra moved to his station, and motioned for him to continue.

“The beacon we put on Senator Addy’s shuttle indicates it was moving away from us for a time, but is now on an intercept course.”

Khephra looked at the sergeant specialist’s view screen. “They’re heading for Everona?”

“That would be my guess, Sir. There’s nothing much else out that way.”

“There could be another destination. Sub-commander Saki is just beyond Everona, searching for the planet the vessel came from.”

“We should let him know the senator is coming, Sir. He can intercept him and recover it.”

The supreme commander shook his head. “There’s something wrong here. Why would Addy go so far out of his way then race back to Everona?”

“No idea, Sir.”

“Come now, Sergeant Specialist. You’re smarter than that.”

“He was meeting someone?”

Khephra nodded. “But who?”

“That’s not far from the Maatiirani neutral zone.”

“But what would he need from them? Everona is a neutral planet and the people he stole the vessel from are primitive.” He tapped his chin. “And what would be the Maatiirani’s motivation?”

The sergeant specialist shrugged. “I think we have to assume they’ve formed an alliance. After all, isn’t he the snake, Sir?”

Khephra smiled while slowly nodding. “You’ve earned your stripes today, Sergeant.” He turned to Captain Praetor, “Engines at full thrust, Captain. We’ve got a snake to squash.”

Praetor shook his head. “But Sir, our fuel level is dangerously low. At full throttle we won’t have anything left to fight with when we arrive.”

"And if we stay at this speed?"

Praetor looked at his screen. "We'll arrive with half-a-*pak* of reserves."

Khephra stared at the main screen with unfocussed eyes as he rubbed his chin. After a moment, he nodded.

"Calculate the difference and transfer that amount to the four lead battleships. We'll race ahead and engage any enemy we find while the rest of the ships follow at normal speed. If I detect an enemy force before I arrive, I'll contact Saki and have him join us."

"That's risky, Sir."

"The alternative is leaving Saki exposed and vulnerable. I've already done that once and it's not going to happen again."

The captain nodded. "But we'll have to stop to transfer the fuel."

"We can't do it at this speed?"

Praetor shook his head. "If one bit of space debris a hundredth the size of a pea hits the transfer line with their engines fully engaged, both ships will be destroyed."

"Cut the engines and coast during the transfer."

"It will take some clever flying to keep the ships from rolling."

Khephra turned to his navigation officer. "Can you keep this ship steady without main engines?"

The officer smiled. "Give me a needle and thread and I'll knit you a lace hanky with her, Sir."

He turned back to the captain. "Good enough, Captain?"

Captain Praetor smiled nervously. "Good enough, Sir."

"Then make it happen!"

102

"Oh really," Kappa cried while holding up his bruised arm. "This is not exactly 'no harm'."

Pana's mouth dropped open. "I did that?"

"You or whatever it is that took over your body."

She shook her head as her fingers moved gently over the bruised surface. "I'm sorry."

"I'm not blaming you, but this is going too far."

"No, I can't stop."

"But he wants you to."

She sighed deeply. "He doesn't understand."

Gently, Kappa slid a hand around the back of her neck and looked into her eyes. "Neither do I."

"I have to get back to my people."

"We are your people," Kappa insisted.

Leaning her forehead against his, she locked eyes with him. "Please."

Sighing, Kappa slowly shook his head. "Where are these people?"

"We're going there now."

Looking at the main view screen, he shook his head. "Pana. There's nothing in this part of space, but a neutron star."

"And that's where we're going."

He sat back, raising an eyebrow. "There won't be a planet around it. All of that stuff would have been blown away millions of *druaks* ago when this thing went supernova."

She pulled back, wiping tears from her cheeks before continuing. "About six-billion *druaks* is more like it."

Kappa barked a nervous laugh. "The universe isn't that old."

Pana shrugged. "Actually, it's trillions of *druaks* old. You just can't see the whole thing from here."

He shook his head in disbelief. "This is crazy. If we can't see beyond the known universe, how can you know it's older than that?"

She motioned to the view screen. "This neutron star proves it."

Kappa looked at the tiny blip on the screen. "Wat Wat?" he called without turning around. "Can we date this star?"

His comrade moved to a control station and pressed several keys. "Hmm. I'll try to get its rotational speed. Since it doesn't have a companion star and there's nothing to interfere with its momentum, I should be able to give you a rough idea of its age."

"Without getting too technical, how?"

Wat Wat smiled. "It's easy. When stars of a certain size go nova, the remaining matter shrinks into a neutron star that typically spins at a rate of several times per *micro-pak*. If nothing interferes with them, the spin slows at a consistent rate. All I have to do is use our sensor readings to get this star's present deceleration rate and have the computer extrapolate back to determine roughly when this helium bomb blew up."

He punched keys for a few *micro-paks* before announcing, "Whoa! Something's wrong here."

Kappa looked at Pana who shrugged.

"What do you mean, something's wrong?"

Wat Wat shook his head. "These numbers don't make any sense. OK. Wait. Let's try using the star's temperature." He leaned over his console again. "They also cool at a consistent rate, so I'll just plug in the averages and see what's what."

Pana shook her head and sighed. "It's not going to make any difference."

"I don't get this," Wat Wat complained. "This star is weird."

"Give me a number," Kappa demanded, "no matter how wrong it seems."

Wat Wat scratched his head. "This damned star is hardly spinning and it's way too cool. No matter how I twist the dial, it can't be less than four-billion *druaks* old."

Kappa's jaw dropped. "You're kidding."

His comrade shrugged while shaking his head.

Pana put a hand on his arm. "Trust me, Kappa. His numbers are low."

"But how?"

She laughed. "Isn't it obvious?" She pointed to the screen. "This neutron star was far enough outside the range of the explosion we call the Big Bang. There were others as well. They're part of what created the turbulence that eventually caused stars to form from the ejected plasma."

Kappa turned to Wat Wat. "Does this make any sense?"

His companion shrugged. "I…suppose it might have happened that way."

He turned back to Pana. "So what does that particular star have to do with you?"

Letting out a sigh, she leaned back into her seat, but continued to face him. "Let me go find out."

She could see a protest form on Kappa's lips as he blinked from sight. All around her the mist was still turbulent: waves crashing, spray flying into the air. At that moment, she seemed to know she was only micro-millimeters tall. The star's massive gravity wouldn't allow more, but it didn't matter.

"Father, I can't remember what happened," she said to the mist forming a tube around her. "Why do I feel like it was my fault?"

The eyes appeared in front of her, and then melted back into the mist. Turning suddenly, she spied them in a different place just as they pulled back yet again. It was then she realized the second pair of eyes were more feminine and wider apart. A third pair appeared: larger and looking angry.

She felt fear again. "Father? How many are there?"

His familiar eyes appeared in front of her. "Thirty-six hundred and twenty-three, but it wasn't your fault, child. You were just too young to know better."

"To know better than what?" she asked as more eyes appeared above, below and beside her father's. She felt conscious of her nakedness again and wrapped her arms over her breasts. "What did I do?"

Her father's voice was soothing, as though speaking to a scared child. "Now don't worry, Dear. I don't think…"

"Tell her!" a male voice demanded angrily.

"After all this time, she should know," a female insisted.

"I don't know," her father waffled. "What good will it do?"

The angry one shouted, "She can get the damned vessel, you silly fool. It can get us out of here."

Her father's eyes moved forward, separating from the whole to form a humanoid-shaped blob of mist.

He turned to face the others. "It doesn't work that way. It will only trap more of them."

"You don't know that," a different female screamed. "You're just trying to protect her."

"What is it, Father?" Pana cried when he kept his back to her. "What can I do to help?"

He shook his head, but remained facing away from her. "It's too much to ask."

Freeing one hand covering her breasts, she grabbed his arm and was surprised to find it solid. "Tell me."

The eyes that faced her were sad, but the others grumbled angrily. She tried to count the pairs of eyes, but the swirling mist kept hiding and re-exposing them.

"You have to destroy this neutron star," her father finally said in a voice so soft she almost didn't hear him.

She shook her head. "That's impossible. Even the last Big Bang didn't do that."

He put his hand over hers. "Actually, it might be..."

"If you do it right," an angry voice interrupted, "it can be done."

"How?" she asked.

The many eyes looked around nervously as her father pulled away and turned toward the others. His face had no particular shape, just a spheroid with two eyes in it, so she couldn't guess what he was feeling. Wanting to ask more, but afraid of what they would say, she remained silent and watched the others.

Finally, her father sighed and turned toward her. "Bring the vessel here," he said, "and let it fall to the surface?"

"It would destroy everything again, like last time."

Another shape partially separated from the mist. "Nothing would be destroyed," it argued angrily. "It's all just energy and matter. The explosion would rearrange things a bit, just like last time."

"Not like last time," her father said as the other shape merged back into the mist. "The neutron star would produce a counter force that could focus the energy in a single direction."

"It might carry us for trillions of light years before it ran out of energy," a male voice speculated.

"So what?" a female argued. "We'd be free. Isn't that what's important?"

"Father," Pana called as she forgot her inhibitions and reached out to him with both arms.

Another voice laughed. "We'd be shot beyond the known universe. How exciting!"

"Compared to what we've already been through, a billion years as plasma would be like nothing," chuckled someone else.

"Father!" Pana shouted. "I can't do this."

"What?" the female snapped.

"You must," demanded a male voice.

"Make her, Anjenet," pleaded a different female. "Please make her do it!"

Anjenet's eyes locked with his daughter's. "Now you see why I didn't want you to come."

Cool tears trickled down Pana's cheeks as Kappa's face appeared in front of her.

She looked surprised to see him, but after a moment, she asked, "Did you hear any of what went on down there?"

He shook his head. "Just your side and that didn't make much sense."

She sighed wearily and leaned into him. "Just hold me."

Wrapping his arms around her, Kappa looked at his companions and sighed.

103

Stitto sat uncomfortably at the café's outdoor table while Addy appeared to be enjoying an afternoon on holiday.

"How you be so relaxed?" she asked indignantly.

Addy shook his heads. "You not impress them if they see nervousness. Our gut churn as much as yours, but Maatiirani smell fear."

Stitto squirmed in her seat. "Then We be Kurdo bait. We sweat so much our ass stick to chair."

"Sweating much is OK, but keep face neutral. They not know our species well enough to recognize nervousness. Just not look scared and they think you not, maybe?"

Stitto closed her eyes and tried to will her hands to stop shaking. To her dismay, it didn't work. As the four Maatiirani appeared from around a street corner, she shoved her hands under the table and swallowed hard.

"They be pussycats," she repeated again and again under her breath as four of the least pussycat-looking characters in the universe approached, dressed all in black leather shirts, pants and boots, with the blood-red image of a large bird embossed on their chests. Their black hair was pulled tightly into thick braids that ran down their backs and contrasted sharply with their shock-white faces.

The Maatiirani wore no jewelry, if you didn't count the teeth attached to their braids. However, on a silver belt around their waists dangled a laser pistol, a wicked-looking knife, and Stitto realized as they drew nearer, a gleaming pair of silver pliers.

Knowing a show of weakness might mean death, she tried her best to look stern, but couldn't resist the occasional break in form to swallow hard.

"Gentlemen," Addy greeted casually as the foursome stopped, and stood shoulder-to-shoulder in front of them. "Please to have seat, maybe?"

The two outside Maatiirani turned only their heads and scanned the area while Ehar shook his. “We prefer to remain alert in public situations,” he sneered. “Our people have more than a few enemies in this region of space.”

“Suit self, but eating dinner standing be difficult, maybe?”

Ehar nodded. “We’ll find something less exposed.”

After taking a slow sip of his drink, Addy chuckled. “There not be murder in town for ten *druak*, maybe? Even peoples crazy to kill Maatiirani keep peace here.”

Ehar jerked his head tersely as his comrades continued to watch those around them. The palpable tension made Stitto so nervous, she nearly dropped her glass. As Ehar glared malevolently at them, the senator looked like he hadn’t a care in the world.

“Suit self,” Addy said while rising slowly, drink in hand and signaling for Stitto to do likewise. As she did, she looked directly at them for the first time, and was surprised to see that the one in charge was the shortest.

Addy motioned toward the café’s door. “We find something inside, maybe?”

As one unit, all four Maatiirani moved quickly into the café. Stitto started to follow, but Addy motioned for her to wait as he tilted a pair of ears toward the door. *Micro-paks* later, there were several anguished cries from inside and three locals stumbled out while cursing the “white-faced bastards”.

Addy sighed and shook his heads before motioning for his companion to follow. Upon entering, they found all four soldiers seated at a large table, their backs to the wall and their hands out of sight. Stitto’s hearts pounded as she followed Addy in and sat across from them. Struggling to breathe, she couldn’t help imagining their fingers on the triggers of unseen laser pistols, ready and eager to kill them both at the slightest provocation.

Her hands went instinctively to her belly, all the while uttering a stream of prayers to any god who would listen.

“Oh, this be muchly better,” Addy exclaimed as though the idea had been his. He motioned to the bartender who appeared to be deciding whether to chance a dash for the door or dive behind the bar. "Kind Sir. Bring drinks for our friends, maybe?"

The bartender hesitated before asking, "What…what will you, uh, have?"

Without looking at his companions, Ehar answered, "Zorsish! If it is not green."

The barkeep's eyes went from Addy to Ehar and back. "I have some that's at least twelve *sirius* old and it's as black as *Quadaffa* coal. Will that do?"

All four growled their assent and the bartender hurried away.

Ehar lifted both hands from beneath the table and rested them in front of him. As twelve razor-sharp claws dug shallow pits into the table's scarred surface, he turned his attention to the senator.

"Where is Khephra?"

Addy slowly sipped his drink and sighed. "If our calculations be correct, he on way now."

Only Ehar's eyes revealed his nervousness at Addy's announcement. "And when do you expect him?"

The senator shrugged. "He be in process of destroying our fleet when We last see his battleship, so two or three *paks*, maybe?"

"And I suppose you want us to deal with him?"

"That can wait. We have something muchly important to do first."

"We?"

Addy nodded. "You want Khephra and he want us. Where We go, he go."

"What makes you so sure he knows where you are?"

The senator barked a laugh that surprised even the Maatiiranis. "Khephra have us pinned down on planet, he send teams of best men to surface and yet, here we be having drink with you."

Ehar's three companions stared blank-faced at Addy as their captain scowled. "He let you get away?"

Addy nodded. "And that why We come to you."

"You set me up?"

"No," Addy said conspiratorially. "We give opportunity."

Ehar's scowl gradually turned into a smile as he pulled a communicator from his pocket. "Brother," he called into the device. "All ships on high alert. Khephra's on his way."

"It is done, Brother," came the terse response. "We'll be ready for him."

Addy shook his head. "Be not forgetting, we be doing something else first."

"Why should I care?" Ehar snapped.

"Because, if you want Khephra, you needs stay close to us."

The teeth on Ehar's braid rattled as he shook his head. "I like the advantage this system gives me."

Addy shrugged. "And you much better like where we be going, maybe?"

"Why?"

"Because lots 'a space junk floats around there. Your smaller craft has distinct advantage over bulky battleships in such a place, maybe?"

"And where exactly is this system?"

Addy looked up to see the nervous bartender approaching. "Your drinks." He turned to Stitto, who seemed on the verge of a seizure. "We think it time to order dinner, maybe?"

Holding her grumbling stomach, the poor female nodded curtly and mentally challenged herself not to faint.

104

"Sir," Akki called as he entered the bridge. "I've got the results of the DNA profile you asked for."

The sub-commander held up a hand as he focused on a monitor screen. Rising to his feet, Tot rubbed his new arm. The scars on his face were gone and his bright, amber eyes seemed to shine as he nervously watched Akki.

"You know where I come from?"

Akki's eyes jerked from his superior to Tot and back, but all he could do was shrug.

Finally, Saki tapped a few keys on the control panel and looked up. "What did you find?"

"Well, this is confusing, Sir," the sergeant specialist answered, but his eyes were on Tot. "He's something new…and yet he's not."

"Please clarify, Sergeant Specialist. I think our guest is going to burst."

Akki shook his head. "When I was very young, my great uncle used to tell a story of the People Before Time. He said they lived even before the universe was created, and unlike us, their bodies lasted forever. According to the myth, we are all descended from them."

Saki shook his head as well. "Go on."

"I think Tot is proof that it wasn't a myth," he said while handing a tablet to the sub-commander. "His DNA is unlike anything we've ever seen, yet it's got pieces of every species we've ever know, including the Humans on the prison planets."

Saki looked at Tot then down to the tablet. "That can't be possible."

Tot's eyes moved from the sergeant specialist to the sub-commander. "What are you saying? I'm your infinitely-great grandfather?"

Akki smiled. "It looks that way."

"But where are the others?" Saki asked while still staring at the clipboard.

When Saki looked up, all eyes were on Tot and once the shaman realized it, he shook his head. “I really don’t know anything before these people found me, but I have this feeling that the rest of them were wiped out by a very powerful force.”

“It could have been what we call the Big Bang,” Akki speculated. “There’s not much that could have survived that.”

“But you think I did?” Tot asked. “And what was I doing between the time that happened and my craft crashed into this planet?”

Saki returned the notepad. “Maybe memory reconstruction can help you remember.”

Akki turned to Tot. “Would you be interested in trying?”

Nodding, Tot gently ran fingers over his new forearm. “I can’t think of anything I’d like more.”

“Sir,” the communications officer called as Akki and Tot left the bridge. “We’ve just received a communication from our operative on Everona. A squadron of Maatiirani ships arrived recently.”

Saki shook his head. “That’s way out of their territory. Any idea why they’re there?”

The officer shrugged. “Four of them went down to the planet and met with two Kokos.”

Saki looked at the screen in front of him. “Captain? What do you think of our odds against twelve Maatiirani ships?”

Fatak shook his head. “It does not promise a favorable outcome.”

The sub-commander turned to the communications officer. “Any word on the whereabouts of Supreme Commander Khephra?”

“None, Sir. The last I heard, he was following Senator Addy, but that was several *paks* ago.”

Saki shrugged. “He could be hundreds of light years away.”

“However, Sir. The senator’s last known heading was toward the Maatiirani region. The report did say these Maatiirani are meeting with Kokos. Maybe that’s him.”

For a few moments Saki stared at the planet slowly revolving below them before pressing an icon on his console. “Lieutenant Partok. How is the conversion of the internees going?”

A frazzled face appeared on the screen. “Not well, Sir. With our limited resources, we can only process a few dozen at a time. This is going to take half a *druak* to complete.”

“How long before the first batch is ready?”

Partok shook his head. “Ten, fifteen *pak*, Sir. And the process is made worse because they are coming out of the memory clamp spontaneously.”

Saki nodded. “We don’t even have enough crew to fully crew one of our ships. How are we going to defend ourselves against a squadron of Maatiirani fighters?”

Partok looked off screen and then back. “I have an idea, Sir. Some of the internees have started recovering their memories earlier than the rest. They’re still in Human bodies, but they’ve stabilized enough to be functional.”

“Why are they still Human? I would have thought you’d have transferred them first.”

The lieutenant shook his head. “Well, Sir…they refused.”

“Why?”

Partok shrugged nervously. “They want to remain Human.”

“That’s not helping,” Saki growled.

“Actually, it just might, Sir.”

“In what way?”

“Staying Human eliminates the adjustment period. Sergeant Specialist Akki thinks it would be easier to convert some of our ships to an oxygen-based atmosphere, boost the radiation shielding and train these people to fly them.”

“Hammond be praised,” Saki laughed derisively. “You’ve got to be kidding.”

Partok shook his head. “The doctors believe we can speed up the training with specialized memory regeneration. We can’t push that too far, but if the Maatiirani take another *pak* or so to get here, we may have one or two minimally trained crews ready to fight. Every *pak* thereafter give them more time to train.”

The sub-commander turned to look at the planet. “There’s no way this is going to work,” he muttered to himself before turning back to Partok. “How long will it take to convert the ships?”

The lieutenant smiled. “Preparations are already underway, Sir. We’ve also had the Humans working with simulators for the last couple of *deca-paks*.”

Saki smiled at his subordinate. “Good work, Lieutenant. Let’s hope the Maatiirani are enjoying their stay on Everona.”

Saki signed off and turned to his captain. “We’ll need to know the minute those ships leave Everona.”

Fatak shook his head. “The Maatiirani have a communications blockade around the entire system. Our agent had to leave the area to report to us.”

Saki nodded. “Tell him to do the best he can.”

“Yes Sir.”

Saki turned to review a message on his screen when the communications officer called. “Sir. I’m receiving a priority communication for your eyes only.”

“Send it to my station,” Saki ordered as he switched his screen to read it.

Captain Fatak watched the sub-commander’s face go pale.

“Sir?”

“We no longer have to worry about the Maatiirani leaving Everona,” Saki’s mouth was a thin line and his eyes wide with worry as he turned to face his captain. “They’re already on their way.”

105

"I still don't see why we're making this side trip," Ehar complained, his angry face filling Addy's view screen. "We need time to scope out the debris field you're taking us to and prepare for Khephra's arrival."

Addy nodded, though Stitto could tell he viewed his new ally as more a dangerous child than a warrior. "We get there soon enough, Commander, but We need something else to assure victory."

"But you said this planet is only occupied by bare-assed primitives. Of what use could they be to us?"

Addy shrugged. "Bare-assed maybe, but they have bit of ancient knowledge we can use to advantage, maybe?"

"What are you talking about?"

The senator shook his head. "That our little contribution to party, Commander. For time being, We keep to ourself."

Ehar started to protest, but checked himself. "I guess that's fair, Senator, but if you try to double cross me, I've got a few secrets of my own."

Addy sighed. "We sure you have, but nothing like that even cross our minds."

At the senator's signal, Stitto cut the connection.

"We hope Khephra blows psychotic bastard to deepest bowels of hell," Addy growled.

"But Sir?" she asked warily. "If Khephra win, do not that mean we be in trouble, maybe?"

Addy waved a hand dismissively. "It not matter. If We get what We want, we rid universe of both at same time."

"You be talking of key you search for, maybe?"

He nodded. "Which give us ultimate power of universe."

"But you really not know what inside box."

The senator shrugged. "Maybe, but we know it energy source greater than anything we ever see."

"A weapon?"

"Who knows? No one can decipher inscriptions on box, and without key, we not can open it again."

Stitto shifted in her seat. "Why did Khephra let us off planet with vessel?"

Addy nodded. "He want it away from fleet."

"But sensors not show anyone follow us."

"He not need to follow close with tracking device attached to our ship."

Stitto reached for the scanning controls, but Addy stopped her.

"We need him to follow."

"To get key, maybe?"

The senator rocked his heads from side to side. "Close, Commodore, but Khephra not have key."

"Is in Ooertfael debris field?"

"No. It once be in medallion around neck of shaman we going to see, but is now part of a Life Force."

"And where it be now?"

Addy chuckled. "On way here, in body of Khephra's daughter."

106

"Sir?" Captain Praetor called as he looked up from his monitor. "We'll be within visual range of the Everona system in one *pak*. I advise a scan of the system for hostiles."

Supreme Commander Khephra shook his head. "If Addy's working with the Maatiirani's, they'll be watching for active scan signals."

"Should we assume the Maatiiranis are in the system, Sir?"

Khephra nodded. "Keep an eye out for a perimeter guard and sensor buoys."

"Will we be approaching from underneath the planet again?"

The Supreme Commander shook his head. "Unlike Senator Addy, the Maatiirani are space pirates and will be thinking three dimensionally when it comes to defense."

"Sir," the scan officer called. "I'm getting readings of thirteen ships leaving Everona's orbit. According to our probe, Senator Addy is with them."

"Change course to pursue," Khephra commanded.

"Sir?" Praetor asked cautiously. "We don't have enough fuel to follow them, let alone fight."

Khephra clenched a fist and shook it at the main view screen. After pausing for a moment, he turned to his captain. "How long will it take us to refuel?"

Praetor shrugged. "Maybe one-and-a-half paks, if all the fueling stations are available."

"Just our ship?"

"We can't take on a dozen Maatiirani pirates with one battleship."

Khephra shook his head angrily. "Saki can come up in support."

It was Praetor's turn to shake his head. "None of his ships are properly manned. He'll be more of a hindrance than help."

"Damn!" Khephra cried while slamming a hand onto his console. "At the very least we've got to warn him."

"If I may make a suggestion, Sir," the communications officer said.

The supreme commander jerked a nod.

"We could send a broad-spectrum transmission in the general direction of Sub-commander Saki's position."

Praetor huffed. "But then the Maatiirani will surely know…"

He stopped and turned to Khephra who was already nodding. "…that we're here."

The supreme commander moved to the communications station. "Not too broad a spectrum," he said while turning toward the view screen. "Their captain has to know I'm not stupid. If it's too easy he'll suspect a trick. Just make it enough to seem like we tried to sneak it past him, but failed." He turned back to the officer. "And use Sotar999 encryption. It shouldn't take them long to break that."

"What shall I say, Sir?"

Khephra turned to face Praetor. "Maatiirani approaching your position. Avoid contact by moving to the Sentar system. High priority."

Praetor smiled. "You're thinking the Maatiirani will split their force and try to take both targets?"

The supreme commander smiled back. "And if my instincts are correct, they'll not be happy with the result."

The captain held up a hand. "I advise delaying that transmission, Sir." Khephra raised an eyebrow, but said nothing. "We'll be arriving at Everona in half a pack. Sending the message then would give us time to at least partially refuel before the enemy arrives."

"What about Saki and the other half-dozen Maatiirani?"

"I think the Maatiirani will stop to assess the situation," Praetor answered. "They'd still be over a pak from his position, so he'd have time to slip away and hide."

Khephra stopped to look at the view screen again then turned back to his captain. "Let's do it."

107

"Sir," Captain Fatak called as he entered the bridge. "The Human teams are ready for their test flights."

Saki's head snapped up. "There's more than one crew?"

Fatak smiled. "Actually, Sir, we have enough volunteers for three and the memory refresh got them up to speed much faster than anticipated."

The sub-commander nodded. "Let's see how they do."

Both officers turned to the view screen as three ships pulled out of formation, starting slowly at first then speeding up to complete a circuit of the planet's nearest moon.

Re-approaching the planet in a large arching trajectory, they flew past ten stationary targets, firing as they did. Each ship managed to hit better than half the targets, but the last ship cut its engines and did a quick end-for-end flip. While still moving away from the targets, its lasers fired to finish off the rest. It then did another back flip, fired up it engines and returned to the formation.

"Who the hell is flying that last ship?" Saki asked.

"Do you recognize the movement, Sir?" Fatak asked.

The sub-commander nodded. "I used it to pass my first flight test. It got me the admiration of my crew and the admonition of our division commander."

"And what will you tell this particular officer?"

Saki smiled. "I'm sure I'll think of something appropriately stuffy to say."

"Then as soon as their ships are back at station, I'll have them report to you."

Saki nodded and returned to his monitor. Before he even realized the time had passed, three Humans in space suits appeared on the bridge and snapped to attention.

Fatak stepped forward. "Sir, I'd like to introduce your Human captains: Captains Effret Attenta, Bottar Wak and Tammabet Ferrisis."

Only Saki's eyes gave away his surprise, but he quickly forced a stern look onto his face. "And I am to assume it was Captain Ferrisis performing those dangerous maneuvers with one of our precious ships?"

Captain Fatak nodded, but his face revealed no emotion.

Saki walked in front of the officers, making eye contact with each of them. When done, he moved a few paces away, turned and faced them.

"At ease," Fatak announced and the threesome shifted into an only slightly more relaxed position.

"Gentlemen, I believe you've been briefed on what's coming our way, so I won't go into that. We're outnumbered three-to-one and from an odds perspective, our position is pretty hopeless. But I don't pay much attention to numbers." His eyes jerked to each person in turn, but they remained motionless and straight faced. "What I have in mind is going to call for everyone following my game plan to the letter. The Maatiirani are pirates, so they know how to fight dirty. Our only hope is for them to initially believe we're undisciplined Kokos, willing to be panicked at the slightest provocation."

He paused to let his statements sink in.

"Do you understand me, gentlemen?" he asked sternly.

"Yes Sir!" they shouted in unison.

He paused again, searching their faces for a smirk or an attempt to catch his eye. None moved.

"Then let's get to work."

108

"Pana, what are we doing now?" Kappa asked as he brought the ship up to speed.

"I have to retrieve the vessel," she said softly, her eyes unfocussed.

"But we don't know where it's at."

She shook her head. "Yes I do."

"How?"

"I don't know. I just do."

Kappa made some adjustments to the controls before turning to her. "Will you tell us what's going on?"

She turned, focusing her large black eyes on him. Though he couldn't explain why, they seemed different to him somehow.

She sighed. "Before time as we know it happened, there was a different universe where this one is now."

"You mean, before the Big Bang?" Wat Wat asked.

Pana turned to him. "Yes, and before that there was another and then another. Trillions upon trillions of *druaks* of existence, interrupted every hundred million *druak* or so by a catastrophic eruption that rearranges everything and starts the process over again."

"How do you know this?" Kappa asked.

She shrugged. "Because there are two entities occupying my body and one of us has been around since before the last eruption happened."

All three looked at her with stunned expressions.

"How did you get into Pana's body?" Kappa asked.

She shook her head. "I've had many bodies since your universe was created. My brother and I traveled around, seeing worlds, solar systems and even galaxies created, destroyed and recreated; the rise and fall of endless civilizations; even the individual birth and death of stars. My last body was destroyed when our ship malfunctioned and crashed on the planet my brother Tot lives on. My

Life Force was transferred to a special amulet, then to a KokoroTetian and finally to this one."

"What is your name?"

She shrugged. "I've long forgotten what my original name was. I usually just took the name of the body I occupied. The most recent one I remember was Et."

Kappa shook his head. "But what happened to Pana?"

"I am Pana. Or more precisely, we're Pana."

"You've merged your Life Forces?"

Her head shook. "Not exactly. We're just sharing the space for now, but our thoughts and memories have merged into one harmonious collection."

Kappa's eyes widened. "That's not possible."

Pana smiled. "Trust me, she's accepted me voluntarily. We are like sisters in one body."

"But how do I know which of you I'm talking to?"

She shrugged. "You're always talking to both of us and we decide between ourselves who responds."

He pulled back and looked at her. "I'm not comfortable with this."

Pana shrugged again. "It doesn't matter. Our goal is to find the vessel and use it to free my father and his colleagues."

"And what of us?"

"If we do this right, it should have very minimal impact on your universe."

"And Pana?"

Her face showed confusion. "I want to stay here with you."

109

"What was that?" Ehar demanded as he rushed to the communications station.

"I'm not sure, Sir," the officer answered. "It's on an old Antrakan communications frequency."

"Military?"

"Yes Sir. It's encrypted, but I can break it."

"Khephra?" Ehar asked rhetorically as he looked at the main view screen. "How long?"

"It shouldn't take more than a few milli-paks. He probably didn't think we'd be monitoring this frequency."

His eyes still on the view screen, Ehar asked, "Does he think we're idiots?"

"He may think just that," Uhua said while moving in to lean over the communications officer's shoulder.

"I wonder," Ehar whispered to himself.

"I've got it," the communications officer announced as he turned to his captain. "The sender is signaling to a ship ahead of us. I think the captain's name is Saki."

"N-Tschester?" Uhua asked, surprised. "What's he doing out of prison?"

"Sir," the communications officer called. "Senator Addy is calling."

Ehar scowled, but nodded. "Senator," he said as pleasantly as his newly-soured mood would allow. "What can I do for you?"

"Did you intercept transmission?"

Ehar indicated for silence. "Yes, we are trying to decipher it right now."

"It gotta be Khephra. He be only one using that kinda military frequency."

"You might be right, Senator, but I'd like to wait until we find out what the message is."

"Are any ships ahead of us?"

Ehar looked at the scan station, but the officer shook his head.

"Nothing as of yet, but we're too far away to see anything at our destination. Another half-pak ought to do it."

"Keep sharp eyes, Commander. We not know how many ships Khephra have."

"I very much intend to, Senator," Ehar said as he signed off.

The commander turned to the communications officer, "What's in that message?"

"It's a warning of our presence and advice to leave the area as soon as possible."

"Destination?"

"The Sentar system, a pak and a half from our destination."

Ehar frowned. "Just out of passive sensor range, but close enough to provide support if needed."

"It might also be a ruse," Uhua warned. "What if they do have more ships and are preparing to sandwich us between them?"

Ehar signaled to his communications officer. "Let's have another chat with the senator."

Bending over his console, the officer worked the controls for a moment before shaking his head.

"He isn't responding, Sir."

"Sir," the scan officer called. "The senator's ship is accelerating away from us at super-light speed. I've never seen anything move that fast."

"Get after him," Ehar demanded as he moved to the navigation console to watch the tiny blip grow ever smaller.

"We can't Sir," the navigation officer announced. "He's moving at over twice our maximum speed."

"He's what?" Ehar cried as his eyes jerked down to the officer's display. "That's impossible."

"Where's he headed?" Uhua demanded.

"The same destination, it seems."

Uhua moved up beside his brother. "Is this a trap?"

The commander shook his head. "He's afraid they'll beat him to whatever he's looking for."

Uhua's eyes followed his commander's. "And if they do?"

Ehar shook his head. "It wouldn't be good for either of us."

"So what are we going to do, Brother?"

"Damn!" Ehar cried. "Politicians are hell on strategy." The commander marched several times around his console station before pointing to the communications officer. "Send a command to the group. Hard to port and full throttle."

Uhua looked confused. "Are we running?"

Ehar's head shook. "I just want time to figure out what's going on."

He moved to the scan station. "Aggressive scan in all directions, but do it quickly so they don't know we've deviated from our previous course."

He returned to his console. "If the force on our right is light enough, we can wheel around and hit them first." He pointed to his screen. "We can cut behind that dusty proto-sun and then skip to the small system just beyond it. Both will hide our approach until we're almost on top of them."

"But Khephra is behind us," Uhua argued.

Ehar nodded. "He doesn't yet know we've changed course and I'm guessing he won't fully reveal himself with an active scan until he's closer." He dipped his head, running a razor-sharp claw slowly down the bridge of his nose. After a moment, he laughed softly. "That Supreme Commander is a crafty dog. I'm going to enjoy taking his teeth."

"Sir," the scan officer called. "I detect four ships coming at us from the right. None from our left."

"None?" Uhua asked.

"I scanned all the way back to Everona," the officer answered. "There are ships in her refueling stations, and a few on the normal trade routes, but none in this sector."

"Hmmm…" Ehar muttered while scratching his nose again. "Maybe the Kokos were right. His ships might really be invisible."

"But if it's the same technology as Addy has, we can see through it," Uhua argued.

His brother shook his head. "Only at close range. Our long-range scans won't detect them."

"Sir," the scan officer announced. "I finished analyzing the data from my scans. The four ships coming from our right are Koko ships."

Ehar smiled and turned to Uhua. "Brother. It looks like we're going to have a little fun before we take on the big guns." He turned to his communications officers. "Get Captain Ojau on the comm."

After a few micro-paks, his station communicator beeped.

"Captain. Take five ships and head back toward Everona until you find Supreme Commander Khephra's fleet, but don't engage them. I'm going to deal with the ships coming from the other direction. When I return, I'll sneak around to Khephra's rear and give him a little surprise."

Captain Ojua smiled. "With pleasure, Sir."

Signing off, Ehar grinned wickedly at his brother. "The supreme commander's teeth are as good as mine."

110

"Sir?" Stitto asked as she watched the Maatiirani ships vanish into the distance behind them. "What we doing, maybe?"

Addy shook his heads. "We not wait for shit-heads to fight this out. If We get first to shaman, we end this for all time."

"How we do that, Sir?"

He jerked a head in her direction. "Surely if shaman got one key, he got another."

Stitto put a hand on her grumbling stomach and felt her eggs shifting. "Would this planet be good place for to have babies, maybe?"

Addy peered at something on his view screen. "They not friendly last time, so no, We not want spend much time there."

Stitto leaned one head over to peer into Addy's monitor. "Be that four ships coming at us?"

The senator nodded. "And they be KokoroTetian light cruisers. What that crazy Khephra up to?"

"Maybe they not his. We be happy for reinforcements about now."

Addy shook his head while playing with the communication controls. "No, if these be our people, We hear plenty chatter."

"Scans show enough bodies to be properly crewed, but they not KokoroTetian."

"He got only six ships. Where extra peoples come from?"

"This be crazy, Sir, but one ship only have Antrakan crew. Other three be manned by…" Her jaws slack, she looked briefly at Addy before turning back to her screen. "They be Human, maybe?"

Addy snorted. "Nonsense! He not have time to train primitives for…"

"Sir?"

"Khephra be using prisoners, maybe?"

"On space ships?"

Addy snorted. "He give crap to us about abusing primitives and now he do same."

"But he tell them to flee, Sir. Why they come this way?"

Both of Addy's heads jerked in her direction. "Let's be sure they not find us. Stay above their flight path and get to planet quickly, quickly."

"Yes Sir," she responded, her stomach gurgling as a reminder that getting somewhere… anywhere as quickly as possible was also important to her.

111

"Sir," Saki's scan officer called as he turned in his chair. "Something just zipped past us at well over light speed."

"That's not possible," the sub-commander exclaimed while jumping up from his station. "What was it?"

The officer turned back to his screen. "It looked very much like the ship we took from the Koko pirates."

"Addy," Saki muttered while slapping the high back of the scan officer's chair. "Do an active scan for Maatiirani ships."

The officer stared at his screen for a moment before reporting, "Nothing within a pak of our position. I do see six of their ships heading back toward Everona."

Scratching his chin, Saki paused momentarily before turning to the communications officer. "All ships on full alert!"

Doing a quick spin around, he hurried to his station. "Captain. Work up the most likely attack vectors."

Fatak was already ahead of him. "A small, dusty proto-sun to our right would provide just such an opportunity, Sir. If they came through it at maximum speed, we'd have only micro-paks to react before they'd be in weapon's range."

"If we can't see them then they can't see us." He pointed at the navigation station. "Go into that solar system. When they come around, we'll be the ones providing the surprise."

"Communications, tell the other ships to prepare for battle. The Humans will need full combat suits so they can reduce the oxygen levels in their ships."

As the ships approached the dust lanes surrounding the proto-sun, Saki watched his crew busily working at their stations.

"Enemy ships straight ahead, Sir," the scan officer cried.

Saki's eyes jerked to the view screen as one ship after another appeared from the dusty screen.

"Full attack formation," he cried as the bridge lurched violently to the left.

112

"Sir, we need to get underway," Captain Praetor insisted as he came onto the bridge. "I've just received word that the Maatiirani have split their group and six are headed this way."

Khephra looked up from his monitor. "That's a bit sooner than I would have expected. Any idea why?"

"None, Sir."

"What is our fuel situation?"

"All of our ships are at least half full, some even three-quarters."

"How long before we're fully loaded?"

"Another quarter pak, Sir, but the Maatiirani ships are less than half-a-pak away. We wouldn't want to get caught just leaving the fueling station. It will take a deca-pak to get our ship out of dock and our engines up to full thrust."

The Supreme Commander nodded. "Quite right, Captain. Order all ships out of dock as soon as possible. Contact the trailing ships and have them head straight for the fueling stations. They are to report to me on arrival. We may need them to take on minimal fuel and then fly out to give us a hand."

"I've already ordered it, Sir," Praetor responded while moving to the communications station. "The tug is moving into position now."

"Scan station," Khephra called. "Give me an accurate status of the Maatiirani ships. While you're at it, see if you can find Sub-commander Saki's ships as well."

"Yes Sir."

Khephra turned back to his monitor as a space tug made contact with the ship, causing it to jerk slightly.

"And Captain, tell that tug operator that if he doesn't want to be caught in the middle of a battle, he'd better get us into the transport lane quickly."

Praetor's head rose as he nodded and then ducked down to speak to his communications officer. A micro-pak later, he popped up again.

"Sir, the marker we put on Senator Addy's ship has gone dark."

Khephra nodded. "It doesn't matter now," he said unhappily. "We know where he's headed."

The captain and his commander's eyes locked briefly before Khephra added, "May the Lord Hammond have mercy on their souls."

Praetor dipped his head momentarily before turning back to the communications officer.

"Sir," the scan officer called. "Six Maatiirani ships are headed our way. So are Sub-commander Saki's ships."

Praetor looked from the scan officer to his commander. "He's headed our way?"

"Where are the other Maatiirani?" Khephra asked.

"I believe I saw them going into the disk of a proto-sun just to the sub-commander's starboard side, Sir."

Praetor shook his head. "We should warn him."

Khephra held up a hand. "It will do no good. They'll be on him before our message arrives."

"But…" the captain said, but the supreme commander stopped him.

"I'm sure Sub-commander Saki knew we needed to split them up to have any chance of winning this battle. We'll have to honor his sacrifice by using the advantage he's given us."

The whole bridge paused with every eye on the Supreme Commander. He also paused for just a moment before turning to his captain.

"Let's get that tug into high gear," he ordered. "We've got some Maatiirani butts to kick."

113

"I can't believe we're going this fast," Wat Wat laughed as he watched the universe zip past. "Who created this ship?"

Pana looked up from her monitor. "The technology came from the Time Before Now."

Wat Wat looked confused. "The what?"

Pana shrugged. "The time before the Big Bang, when my people lived as scientists. I helped my father create something like this and built one for us later."

"You gave it to the Kokos?"

She shook her head. "I intended to use it to free my brother from his self-imposed exile, but the one I was flying crashed when I tried to land it. My body was destroyed and I was forced to live in his Exdansta jewel."

"His what?"

She waved a hand dismissively. "You'd call it a large gem, but it's actually a vessel that can hold Life Forces. The people living on that planet weren't suitable for hosting me, so I went there to avoid being consumed by the Samhain."

"But why didn't Tot help you build another one?"

Pana shook her head. "My brother's body wasn't seriously damaged in the crash, but the trauma made him lose his memory. I had no physical form, so naturally, I couldn't build another craft myself, nor could I convince him to do so."

"So you were trapped there."

"Until that two-headed creep, called Addy came down. I tried to move to one of their bodies, but found the KokoroTetians have two life forces and are far too self-centered and impulsive to easily control. In the end, they took me away in my own ship. Then after the box had been opened, and their bodies destroyed, I was transferred to Pana."

"But why did you let her be imprisoned?"

Pana sighed. "Your friend wanted to stop a war, and in case you hadn't noticed, she has a very strong will."

"You can say that again," Kappa laughed.

"Could you show us how to build something this fast?" Wat Wat asked.

Pana shook her head. "The technology in this craft could be modified to allow it to reach warp ten, at which, theoretically, you transcend space and time. I think that right now, your people should be limited to this space you refer to as the 'known universe'."

"Why?"

"Not all of the real universe is as violent and aggressive as you are."

"We're not that violent," Wat Wat protested.

"You are threatening a galactic war over a vessel you believe contains the ultimate source of power, are you not?"

Wat Wat stiffened. "We just want to make sure it's not misused."

Pana smiled. "And who among you can be trusted with it?"

Kappa laughed. "I think you just asked the ultimate question."

An alarm sounded on Kappa's console, startling him. "What's this?"

Pana leaned over to look at his console. "We're dropping out of warp. Something in this area is destabilizing our engines."

"What do you mean?" Wat Wat asked.

Pana checked her own monitor. "High-energy discharges like those coming from this young proto-star we're passing."

Kappa shook his head as he looked at his scanner. "There's a battle going on over there."

"Who?" Ba' Roque asked as he moved up behind Kappa.

"Oh sweet Hammond," Pana cried. "Those are Saki's ships."

114

Saki scrambled up from the floor of his bridge and yelled. "Damage report!" as he heard his own ship's weapons discharge.

Captain Fatak swiveled his monitor around and scanned it. "Cargo hold two has ruptured, but we're otherwise sound, Sir."

"So much for the element of surprise," Saki muttered, but then asked, "Where are those Maatiirani ships?"

"They came out too close to fire more than one volley each," the scan officer announced. "We took one hit and Captain Attenta's ship took two. One of the Maatiirani ships is spewing smoke from the engine, I think."

"Is Attenta still operational?"

The scan officer nodded. "He's coming around with the rest of us to face their next attack."

"Tell him to wait and pretend to be disabled. Have Captain's Ferrisis and Wak move away from him. The enemy will likely send a ship or two to finish him off and we can split their force enough to give us an edge."

"That won't really gain us much, Sir," Fatak announced. "It looks like their damaged ship is also still operational."

"Fire in cargo hold one," someone yelled over the comm link.

"We have to shut down the port engine or the whole ship's going to go."

"*Shendtada*," Fatak swore. "We can't fight with only one engine."

"Into the dust lanes," Saki ordered. "We'll play hide-and-seek until that fire is under control."

"Too late, Sir" the scan officer announced. "They've already started their turn."

Saki looked around for a solution, but finding none, leaned toward the communications officer. "Tell Attenta to come up with us. It looks like we're going to have to make a stand here, even with only one engine." He leaned on the comm icon. "Damage team? Let me know the instant that fire's out. I don't have to tell you how badly we need that engine."

"Will do, Sir."

"Communications? Give me a secure channel to the other ships." Micro-paks later, the officer gave him the thumbs up. "Captain Ferrisis, it looks like we're going to need a bit of that fancy flying you exhibited earlier."

115

"We be landing in couple milli-paks, Sir," Stitto announced as they dropped through the deep layer of clouds covering the planet.

"Be that rain down there?" Addy asked while peering through the side window.

"Yes, Sir," she answered. "Big storm at landing site."

"Have you found natives?"

Stitto looked at her monitor. "We think so, maybe? They be clustered around refuse pit."

Addy nodded. "They be hiding in shelter covering opening, maybe?"

"We sure not want be caught long outside in this crap."

"Let's be getting in and out quickly, maybe?"

Stitto looked at the senator. "We thought shaman you kill be only one who know about key."

"He live with them for long time. Maybe someone else know how to open vessel."

"But if it do so much damage when our scientist open it only tiny bit, what use is it?"

Addy smiled wickedly. "Best weapon be so deadly nobody ever want it be used."

"But opening vessel mean we all be destroyed."

He nodded. "Then everybody gotta believe We be crazy enough to do just that."

"We not see you as self-destructive."

Addy grinned. "Keeping that secret to ourselves be OK, maybe?"

Stitto frowned nervously. "Yes Sir."

Closer to the ground, Stitto struggled to steady the craft as high winds raged around them.

"Sir, we not be going out in this storm safely," she protested. "We not even be sure of landing safely."

Holding tightly, Addy shook his heads. "We got no choice."

Stitto gulped down a breath and struggled with the little craft until it thumped noisily onto the ground. The craft continued to shudder in the high wind as she completed her shutdown procedures.

Addy took a deep breath, pried his fingers from the stabilizer bars, and climbed from his seat.

"We be thinking there be rain gear in storage locker," he announced while unlatching the vessel behind his seat. "Bring laser weapons too, maybe. This not likely be cordial visit."

Stitto shook her heads as she struggled to extract herself from the seat. "Just what expectant mother needs be doing," she muttered while moving toward the back of the ship, "waddle around on stormy, muddy, gods-forsaken planet looking for unfriendly natives."

"What that, maybe?" Addy asked as he lifted the vessel.

"We just getting laser pistols, Sir."

The rain-laden wind was colder and more forceful than she expected and the ground muddier. However, with ten short legs to distribute their weight, the KokoroTetians were actually better equipped to walk in mud than bipeds.

Ducking their heads against the wind, they hurried down the path to the village without seeing a single soul.

"Where be everybody?" Addy cried over the howling wind.

"They probably not even know we come," Stitto grumbled while slogging through down the muddy path.

"Not be worrying," the senator said while gripping his weapon in one hand, and holding the vessel with the other three. "They know lot more than we give credit for."

Stitto's stomach grumbled as her eggs shifted position. "Sir, We be thinking maybe our estimate of..."

She stopped as they entered a sheltered clearing filled with people, and beyond them, the covered pit that was Addy's destination.

Addy raised his weapon, sweeping it in front of his body. His companion held her two weapons pointed at the people's feet.

"We talk to shaman," Addy squawked and then waited for his translation unit to repeat his demand.

As the people in front of them agitated, he could hear grumbling and cries through his ear piece, but no words.

Finally Tot stepped forward looking wet and cold. “We have nothing left to give you.”

Addy looked at him in amazement. “How you do that?” he asked. “You buncha’ tiny people and yet shaman always bigger. Be you taking something to stimulate growth, maybe?”

When Tot gave his head a sharp jerk, water flew out from the ends of his long hair. “I’ve always been their shaman, and there’s only ever been one of me.”

“But that not can be,” the senator argued. “Last time here, We kill shaman.”

Tot shrugged. “You tried, but they saved me.”

“And reattached arm?”

“No. That was done by the one they call Saki.”

Addy looked at him warily. “You know We coming, maybe?”

Tot nodded.

“Then why you not escape with him?”

Tot spread his arms out. “My place is with my people.”

Addy laughed. “We love heroes. They be such suckers.”

Shifting the vessel, Addy pointed his weapon at Tot and prepared to vaporize him when an acrid smell assaulted his nostrils.

“What?”

Stitto jumped forward. “Sir, something flowing down path.”

“What?” he cried again while stumbling forward, all the time waving his weapon at the crowd to ward off attack.

“It is accadity oil,” Tot answered. “It will burn the flesh right off your bones.”

“Hammond’s balls,” Addy cried as he reached the front of the crowd. “Make it stop or We kill your people.”

Tot shook his head as the crowd parted, exposing a path to the shelter. “There’s no time. Inside quickly or you will die.”

Addy leveled his weapon at Tot. “What traps be there for us?”

Tot motioned to the liquid flowing toward them. “Nothing as bad as that.”

As Addy took another look back, a dog-like creature dashed into the path. As soon as its forefeet hit the liquid, it cried out and collapsed head first into it. A cloud of mist rose up around the beast as it melted into the path. Within seconds, nothing remained but bubbling liquid and puffy patches of yellow mist.

"Ahh," the senator screamed as he dashed for the shelter with Stitto close behind.

"Senator," his companion called as they stepped inside. "Walk carefully. There may be loose boards…"

Her warning was cut off when the floor under her boss dropped from sight, carrying the screaming Addy down with it.

Spinning around as fast as her egg-laden body would allow, she pointed both weapons at Tot as he stood alone in the entrance.

"You kill him," she cried.

Tot shook his head. "We only stopped him from hurting us."

Only then did Stitto hear the whizzing pulleys."

"He on elevator, maybe? How far down it go?"

Tot moved slowly to the edge of the opening. "It is about a hundred meters to a ledge that opens into a small cave. That is where they discovered the vessel all those lifetimes ago."

Aiming her gun at his chest, she did her best not to look terrified. "Bring him back."

Tot shook his head again. "It would not be in his best interest." He waved a hand toward the ceiling of the hut. "Up there, a great battle is being fought. If your allies win, they'll likely kill us all, and you as well, to get what your companion possesses."

Keeping one face toward Tot, Stitto turned the other up and imagined the battle. Suddenly, Ehar's excited, blood-smeared face appeared in her mind's eye.

She lowered her weapons as both faces drooped toward the floor. "What in Hammond's Name we do?" she cried. "This go badly for us no matter who win, maybe?"

Tot smiled. "The battle will probably be indecisive, but your enemies will likely return before your allies."

"Khephra kill us both."

Tot shrugged. "I am told he only wants to make sure the vessel isn't used improperly."

"And if Maatiirani win, maybe?"

Tot nodded toward the opening Addy had dropped through. "They can't kill what they can't find."

Stitto suddenly realized the crowd had begun filing through the doorway and were gathering around them. After a few milli-paks, an ancient-looking female appeared from among them, and stopped just in front of Stitto. She stood quietly for a moment and looked the KokoroTetian over before saying something to Tot.

"What she say?" Stitto demanded.

Tot nodded to the female, who gave Stitto a toothy grin before moving back into the crowd.

"She is Aha, one of our wisest healers," Tot explained. "She tells me you have more than one life to protect."

Both of Stitto's heads turned to follow the vanishing healer. "How she know that? We be different species totally."

Tot chuckled. "I've long stopped wondering about Aha's wisdom. She just knows these things."

Stitto grabbed her stomach as a contraction rippled through it. "We gotta get off planet."

"You are safer here than anywhere in the universe."

She shook her heads. "We know senator kill many people last time he be here. Why you help me?"

Tot shrugged. "He who did these terrible things, not you."

"So you wanna kill him, maybe?"

He shook his head. "The one called Saki promised he would not be hurt if they came for him. I've seen their rehabilitation process. It is very humane."

"You want revenge?"

"Revenge only brings an endless cycle of retaliation that accomplishes nothing and destroys much. Forgiveness is the only way to end that destructive cycle."

Stitto shook her head. "You all be nuts."

Tot looked confused. "Your translation device was unable to interpret that last statement."

"Not to worry," she laughed dryly. "Just get us down there."

116

"Sir," the scan officer called as Saki watched the Maatiirani ships swinging around for another pass at them. "Captain Ferrisis has broken from the formation." He turned back to his screen. "Two enemy fighters are pursuing her."

"What is the status of our remaining ships?"

"They are approaching our position, Sir."

Saki looked up at the view screen to see four Maatiirani ships almost within weapons range. "Engine room. What's happening with that fire?"

"Not good, Sir," the response came back. "The fire is approaching the fuel lines. We're going to have to vent two more holds into space or lose the whole thing."

Saki nodded. "Get your people out of there and vent them now."

"Already on it, Sir."

"Engineering, get that engine up as soon as you can," Saki yelled. "Immediately may not be soon enough."

"We've already started priming the ignition," the engineer responded.

Saki shook his head. "Let me know when I can do more than sit here like a fat cow."

117

"Two of them are venting, including the lead ship," Uhua announced as he fondled the silver pliers on his belt. "I can almost taste their blood now."

Ehar snorted derisively. "Do not write off these Kokos so quickly, Brother. They sometimes put up a good fight."

Uhua laughed. "That would make their teeth more valuable."

"One of the ships is breaking ranks," the scan officer called.

Ehar's eyes jerked to the view screen. "Send two of ours after it." Shaking his head, he turned back to Uhua. "These Koko commanders can not even keep their ships in formation. You may be right about this being an easy win."

"The lead ship is venting even more, Sir," the scan officer called. "Thermal scans show he is only running on one engine and rotating out of firing position."

"Could this get any easier?" Uhua laughed.

"Bring up two ships to keep their companions occupied," Ehar ordered. "We will focus on the lead ship, and disable its remaining engine." He turned to his brother. "Prepare our sons' team for boarding. We will let them have first kill while we finish off the others."

"Will you not participate?" Uhua asked.

Ehar shook his head. "I will wait for the Supreme Commander's ship."

Laughing, Uhua left the bridge.

"We are almost in weapon's range, Sir," the scan officer announced.

Ehar nodded, leaning forward as though he were ready to leap from his seat.

"Hold fire until I give the order," he said while remaining mesmerized with his objective. "I want to get close enough to see their eyes when we take out their last hope of resistance."

One officer laughed, but the others remained quiet as Ehar twitched in his chair, straining against the slow pace of time as the anticipated engagement approached.

Slowly lifting his hand, Ehar watched the distance-to-target display on the view screen. As his eyes jumped from the display to the ship foundering before him, the scars on his face turned a brighter shade of crimson.

"My enemy's blood will flow this day and defeat will be his supper," he quoted from an ancient Maatiirani poem. "Victory is a soldier's game, given to the best of us. As blood of the vanquished pools at my feet…"

The ship shuddered.

"Sir, the fleeing ship is firing on us."

Ehar looked toward the scan officer. "The fool! It is too far away to do any serious damage."

As his attention was momentarily drawn from the screen, his foundering opponent suddenly jumped to life, its second engine firing flame. Ehar jerked his eyes back to the screen and was just preparing to order a course change when two fists of energy slammed into his own right engine.

The view screen became a blur as Ehar cried, "Ya Ya's ass!", but all he could do was hang on to his seat as his navigator struggled with the controls.

"Our right engine's out," the officer announced. "We are pushing too hard to hold her steady."

"Kill the engines and bring her about," Ehar screamed. "Who is watching our flank?"

"I can not see anything," the scan officer complained while holding onto his console. "We are spinning too fast."

As the ship's spin started to slow, another blast jarred it.

"We've lost navigation," the navigation officer announced. "I can bring her around under manual control, but we will be flying without sensors."

"The Great Warrior's ass you say," Ehar swore. "Get this ship back into the battle. No Koko puddle jumper is going to defeat me!"

His ship spinning at a disorienting speed, Ehar caught only a glimpse of the opposing lead ship attacking his wingman.

"Narrow the view screen window and center that ship in it. We can help our wingman by distracting them."

"That will limit our view of the battle," the navigations officer complained. "We will not be able to see anyone else coming at us."

Ehar jumped from his seat as the ship's spin slowed. "I have three other ships to deal with them. I want this Koko's teeth!"

"It's not a Koko commander, Sir," the communications officer announced. "They are using Antrakan frequencies."

"Antrakans on a Koko ship?" Ehar cried. "What is this?"

Ehar rushed to the weapons station as the Koko lead ship turned sharply and passed in front of his wingman. Though the wingman fired, his shots fell just behind the faster light cruiser.

The cruiser then flew above his attacker, and fired a shot into its hull in front of the port engine. The cargo hold burst open, disgorging equipment and bodies into space. A second shot ruptured the engine, sending the ship spinning in Ehar's direction.

"Fire at that damned ship," Ehar screamed.

"But Sir, our wingman's in the way," the officer argued.

"He is dead anyway, so fire away."

Several beams of light surged from their laser cannons, but all missed the mark as the enemy ship flew across their field of view. Their last shot punched a hole in the wingman's damaged engine.

"Damn!" Ehar screamed. "Where are the rest of our ships?"

The scan officer held up his hands. "We are blind, Sir. I can not see anything more than this view screen shows."

"Open it up to wide screen and let's see who can help us."

The screen's view changed in time to see two of their ships being outmaneuvered by Bottar's light cruiser. To the far left of the screen, a fourth ship was making progress with Attenta's cruiser, but Tamm and her two pursuers were out of sight.

"This is a damned mess," Ehar moaned as he turned to his communications officer. "Bring back the two chasing the break-off ship back. We will worry about the coward later." He started to turn away, but changed his mind. “Get the status of our wingman. Navigation: Get us into position to fire on that lead ship.”

The navigator shook his head. “He is moving too fast to follow with only maneuvering thrusters.”

“What about aft sensors?”

“Disabled along with our starboard engine.”

“Then flip over, nose to tail and make him come to us.”

The view screen filled with star trails as the navigator made the required move. When the ship achieved the one-hundred-and-eighty degree rotation, the enemy ship appeared at the left edge of their screen.

“Fire when ready,” Ehar commanded.

As the sizzling balls of energy flew at the enemy ship, Ehar’s own ship shook violently.

“Sir,” the engineer called over the intercom. “Our laser generator just exploded. All weapon systems are down.”

“Ya Ya’s ass,” Ehar swore while watching his shot hit the enemy mid-ship. “What else can go wrong?”

“Sir,” the communications officer called. “That blast took out our communications as well. I was just able to call our two ships back, but it went dead before I could contact the wingman.”

Slamming both fists against his console, he screamed. “Emergency power to those stations. I am not turning tail on Kokos!”

“It looks like the enemy ship has gone dark. Our last shot must have taken out his power conduits.”

“What is happening with our other ships?” Ehar bellowed. “Communications?”

“I am working on it, Sir!”

Ehar waved an arm impatiently. “Navigation, bring us around so I can see the whole field.”

The ship turned to show their damaged wingman sitting dark in space with two KokoroTetian light cruisers hovering above it. As they came fully about, four new shapes filled his screen: fully-armed Antrakan battleships in attack formation.

“By the Gods,” the navigations officer cried. “We are dead.”

118

"Sub-commander Saki N-Tschester, as overseer of the prison colony at Secor-Alpha Four, I hereby arrest you and your crews as escapees from Prak a'Terra." Sub-commander Petish shook his head as he turned to face the view screen. "Now that we've got the formal shit out of the way, maybe you'd like to explain what in Ceratha's name is going on here."

"How did you…?" Saki started to ask but was stopped by a wave of Petish's hand.

"You may think I'm stilted as a commander, but I'm not stupid."

"I would never say that."

"I don't intended to be insulting here, N-Tschester, but you make a lousy Koko captain."

Saki looked surprised. "But why didn't you intervene?"

Petish moved close to Saki. "I know the supreme commander removed you from Prak a-Terra. No one in this fleet has more respect for our leader than I. I served under him for ten *druak* just after you were interred. Someone like that doesn't spend his entire life supporting our way of life and then suddenly abandon those beliefs without good reason."

"But how did you follow us without being spotted?"

"I'm a technical person," Petish said while turning toward the view screen. "I like my life ordered and things where they should be. But serving under the supreme commander teaches you that technical precision does not always win out over creativity." When he looked at Saki again, he was smiling. "I used one of Khephra's tricks, and put a marker on your ship. That made it easy to follow you anywhere without exposing myself."

Saki's attention was distracted by a shadow at the edge of his vision, but by the time he turned to look, he only caught a glimpse of a brown robe vanishing through a door.

"I'm guessing you had a little help, Sub-commander," he said while turning back to Petish, "from the Ghostman?"

Petish didn't try to hide his surprise. "For someone who's been locked away for so long, you know a lot of influential people."

Saki smiled. "Like you said, you can't hang around the Supreme Commander long without picking up a few of his tricks." Saki's smile vanished. "This is only half of the Maatiirani ships. Where are the rest of them?"

Petish laughed. "They've taken on a worthy opponent, but just the same, my light cruisers are providing him support. The Maatiirani shouldn't be much trouble."

"He'll likely fare better than we did," Saki sighed.

Petish shook his head. "You fought six Maatiirani ships to a stand-still with only four of those worthless Koko cruisers, three of which were manned by Humans. Hammond's ass, N-Tschester. Humans! Such use of primitives has never even been conceived of before now."

"Most of them are internees, but regardless, they fought well."

Petish shook his head. "This is definitely one for the history books."

"So what happens now?"

Petish shrugged. "I'm neither a lawyer nor a policeman. Since the Councils have taken no action against the supreme commander, nor have they appointed a replacement, he is still my commanding officer. I will wait for his instructions."

Petish swept a hand at the view screen. "Until those orders come through, I'm going to spend my time cleaning up this little mess."

"With all due respect, Sir, I'd like to request permission to continue a mission the Supreme Commander assigned to me before the Maatiirani interfered."

"And what assignment would that be, Sub-commander?"

"I need to rescue some bare-assed natives and possibly save the universe."

119

"Sir," the scan officer called as they entered orbit. "Senator Addy's ship is right where you expected it to be."

Saki looked at the cloud-covered planet filling his view screen. "And where is its crew?"

"I found one Koko in the middle of Tot's village, but can't find the other one."

"Try looking below the surface."

A slight pause was followed by, "You were right, Sir. He's about a hundred and fifty meters down in a small underground cavern and he's alone."

"And the other one?"

"She's surrounded by natives, but I don't detect any weapons fire, so either there's a standoff or they're cooperating with her."

Saki shrugged. "Maybe pacifism is the way to win against an overwhelming enemy."

"Sir?"

Saki shook his head. "That doesn't mean we're going to play it that way. Get the assault team into the shuttle. We're going down."

"Sir, we've got company," the scan officer announced.

"More Maatiirani?"

The scan officer shook his head. "You need to see this Sir."

Saki looked at the view screen. "For all the Gods hold holy," was all he could think to say as he looked out at Khephra and Petish's combined fleet.

120

Addy's hysterical stereophonic howls followed the elevator down, decreasing slowly to a whimper after it came to an abrupt stop. Gasping for breath, the terrified KokoroTetian remained frozen for nearly a milli-pak before he opened his eyes to see a gaping black hole in the cliff face. Even then, he had to work at unwrapping his fingers from the elevator railing.

Reaching a shaking hand into his broad fanny pack, he extracted a small flashlight and flicked it on.

"Be anybody here?" Addy called as the beam of his light slashed jerkily from side-to-side within the large cavern until it illuminated someone near the back.

The senator's eyes bulged.

"Shaman? How you get here?"

Setting something on the floor, Tot waved a hand over it and stood back as it rose to the ceiling. Though the device did not appear to give off light itself, the entire cavern was suddenly illuminated.

Tot shook his head. "Unlike you, I can be in two places at once."

"How?" Addy asked as he scrambled to solid ground just inside the entrance, and pointed at the device illuminating the cave. "Is that projection device?"

"No," Tot laughed. "It just lights up the room."

"We got weapon," Addy threatened as he yanked a pistol from his belt and waved it.

"You have to know by now that you can't kill me."

The senator aimed his pistol high and to Tot's left, firing a short burst into the rock. Instead of dislodging a small amount of stone, the whole cavern began to shake as huge slabs of stone fell from the ceiling.

"*Shendtada*," Addy screamed as he struggled to avoid being overwhelmed by the hail of stones.

It was several micro-paks before he realized the Aken vessel had slipped from his grip.

"No," he screamed as rubble accumulated against the vessel's side, slowly pushing it toward the cavern's opening.

He started to run after it, but a sizable rock whacked his left head, knocking it unconscious and sending him stumbling off course. Not even hesitating to see if his other half were alive or dead, Addy turned back toward his objective, dragging his unconscious half around a pile of stones.

On the other hand, Tot seemed unperturbed by the falling rock as he made his way toward the vessel.

Knowing he wasn't going to get to it before the shaman, Addy pointed his weapon again.

"Stop or We shoot," he screamed over the noise of falling rock.

When Tot didn't respond, he fired directly at him. Though his intended victim seemed surprised by the assault, the bolt of energy went right through him and into the far wall, sending more rock spurting from the impact point. Some of the debris even struck the vessel, pushing it ever closer to the edge of the precipice outside the cave's opening.

Tot hesitated momentarily as Addy's unconscious side seemed to come around. After a brief shake of its revived head, the senator lunged at the vessel, wrapping all four arms around it and scrambling to his feet only centimeters from the opening's ledge.

As the senator rose he suddenly realized he'd dropped his weapon. Turning quickly around, he saw it in Tot's hand.

His left head still looking dazed, the senator hugged the vessel to his chest. "Shoot us and you destroying Aken."

Tot smiled at the absurd sight of Addy clutching the pyramid-shaped vessel, his belly protruding below it, two heads towering above, four fat hands gripping so tightly, their gray skin was white.

Sighing sadly, the shaman tossed the weapon past the KokoroTetian and into the blackness of the abyss.

"I'm not here to hurt you, Senator," he said softly as the cascade of rocks became a trickle. He waved a hand around the cave. "You seem to do enough of that on your own."

"Aken be ours," Addy protested desperately. "You gotta kill us to get it."

Tot moved to a large bolder and leaned against it. "There's no need for that. I'll just wait for you to release it."

"That We not ever do."

Tot shrugged, but said nothing as the elevator platform rose.

"What?" Addy cried. "Nooo..."

The senator ran to the opening, but the elevator was already far overhead.

Shaking his head, Tot moved to a smaller rock and sat.

"This not fair," Addy screamed as he gripped the edge of the opening with one free hand, leaned out and turned both faces up toward the small point of light above. "We steal it fair and square."

Moving away from the edge, he flailed two arms. "Our allies be Maatiirani. They bloodthirsty warrior race who will kill all peoples on planet."

Tot shrugged. "Death is but a transition from one existence to another. My people will accept their fate, but the Aken stays here."

Hugging his prize tightly, Addy quickly scanned the cave as realization dawned on him. "If We trapped here, so be you."

Tot settled back on his rock and sighed, "Then that's how it must be."

Shaking both heads violently, the senator stepped around a boulder and ran further into the cave. "No, no! There gotta be other way out."

"For you, the lift is the only choice."

Finding Tot's statement to be true, Addy moved back to the opening's edge. "Maatiirani got small shuttles that fit in here easy. They come get us."

Without comment, Tot closed his eyes and seemed to slip into a trance. After a moment, he opened them again.

"Your friends are not coming, Senator."

Addy lurched from the opening, yanking a communicator from his fanny pack. The display read, "No signal."

"How you can know that?" he demanded. "We not get nothing."

Tot shrugged. "My other half on the surface has told me this."

Addy looked at him incredulously. "You communicate telepathically?"

Tot nodded. "That's a close enough approximation. We are, after all, the same person."

"You say, but it not possible, maybe?"

"Not possible for you," Tot laughed, "but it is true just the same."

"But you lose all memories. How you know this?"

"Isn't it enough that I do?"

Addy glared at him. "So now you can open vessel, maybe?"

The shaman shook his head. "But I know what you will find when you do."

Eyes wide with anticipation, the senator shouted. "What? What? What? You gotta tell us."

Tot opened his mouth, but stopped when he heard someone else talking. A moment later, the crowded lift stopped in the opening. Saki, Stitto, Pana, and Khephra went silent, their stares shifting from Tot to Addy and back.

Pana rushed from the lift, heading toward Addy with both hands held up, palms out.

"You don't understand, Senator," she cried. "The Aken won't solve your problems."

Moving slowly, as though listening to her, Addy kept one face toward her as the other searched for a safe place to put his precious package.

"How you know that, maybe?" he asked.

"Do you know who I am?" Pana asked.

Addy nodded toward the vessel. "You got key to open this?"

Before she could answer, several large stones fell from the ceiling to Pana's left. As they slammed onto the cave floor, sending a spray of smaller debris flying, she stumbled to her right, shielding her face from the flying stone chips.

Addy released the vessel and ran to her.

"Pana!" Saki cried as the KokoroTetian wrapped two arms around her. In the same move, Addy pulled another weapon from his fanny pack.

"Lies not help you," he screamed while pressing the weapon to his captive's head. "Vessel be ours, and We want key!"

"What good will that do?" Tot asked as he moved in front of the others. "Her Life Force is not dependent on the physical body."

Addy grinned malevolently. "This weapon be in red box on our ship. Warning message say it use Anderfor energy."

"What's that?" Khephra demanded as he stepped off the lift.

Addy pressed the weapon's muzzle tighter against Pana's neck. "It destroy Life Force."

Khephra's eyes jerked from Tot to Addy and Pana.

"What do you want, Senator?"

Addy nodded one head toward the box behind him. "We want key transferred to us."

"If you pull that trigger," Tot cried, "you'll be destroying the only one who can open it."

Addy shook his other head. "We think you know other way, maybe."

Tot looked stunned. "There is no other way."

The KokoroTetian tightened his grip on the weapon. "Well, it be time to find out."

"That won't be necessary," Pana said. "I'll give you the key."

"Pana! No," Khephra cried.

"Et! You can't," Tot pleaded."

Pana nodded slowly. "But I can, Brother."

"But last time…"

Her head shook. "This time will be different. I know what will happen."

Addy looked at her cautiously. "What you say?"

"Let me show you," she said as a ghostly figure rose from Pana's body.

When the apparition rose from her, Pana slumped in Addy's arms. Looking stunned, he releasing his captive and let her fall to the floor. Only Stitto saw the Aken transforming into a glowing boxlike shape, because everyone else's attention was on Et's beautiful ethereal form shimmering in front of Addy.

"What we do now?" Addy asked uncertainly.

Et nodded curtly. "You can kill me, Senator. She's no longer of any use to you."

"W…We not want to kill. We want to…join you." Pointing toward Pana, he added, "Like you do with her, maybe? We want to know all there be to know of universe."

Et shook her head. "You might want to rethink that request. It's a very painful process. Especially for a male."

Looking uncertain, Addy squeaked, "Huh?"

As the senator hesitated, Et transformed into a ghoulish specter and lunged forward. The startled Addy took several quick steps back, bumping up against the edge of the opening. Before he could recover his balance, she lunged again. Addy tipped backwards, expecting to land on top of the vessel, but the opening seemed to grow as he fell.

Flailing his arms desperately, he managed to grab the lip with both right hands, but it left him dangling helplessly over an endless expanse.

"Eewaaak," he squawked in stereo.

As everyone else watched in stunned amazement, Stitto lunged at the opening. "We got you," she cried as her fingers wrapped around his forearms.

She tried to stop her forward momentum, but the strong gravitational pull from inside the opening tugged on her body, causing her eggs to shift forward. Instead of halting at the edge, she lurched into the aperture, wrenching Addy's hands free. Grabbing desperately, the senator clamped onto her flailing wrists, yanking the top half of her body into the opening.

As Et's ethereal form floated above them, the rest of the room's occupants watched Stitto's feet go up and disappear over the rim.

121

Expecting certain death, Stitto was surprised to find the landing much like dropping off a short ladder. She landed on her rump, and found herself sitting in a field of green grass with birds twittering overhead. A herd of cattle grazed off to her left, and a small barn sat a short distance to her right. The field ran to the horizon in every direction, and as far as she could see, the place was devoid of any other beings or plant life.

No longer willing to be contained, her tennis-ball-sized eggs spurted one-by-one onto the ground. As soon as each egg made contact with the air, its slimy coating jelled into a glue-like substance and stuck to anything it came in contact with. The palms of Stitto's hands oozed a similar fluid that allowed her to handle the eggs without sticking to them. She pushed them into a rough spheroid shape containing several dozen eggs. As she concentrated on organizing her offspring, several bipedal beings suddenly appeared next to her.

"She fell from the sky," one of them exclaimed.

"Look, a portal has opened," another cried excitedly.

Stitto's attention was drawn to a dark square in the sky above her.

"Hurry," the first person exclaimed. "It might close at any moment."

"What be happening, maybe?" Stitto asked as she struggled to keep up with the steady stream of eggs.

The crowd quickly grew from dozens to hundreds to thousand, all ignoring her as they shouted to each other and pointed skyward.

Pushing at the people closest to her, she cried, "Give us room."

A person separated from the crowd, looking down at her and the accumulating bundles of eggs. "Are you injured?"

She shook her heads. "We be giving birth."

"Do you need assistance?"

"No," she snapped irritably while elbowing someone crowding in on her left.

"How did you get here?"

She completed another bundle and set it aside as two more eggs popped out. "We fall into vessel and…" She slapped at a female who stumbled close to an egg bundle. "…we end up here."

"You opened the Aken?" he asked incredulously. "How?"

She patted more eggs into the fresh bundle while shaking her heads. "I not know how. It just open."

The crowd parted slightly and the person pointed to a familiar figure struggling to extract himself from a manure pile next to the barn. "Did you fall through with someone else?"

"That be appropriate," Stitto chuckled as she watched Addy wallow in manure. "Where be this place and what everyone doing?"

"We call ourselves the Biquicha. You're in a simulated world we created on the surface of this dead star."

Puzzled, Stitto looked around at the pasture: peaceful except for the excited people around her. "We be on star? How that possible?"

The person sighed. "Our bodies were destroyed in an explosion a very, very, very long time ago. Though our Life Forces survived, we have been trapped in this star's massive gravitational field ever since. Over time, we figured out how to manipulate matter to make anything we wanted."

"This be nice."

Shrugging, he pointed to the struggling Addy. "Is that your mate?"

"God no," she exclaimed. "He our boss."

"Pity," he sighed while moving away. "It's going to be a long time before you see another of your kind."

"What you mean, maybe?"

The person tilted his head toward the dark square. "The only way off this star is through that portal. The last time it opened was the day your universe came into existence."

As her jaw dropped, the people around her began to dematerialize, their ghostly shapes rising toward the opening.

"And you be here…" she started to ask, but the question faded from her lips.

The person sighed as his body became more and more transparent. "…far too long to keep track." The features of his face blurred slightly as he shook his head and began rising. "You might think not dying is one advantage of living here, but you'll soon realize it's the worst part."

"But We not want to stay here with him," Stitto cried as she waved a gooey hand toward Addy.

Without responding, the person continued to rise, his attention on the dark square in the sky.

Terror filled Stitto as the last of the ghostly forms disappeared through the opening. She started to rise, but several more eggs fell onto the ground, drawing her attention back to them.

"Where everyone go?" Addy asked as he shook offal from his hands and arms.

She ignored him at first, but the smell of manure finally penetrated her stunned senses. With one head still watching the last of her emerging eggs, she turned the other toward her boss.

"They escape."

Addy looked around incredulously. "Escape what?"

"This place," she answered as he continued to wipe offal from his clothes. "They say you not ever die here, but only way out is through portal in sky."

Addy tilted his heads back and stared upward. "Portal?"

When Stitto looked as well, all she saw were puffy white clouds in a blue sky. Gasping, she lowered her gaze the horizon to see a boiling mist flowing over the grass toward them. She turned her heads in opposite directions to find that no matter where she looked it was the same.

"Lord Hammond save us," was all she could think to say.

122

The group in the cave stared in wonder as each ghostly apparition rose from the vessel. They started coming out singly, but their numbers increased until a solid stream flowed through the opening, climbing rapidly until they vanished into the rock overhead. None of them acknowledged the bystanders until the last one appeared.

Tot and Et both cried, "Father!"

The apparition stopped just above the opening as his children approached. Et floated to him, but Tot stopped just long enough to flip the lid closed before his own body faded to the same ghostly form. When he did so, the vessel regained its pyramidal shape and stopped glowing.

"I'm sorry I doubted you, children," Anjenet stated.

"Ceratha's boiling bowels," Khephra exclaimed. "What just happened?"

Tot turned to face the others. "This is our father. He's been trapped on a magnitar neutron star since your universe was created."

Et laughed. "The Aken allowed us to free him."

Tot turned to his father. "That's where we were wrong, Father. We thought the time machine was tied to the age of the person who opened it."

The father nodded. "And it's not?"

"No," Tot laughed. "No matter how old you are, it takes you to where ever you want to be."

Et nodded. "When I first opened it, I must have wanted to go back to the beginning of the whole universe, and that's where it took me."

Anjenet looked at Khephra. "All I remember is a brilliant flash of light and we found ourselves on that neutron star."

The siblings nodded energetically, before Et spoke,

"In the explosion, we were thrown far away, but we never stopped looking for you."

"And it took you all this time?" Saki asked as he moved closer to the ethereal trio.

Tot shrugged. "Even traveling at faster-than-light speed, your part of the universe is enormous and the last place we thought to look was on a neutron star."

Et turned toward the group. "If it hadn't been for the KokoroTetians opening the Aken, we'd have never figured it out."

"What did that have to do with it?" Khephra asked.

She shrugged. "If it had been based on age, the Koko scientists who opened it would have been too old for it to take them that far back in time. The powerful discharge had to have happened because that's what they wanted.

"Before we reasoned that out, I was already in Pana's humanoid body and trapped on your prison world."

"And I suffered a memory loss after being attacked by the Pandani," Tot added.

Et floated to Pana. "It seems my bonding with Pana created some kind of psychic connection with father. It was only then that I knew where he was." She floated back to Anjenet. "And until I knew that, I couldn't ask the Aken to take me there."

Saki motioned to the vessel. "So now Addy and his companion are trapped on a neutron star? Can we get him back?"

"Only his Life Force can be recovered," Anjenet said. "Though he doesn't realize it, his body was crushed to atoms before he even reached the surface."

"We could transport him directly to a prison planet until he is reformed," Khephra stated. "That shouldn't take more than two or three hundred *druak*."

"It doesn't matter either way," Anjenet said. "Now that we have control of the Aken, I can go back and stop my daughter from opening it. Our part of the universe will never have been destroyed, and the Biquicha can have their lives back."

The three Antrakans stared at Anjenet.

"The Biquicha?" Saki asked.

Anjenet nodded. "That is what we called ourselves before this happened. And it's not just about us. There were trillions of species that lived before that time. They will all be restored to existence."

Khephra shook his head. "But what does that mean for our universe and all those who exist now?"

Anjenet shrugged. "I would think that is obvious."

Before anyone could react to his statement, the ground shook. Toward the back of the cave, a massive chunk of stone fell from the ceiling, smashing into thousands of smaller pieces on impact. All the corporeals were knocked to the floor by flying rock. They rose to see Tot floating toward the vessel, still lying next to the entrance where Addy had left it.

Jumping up, Pana scrambled across the rock-covered cave floor toward the vessel. Though she had to dodge falling rock, Tot's ethereal form passed right through it.

However, as he approached his objective, a shadowy figure appeared seemingly from thin air and blocked his way.

Stopping, Tot released a sharp cry, "Pandani!"

Pana blinked several times while trying to focus on the indistinct figure, but the only part of it she could see clearly was a single large eye glaring at Tot. She grabbed a rock as she moved forward and threw it at the figure. Her aim was dead on, but the projectile passed right through it like air through coal dust.

The eye turned in her direction and an ear-splitting hiss caused Pana to cover her ears and fall to her knees.

"It's an inter-dimensional creature," Tot warned. "There's nothing you can do to harm it."

"Don't let it take the vessel," Khephra demanded as the Pandani scooped it up and started to fade away.

Pana rose from the floor as Tot lunged forward, his body taking a more material form just before he impacted the shadow creature. As Pana scrambled up, Tot and the Pandani fell toward her, and the vessel flew from its grip. She jumped forward to catch it, passing through both combatants as she went. Though she reached the vessel in time, it went through her hands, and vanished into the floor.

Screaming as her body impacted the rock-covered floor, Pana slid to the opening and vanished from sight.

Khephra ran to the opening, fell on his stomach and scrambled to the edge. Just below it, he found Pana hanging onto a slim ledge of rock, her feet dangling over a black abyss.

Reaching over the edge, he just managed to grab Pana's wrists as another earthquake caused the narrow ledge to break away. With the ground still shaking and Pana's added weight, Khephra found himself being pulled over with her as she struggled in vain to find a foothold in the smooth rock.

Saki landed on Khephra's legs as Anjenet joined his son in attacking the Pandani, but despite their efforts, the shadowy creature wrenched free and flew into the cave's wall with the two Biquicha close behind.

Though Saki had stopped Khephra's slide toward the abyss, the supreme commander was too far over the edge to pull himself back up without releasing his daughter.

"What do we do now?" Saki asked desperately as he struggled to get a foothold in the cave floor. "I can't get enough purchase to pull you back."

"I'm slipping," Pana screamed.

"Not on my watch," Khephra bellowed as he tried to heave her higher, but instead her right hand slipped free.

Pana reached up with her free hand and tried to grab higher on her father's wrist, but the movement only caused her left hand to slip more. As Khephra struggled to get a better hold, she slipped from his grip and vanished into the darkness.

"Aaarrgghh!" he cried while spasmodically grabbing at the dark as though he might catch her invisible hand and still save her.

Feeling the pressure lighten, Saki pulled the supreme commander back from the edge before the reality sank in.

Both men stared at the empty opening in stunned silence until Pana's startled face appeared with Anjenet holding her.

He floated into the cave and set her down before stating blandly, "The Pandani got away, but at least it didn't get the Aken."

Khephra and Saki jumped up and wrapped their arms around Pana. Tot appeared from the rock wall and moved to his father's side. Both Biquicha stared at where the vessel had vanished.

As the three Antrakans struggled to cope with their near loss, Anjenet turned to his son. "We must find it before they do."

Tot shook his head. "It could be anywhere in an infinite number of dimensions."

Anjenet shook his head as well. "But we know which ones they normally travel through. We can start there."

Et appeared from the ceiling above the three corporeals. "We might find it faster if I can occupy her body again."

Tot shook his head. "Inter-dimensional travel would destroy her corporeal form and their Life Forces don't function as well as we do without a physical body."

Et looked from Pana to her brother. "It would be worth a try."

Pana stared at Et opened mouthed, but Tot did not respond. Finally, Anjenet moved beside his daughter.

"We won't do that," he stated. "We cannot ask such a sacrifice of her."

Khephra gave his head a sharp shake as he grunted angrily. "And that's worse than wiping out our entire universe?"

Anjenet turned to him and nodded. "To murder an individual to further our goals is immoral because she exists now and if we never find the Aken, we have denied her future potential. On the other hand, if we do restore our part of the universe, it won't be murder, since you'll not have existed in the first place."

"That's just a convenient lie," Pana protested. "We do exist. Erasing us from history doesn't make our destruction any less wrong."

Anjenet opened his mouth, as though to argue, but instead shook his head and announced, "We must go," and floated up into the cave's ceiling.

Et quickly followed, but Tot hesitated.

"You have to stop him," Pana pleaded.

He shrugged. "He's my father." He pushed off and floated into the ceiling.

Just as he disappeared, the ground shook and rock once again began crashing all around the threesome.

"To the elevator," Khephra commanded as he dodged to one side to avoid a large stone that exploded on the floor only centimeters behind him.

Saki took a glancing blow on the shoulder that nearly knocked him down. Stumbling along behind his father-by-law, he managed to leap into the elevator beside Pana as another slab fell from the ceiling and slammed onto the ledge behind them.

The elevator rose slowly as ever-larger rocks began falling from the tunnel's walls. All around them floated the ghostly, nearly shapeless Life Forces of the Biquicha. Anjenet moved to each in turn and barked instructions. Micro-paks later, the recipient vanished.

"We've got to stop them," Pana demanded as she gripped the elevator's railing and watched for falling rocks.

"What can we do?" Khephra grumbled, more to himself than his companions.

"We need to find these Pandani, and try to enlist their aid," she stated.

Khephra shook his head. "What good will that…"

"Mother ship to Supreme Commander."

"Khephra here."

"Sir," the voice said nervously. "Long-range scans indicate the bulk of the Maatiirani fleet has crossed their border."

"Projected destination?"

"Many, Sir, but one group is coming this way."

Khephra's eyes locked on Saki. "Hammond preserve us!"

A cold silence blanketed the elevator, as each person stared in disbelief at his companions.

"Estimated time of arrival?" Khephra asked.

"To our location, approximately two-point-three pak. Prior to that, they will make first contact at Angrolicat in about a pak, and then Prak a'Terra."

"All this trouble," Khephra muttered, "and we're going to war anyway."

"There's one more thing, Sir."

"Yes?"

"We're detecting more than just Maatiirani ships in the attacking fleet. There appear to be KokoroTetians and another…uh… we don't know what species they are."

Khephra finally broke the silence, "Pandani?"

When no one answered, Saki moved forward. "What in Ceratha's name are these creatures?"

Khephra shook his head. "That's a question for another time. Right now we have to come up with a plan to defend ourselves."

Tot floated up over them, somehow creating a shield that deflected the falling stone. "I'm really sorry about all of this. I'd like to help you with your problem, but Father says it is your problem. Ours is to find the vessel."

"What do you know about these Pandani?"

Tot shook his head. "Let's just say they were an experiment gone wrong."

"You created them?" Saki asked.

Tot jerked a nod.

"Then tell us how to defeat them," Khephra demanded.

Tot shrugged and looked at Pana. "You have all my sister's memories. That's the best I can do for you right now."

Anjenet moved up beside his son. "We must go. The Pandani are already searching for the vessel."

"And when you find it," Khephra growled, "you will destroy the very people who helped free you from your prison."

Anjenet locked eyes with the supreme commander for a long moment before he shook his head. "I have an obligation to my people."

Though Anjenet quickly moved away, Tot maintained his shield until they reached the top. As they moved out of the hut, the ground continued to shake as panicked natives rushed around trying to avoid falling tree limbs and head-sized fruit.

"Mother ship to Supreme Commander."

"Khephra here."

"Sir, six Pandani ships are coming this way, traveling at two-point-three light speed."

"Stand by," Khephra said with a steadiness not reflected in his face. "We don't have anything to deal with something like that."

Pana nodded. "I have an idea, but I'll need Senator Addy's ship. It's the only thing that can match their speed."

"But what about weapons?" Saki asked.

She smiled. "If my plan works as expected, we won't need any."

123

The two priests sat on a bench in the rooftop balcony. One stared up at the night sky, but the other only listened to his companion, Ansen Paraka shiver as he pulled his heavy cloak close.

"How many did they say were coming?" the Shendeah asked calmly.

Ansen shook his head as his trembling shrug was offset by sweat beading on his forehead. His companion, though dressed only in his usual light linen shift, looked neither cold nor nervous.

"I'm not exactly sure. The last report said over three thousand ships, but they may not all be headed here."

"Such a massive buildup. How did they keep it a secret?"

"I've no idea, Father. I'm just a healer," Ansen sighed. "Maybe that other race – the ones they call the Pandani – helped in some way."

"Is everything ready for their arrival?"

Ansen barked a hollow laugh. "Even if only a thousand come our way, it will be a hundred times more than we've ever faced before. As I see it, we've nothing left but to pray for a miracle."

The Shendeah stood abruptly and moved quickly to the exit.

"Where are you going, Father?"

Pausing at the doorway, the small figure turned his head to reveal a heavily shadowed face that hid all but wide, unfocussed blue eyes reflecting the light of Ansen's small lantern.

"To take the advice of my healer."

124

The small armada followed Pana to the long-since-dead fourth planet of the small yellow star. Chunks of the plant's moons mingled with the debris of partially obliterated space ships that still orbited the dead planet's cold, barren core. Her heart ached as she saw dismembered Maatiirani and Ooertfaelian corpses float by.

"What are we doing here?" Khephra's voice growled as his stern face appeared on her communications screen. "I don't hide in graveyards."

"We're not hiding," Pana answered through the tears streaming down her cheeks. "This is where we make our stand."

"Why here?"

"Because we need something to blow up."

"You've lost me."

"When I flew over Saki's battle with the Maatiirani, the explosions interfered with the warp bubble protecting my ship and I had to slow down. Fortunately, there wasn't much activity, so the warp bubble didn't collapse completely. If it had, we'd have been destroyed."

"You mean we fire at them and they'll spontaneously explode?"

Pana shook her head. "It's not the lasers that cause the interference, but the energy they give off when destroying any kind of metal. I don't know the specifics, but it interrupts a ship's warp field."

"Will it also interfere with their shields?"

"I don't know, but remember, I have all of Et's memories and she knows nothing of this, so I am assuming the Pandani don't either."

"That puts us on very shaky ground," Khephra growled.

"We don't have time for anything else."

"I'm not about to…"

"Father!"

When he hesitated, Pana began tapping a fingernail on her console. Khephra started to protest, but stopped as he appeared to recognize the pattern of her tapping.

After she stopped, he let out a heavy sigh and nodded. “Supreme Commander to all ships. Sub-commander Khephra has what may be our only hope of coming out of this alive. You are ordered to follow her orders as though they are mine.”

Ba’ Roque moved up behind Pana. “What was that?”

Turning toward him, she smiled sadly. “It’s an old code of dots and dashes one of my Human fathers and I worked out when I was a child.”

“And what did you tell him?”

She sighed. “To trust me.”

125

The entire bridge crew watched the six blips on the screen.

"Sir," Captain Praetor almost whispered. "They're traveling at greater than twice light speed."

Khephra snorted derisively. "But that separates them from their allies, and gives us an advantage."

"What kind of shielding do they have?"

Shaking his head, the supreme commander tapped his console. "Sergeant Specialist Akki?"

"Yes, Sir."

"What is the status of Pana's inertial dampener changes?"

"We're finishing up now, Sir."

"What will you need to test them?"

There was a pause before Pana spoke, "There won't be time for tests. We'll just have to hope they work."

Khephra's eyes jerked to the main screen to watch the six growing blips before he looked around his bridge at the quiet crew waiting for his command.

"Then God go with you, Daughter."

In less than ten milli-paks, Pana's ship flew across the view screen and turned towards the enemy.

As Khephra watched, he said, "Once we've beaten the crap out of these bastards, I'm going to take every surviving Koko in the universe and put them on that neutron star with Addy."

"Sir," called the scan officer. "Captain Khephra has reached the halfway point and is turning about. The Pandani ships have increased to two-point-six light speed."

"All hands to the ready," he called. "Communications: let all the other ships know to follow my lead. Weapons control: lock on target."

"Target locked, Sir."

"Now pray hard, Son," Khephra sighed. "We're going to need it this time."

126

Kappa strained against the resulting G-forces as he pulled the ship into a sharp left turn.

"Thank Hammond the inertial dampeners are working," he said because he needed to say something to control the agonizing terror in his head.

"Thank Akki," Pana corrected while staring at the screen showing the six ships bearing down on them. "I only hope we turned soon enough."

"Surely they're not stupid enough to follow us right to our fleet."

Pana shook her head. "The fleet is irrelevant. Our weapons are useless against their warp bubble. If they eliminate this ship, our people will be defenseless against them."

Kappa shook his head while looking toward the solar system that concealed their armada. "How close do they have to get to our fleet?"

Pana shrugged while watching the rear sensor data on her screen. "No idea," she said with a casualness not reflected in her eyes. "We just have to get them as close as we can."

"Why don't they know about the interference our weapons cause in their warp field?"

Pana shrugged. "Because they use a different type of energy than we do, their weapons don't generate the same interference."

"Can they fire from within the warp bubble?"

"I'm afraid so."

Kappa grabbed the throttle. "Then I'm not taking any chances."

Pana put her hand on his. "We have to wait a few more micro-paks."

He started to object, but Pana's attention had already moved to her monitor. Sweat dripped from Kappa's nose as he watched the blips on his screen slowly transform into recognizable shapes.

"Three-quarter light speed," she announced finally.

Kappa pulled the throttle back, and felt his body press into the seat-back. To his consternation, the enemy ships on his monitor continued to grow at a disturbing rate.

"Prepare to make a sharp right," Pana ordered.

"How sharp?"

"As much as we can stand."

Kappa gave a nervous tug on his seatbelt harness.

"Ten micro-paks to turn," Pana called.

Kappa looked at the screen, puzzled. "They're too far away."

"At greater-than-light speed, things always appear further away than they really are," Pana explained. "Five micro-paks."

Without speaking, she fired a laser canon toward the hiding Antrakan fleet.

"Three. Two. Now!"

The ship banked into a tight turn, and despite the added inertial dampeners, centrifugal forces pulled Kappa's body tight against the seatbelt harness. His head involuntarily turned left, and it was all he could do to keep his hands near the controls. As he slowly brought his head back around to look at the monitor, a bright flash filled the cabin.

"They're in weapon's range," he groaned.

"Four. Three. Two. All Stop!" Pana cried.

As he cut the engines, the ship immediately started to tumble. The effect was quite dizzying, but with some effort, Kappa managed to right it again. As the tumbling slowed, the twosome stared out their windows at the glowing vapor trails around them.

"Son of a farting pan-lizard," Kappa swore. "We did it."

127

A nervous silence fell over the bridge as the crew watched Pana's ship gradually increase speed in front of the approaching Pandanis. Just as she neared the solar system, her ship jerked sharply to the right and quickly slowed.

"Fire," Khephra bellowed as a pulse of light flashed from Pana's craft.

Each vessel glowed brilliantly as the solar system flared up. At the same instant, a sphere of invisible energy radiated out at the speed of light. When the shockwave reached the enemy ships, their protective warp bubbles dematerialized, and their hulls disintegrated.

"God Almighty," Captain Praetor cried as everyone watched the bright flaring remains of the vaporizing ships.

Khephra jumped from his seat. "Navigation: get us out of this solar system. Communications: bring everyone into battle formation. We've still got a fight ahead of us."

The bridge was suddenly a bustle of energy as the crew worked to prepare for the hundreds of Maatiirani and KokoroTetian ships growing ever larger on the view screen.

"Father," Pana called as Khephra watched his fleet pass the remains of the Ooertfaelian planet. "I need to borrow these two light-speed ships and Saki."

"What for?"

"Et's memories may give us some hope of getting the Pandani to change sides. There is a reason they were hiding in their region of space for so long."

"What was it?"

"She believed they were hiding from something or someone. If we can figure out what it was, we might use it to get them to change sides."

"I could use those ships in the upcoming battle."

"And it will all be for naught if the Biquicha find that vessel before we do."

He thought of protesting, but stifled it. "I'm going to trust you on this, Daughter. Take what you need and may Hammond guide your way."

Out of the corner of his eye, Khephra saw a shadowy figure he immediately recognized.

"Besides getting rid of those shadow ships, what did this gain us?" AnKat Ta-Tschester asked softly as the supreme commander moved in close.

"They just threw the best they had at us and we destroyed them," Khephra growled. "If we can play that advantage, the Koko commanders may well bolt."

"But the Maatiirani are not a trivial opponent."

Khephra turned toward the view screen. "And neither are we, AmPheet," he snarled. Looking back to find the shadowy figure gone, the supreme commander shook his head. "I'm glad your son doesn't take after you," he sighed before turning back to his busy bridge.

128

Cold winter winds whipped the tall damp grass, offering a chilling welcome for his return. Dark clouds threw a pall over his mood as Marrett and his four companions stared down from their hilltop perch at a small farm house, partially blocked by a larger barn.

"This was my grandfather's place before…" His voice trailed off, but his comrades knew the rest. "We're far enough from the city now. No one will be looking for us out here."

Moving off the hilltop, he led them along a line of bushes, snaking down the slope until they reached a fence bordering a field overgrown with weeds. Moving right, the small group jogged along a path parallel to the house until they reached a small cluster of young trees thick enough to block their approach.

As he moved close to the fence, the others extracted laser pistols and held them at the ready.

"This way," he called while lifting his own pistol, climbing through a barbed-wire fence and heading straight into the trees. "We should be able to see the whole house from this angle, but let's keep it quiet until we know there's no one inside."

"You're the only one talking," a tall, thin blond woman sneered.

When Marrett looked back at Bouche, her narrow face was tense, but a tell-tale smile told him she was teasing. He smiled back, or at least hoped he had.

At the far edge of the trees, he waved for them to stop and stared at the sprawling ranch-style house.

"What are those cars doing here? This place has been abandoned for over a year."

Marrett listened for voices, but heard only the white noise of wind rushing past his ears…and a hint of something else.

Suddenly, the breeze stopped and the something else became more distinct: the soulful wail of a woman, venting her pain into the uncaring wind. Marrett shook his head and sighed nervously. They'd heard that sad cry so many times in the last year. So much death and the wild, inconsolable bereavement it brought.

His four companions watched as Marrett squatted, looking indecisive. This close up view of the farmhouse brought a flood of fond memories that were quickly replaced with the pain of what had been lost. As his comrades began to fidget nervously behind him, the bereaved woman cried out words Marrett could not make out because her voice was drowning in the pain flowing from her heart. However, it wasn't the words that grabbed his attention.

Bouche barked a whispered alarm as Marrett started to run, but his brain refused to comprehend anything beyond the thumping of his heart and the woman's mournful wail.

He crashed through wet grass, and clambered over a wire fence that tore his soggy shirt. His weapon was gone, as was his backpack. They didn't matter as he rounded the house and slid to a stop. A small cluster of people were locked arm-in-arm in a small fenced cemetery containing half-a-dozen older headstones. The wailing woman was on her knees, her forehead against a new one.

"Mother!" he screamed, or at least thought he did, as his heart pounded and his feet began moving again.

The people around the woman turned to look at him. One of them said something that made the woman look up. When her eyes focused on him she froze, but he didn't stop.

Suddenly, she was on her feet, running toward him and screaming, her arms spread wide. None of the others moved as the twosome drew closer. The woman was releasing a wordless, high-pitched squeal that matched a noise coming from someone else. After several strides Marrett realized it was him.

They met with a thud as he picked her up bodily, carrying her with his momentum. Her arms were wrapped around his neck, her face smashed into his. For a time, he knew not how long, there was nothing but her in his existence.

Eventually, shouting voices made him look up to see his companions standing at the corner of the house, their bodies tense, faces confused, and weapons drawn. He looked back at the crowd in the cemetery and saw that they too were prepared for a firefight.

"Wait," he cried while the woman continued to hang from his neck. "Everybody, hold your fire."

A dozen or more pairs of eyes were on him as the woman finally released her grip and pushed away, though still tightly gripping his arm with both hands.

"It's Marrett," she sobbed to her people. "My son is alive!"

From a branch high up on of a nearby tree, a bird spread its wings and lifted off, flying high over the scene while watching the two groups come slowly together. As it soared ever higher, an antenna lifted from a tiny box on its small back and its eyes glowed red. The bird banked left, catching a rising current that would lift it above the hill blocking its line-of-sight view of the nearest Maatiirani camp.

The valley beyond was just coming into view when a flash of light vaporized the tiny body, leaving nothing but a puff of burnt feathers floating in the cold wind. On the ground, the young blond woman shivered while pocketing her weapon.

"We need to leave now," Bouche insisted. "They may have spotted us."

"Come with us," Ba' Roque said. "Our ship is on the other side of that clump of trees.

For the first time, Marrett realized Ba' Roque was wearing an environmental suit.

"You're an alien," he said more matter-of-factly than he felt.

When Ba' Roque didn't respond, Tamm turned to her son. "They're on our side."

Marrett felt an instant flash of anger as he looked from his comrades to his mother. "We've seen a lot of killing done by aliens."

"Not these aliens."

"How are we supposed to know?" Bouche asked angrily.

"Please, Marrett," Tamm pleaded. "We have to get out of here, now."

Marrett looked into his mother's face for a moment before turning to his comrades.

"What do you think, guys?"

Bouche shook her head. "Are you sure this is your mom?"

Marrett turned back to Tamm. “What was the name of our dog?”

She smiled. “We never had a dog, but our last cat’s name was Fuzzy Wong.”

He laughed and nodded to his companions. “Pretty sure, yeah.”

Bouche sighed. “I guess if you were with those white-faced bastards we’d already be dead.”

Marrett pointed at the house. “If you have a ship, where did those cars come from?”

Tamm shook her head. “There are six skeletons inside the house, another in the grass out front. They must have belonged to those poor souls until the Maatiirani got them.”

“The who?” Bouche asked.

“Those white-faced bastards you were referring to. In our…” She turned toward Ba’ Roque. “…his language, Maatiirani means something like ‘space pirate’.”

Marrett shook his head. “Even pirates would hate these assholes.”

Bouche shook her head as well. “How can your ship get past them? The planet is surrounded.”

Ba’ Roque nodded clumsily in his environmental suit. “Our ship is invisible to their sensors.”

Bouche frowned. “That’s not possible.”

“How do you think we got here?”

After a tense moment, Marrett nodded. “Then let’s go.”

As the small group moved toward the trees, another bird floated overhead. After Bouche lifted her weapon again and fired, Marrett and his mother stopped to look up at the puff of feathers.

“That one probably got high enough to connect with their listening station,” Marrett warned.

Nodding, Bouche took a nervous look around. “Then we should hurry.”

After a moment, Ba’ Roque signaled for them to stop as he pulled a device from his pocket. Micro-paks later, an opening appeared where there had been nothing. A staircase unfolded from the opening, and when it reached the ground he motioned for them to enter. Marrett and his comrades hesitated as the others rushed inside.

Tamm stopped at the stairs, and motioned for them to follow. “Let’s go!”

Marrett’s comrades watched him as he looked from one to the other.

Bouche looked up. “I wish I’d spotted that bird sooner.”

“It wouldn’t have mattered,” Marrett insisted.

When she hesitated, he shook his head. “Nothing but death waits for us here.”

Without another word, Marrett followed his mother. The remaining four hesitated briefly before doing the same. As soon as they were in, the stairs folded up, and the opening closed, leaving nothing but the fading whine of engines as the chilling breeze tumbled dry leaves across the bare ground.

THE AUTHOR

Growing up on the Oregon coast, Cliff has enjoyed telling the stories rattling around in his head. This book is his first chance to share an out-of-this-world adventure with a wider audience.

A fifth-generation Oregonian, Cliff has been a farmer, logger, and business owner. He now lives in the small town of Jefferson, working as a computer support consultant for small businesses up and down Oregon's beautiful Willamette Valley.

For more information on Clifford M. Scovell, please visit:
www.prisonearth.com

Photo by Andre Lindauer

www.ingramcontent.com/pod-product-compliance
Lightning Source LLC
Chambersburg PA
CBHW020834030726
47496CB00001B/238
9780984732463